Year of the Decree Absolute

Penny Destro

A Purple Pen Publication

First Published in 2014 by Purple Pen Publishing Ltd

All characters in this publication are fictional and any resemblance to real persons, living or dead, is purely coincidental.

ISBN 978-1-908616-68-5

Printed and bound by Berforts Information Press
23-25 Gunnels Road
Hertfordshire, SG12BH

Published by Purple Pen Publishing Ltd
145-157 St John Street
London EC1V 4PW

www.purplepenpublishing.net

Acknowledgements

With grateful thanks to many friends for their input and advice, and to my husband, Hugh, for his unfailing support.

JANUARY

I'VE always been of the opinion that if something's sufficiently memorable, I'll remember it. And this year – to the Chinese the Year of the Pig, to me the Year of the Perfidious Swine - is one I know will be notable if only because I am on my own for the first time ever. I am soon to be the reluctant recipient of a Decree Absolute.

I therefore feel I owe it to myself to record my transition into the world of the divorcée. Also Leah, my daughter, presented me with this blank tome for Christmas and suggested I use it to appraise my life or as she put it, sort my head out.

'Seeing things in hard copy helps you to evaluate them,' she said, contradicting her computer-age principles. 'Write as if you're talking to a stranger - you'd be amazed at how visualizing your anxieties can influence how you feel about them.'

As I've been in advertising for over 22 years she was preaching to the converted (i.e. brainwashed), but I've started writing, mainly to gain my obstreperous offspring's approval and if as a side effect my head gets "sorted" it will be a bonus.

My account shall be dateless. This is to save myself a guilt trip when I don't feel inclined to put pen to paper. To be absolutely honest, this is not my first attempt at my memoirs: I started to chronicle my (very basic) thoughts the year I fell in love and gave up my most treasured possession - Simon couldn't stand me practising the oboe. Needless to say, the attempt was aborted when I found it more exciting to experience life than write about it.

But that was decades ago, and now I'm older and theoretically wiser, perhaps this time I'll be more successful – even if it only serves to show me the error of my ways.

Anyhow, I meant to begin writing yesterday but had a

troupe of steel-toe capped elves inside my head. I had intended a quiet and sophisticated New Year's Eve as befits an almost divorced woman of 46 who is the mother of 20 year-old twins, so a night at the Queen's Head with Linda and Ron from next door, playing Twister and being groped by Minty Mike the landlord, was not what I had in mind.

So where do I start? On Christmas Eve, with incredibly ill-timing, it was only when my Decree Nisi was delivered among the festive post that I acknowledged my marriage was well and truly over. Until that moment, in the furthest reaches of my mind I naively imagined that Simon would have an epiphany, realise the error of his ways and rush to my side full of regret, goodwill and seasonal spirit.

I was right about the Christmas spirit as was apparent when I answered his phone call. He was rat-faced and any illusions I may have had were shattered faster than a glass bauble on concrete.

'Did you get your piece of paper?' he slurred.

I bristled instantly. 'You mean the piece of paper that ends our marriage: the Decree Nisi? Yes, I did.'

'Tha's good, 'cos I wouldn't want you to think, you know… tha' I wouldn't go through with it…ya know I'll always l-love you, Rosie, but I don' want you to think' tha' I might come back to you.'

I could barely get the words out. 'Why would I think that, Simon, when you've been screwing your secretary for the past year? And why would you imagine for one second that I'd want you back?'

'Well if that's how you feel…' He had the gall to sound *hurt*!

'That's exactly how I feel – and let me tell you that *piece of paper* is the best Christmas present you've ever given me. And definitely the most expensive. It beats the tumble dryer hands down.'

I cut the line and threw my mobile halfway across the room; not just because I was angry, but because I knew I was about to burst into tears. Until recently I had never realised what an insensitive, insufferable idiot he could be. But when I think back, there have been many incidents that could be categorized as such, and for some reason I either failed to notice or chose to ignore them.

I thought I was a pretty good wife – and that he was a good husband. I was quite content with my wonderful children, modest home and annual holiday. I didn't want to be fashionably divorced, or fashionably single. The only thing I wanted to change was my job, and though I can't actually pinpoint the moment when things started to head for those mythological rocks, I have realised, thanks to the 20-20 vision that retrospect allows, that the real problem stemmed from my desire to further my education.

My mother didn't believe in higher education for girls and refused to allow me to contemplate a place at college or university – and my father never could stand up to her. Happily for both of them she met someone else, divorced Dad and took herself off to America, but not before she had forced me to endure a secretarial course and witnessed me begin my first job.

Naturally I missed her – she was, after all, my mother. Still is, god help me. But without her negative influence I decided to save up and do what I really wanted, which was to go to art college, and within a year I'd saved enough to enrol at Kingley College of Art where I studied graphic design and photography. Working and studying didn't leave much time to think about my absent mother or my father's unhappiness, and eventually enabled me to get a (very junior) job with an advertising agency known as The Company.

Actually, at present I'm still there, albeit in a (purportedly) more senior role, but biding my time until something better comes along. Undaunted by their penny-pinching ways, I went back when the twins went to playgroup because it was convenient and familiar. I also needed the money as Simon was becoming increasingly tight-fisted: if he'd been at home all day he'd have known that the occasional aromatherapy massage was a necessity, not an extravagance. Ditto the extra bottles of wine. Also I found the adult company something of a novelty after being at home with toddlers, though nowadays there are times when I feel some of my colleagues would benefit from a few hours playing with Fuzzy Felt and an afternoon nap.

Anyhow, to cut a long story short, when the twins were studying for their GCSEs it reignited my long-buried desire to get a degree: mentioning it to Simon caused our first major marital rift. Probably because I refused to admit it was a stupid idea, that it was something I didn't need, and that it would be a waste of his hard earned cash because I wouldn't finish it.

Obviously my hard earned cash counted for little, but his patronizing attitude only spurred me on. I knew I had a brain, and I knew I didn't want to be stuck at The Company for the rest of my working life, so I embarked on five years with the Open University.

It was far from easy juggling work, family and study but I did it and earned my BA (Hons) in English Literature & Language. I think it probably earned that Decree Nisi as well, because Simon never really forgave me for going against his wishes and refused to lift a finger to make life easier for me, substantiating the adage that women who want to have it all end up doing it all. And, of course, my "lack of attention to his needs" turned out to be the perfect excuse for his infidelity. Not the most original reason for a marriage break-up.

So yes, it still hurts because we'd been together since we were 20. But want him back? Never!

Happily the twins made up for Simon's lack of enthusiasm, and when I graduated, they were there at my side, proud as punch. In fact they really are my saviours in all this messy business, and it hasn't been easy on them: no matter what your age or the reason, the breakup of your parents' marriage is a life-changing experience as I myself discovered - and I've never been very close to my mother. Jamie seems to be coping quite well, but though Leah doesn't say much, she was the apple of her father's eye and I know it has hit her hard. As for me, my emotions have leapt from anger to sadness and back again – and it's not always Simon who's the target of my wrath. Not directly anyhow.

Gina, my best friend, who's been divorced for 25 years and is engaged for the fourth time since, says men think all divorced women are suffering from sexual deprivation. She also says that after the split, the first man to hit on you is your husband's best friend. Yesterday proved her right.

Alan has been Simon's buddy since school: he was best man at our wedding, yet there he was on my doorstep last night, calling round "just to make sure you're OK, and wish you a Happy New Year".

I should have been suspicious as he'd shown precious little concern for me when he was busy covering Simon's faithless backside, and I haven't had sight nor sound of him since the man walked out on me.

Grudgingly I invited him in for a coffee, and within five minutes he was whingeing how his wife didn't understand him "even though she was a wonderful mother, of course", and working one hand round the back of me on the sofa, all the time regarding me with pathetic puppydog eyes.

I almost fell for it too, until his other hand landed on my thigh.

He was most put out when I whacked it with a handy copy of The Feminist's Bible, and tried to tell me he was just being a good friend. I said I didn't think Cindy would agree and he left in a righteous huff. I always thought he was as slippery as a sackful of ferrets.

It's funny but I've noticed one or two neighbours who've been keeping their distance recently, and the attitude of their husbands has discernibly changed too. They ignore me when their wives are about and make ambiguous remarks when they're not. Perhaps the offer to come and sort out my plumbing was genuine, but how Sid Roberts knew my ballcock was sticking beats me.

It must be contagious. First thing this morning Seth Barker,

Office Lecher, offered his services should there be a shortfall in my sex-life.

'The only shortfall I know of is in your brain – half of it's missing,' I snapped.

He still leered. 'Rosie, darling, you don't know what you're missing until you try it.'

'I don't have to be bitten by a black rat to know it's revolting and would probably leave me with a nasty disease.' I lasered him with my look that kills at twenty paces and he scuttled back to his corner.

Just before lunch I was trying to sneak out fifteen minutes early to satisfy my shopaholic urges at the January Sales when I received a summons to the boss's office, and was surprised to find Roman Doyle, Client Service Director, there. He was posing against the filing cabinet with a paper cup in his hand looking as if he were enjoying happy hour at his country club.

Roman is the firm's fantasy male, except he's married to the chairman's daughter, Lady Anna, who's said to rule him with a silver tongue, gold handcuffs and a platinum credit card. But there's no getting away from it, he is rather gorgeous…weak-willed, with a closed wallet and ever open zip (if rumours are to be believed), but very fit nevertheless. And very aptly titled as I doubt there are many clients he hasn't serviced.

It transpires I have the dubious honour of being picked to accompany him to a client conference in Bournemouth next weekend. My initial euphoria soon dissipated when I realised I was replacing Sharon, the dizzy blonde account manager who, amazingly, was last year's top earner. God knows how: she spends half her working life in front of the mirror in the Ladies and the other half in Zara.

According to the Creative Director, Big Ted (my immediate superior – and I use the term loosely), Sharon is flat on her back having taken a tumble at her New Year celebration and dislocated her hip. Quite surprising as she's said to be as flexible as knicker elastic. Especially hers.

As I am now unencumbered, I was the obvious choice of replacement. In fact the only one as it appears all my colleagues have prior engagements.

Looking at this positively, spending the weekend at a five-star hotel with a handsome younger man has to be a more exciting prospect than Breakfast at Tesco with Linda – especially as I have just started my diet and their Red Velvet Cupcakes were invented by the Calorie Devil himself.

In preparation for my trip I purchased a little black dress that had 40% off. I tried one boasting a 60% cut, but it was so skimpy I think it referred to the material - it was definitely my size. I also acquired half-price matching makeup and toilet bags. Bournemouth, here I come!

It's just dawned on me that next weekend starts tomorrow evening when Roman is driving me down to the venue in his company Mercedes, and I've had to bribe Wayne, next door's teenage brat, to feed Geoffrey, cross Siamese (half breed cat, not irate Oriental).

Today started badly and got steadily worse. I woke late, then halfway to work realised that having painstakingly transferred everything to my new make-up bag, I hadn't packed it, so had to turn back. When I eventually arrived at the office I was accosted by Big Ted (so called, by the way, because his name is Edward, and there the reality ends: he's a midget and about as cuddly as a frozen porcupine). Anyhow, he was foaming at the mouth as he thought I'd forgotten the pitch I was doing for some prospective clients at 10.30am. He was right. I had, and only just made it.

It did not go well. My flipchart stand collapsed and I knocked over a cup of coffee with my hip as I bent down to rescue it. Big Ted was now puce with rage and I distinctly heard him mutter something that included the words "useless" and "fat", which didn't help.

I don't think we'll get the campaign, and I'm not sorry as I wasn't looking forward to persuading Joe Public that reconstituted lettuce is a viable alternative to the real thing. Even a rabbit would turn up its nose at slimy green leaves optimistically named Salfresh. It sounds like a toilet cleaner.

Anyhow, as my colleagues departed to enjoy their weekend, I waited in the foyer with my suitcase and a carrier bag containing the sandwich and Diet Coke I hadn't had time for at lunch. I was hoping to consume them on the drive down to Dorset.

I waited. And I waited. And my stomach rumbled so loudly it evinced an irritable glance from Eric, the night security guard, who was in his glass cubicle squinting at the Evening Echo and toasting his feet by a small electric fire. It was then I realised the heating had been turned off and I was beginning to feel cold as well as hungry, and Roman was now 25 minutes late. Had he forgotten me?

I delved into the bag and eventually prised a tuna sandwich from its user-unfriendly packaging. Salivating, I took a massive bite, forgetting my anxieties for a moment... and there was Roman, just managing to wipe the distaste from his face as my eyes met his, and he forced a smile. I almost choked in my haste to swallow my mouthful while he stood expectantly, his spotless Aran sweater giving the impression he was modelling for a 1950's knitting pattern.

'Sorry I'm a bit on the drag,' he drawled without explanation. 'Let me take your suitcase.'

He made a grab for it while I composed myself as best I could, stuffing the remainder of my lunch back into the bag.

'God – what have you got in here? It's two days in Bournemouth, not a fortnight in the Bahamas.'

If it was the Bahamas, you jerk, I wouldn't need six sweaters and a pair of fur-lined knee boots…is what I should have said… "Sorry" was the only word that emerged. Pathetic!

The car was warm and comfortable as he weaved his way through the weekend traffic, singing along tunelessly with Cher. Apparently he isn't allowed to indulge his taste in popular music when his wife is in the car. Lady Anna, he calls her. Lady Anal according to Gina, who does her nails.

It was too warm and comfortable and I must have dozed off because the next thing I remember was his voice, slightly shrill, asking 'What is that awful fishy smell?' and glaring at me accusingly.

I straightened up, my senses returning in a rush, mortified to think I may have been snoring – or worse still, dribbling. And then I became aware of the fishy smell and scrabbled around my feet knowing my tuna sandwich had somehow escaped and got too close to a heating vent.

'We *never* allow food in here,' he barked when I admitted my sin. 'Chuck it out!'

'What? Out of the window – in a built-up area? How would you like it if someone threw their rubbish in your back yard?' I was angry at his anti-social proposition. And because I am known to be peevish when woken abruptly.

He cast me a frown and then grinned. 'Of course, you're right.' Taking his attention from the road again he gave me the benefit of his sexiest smile, dark eyes glinting in the dashboard light. 'I'll stop at the next lay-by. You know you're very appealing when you're asleep.'

Did that mean I wasn't appealing when I was awake, or that I was *only* appealing when I was asleep? Why should I give a stuff what he thought? He's a renowned philanderer and just because I was there as Sharon's stand-in didn't mean I had to take her place in his sordid sex-life. Even if I wanted to, which I definitely didn't. I have enough troubles, as well as a vendetta against men in general, in case you hadn't noticed. But that lay-by suggestion could have been misconstrued.

Unsurprisingly our rooms were adjoining and had connecting doors, but under the circumstances I didn't feel I should complain. The first thing I did was approach the connecting door to ensure it was locked.

I was therefore rather put out to hear the key in the other side being turned.

We were late for dinner but nevertheless in time to be issued with name badges to help us "bond" with our colleagues. Naturally mine still had Sharon's name on it and Roman was not thrilled when I refused to go along with his suggestion to pretend I was her for the duration.

I told him I wasn't about to act like a nympho airhead for anyone. He muttered something that sounded like "you wish" and with a rueful smile and shrug of his broad shoulders, slithered towards a redhead with hair like a poodle, and from whose bony promontories hung a pair of skin-tight silver leggings. She reminded me of one of those long-lasting batteries; perhaps she'll wear out Romeo Roman. In fact I can hear squeaking springs and squealing woman coming from his room as I write.

I know why I feel so hostile towards him. He's too good-looking by half, and my sympathies are most definitely with his long-suffering wife, anal or not.

I know what it's like to be on the receiving end of such treachery. It's only five months since Simon broke the news of his joyride with his secretary. I was horrified as he'd inherited Betty with his promotion - she was ancient and almost due for retirement back then. But of course, she *had* retired - and been replaced by a child barely out of college with legs up to her armpits and skirts round her neck.

Naturally Simon had mentioned the change, but it hardly registered, though I do remember the Freudian thought that Angelica was a bit of a mouthful. He calls her his Angel now. She's a year older than the twins and he says he's going to marry her.

I'm still having difficulty getting my head round the whole disastrous affair.

Christmas was different, but not as difficult as I imagined. Leah, Jamie and I went to the farm in Devon owned by my sister Lizzie and her husband, and Jamie decided to remain there until term starts. Jamie's always been very fond of his Uncle Bill and jumped at the chance to stay when he was told he could do some painting. Knowing Bill he probably means whitewashing the barn or cowsheds, but I wasn't about to spoil Jamie's pipedreams.

Leah came back home with me and went to stay with a new friend. She says it's a female; I suppose I'm lucky she told me that much. I dropped her off at the station and she told me not to worry, but I can't help recalling what I got up to at her age – mainly with her father, and he's certainly turned out to be a poor role model.

Leah is at present refusing to say a civil word to him, though she manages to wheedle extra cash out of him at every opportunity. He can hardly blame her: she's always been the light of his life, and now he's sleeping with a girl who could be her contemporary. Or not. Leah has always been extremely bright and I can't imagine that bimbo being in the same league. However, I suppose it depends on your predilections.

My fear is that this betrayal and its subsequent disruption will hamper Leah's studies to become a rocket scientist, or more precisely, an astrophysicist. I don't know where the science gene comes from – certainly not from me, and Simon's only foray into the world of science was brewing his own beer, yet Leah first showed an interest when she was eight years old. I think she'd been watching reruns of Star Trek. Anyhow, she's already more than halfway to her BSc and is due to spend her third year with NASA in Florida. To me she's always seemed to be on a different planet.

I've noticed that boy/girl twins often practise role reversal, albeit subconsciously. Leah has consistently been the dominant, athletic one, whereas Jamie is soft hearted and artistic. Not that there's anything wrong with that, but I've occasionally found myself wishing Leah were a little more feminine, and Jamie more assertive. Anyhow, he's very creative and belongs to a band at Art College. I adore them both – and our relationship is so much smoother now they're living away from home much of the time. I've been too occupied to experience the empty nest syndrome, but I do miss them, and the house sometimes feels unbearably empty.

Anyhow, I'm going to try to get some sleep now - if I can deaden the sounds still coming from next door and black out the unpleasant images they conjure up. Whoever said sex was a beautiful experience should listen to this pair: even Howler Monkeys must do it with more finesse.

This morning I had to sit through a presentation with lots of cheering and self-congratulatory ovations led by one of our counterparts from America who sported a glorious silver mane and evangelical charisma. At the height of his fomentations I half expected his inflamed flock to rush the rostrum and prostrate themselves before him. And all in the name of Salfresh and its ilk. What a way to earn a living.

As I'm not usually invited to client conferences it was a bit of a culture shock to experience the fevered adulation that a box of dishwasher tablets inspired, but I have to say I was more interested in the attempts of Poodle-head to make eye contact with Roman across the auditorium. He was doing everything bar feigning blindness to avoid her, and when we broke for coffee he grabbed me with a vice-like grip and dragged me to a table so minute it would barely hold two cups. He then charged to the head of the queue and, excusing himself with a dazzling smile and silky words, managed to get us some coffee before sitting down with his back to the crowded room.

'Tell me if you see that awful woman coming towards me,' he hissed.

'What awful woman is that?' I asked innocently.

'You know…the one with the big hair who wouldn't leave me alone last night…'

'Oh, *that* woman,' I said, and his hunted expression relaxed slightly. 'The one you kept screaming to "do that again, baby, don't stop" all last night?'

He flushed, but immediately recovered

'Aw, come on, Rosie, give us a break – she was all over me a like a rash, begging for it…you know what these divorcées are like.' he flashed his most devastating smile. 'I couldn't really turn it down, could I?'

I shrugged wordlessly. Of course you couldn't, you unprincipled pillock.

The rest of the morning was much the same, and at lunchtime Roman insisted I dine with him and a couple of male friends and that I take a notebook to the table "so it would seem like a real business lunch". Actually, so that Poodle-head couldn't barge in and join us. Except she did.

Her name was Rita and she squeezed in beside Roman forcing me into close contact with one of the friends whose thigh tautened meaningfully against mine. That was before he glimpsed Rita's cleavage. I thought it singularly unimpressive, but a balcony bra under a miniscule crocheted top displayed it to full advantage. Men are so shallow.

Anyhow my appetite disappeared having to watch Roman gradually succumb to Poodle's obvious charms, and trying to field his creepy colleagues' ambiguous suggestions for an afternoon session.

As it happened the actual afternoon session was only slightly more appealing with the same boring pep talks and a video thrown in. Roman and Poodle were noticeably absent until after tea break. He came to join me, cup in hand (perhaps that should be cap in hand, recalling his sheepish expression).

'Oh, you're here,' he said.

I glared at him. 'Of course. I see you couldn't resist *that awful woman* again.'

He smirked. 'Do I detect a hint of the green-eyed monster?'

I almost spluttered my tea.

'You're in with a good chance Rosie. There's still tonight.'

'My god, you're insufferable. Just because I'm divorced doesn't mean I'm desperate. I wouldn't go near your...bits...if you scrubbed them with a Brillo pad.'

The insult seemed to go over his head, but his entire demeanour was instantly on full alert, like a gundog that had spotted a falling pheasant. 'You're divorced? Nobody told me that.'

'Why should they? Besides, it's not final yet.'

'Then I'm sorry. Divorce is a messy business,' his brown eyes were limpid with sympathy. What a player! He took my hand. 'I really am sorry Rosie. Perhaps...later on...I could take you out for a meal to commiserate?'

I pulled my hand from his, seething. 'You just can't help it, can you? You are married. With children. Don't you think your family deserves some loyalty? Or do you have to prove yourself with every woman you meet?'

For a moment he looked shocked. 'Is that how you see me?'

'It's how everyone with more than half a brain sees you. Wise up, Roman, before it's too late.'

The bell went, signalling the return to the auditorium and Roman turned on his heel and stalked to the foyer.

Perhaps I should have kept my mouth shut. The following morning I found a note at reception telling me to take the train home. When we get back to the real world he could have me sacked. That's all I need.

It never ceases to amaze me that companies fund these orgies, for that's all last weekend's debacle appeared to me. But I shouldn't be surprised because I've had my share of the low-level sexual harassment which is par for the course in the advertising world: it's full of people who think monogamy is something you make sideboards out of.

I spent the entire evening of the farewell Dinner & Dance fending off drunken idiots who seemed to imagine I was part of the entertainment which was hardly surprising as most of the women behaved worse than the men. I saw at least four complying with chanted requests to "get yer boobs out for the boys", and one full striptease. Perhaps I am a miserable killjoy (to quote one particularly obnoxious groper) but I went to bed well before the end.

I guess I never realised the extent of the debauchery. Though given my present situation, who's to say my conventional views on matrimony are unblemished?

Maybe I should have taken up Roman's offer then I wouldn't still be worried about losing my job. I bet he had the mother of all hangovers and I hope his children screamed and jumped all over him when he got home.

Anyhow, having not been delayed in the Xmas mail, all else pales into insignificance against the arrival on Wednesday of my Decree Absolute.

I am now single. I expect the young and free bit will come later. Ha!

Joking apart, and though I went out for a "celebration"

drink with my three closest friends, I am still grieving that something which started with such hope has ended so bitterly. Because I *am* bitter. Even a saint would have the beatific smile knocked from its face after being thrown on the scrap heap and usurped by a newer model. It makes you feel no more important than a washing machine or an electric carving knife.

Compared to many discarded wives – my friend Heidi for a start - I know it could be worse. I have the house, which was awarded to me in lieu of foregoing my claim on Simon's pension. Now all I have to do is pay the mortgage. And all the running expenses. Thank goodness I still have my job: demoralizing it may be, but it gives me an (almost) liveable wage.

Simon is contributing towards the twin's expenses until they leave university.

My friends optimistically labelled the gathering my "Freedom Party", but quite frankly, being on my own with half the income and twice the hassle, at present I can work up very little enthusiasm for my new found emancipation.

Heidi is selling her family home because her youngest son, Martin, is now sixteen and has left school, and her ex is enforcing the divorce settlement. She works as a care assistant so can barely afford a bedsit unless she goes deeper into the countryside, and then she'll have further to drive, which means more petrol. It's a vicious circle.

She was telling us that on top of this, Martin hasn't yet found a job and though the Family Allowance has ceased, he's not entitled to unemployment benefit so she still has to support him too. Where is the justice in that? Where is the joy in being divorced? Gina's (current) fiancé, Lloyd, owns a building firm and she's promised to ask him to find Martin a labouring job.

Heidi saved my sanity when I had the twins. She hasn't had an easy life yet she's the most sweet-natured person imaginable - which isn't a description I'd bestow on all of my friends. Madeleine, for example: she's great; she's supportive, glamorous – but not a bone in her body that could be designated as "sweet".

Anyhow, Maddy was there, resplendent as usual in designer gear, and looking on as if we were speaking an alien tongue. She's been married and divorced three times, but her exes have all been wealthy, and her settlements have taken her on an exotic journey from council house in Colchester to pied-à-terre in London, duplex in New York, villa in Cyprus, small yacht on the Hamble, plus a gargantuan mansion in the Essex countryside. And that's just what she owns now, all part of generous settlements from accommodating ex-husbands. I don't know why she still bothers with the rest of us unless it's to remind her of what life might have been.

We all met at primary school, and were a foursome long before we embarked on our secondary education. We shared our first cigarettes, our first discos and the secrets of our first fumblings, and though there have been times when life took us our separate ways, somehow we've always been there for one another, if only to give moral support. Or perhaps that should be *im*moral support in the case of Maddy's chequered love-life.

Heidi started nurse training but had to leave when she became pregnant and married the father, Peter "Dingo" Fox, embarking on twenty years of domestic hell. We all tried to persuade her to leave the no-good waster, but she hung on until just before Martin left school. In retrospect, I guess her situation made me feel complacent about mine. Big mistake.

Gina trained as a beauty therapist and married at nineteen. Luckily she didn't have any children, for two years later her husband, Graham, a former high school heartthrob, decided that he preferred the opposite sex (opposite to women, that is) and she dumped him like a hot brick when she came home and found him canoodling with an ugly macho brute, a former prefect who had made the lives of us juniors a living misery. We felt we'd been sweetly avenged when his secret life was revealed. Especially regarding his penchant for pink tulle.

Anyway, it didn't actually make Gina wary of men, more the reverse. Some people think she's a bit of a strumpet, but the fact that she keeps getting engaged and then cries off, tells us, her friends, she's insecure and afraid of making another mistake.

Though I don't believe I'd feel so aggrieved if Simon had discovered his feminine side and run off with a raving poofter: at least I could understand the attraction.

Madeleine (she's prefers not be called Maddy nowadays) was always stunning and smart enough to make it work for her. She became a top model and sometime actress - and my claim to fame is that I took the photos that interested her first agency. She married an American who was heir to an enormous fortune and whose father fortuitously died just as he was about to file for divorce. She then wed a Greek millionaire who died eighteen months after their wedding and to whom she has a son, Andreas, and went on to capture the heart and half the assets of a Formula One driver who dumped her for a statuesque Swede. Her latest squeeze is a minor soap star who is twenty years her junior. We think he's after her dosh – not to mention the publicity. Time will tell.

As for me, I wanted to be a photo/journalist or an artist, but as I've already said, my mother never saw the necessity for a woman to be well-educated, so my dreams of going to university were stunted before they had a chance to blossom.

Actually the secretarial course she forced me into turned out to be very beneficial – particularly for The Company because when they took me on as a trainee graphic artist it enabled them to incorporate my secretarial skills without the necessity of paying an extra wage.

This parsimony taught me little because of course I returned to full-time employment when the twins started school and progressed to account executive/copywriter/graphic artist, which makes good use of my creative skills, and still saves them barrel loads of cash.

Completing my OU degree seems to have made little difference to my career as The Company has refused to give me a rise in pay or status, and I started to look further afield as soon as I realised nothing was ever going to change. Ironically, I was due to go for an interview at the only decent agency in town when I discovered Simon's duplicity. I wish I'd gone, but at the time I was in no state to persuade anyone that I had the nous to sell ice to the Inuit, let alone run a national campaign.

But in the early years I was happy enough with my job and loved being with the twins. We'd been married a year and I was almost 27 when I had them – and what a shock they were! It was wonderful until I found myself home alone with these two screaming bundles – well, one screaming bundle who always managed to wake up her ever placid brother.

It was then I rediscovered my true friends. Heidi, who already had three children and was pregnant with her fourth, came over as often as she could and guided me through the minefield of child rearing. It wasn't easy for her as she had to come by bus with her two youngest. It was obvious to me even then that her marriage was not like ours, because although Simon was hardly a New Man in the nappy changing and night feed department, we were good together in those days.

Anyway Gina, who to my knowledge has never left the house without a face full of make-up and never had a bad hair day, would also come over at the weekend and do her best, even though her talents peaked at pram pushing. She has always been the twin's favourite auntie though, and spoils them rotten at birthday and Christmas time.

I was quite ruffled when they were at that awful pubescent stage as Leah turned to Gina more than she ever did me. Gina reminded me how we went through a phase when we'd no more confide in our mothers than eat broccoli, and of course, she was right, and Leah gradually returned to human form. As near to it as she's ever been, that is. I just wish she'd get out of those jeans every now and again and smarten herself up a tad. If she's ever had a proper boyfriend, I haven't heard about it. Not that I'm advocating marriage - god forbid – I just want her to get out and enjoy herself.

Madeleine visited once or twice over the years, always impressing us with her latest car/clothes/man and bearing extravagant gifts for all. Her visits caused a stir in the surrounding area as she was a genuine supermodel in her day, and more than once we found photographers at our gate within minutes of her arrival.

Once, when she was married to Andreas Senior, she arrived on the local football pitch by helicopter along with Andreas Junior and his nanny, and a picture of them leaving our three-bed semi appeared in a tabloid under the headline "Maddy drops in" which didn't please her anymore than the ensuing blurb pleased me (or our neighbours) when it was described as the "poverty stricken area she left behind". House prices dropped to an all-time low.

In actual fact the estate where Maddy was raised is ten miles away and ten times scummier than our quiet, clean neighbourhood. But at least she kept in touch, and in recent years we've all seen a lot more of her, especially in between divorces (also in Playboy, Loaded and FHM – but that's another story). I can't understand why she's always so quick to replace her husbands (or do centrefolds) – she certainly doesn't need the money. Or the exposure.

It's ironic because now we're all over forty-five (though Maddy's publicity says she's thirty-nine) - and since I've joined the realms of the singleton, none of our quartet actually has a husband. Gina's is pending - or *de*pending on whether or not she makes it to the altar.

I had a phone call from Jamie saying he's coming home tomorrow and bringing a friend. I wondered how long he'd last at the farm after my brother-in-law told him the vet would be coming to castrate the calves. Bill also complained about the modern art/graffiti covering his cowshed walls – he says his milk-yield is down. Serves him right for using my son as cheap labour! Jamie's due back at college next week anyway.

I must remember to make up Leah's room. I have no idea what gender the friend is, but it's equally suitable for either; her only poster is of Baywatch and there are models of Starship Enterprise and the Columbia space shuttle hanging from the ceiling along with an assortment of luminous stars – stuck in their correct astrological pattern, of course.

I only caught a fleeting glimpse of Roman Doyle this week. I had just entered the lift and he seemed to be heading for it too, so I held the door but he veered away suddenly. If I didn't know better I'd think he was trying to avoid me. Apparently dizzy Sharon returns to her duties next week. It will be interesting to see if there's any contact between them.

On Saturday morning, just as I was relaxing at the kitchen table with a mug of coffee, wearing my sloppy tracksuit and surrounded by assorted piles of washing, Jamie burst in followed by Adonis.

I can honestly say it's a very long time since I'd had my senses stirred by a vision of male beauty, but young as he was, Joshua was exactly that. He was tall, broad shouldered, had a six-pack visible through his T-shirt, and the face of a slightly rugged cherub with sparkling blue eyes and fair hair moulding his perfectly shaped head.

When he spoke his voice had the timbre of a mature male, beautifully modulated, which coupled with an all pervading look and a lingering, far-from-limp handshake, sent a shiver right down to my boots. Or Garfield slippers, to be precise.

'Mrs Grant, I'm delighted to meet you. Jamie didn't say you were so…young and attractive.'

Smarmy little wretch! He was well aware of his assets and obviously had much practise at capitalising on them. I imagined the trail of brokenhearted females in his wake.

Then, as Jamie led him upstairs to show him Leah's room, I saw him put his hand on my son's bottom. And Jamie just grinned.

Oh – my – god.

Josh, of course, was much too pretty to be straight. But, what about my Jamie? Did it necessarily follow…? I'd long been aware he has a very soft streak – at least, he's always been kind-hearted and cried at sad movies, and he's tidy, and very fussy about his clothes (he's been ironing his own shirts since he was thirteen as he doesn't like the way I do them). Had he invited Josh here because he couldn't face telling me he was gay? Oh my poor baby...but no, surely there'd have been some tangible sign before now?

I heard them bumbling around upstairs and had to stop myself from rushing up to see what they were doing. Instead, in a flustered attempt to get them where I could see them I shouted up to ask if they wanted any coffee. They did, and I was pouring it in seconds.

They went out as soon as they'd finished their drinks saying they were going shopping then meeting up with some other friends. They would probably end up at a club and expected to be quite late. Visions of dimly lit basements, smoochy music and grown men dressed as shirtless builders and firemen filled my mind, but I followed them to the door, limiting myself to saying "Have you got your key?" and "Have a great time" and withholding the urge to drag my son back or thrust a packet of condoms in his hand. If I had any, of course.

I spent the rest of the day in a state of anxiety. Was it my fault? Had I been too soft on Jamie when he was growing up? Simon always said I was, but it was just that Leah was always so difficult, and Jamie never gave me a moment's grief. Not that I am in the least homophobic – one of my best friends at work is gay - but it's not something you'd wish for your son, is it? I mean, life must be much easier if you're "normal". Whatever that is.

I drank almost a full bottle of wine, and when I eventually went to bed had not slept a wink when I heard them stumbling up the stairs at five past three. I breathed a sigh of relief as I heard them say goodnight and go to their separate rooms, then like a cross between the Pink Panther and Miss Marple I lay there listening to ensure there were no musical beds before allowing myself to fall into a fitful slumber.

I was in my dilapidated dressing gown in the kitchen just fixing myself a slice of toast when I was startled to find Josh, clad only in silky boxers bearing an image of Minnie Mouse, standing in the doorway and regarding me with those sultry eyes. Too early and much too disturbing for a Sunday morning.

'May I make some coffee, Mrs Grant?'

'Of course.' The fact he was my son's age and probably gay didn't make it any easier to ignore that golden, practically naked torso – which somehow he managed to keep brushing against me as he moved to refill the kettle and get the milk from the fridge. Even his smell exuded testosterone.

When the coffee was made, instead of taking it upstairs as I expected, he seated himself opposite me at our compact kitchen table, his bare knees touching mine.

'I hope you don't mind, Mrs Grant, but I love to sit in the kitchen. It reminds me of when I used to do it with Nanny – my parents were frequently away, you see…'

The angelic features looked wistful and my heart went out to him as I imagined this sad little boy. I patted his hand and he grabbed it…

'…she used to let me come into her bed sometimes and, like you, she had magnificent breasts. I so liked to lay my head on them…' the slender fingers of his free hand were reaching hypnotically towards by unharnessed chest…

I sprang up, shocked not only by the turn of events, but by my treacherous body's reaction to them.

'Joshua, I really don't think you should be speaking to me like this.'

He immediately stood and I had to drag my eyes from the increasingly pregnant Minnie Mouse.

'I do apologise, Mrs Grant. You are just so-o sexy. Please don't take offence…' he was completely unabashed.

With a regretful expression he closed the door and I plumped back down on my chair. Cheeky little so-and-so! But there was nothing in the least gay about that tumultuous display.

I knew I had a stupid grin on my face. Audacious he may have been, but he was young and beautiful. And, apparently, found me sexy!

I no longer believe I'm totally frigid (as Simon was fond of telling me) as I've had more than a few "what if" moments about that little incident, I can tell you.

Not that I ever really believed my ex-husband's assertion. Ex-husband! That's the first time I've actually thought of him as that. But I suppose that's the reality and I'll have to get used to it. Anyhow, I am now certain that frigid was the wrong description for my lack of enthusiasm in the bedroom. Fatigue, familiarity and fed-up with his lack of moral support, maybe. And dare I say boredom? But frigid? No.

Later that afternoon after Josh got into his MG and zoomed off to town, Jamie said, 'He's a nice guy, isn't he? Bit of a prat though – he's got a great girlfriend, really hot, but there's always some crumpet throwing herself at him and he just can't seem to resist it. Mind you, it's handy knocking about with him as there's always plenty of spare. And he thinks you're a real milf.'

I must remember to let Jamie know I disapprove of him referring to the fairer sex as "crumpet" and "spare". Also I really should check on the condom situation. And not just for my son. And what on earth is a milf?

FEBRUARY

Lately my life seems to lurch from one crisis to another. Gina was on my doorstep in tears the other morning: the wedding is off. Surprise, surprise. Except this time it was *he* who got cold feet, not her. Lloyd, apparently, is not sure he's ready to make the ultimate commitment. And in keeping with my new policy to stop saying what people want to hear, whilst drying her eyes I remarked that it must be very hurtful to find oneself rejected in this way – as she had her last three fiancés.

She looked shocked, 'How can you be so cruel, Rosie? This time it's different. I really love Lloyd...a-and ...I-I don't th-think I can l-live without him...' she dissolved into shuddering sobs.

My entire Saturday morning was voided as I tried to find comforting words for my heartbroken friend. So much for forthright speaking. To appease her I agreed, very reluctantly, to accompany her that evening to a singles' club where she was sure she'd find Lloyd.

I knew it would be a mistake. When Gina came to pick me up, gone was the wan, crushed figure of earlier and in its place stood Miss Congeniality, glorious in a short red number that mysteriously enhanced her copper-coloured hair. She was in man killer mode and my heart sank: I was still in the mood to man-kill. Literally.

She insisted on starting off at a nearby pub where we were supposed to acquire some Dutch courage before making our grand entrance at the Popinjay Club, the plan being she would totally ignore Lloyd. I'd never been to the Popinjay before, it being proclaimed as a venue for "over-35s singles". But I was well aware of its reputation – or should I say notoriety - as a hunting ground for the not-single-but-looking-for-an-affair/one-night-stand type. But it was where Gina met Lloyd, so I knew her strategy to ignore him meant she would flirt outrageously with every other man in the room in an effort to make the erstwhile fiancé jealous. I just hoped it wouldn't backfire.

Fortunately, Lloyd was nowhere to be seen, and nor did he make an appearance all evening. I spent uncomfortable hours in this meat market fending off Medallion Man clones and being glared at by supposedly mature women dressed like teenagers who obviously feared I might be in competition for one of these ageing Lotharios. Not if it were my last night on Earth, believe me! Gina became more and more manic as time passed, so when I realised she was on the point of accepting a lift home from a slimebag I knew she wouldn't look at twice when she was sober, I dragged her into a cab and took her home. I then sat on the side of her bath as she sobbed (again) with her head down the toilet.

It took me back twenty-five years, and I realised with a sense of dread that if I ever overcome my aversion to the opposite sex, this miserable scenario is par for the course in the mating game.

Put the condoms on hold. Indefinitely.

Lloyd, by the way, has found a job for Heidi's lad, so something good came out of the relationship.

It's been a strange week at work. Big Ted has been quite nice to me as we won the Salfresh account, despite my inept presentation. I still cannot think of a way to persuade anyone to buy it: all I can picture is a slogan saying *"9 out of 10 rabbits prefer Salfresh – when the other choice is a 12-bore shotgun".*

I saw Roman Doyle having a tête-à-tête with Sharon over the photocopier. He spotted me and leapt away from her as if she'd burst into flames. Instead of pretending I hadn't noticed anything I couldn't resist raising a disdainful eyebrow, and he actually seemed embarrassed. I think he's scared I might open my mouth about his client conference sexploits.

Well I didn't open my mouth, but somebody did, because Monday morning saw Lady Anna storming up to the third floor. Apparently she swept past the secretaries and flung open the door to Roman's office, slammed it shut, and proceeded to give him a dressing down as only the public school educated know how. Which is why, despite having their ears glued to the door, the secretaries only overheard the occasional venomous "little shit" and "complete wanker" and "Daddy says" followed by muttered cajoling from Roman, a series of dull thuds and then the sound of breaking glass.

The angry wife swept out, scattering secretaries like ninepins and was followed a while later by a very meek Roman, limping slightly.

I went to the Ladies in time to see Sharon poking her head round a cubicle door, an expression of terror on her face. So, Roman had been caught dipping his hand in the honeypot. Someone's going to pay.

I'm trying to record this is in a coherent manner so that if I ever want to remind myself of this time, it will be intelligible, but all I want to do is scream and give way to hysteria. I am shattered. I cannot believe it. *I have been sacked!*

I was called into Big Ted's office at 4pm on Friday afternoon and told the department was being downsized and that my services were no longer required. I was speechless, but the thought kept swirling round my head that Roman Doyle had engineered my demise: he obviously blamed me for his wife discovering his extra-curricular activity with Sharon. But that's the least of my worries as I have just four weeks to find another job.

Though there have been rumours that The Company's profits were down, and there was some downsizing six months ago, there had been no hint further cutbacks were on the cards. I have given over 20 years service to that underhand outfit, and this is how they repay me. I am to get a statutory redundancy payment – which might pay the mortgage for a couple of months, and that's it.

I am now over forty-five and the one qualification advertising and PR agencies require is Youth, with a capital Y. Enthusiasm is more important than experience. It doesn't matter if you can't spell, or draw because the computer can do it for you, and these fledglings then become whiz kids and are soon earning megabucks. It's not fair. Yet another master has thrown me on the scrap heap.

I rang Gina after a sleepless night during which I tried to imagine having to exist on the wages of a supermarket shelf-stacker - if I were sufficiently fortunate to find a vacancy. I must have sounded like a gibbering idiot because she came round and had rallied Heidi and Madeleine to attend with bottles of wine.

It wasn't exactly what a person on the verge of becoming a bag lady needed, but by the end of the afternoon I was feeling much more positive about my situation. Not to mention inebriated. I love my girlfriends.

I had also learned that I wasn't the only long-serving employee to get the boot – Seth Barker was also out on his ear, so my paranoia at being the victim of an avenging husband has diminished slightly. Unless Seth was also a suspect in the hiss and tell saga - which I doubt or the whole building would have known about it.

Sunday morning I forced myself to take stock of my situation. Since Simon went I've had to get used to tightening my belt, and after the initial shock of existing on less than half my previous disposable income, now have a sense of satisfaction that I am managing (almost) and enjoy the sense of independence it gives me. This was something I'd never really known: when I was young, I was never free and single in the proper sense as Simon and I started saving for a house soon after we met. But as I was about to join the world of the unemployed, I did my sums and wanted to hide in a corner and cry like a baby. Actually, that's what I did.

When it comes down to the nitty gritty – and it has - unless

I can find a position that pays within £5K of what I earn now I cannot afford to stay in this house. And the chances of that are nought to nothing. Not only am I jobless, I shall soon be homeless too.

I took a sickie today, something I've never done before unless I was genuinely ill. When I think of how I've crawled to my desk on the verge of collapse I could spit. I should have stayed at home in bed watching game shows on TV until the alcohol dispersed naturally, like everyone else does. I even missed the twin's sports' day once as a favour to The Company. My loyalty was sadly misplaced.

Anyhow, I feel positively sick now: I spent the afternoon contacting the specialist employment agencies I knew might have something in my line, and drew a complete blank. I then toured the High Street agencies and there was only one situation even vaguely suitable. It's with a PR company and the money is laughable, but I'm going for an interview tomorrow, so will be taking another sickie. In fact I think I'll go for the full week of self-certification, and after that, if they want a doctor's note I'm pretty sure I can simulate a nervous breakdown. Though simulation will probably be unnecessary.

I have never been an aggressive person, but when the babe-in-arms who interviewed me for the PR job, having glanced briefly at my CV, suggested I might find the post too challenging, I wanted to drag him over the desk and knock the spots from his face. Challenging? It entailed copying blurb and turning it into press releases – something I used to do when he was still in Pampers.

But I managed to keep my cool. Just. No point in antagonising the agency. I stood up and uncurled my fists.

'Actually, I think perhaps you're right. I don't believe this position would be suitable for a woman of my experience. Have a nice day.' *Actually, have a crap day and may your zits multiply abundantly.* Outside again I wanted to scream my frustration. Instead I went into the nearest coffee shop and treated myself to a cinnamon latte and a large choc-chip muffin.

I went home with a copy of the local paper and scoured the Sits Vac. There was nothing at all faintly appropriate – and to be honest, I think I would rather stack supermarket shelves than work for the likes of a juvenile who thought I'd find concocting a press release too demanding. Yet have I really progressed so far from there - persuading people that products made from chemicals and E-numbers are good for them? How many times can a soap-powder or cleaning fluid be "new and improved"? What will I tell my grandchildren - that Granny's life was spent thinking up stupid slogans and conning people?

I am thoroughly confused, not to mention depressed.

to go for an interview.'

'But I thought it was temporary?'

'It is. Do you want an interview or not, Mrs Grant?' Her tone was verging on the impatient.

'Yes.' I withheld the urge to tell her where to stick her job.

'Wednesday afternoon at 3pm then. You have to see a Mr Mike Robbins.'

Despondently I wrote down the address then looked again at the possibilities I'd marked in the paper. There was nothing in the least creative about any of them. One was for a sales assistant in an upmarket fashion boutique, one for a customer service assistant a - "mature, sensitive person" was required but it didn't hint at the nature of the business, and the third for a Girl Friday for a small publishing company.

I started with the third.

'Good morning. I'm ringing about the Girl Friday vacancy advertised in the Gazette.'

'Sorry, it's no longer available. Our Saturday girl has decided to take it.'

Was this some kind of a wind-up? I stood open mouthed before I realised I'd been cut off.

I tried number two, preparing to use my "mature, sensitive" tone.

'Smith & Sons Funeral Services,' said a sombre voice. 'How can we be of service to you?'

A funeral parlour. No, I'm not that desperate.

'Sorry. Wrong number.'

Two down and one to go. I dialled again.

'Esmeralda, *Haute Couture Boutique*. May we help?'

This time the voice was exactly what I expected; she was bound to call customers "Modom".

'Good morning. I'm ringing about the vacancy for a sales assistant.'

'Oh. Have you any experience in the fashion trade?'

Yes, I design an annual Paris Collection. 'Um, well not exactly. But I'm willing to learn – and I buy a lot of clothes.' Well, I used to.

'Humph. We have some very wealthy customers who require special, individual treatment. How old are you?'

I told her.

'Come for an interview at 2pm. Your name...?'

I gave it and as the phone went down heard her gushing 'Good *morning,* Lady Anna...'

Lady Anna? Things can only get worse.

At 2pm, wearing my most fawning expression and a Jaeger suit given to me by my ex-sister-in-law, I opened the imposing door of Esmeralda. I've passed it many times but neither the styles nor the designer labels have ever enticed me through its portals.

Inside it was plush, with thick carpets, mirrors that made me look like a stick insect, and a few sparse rails of clothes too expensive to warrant price tags.

Before I could close the door I was approached by the archetypal upmarket sales person of yesteryear, an older woman in a suit with her hair in a neat chignon and an expression more grovelling than mine that instantly turned into all-encompassing scrutiny as she realised I was not one of her "Modoms".

I smiled and extended my hand. 'Hello. I'm Rose-Anne

Grant. I've come about the job.'

'I could tell you weren't a customer. Follow me.'

I had a childish impulse to stick my tongue out at her ramrod straight back as she led me to a tiny office filled with ledgers and invoices and no computer. It was positively Dickensian: the only things missing were an inkwell and quills. She bade me sit opposite her.

'Here we do not sell *clothes*; we sell an *image*, a *concept*. Our customers are *very* particular, and are *always* right. Do you understand that?'

I nodded meekly.

'How are you with money?'

I know how to spend it. 'Fine.'

'I meant, how's your arithmetic?'

'It's fine. Accurate, normally.'

'Credit cards?'

'I have two.' I could have kicked myself.

She glared at me. 'Do you know how to *process* them?'

'Well, not actually. I know they're swiped and you put in your PIN number then it's authorised - or not, if your account's over your credit limit.'

She looked appalled. '*Our* clients would *never* have problems with their credit limit – and we don't have new-fangled machines because they still know how to write their own names.' Her scathing words reminded me of my old headmistress and I was half ready to repeat them to prove I'd been paying attention.

'Would you like to ask me anything?'

'Er, yes. What is the salary?'

She gave a disapproving sniff. 'We pay National Minimum.'

God, I don't want to work here, that decided me; I wasn't even sure what National Minimum was, only certain it would be a pittance.

She rose as the doorbell tinkled delicately, indicating a customer.

'Well you seem suitable, Mrs Grant. At least you're presentable. You can't beat a good Jaeger. I'll call you tomorrow with my decision.'

'Thank you,' I said as I backed out of the door, but she'd already dismissed me and was wringing her hands obsequiously as she greeted an elderly Modom.

Yuk! Am I that desperate?

Maybe.

Gina came round yesterday evening to give me moral support and two bottles of Tesco's Wine of the Week. She was in high spirits as Lloyd had called her and they were meeting at the weekend to talk. In preparation for this talk she showed me the French underwear she'd bought and described the purportedly aphrodisiac Ylang-Ylang spray she'd acquired for the sheets. I think she's missing the point as I don't believe sex is the problem.

Over the first bottle I told her about Esmeralda's. She shook her head immediately.

'Oh Rosie, you can't. It's not you at all. God, imagine having to spend your day kowtowing old crones with too much money and being watched like a hawk by a mini-Hitler.'

'Ha! I've been doing that for the past 20 years!' I retorted picturing Big Ted. I really must think of a suitable gesture for him before I leave – one not recognised as universally crude. 'Besides, I might not have any choice. I suppose I could always try the funeral parlour.'

This was the catalyst to fits of inane laughter as we pictured me screwing up funeral arrangements and ultimately falling into a freshly dug grave. Gina was right: my demeanour was not suited to hours of solemnity. Under present circumstances doom and gloom are the last things I need.

Gina said she thought I should try my luck in London as there are more jobs there and the money is better. She's probably right, but that option has always been a last resort for me as I can't bear the thought of travelling for two hours a day on trains packed like sardine cans. But if my interview tomorrow comes to nothing, I might have to bite the bullet and face the possibility of commuting.

Over the second bottle we talked about Lloyd and Simon

and Roman and…well it was girl-talk, the usual mixture of love them/hate them. I would love to know if Roman Dickbrain had any part in my demise at The Company. Perhaps I should anonymously drop Sharon's address through Lady Anna's letterbox. Though if anyone is asking for the chop, it's him. And not just in the job department.

Big Ted has just rung. He practically accused me of faking illness, and then said just because I'm leaving doesn't mean I can forget about my campaigns, and what was I going to do about Salfresh? Heartless little tyrant.

I told him I was genuinely sick with women's problems (i.e. men) and that I would have a doctor's certificate on his desk on Monday, whether or not I was fit to work by then. As for Salfresh, I was putting a lot of thought into it from my sickbed.

In fact, as I put down the receiver I had a very good idea. But it requires some refinement.

I was so into thinking what I was going to do with Salfresh that I almost forgot about my three 'o'clock interview and dashed to get ready. I decided on my normal smart clothes; a plum-coloured trouser suit and crisp white blouse. The Jaeger could stay in the wardrobe for another ten years - which reminded me that Esmeralda hadn't rung, and suddenly I knew I didn't want to hear from her because I was not yet in a position to turn down her job – if she offered it – though I really didn't want it. So when the phone rang as I was going out of the door, I let it.

If I'm sufficiently wretched to need a job at Esmeralda I expect I'll be sufficiently chastened to beg for it.

I reached the address in the town centre with two minutes to spare. It was the Shalimar Hotel – so small that I'd never noticed it before, though the name rang a bell - and a mountainous, dishevelled porter looked at me suspiciously then directed me to an empty lobby with well-worn decor and sparse groups of tired looking seats. He told me Mr Robbins was expecting me and would be with me shortly.

Ten minutes later I was still waiting, and becoming

increasingly dubious. As I sat there it came to me where I'd heard of this establishment before: in the section of the local paper where they report Court cases. And if my memory serves me correctly it had something to do with a guest being fleeced by a woman of ill repute – or sex worker as they are now euphemistically known.

What line of business was Robbins in that he stayed in a fourth-rate hotel and needed a mature secretary? For how long? Where would the work be carried out?

I was just thinking that I should hot foot it before I found myself propositioned by a man in a dirty mac, when all at once a figure appeared in front of me. My first impression was of a tall, anxious skeleton. But he was smartly dressed and his smile was warm so I took his outstretched hand.

'Mrs Grant? I'm Mike Robbins.'

Was that an American accent? I nodded, further unnerved by the way he turned his head furtively to either side like a pantomime villain.

'So sorry I'm late. I couldn't get parked. Now, let's get started. Do you have your Résumé - er -CV?'

Yes, American. His voice was deep and deliberate and he took my folder and sat immediately, scanning it and every now and again nodding and muttering 'Great. Excellent.'

Eventually he looked up and smiled.

'Well, this all seems to be very impressive, Mrs Grant, but what I really need is discretion…I guess I mean, how discreet are you?'

Discreet? I glanced at my seedy surroundings and my misgivings increased tenfold. What sort of job was this? Booking-taker in a bordello?

He must have noticed my disquiet. 'Sorry to have to ask you to come here. I just needed somewhere out of the way.' He waved his hand. 'You won't have to work in such shabby surroundings. My client normally uses only the best hotels.'

His client? Hotels? Was this man a procurer?

'Mr Robbins, before we go any further, could you please tell me what this job entails?'

He looked surprised. 'Didn't the agency tell you anything?'

'Only the wages and that the position is temporary.'

He hesitated for a moment. 'My client is a well-known... performer, and that is why we require absolute discretion.'

I stood up, rehearsing what I would say to that so-called employment agency. They were nothing more than pimps.

'I'm sorry Mr Robbins, but I really don't think this is for me.' I was already edging towards the exit.

He looked crestfallen. 'Is it the salary, Mrs Grant? Because Mr Hammer has given me leave to negotiate.'

Something made me stop my flight and he almost collided with me as I turned round. 'Mr Hammer...?'

'Ethan Hammer, Mrs Grant.'

'*The* Ethan Hammer?'

'Of course. He's in town to record at Rockall Studios – and he's writing his autobiography. He needs a secretary – and your editing skills would be great.'

'I see.' I swear my stomach flipped.

'Hence the need for discretion. If the public found out where he was staying, the press and half the female population would be pounding on his door, so obviously he needs someone of sufficient maturity not to be fazed by his fame.'

Ethan Hammer! England's answer to Tom Jones. I forced my voice to sound casual. 'Mr Robbins, I can be the soul of discretion. I *am* the soul of discretion. And Mr Hammer would be just another boss as far as I'm concerned.' *Liar, liar.*

'In that case, Mrs Grant, I take it you're interested in the position? It's for three months initially.'

'Well, it sounds intriguing. And I'm particularly keen on biographical works.' As of thirty seconds ago.

'Great. I'll put your name forward to Mr Hammer and I'll call you tomorrow morning for a meeting with him. I'm sure he'll approve your appointment.'

He stooped forward and shook my hand. 'Thank you so much for your time, Mrs Grant.'

'It's Ms.' Also as of thirty seconds ago.

And he was gone as speedily as he appeared, leaving me

staring after him. Gobsmacked. (I know it's not good English, but it's the most appropriate description, believe me.)

I was bursting to tell someone of my change in fortune and was on the point of ringing Gina when the phone rang. I grabbed the receiver ready to broadcast my news (discreetly, of course) when I was halted by Esmeralda's hallowed tone.

'I've been trying to reach you all afternoon, Mrs Grant,' she admonished, obviously expecting me to have been waiting by the phone for her decision.

'I am delighted to inform you that the situation as sales assistant in my *Haute Couture Boutique* is yours.'

She sounded like the Queen bestowing a knighthood. I grinned stupidly. 'That's very kind of you, but I am delighted to tell you that I no longer want it. Good afternoon, Esmeralda.'

I heard a spluttered "Well *really*!" as I replaced the receiver. I bet her real name's Agnes or Peggy or something equally mundane. I dialled Gina's number.

'You'll never guess what happened this afternoon...'

She didn't, and was suitably impressed. However, as friends are wont, she pointed out that I hadn't actually been offered the job yet – or met The Man.

Ethan Hammer was our idol when we were teenagers, but unlike many of our youthful deities, had endured. His style had changed with the times, and he was still a popular performer, albeit with a different age group: he had grown with us – well, almost – not many men in our age group still wore leather trousers and long sideburns. But I have to confess I hadn't heard much about him recently, not since, according to the tabloids, he'd been through a very messy divorce – his second - and I haven't actually bought one of his recordings for a good few years. Now I had an overwhelming urge to find out every last detail about him. I wondered if Maddy knew anything: she was always a wonderful source of celebrity gossip.

When her phone was eventually picked up I was nonplussed to hear a breathless youthful voice. 'Madeleine's sex slave.'

A girlish giggle was followed by a muffled admonition. 'Hello. This is Madeleine.'

'Shame on you, you cradle snatcher!'

'Thank god it's you Rosie – it could have been someone from Screws of the World.'

'I'm amazed at your stamina,' I said, thinking fleetingly of the days when sex was more than an annual occurrence. 'How do you keep it up? No – rephrase that, you hussy.'

She laughed. 'You know what they say, Rosie – you're as old as the man you feel!'

After swearing her to secrecy, I went on to tell her my news.

'Oh, *Ethan*,' she said meaningfully. 'Well, darling, be careful. He's an absolute tart. He'll say anything to get you between the sheets – and while you're still recovering he's slung his leg over the next victim.'

'Did you ever…?'

'Well, yes, darling. A very long time ago.'

'You never told us!'

'No…it was a very short-lived thing – and I didn't want to spoil your illusions.'

So he'd dumped her.

'Darling, I've heard he's been almost cleaned out by his recent divorce – that probably explains the new album and the book. The ex-wife – Marnie - is an absolute slapper and should be avoided like the plague. He also has hassle with his first ex, Bianca - and he had a drink and drugs problem. Don't know if that's still ongoing. Anyhow, he's not a good bet, so don't trust him any further than you can throw him.'

I didn't point out that I would (hopefully) be hired to work for him, and not having the assets of a super-model or mega-boobed showgirl, hardly likely to be asked to trust him with anything other than my secretarial and English skills.

'Point taken. Maddy?'

'Mm?'

'Was he go-ood?'

She paused briefly. 'The *best*, Rosie. The *biggest* and the best.' We both laughed and hung up.

I mulled over the information, but decided I had little to worry (or daydream) about: if he dumped the likes of Maddy it was implausible to imagine he'd give me a second glance. Though if he were as plagued as she suggested with bitter ex-wives and possible dependency on stimulants, would it be a smart move to even consider working for him?

One thing is for sure – I'm not about to miss the opportunity to meet him. Even if it does demolish all my teenage fantasies.

The call came at ten this morning.

'Ms Grant? Mr Hammer would like to meet you. He's at The Crown. Do you know it?'

'Yes. What time?'

'Will 2pm be OK with you?'

'Absolutely. Shall I meet you there, Mr Robbins?'

'Er, no. I have to be elsewhere – he'll see you alone. Just check with reception. They'll be expecting you.'

'Fine. I'll be there.' Absurdly my heart had started to pound. Despite everything, the thought of coming face to face with Ethan Hammer still had the power to roll back the years and regress me to quivering pubescence. Briefly. I soon returned to the stark realisation that I needed this job and would be in dire straits if he turned me down: the one thing guaranteed to ensure rejection was if I acted like a star struck groupie.

I decided to play safe with the white blouse and plum trouser suit, topped off with a toning silk scarf – a Christmas present from the twins. I restrained my unruly auburn hair with a matching scrunchy, and put on my new black patent mock-croc ankle boots – a Christmas present from myself.

At five minutes to two I presented myself in the sumptuous lobby of The Crown Hotel, newly refurbished and the town's only five-star establishment.

'I have an appointment with Mr Ethan Hammer.'

The sleek blonde receptionist scanned me with a scornful expression. 'One moment, I'll check.' She picked up the phone.

Seconds later she forced a smile. 'Fine, Ms Grant. Mr Hammer would like you to go to his suite. It's the penthouse

– take the lift to the 6th floor. You'll need this security card.'

I pushed the card into the slot under the "Penthouse. Private" notice and was whisked silently to the top of the building, alighting right opposite a door that was already ajar. I took a deep breath, pulled in my stomach, and knocked.

'Come in.'

As I did so he walked slowly towards me, his lithe body cat-like, his welcoming smile as familiar as my own reflection. His handshake was at once gentle and strong – and a little too long.

'Ms Grant, thanks for coming. Please sit down.'

I forced my mouth closed and striving for some semblance of sophistication, dragged my eyes from him and looked about me.

The suite was even plusher than I expected. The room we were in, obviously a lounge, was bigger than an entire floor of my house and furnished in ultra modern style with white sofas, animal skin accessories, smatterings of stainless steel and a plethora of tinted mirrors.

He indicated a chair and sat opposite me. Though I was still struggling to appear at ease and underwhelmed, I had the strangest sense of déjà vu: it was as if I had been reunited with an old acquaintance. Old, partly because on closer inspection the copper-tanned complexion bore the scars of his well-documented journey through the hazardous world of sex, drugs and rock 'n' roll, though his gorgeous green eyes were still fringed with long, dark-gold lashes and his luxuriant hair the trademark dirty blond - though I suspected he'd had a few highlights and had to shake off the image of him with wedges of kitchen foil clinging to his head.

'Can I get you a drink?'

I shook my head, determined to keep it clear.

'You don't mind if I do?'

'Of course not.' I watched him lope over to a built-in cabinet that held a number of bottles. His back turned from me as he took a glass, and my gaze was glued to his wonderfully taut buttocks. Too soon he returned to his seat with a tumbler full of clear liquid.

'Soda,' he said. 'Helps my digestion.'

If you say so.

'Now, Ms Grant – Rose-Anne – may I call you that?'

His smile was knee-trembling.

'Er, I'm usually known as Rose, or Rosie,' I told him.

'Rosie, that's nice. Mike tells me your qualifications are excellent. But you realise the position is only temporary?'

'Yes.'

'Would you be able to work out of town?'

Timbuktu, if necessary, but I didn't want to sound too desperate. 'It would depend on how far out.'

'Oh, perhaps ten miles – I'm thinking of taking a house for a few months. I'm recording an album at Rockall Studios, and doing a few gigs, and to be honest I'm fed up with hotels – they're so impersonal, aren't they?'

'I suppose they must be after a while. The longest I've ever stayed in one was for two weeks on my honeymoon and never one as sumptuous as this.'

'You're married then?' His question seemed almost wistful.

'No. Just divorced. The bastard ran off with his secretary.' My hand flew to my mouth, appalled: how did that come out? 'I'm sorry.'

He laughed. 'No worries – I'm pretty bitter about exes too. I think you and I will get along fine.'

Whew!

'Now, I'm sure I don't need to ask, but you understand about the need for discretion?'

'Of course, Mr Hammer.'

'Ethan. Call me Ethan. Anyhow, my publisher will want you to sign a document agreeing not to disclose anything you learn from my autobiography – and I'd like you to sign one preventing you from speaking to anyone, particularly the media, about me or my personal life – both past, present…and future,' he grinned boyishly as he said the latter. 'Will that be OK with you?'

'Fine, Mr…Ethan. Thank you.'

'Did Mike speak to you about wages?'

'Well…yes.' The survival instinct kicked in.

'And you thought the original offer was a bit short?'

'Well, as the job is temporary…'

He nodded. 'Then I'll pay ten per cent more. OK?'

'That's great. Thank you.' I was thrilled, then remembered… 'You know I can't start until next week?'

He scowled. 'I'd have preferred to begin right away, but needs must. OK…' he was interrupted by the phone. He picked up the receiver and began to purr sexily.

'Darling! Where are you? Really? What colour are they? Well think of me when you're doing that honey-pie…Mmm.'

I cleared my throat, sure he'd forgotten my existence.

He turned in my direction. 'OK then, see you next Monday at 8am. Mike will let you know all the details.'

I was dismissed, and as I reached the door I heard him say, 'Oh, just an old biddy I've hired to do my typing…'

An old biddy! I didn't know whether to scream or spit.

My final day at work was a mixture of laughter and tears. I had, after all, been there a long time and though I had little respect for my present bosses and a positive dislike of current company policy, I also had many friends. I discovered this when I found my leaving card had been signed by *everyone* except Big Ted who has always refused to contribute to farewell collections "on principle" – the principle being he was the role model for Ebenezer Scrooge. By a simple process of deduction it followed that he had not contributed to my leaving present, a very respectable DSLR camera.

"Everyone" included Roman Doyle – who took the time to let me know my sacking had absolutely nothing to do with him, even though he'd originally believed it was me who dropped him in the dirt with his wife. Apparently one of her friends had spotted him canoodling in an out-of-town restaurant with Sharon. He was currently, he informed me penitently, on a very short leash and his final warning. He then gave me his card and said if I was ever lonely to give him a call. I dropped the card deliberately into a waste bin and told him I was sure I'd never be *that* lonely.

I was summoned to Human Resources who offered me counselling and help in finding another position – rather late in the day, I thought. I could have done with the counselling immediately after they dropped the bombshell, and if I'd waited until now to think about future employment I'd be working as a hooker at the Shalimar Hotel by next month. I wish I'd had the camera handy to record the cynical looks on their faces when I told them I had a job with a rock star.

Anyhow, I'd signed for my Redundancy Package, and certain that it had been processed and was even now sitting in my bank account, felt safe to wreak my revenge on Big Ted.

To the last he was his unsympathetic, supercilious self. Mind you, he was still nettled that I hadn't come up with a suitable slogan for Salfresh. Not one of which he approved, anyway.

Salfresh, as I had discovered, was revolting. When reconstituted it had the consistency of over-cooked spinach, and if you left it for a day unrefrigerated, had the stink of rotting vegetation. If the atmosphere was hot, this became akin to decaying flesh – as was apparent when I inadvertently left a bowl of it near a radiator overnight.

So before I left the building I entered Big Ted's lair and stuffed it into every orifice I could find. It was in his filing cabinet and his cupboard, secreted in his executive washroom and taped to the motor of his executive fridge. I know it was childish, but I never want him to forget Salfresh, or the day he couldn't even be bothered to offer his good wishes to a longstanding and loyal employee.

In fact his final words to me were "Rose-Anne, I hope you realise how you've let me down with Salfresh. Neither one of us is going to come out of this smelling of roses."

Certainly not you, you vertically challenged despot. Or words to that effect.

It wasn't particularly late when I arrived home after the do in the Red Lion – at least I don't think it was because I can't remember looking at the clock. In fact, I can't really remember coming home. I do recall waking up on the sofa at 1am, fully dressed and with a tongue like sandpaper.

I eventually surfaced towards midday and after devouring a huge plateful of cholesterol, staggered to the supermarket where I bumped into Gina. Her trolley was overflowing with goodies from the cordon bleu section and included oysters and champagne. Obviously the dialogue with Lloyd is continuing.

We went for a coffee as she wanted the lowdown on Ethan. Naturally I passed on what Maddy said.

'The sneaky mare!' Gina said. 'She slept with Ethan Hammer and didn't even tell us.'

Remembering the Non-Disclosure Agreement I'd just signed I put my finger to my lips as heads swivelled towards us: at this rate I'd be out of a job before it began.

'I think it was just a one-night-stand,' I muttered. 'I reckon he dumped her. She wouldn't want to brag about that, would she?'

Gina lowered her voice. 'Rumour has it he's always been a bit of a dog. I was reading about his latest divorce: his ex has taken him to the cleaners. Apparently she caught him being given a blowjob by his secretary…' she stopped abruptly.

'His *secretary*!' we chorused hoarsely. For a moment we stared open-mouthed at one another. Then Gina grinned slyly.

'You'd better ask him for a blow by blow job description.'

'That's the reason for the privacy clause - he's afraid of kiss and tell…'

'Or suck it and see…'

'Gina!' We sniggered into our cappuccinos.

'I don't know why I'm laughing,' I said. 'I don't relish spending my working hours fending off a sex-mad singer. Oh, I don't know, though…!'

We carried on in this vein until our coffee was finished and Gina had to rush off to her hairdresser. She's still the most well-groomed person I know.

'You should let Julio have a go at yours,' she said, 'some lowlights would look fantastic, especially if you had some long layers cut into it. Hey, why don't you come with me now and make an appointment?'

'Oh I couldn't. Maybe another time.'

'Come on, Rosie, new job, new image. And I'll wax your bits and do your nails for you – for free!'

This was an offer too good to refuse, though Gina has always given me a good discount on any beauty treatment - not that I'd had any lately. Perhaps it was time I did.

Anyhow, it so happened that Julio had his knickers in a twist as he'd had two cancellations – almost unheard of as you had to wait at least a month for an appointment at his salon, so he fitted me in there and then.

He regarded me sadly through the mirror, his delicate fingers rubbing a handful of my hair as if it were rather low-grade straw

'It is very dry, Mrs Rosie. It needs much conditioning. Also it needs to be cut and thinned…' As he spoke he shaped my head with his hands. 'So!' Decision made, he clicked his fingers and a minion wheeled over a trolley. 'First we colour and condition, and then we cut.'

I opened my mouth to ask him not to cut off too much, but he had already flitted over to supervise Gina's operation. Ah well, it would soon grow. I'd kept it long for years because that was how Simon liked it - and he didn't approve of hair colours, highlights and false bits. I wonder if he realises that his Angel is a bottle blonde with hair extensions and acrylic nails? Yes, it was definitely time for a change.

Two hours later as we made our way back to the supermarket car park I was unable to prevent myself glancing at my reflection in every shiny surface we passed, and received a particularly strange look from the occupant of a parked car who rolled down his mirrored window as I pouted into his face. I was transformed. When Julio announced his satisfaction with the deep auburn lowlights his assistant had applied and got to work with his golden scissors, I wanted to scream at him to go easy as huge skeins of my hair fell to the floor, but his fierce, almost manic look as he whisked his blades around my head dared me to comment: a master was at work.

As indeed he was, for under his skilful hands I went from

wild-haired ex-wife to sleek, shiny divorcée. My head felt light, and with subtle changes of shade my glossy mid-length bob fanned around my face with every move of my head.

Gina seemed as impressed as I was and insisted I went home with her to have my nails done. She hadn't time to do my waxing right then but I was pleased about that as I wasn't in the mood for S&M. Besides, I've had a tub of microwave wax in my bathroom cabinet for months and to celebrate my new image, determined tomorrow would be the day to try it. I plan to follow this particular bout of torture with an aromatherapy bath and a session with a bottle of fake tan.

Heidi rang just after I got home. She sounded a bit down, so feeling much too glamorous to stay at home I recklessly suggested we went out that evening.

We decided on a film and a Chinese. It was a toss-up between a romance with a happy ending and a re-run of Stepford Wives. We plumped for realism and went to see Stepford Wives.

Over (very mediocre) sweet and sour king prawns, Heidi told me she may give up her work in the home for geriatrics, and is considering private care. Apparently a friend of hers has a job that entails helping an old lady get ready for bed, then sleeping over in case she's needed during the night. The friend had given her the name of the agency that employs her and Heidi said the money was better too. I told her to go for it.

Her son Martin is doing very well on the building site according to Lloyd, and there's a possibility he may get an apprenticeship with a carpenter. However, he's hardly ever home now and Heidi's worried he's getting into bad habits as she suspects he may be going to the pub at lunchtime as well as after work. She's afraid he's going to turn into a beer-swilling replica of his father.

I could only make sympathetic noises as I have personally seen Martin with a group of fellow lager louts, drinking in the shopping centre and haranguing passers-by, and have always thought he was his father's son. But it wouldn't have helped Heidi to tell her this.

Poor Heidi has never had much luck and she's so kind-hearted. She's going to visit her five grandchildren tomorrow and, fearing I'd be lonely, asked if I'd like to accompany her. I declined - without indicating that I'd sooner spend the day incarcerated in the chimpanzee enclosure at Colchester Zoo.

Though it's Sunday, I rose reasonably early and, having combed my new hairstyle back into place, decided to go through my wardrobe. I was elated to discover that some outfits which had become very snug now fitted perfectly. The spectres of homelessness and poverty obviously have their compensations.

I had just put my wax-pot in the microwave when my mother rang. She still lives in the USA with her third husband, a poor (but very wealthy) sap inaptly named Sylvester, and was on holiday in Las Vegas - where it was 4am. I soon sussed she was more than three sheets to the wind when she started asking if Simon and I had made up our little differences.

Considering she divorced my father citing a supposed one-night stand that happened ten years previously, and had already started an affair with her next husband, I cannot fathom her concept that Simon's on-going affair with his secretary counts only as a "little difference". Particularly as she's always claimed to loath him and wouldn't have bothered coming over for our wedding if my father hadn't put his foot down – a first.

However, I think I managed to convey my displeasure without being too churlish. My sister had told her I'd been sacked, yet she didn't even ask about my job situation, just gave me a lecture about standing on my own two feet – which is rich coming from a woman who never worked from the day she married, and now has a husband sufficiently wealthy to keep her in the style she's always imagined she deserves.

As is the norm with children, it was many years before I realised what a terrible life my father had with her. He's a gentle and considerate soul and was never strong enough to stand up to her. He told me he stayed because of my sister and me: my brother is my mother's favourite and could never do any wrong. He has grown into a fat, layabout who was still hanging onto her apron strings when she crossed the Atlantic, and leeches off her even now. I haven't seen him for years except on a Christmas card – along with his obese wife and two overweight children: in their matching green and red elf costumes they look like the Weebles. But that's unfair. To the Weebles.

Dad, bless him, is now married to Edna, a homely woman who adores him and is a brilliant grandma to Leah and Jamie, not to mention a surrogate mother to me. Sadly they live in Cumbria so we don't see much of them

Anyhow, by the time I'd eased the woman who purports to be my mother off the line, the wax-pot had cooled down again, so I heated it for another few minutes, having prepared the area in front of the TV with a towel and a packet of wipes. (I hoped to take my mind off the discomfort by watching an old movie).

Carefully I carried the bubbling pot – with oven gloves – to the sitting room and sat myself on the towel, exposing a leg like a Christmas tree. I've seen this done many times, of course, both in Gina's salon and on the TV advert for this stuff, and knew it was a very simple procedure: with a spatula you spread warm wax on the area to be defoliated, smooth on a small oblong strip of material ensuring it's pressed firmly to the wax in the direction the hair is growing, and then you rip it off in the opposite direction, leaving the skin silky and smooth. What could be easier?

Anything.

For a start, the wax, though hot, was too thick – probably the result of overheating, so I waited for it to cool down a bit and it became even thicker. I knew then that I had to work quickly as once it cools it is impossible to spread. So I tried smoothing the treacly gunge onto my shin – only to drop a big dollop on the only square inch of rug not covered by the towel.

I reached for a wipe and rubbed at the spillage, but the

more I rubbed, the stickier and more widespread it became. By this time the wax on my shin had started to harden and I slapped a strip on it, gritting my teeth as I yanked it off. It barely removed the wax, let alone any foliage.

In desperation I dipped my spatula back in the pot only to discover Geoffrey approaching it nose down, and as I frantically waved him away, dripped another dollop on his creamy head, causing him to back off hastily. I made a grab for him, not realising I'd managed to get wax on my hand, and found myself stuck to a very cross cross-Siamese. Naturally he struggled and eventually escaped leaving my palm sprouting cream fur.

I looked like a Yeti. I must be the only person in the country who can defoliate and end up with more hair than they started with.

By now, of course, the remaining wax had completely lost its viscosity and I took it to the kitchen to hurl it in the bin. That is, I tried to hurl it, but it was stuck to my hand and the resulting hiccup caused the pot to fall down the side of the bin-liner. I slammed the lid, too exasperated to stop the resulting glutinous dribble which I knew would ensure a major cleaning job. It will probably take a hammer and chisel by the time I get round to it.

I retired to my bath with my trusty Gillette, trying not to contemplate my ruined rug and traumatised cat. God only knows what I'll find stuck to him when he eventually comes home. Probably a Court Order from the RSPCA.

MARCH

As nervous as a child starting school, I presented myself at the Crown Hotel at 7.55am on Monday morning and was waved up to the penthouse with only a hint of a sneer from the brittle receptionist.

I knocked on the door, and waited. After a decent interval I knocked again. No reply. I couldn't stand there indefinitely, so warily I turned the handle, calling out as I pushed it open.

'Hello? Mr Hammer? Ethan…?'

All at once one of the inner doors opened and my new boss appeared. He was rubbing the sleep from his eyes – and stark naked.

I gasped, not least in appreciation of a very fine example of masculinity.

He cursed and turned back unhurriedly, closing the door behind him.

Completely flustered and unsure what to do next I walked over to the window so that I had my back to his bedroom door should he – or anyone else – decide on another full-frontal. A minute later I heard the door open and close.

'Rosie, good morning. Sorry about that – I forgot to ask for a wake-up call.'

Gingerly I turned to find him clad in jeans and a T-shirt, his hair still tousled.

'No problem. Good morning, Ethan.' My professional front kicked in. 'Can I order you some coffee?'

'No, but you can make me some. And maybe a slice of toast or two? By the way, I love your new hairstyle.' Despite myself I couldn't prevent my insides melting at his little-boy look and wheedling smile. And that he'd actually noticed my hair! The fortune I'd thrust into Julio's grasping fingers was money well spent.

'You'll find everything you need in the kitchen. I'll shower while you make it, and then we can get down to some work.'

He took my compliance for granted and slid back to the bedroom, and I unenthusiastically hunted for the kitchen. Gina was right, as usual: I should have asked for a job description (I tried not to think of our original notion). The one place I have never been creative is in the kitchen; in fact, to me c**k is a four-letter word. I therefore feel quite smug that I was able to feed and nurture a husband and two children – keeping in mind that ready-meals were not so readily available when the twins were young, and takeaways strictly an occasional treat.

Anyhow, I found the kitchen cunningly concealed in a mirrored recess. It was compact but well equipped and I opened the fridge to find it almost filled…with beer, wine and vodka. And a slab of butter. Further investigation showed most of the cupboards to be similarly stocked, but there was half a loaf of wholemeal bread and a large jar of Marmite. My rumbling stomach reminded me that I hadn't eaten either; well, if I had to feed him, I'd feed myself too.

Ten minutes later I was sitting opposite my teen-idol eating toast with Marmite (he loved it too) and drinking coffee. I've had worse Monday mornings.

Ethan Hammer seems to be an all-or-nothing sort of guy: as I discovered when we started work, he doesn't do anything by half.

He'd dictated a number of tapes and asked me to input them as he wanted my opinion before continuing with his life story. I couldn't wait to start, not only for the content, which I was sure would be enlightening, but because I was being paid for doing something I really enjoyed.

Once I'd figured out how to use his state-of-the-art recorder I was left alone in the suite while he went to the gym in the hotel's basement, something he said he did at least five times a week. I guessed his physique wasn't built solely on Shredded Wheat. It was certainly easier to concentrate on my work without him hovering, playing music and answering numerous phone calls. Even with headphones on, I couldn't help being aware that the content of some of his calls needed an X certificate: if ever he gets fed up with the music business he could make a fortune on one of those sex chat lines.

However, his style of dictation and of storytelling is surprisingly good. I don't know why it was a surprise other than that I'd long listened to him sing inanities he'd composed such as "You're so f-fine, ya make me wanna, make me wanna ,Oooh-Aaah", which didn't exactly amount to an in-depth appreciation of the English language. Though I suppose it would be classed as poetic license and undoubtedly made him a pile of cash.

The thing that slowed me down was the content. As a fan, in the early days I'd read every snippet ever written about him, but was fascinated by the facts coming from the stallion's mouth, and found myself storing details to impart to my bemused compatriots. Except that I was sworn to secrecy. Yet how could I keep to myself the knowledge that Ethan Hammer was an adopted child who was at present in the process of tracing his biological parents and hoped, before the book was finished to be able to reveal them? Or that he was scared of the dark? Or that he wet his pants on his first day at school?

Whatever my new boss's shortcomings, I can see myself racing to work every day just to catch the next episode. It will be like a private soap opera.

My enthusiasm was not dimmed when lunch turned out to be beans on toast – prepared by me - and I was home by 4pm, though I would happily have stayed for longer.

During my extra two hours of leisure my thoughts strayed to my ex-colleagues at The Company, and I prayed that Big Ted was totally nauseated and overpowered by the aroma of rotting Salfresh.

The following day was very much the same (minus the full frontal), and I found myself fully committed to my unconventional boss's autobiography, though I still had to pinch myself at regular intervals to ensure I wasn't dreaming.

When I got home I had a phone call from Jean who'd taken over the unenviable task of working with Big Ted. She was bursting to tell me how he'd called out the Gas Board before he discovered my sabotage. Apparently he nearly burst a blood vessel and is threatening to sue me. What for - loss of dignity? He'd hang himself before a jury.

I know I should feel at least a twinge of guilt or shame, but every time I imagine the scenario all that comes over me is a warm glow of satisfaction and the fervent hope it was caught on the CCTV he had installed when he thought someone was stealing his Blue Mountain coffee. (There was a hole in the packet). I can think of dozens who'd buy the DVD. Or better still, it could be sent to that TV programme that shows clips of people making idiots of themselves.

Yesterday Mike Robbins called to say he'd found a house for Ethan to rent and they both went off before lunch, leaving me to my typing. I was just embroiled in his first sexual encounter (age twelve, with a girl of sixteen) when the phone rang.

'Hello?' I'd been told not to reveal this was Ethan's suite.

'Who's that?' The voice was female and sounded very young.

'May I ask who's calling?'

'I asked you first.'

I sighed and put on my ultra-official tone. 'Who would you like to speak to?'

She tutted. 'Ethan, of course.'

'I'm afraid Mr Hammer's out.'

'Where is he?'

'I'm not at liberty to say. May I take a message and get him to call you back?'

'Ai'm not at liberty to say,' she mimicked, and I guessed she was not much more than a child. This was confirmed when she added stroppily 'Tell him his daughter rang – and tell him if he expects me to live on this CRAP allowance, he can forget about visitation rights – AND I'll be calling the press. Have you got that, you stupid old tart?'

Ethan has mentioned a daughter of fourteen by his first

wife, and a son, aged six, from his second. The charm-school dropout was obviously Allegra. Her mother, Bianca, was a former dancer-turned-game show hostess who divorced Ethan because of an alcohol problem - he said it was hers, but I'm only recalling reports in showbiz rags: soon I hope to learn the inside story.

Meanwhile, having had my share of teenage melodrama, my sympathy is leaning acutely towards my boss, though one can't help but wonder what has caused a privileged young girl to become quite so obnoxious. When I was her age I was drooling over her father, and I can still remember the physical pain I experienced when he announced his intention to marry the blonde showgirl who became her mother. Makes you glad you were unable to jump into someone else's shoes, doesn't it? Funny how time heals. I wish I could fast forward it until I lose this awful feeling of betrayal Simon has left me with.

Ethan's brat makes Leah seem positively angelic. My daughter is an enigma to me: I have never been even close to her wavelength, and have no inkling as to where she inherited her scientific genius, but only in affectionate jest has she ever called me an old tart - and never a stupid one.

Anyhow, Ethan hadn't returned to the suite before 4pm so I left him a note of his daughter's call. My first draft included her insult: my second was written after I'd realised I'd be playing right into her hands if I reported her insolence. She was obviously angry and seeking attention from her father, and I was not about to play piggy-in-the-middle.

Leah must have known I was thinking of her as she rang yesterday evening. She's going skiing with her friend's family and wanted some extra cash. I told her she had to be joking and to ask her father. She said she already had, but he hadn't donated enough – couldn't I just give her another £100 as she didn't want her hosts to think she was a pauper? I told her she'd most certainly be a pauper when I had to sell the family home.

For a moment she was quiet, then she said in a small voice,

'Don't joke about things like that, Mum.'

'It may not be a joke, love.'

'Oh Mum, things can't be that bad. You've just got a new job. How is the great Ethan Hammer, by the way? I've heard he's a bit of an old tart.'

'Don't you start!' I said, glad of the diversion – I hadn't intended to worry my children with woeful predictions of penury, particularly as they both have exams coming up. 'He's been a perfect gentleman – and he likes Marmite.'

Leah giggled: it was a family joke that you should never trust a man who doesn't like Marmite. Simon hates it. Let that be a lesson to me.

I went on to tell her about the call from Ethan's daughter -and rashly said I'd send her £50.

As she put down the phone, she said, 'Thanks, Mum, and you know what? You really are the best old tart.'

It was said with affection. I think.

Mulling over my first week as Ethan Hammer's secretary, things have gone better than I expected. I miss some of my colleagues, and it's strange working most of the time on my own, but I don't feel so stressed every evening. Not about work anyhow. I really wasn't joking with Leah: my finances are very strained, in fact they've been put through a sieve and come out as purée – liquid, but only just.

While I have this job I can manage, but barely; one crisis and the bank manager will be hammering at my door, closely followed by the bailiffs. It's an unsettling thought, to put it mildly.

I had a good chat with Heidi this morning. She's given notice at her Care Home and is starting with the agency she was telling me about. Her first assignment is a week of nights at the residence of an old lady in Dedham. Apparently it's in a huge house that's really ancient, and she has her own suite – including private bath and satellite TV, so is praying the old girl is not a doubly incontinent battleaxe. Ditto that.

That was her good news. The bad news was that Martin was

brought home by the police for causing a disturbance in the town centre. This time he got off with a verbal warning, and was told next time he'd be charged. I almost felt responsible: perhaps I should have warned her? I advised her to encourage him to join a club of some sort, but she said she'd already suggested that and he just laughed in her face and said perhaps she'd like him to take up pottery classes. I refrained from remarking that his only affinity with pot would be smoking it, not firing it.

Jamie rang to tell me he was on his way to have Sunday lunch with his father who's now living with the Bimbo in Twickenham, so is quite close to the college. I could have bitten off my tongue but I couldn't resist asking if they'd be going to McDonald's or Kids' Stuff.

'Oh Mum,' my son said sadly. 'I couldn't refuse, could I? He's still my dad.'

You nasty woman!

'Of course not, I was only joking, love. You have a good time.' And don't forget to take a spare bib.

I can't help it. Sometimes I feel so *worthless.* I can't pretend our marriage was perfect, in fact I know we'd both been discontent for a good while before I was faced with Simon's infidelity, but I'll never forget the first time I saw him with that *child.* She's not even pretty. Unless you're into blue-eyed blondes built like racing snakes. And I suppose most men are, especially when middle age is creeping up as fast as their waistlines. I should have been suspicious when he started going to the gym and buying trendy clothes: they're classic signs as described by any agony aunt worth her salt, yet I ignored them.

I am not stupid: I have a Diploma in Graphic Design as well as my BA (Hons) for goodness sake, so in my hyper-analytical state of mind following D-Day, I had to concede that part of me – my subconscious at least – chose to turn a blind eye to the writing on the wall. And the thing is, although I sometimes miss his physical presence, I don't really miss him very much at all, except for having someone to talk to. Mind you, I have some major conversations with Geoffrey, and he's a much better listener. I just wish Simon had had the guts to leave because he was unhappy - and before he made a fool of me by screwing his secretary all over the county. His *secretary!* Talk about a cliché.

When I arrived at The Crown on Monday morning amid a flurry of snow that indicated last night's fall was not a fluke, it was to find Ethan standing beside a pile of bulging suitcases.

'Hi, Rosie. We're moving today. Any chance you could take some gear in your car? Mike's is in the garage and I've only got the Porsche.' His smile was appealing.

'Of course – but where are we going?'

'Great Ashley. Do you know it?'

I nodded. It was some ten miles out of town. That wasn't too bad, though I'd miss my lunchtime shopping - which could be a blessing in disguise as I no longer have the wherewithal to sustain any vices.

I must have looked worried at this point because Ethan's expression became concerned. 'Will this be a problem for you Rosie? I know it's a bit out of town.'

I shook my head quickly: if it had been the other side of the moon I'd have found a way to get there.

'No problem at all,' I said brightly. 'It's only a twenty minute drive through the back roads – providing you don't get stuck behind a tractor. But I've just realised I need some petrol or I won't get home again. I'll stop at the Esso on the way out of town.'

'Fine. Mike – you'd better go with Rosie to show her the way. See you there.' With that my boss disappeared into the lift with the smallest of the suitcases.

Mike shrugged. 'That's the trouble with sports cars – they look the business but are never practical. I hope you don't mind this, Rose? It surely doesn't come under normal secretarial duties.'

'Course not. But it's hardly a normal secretarial post, is it?' And perhaps I *should* ask for a job description. Just to be safe.

But I didn't, I simply followed Mike into the lift, wheeling a suitcase and wondering if the rest of them would actually fit into my modest vehicle. They did – just. Luckily it's a hatchback and the back seats fold down, but I swear I heard it groan as we finally got in and drove off.

I pulled in at the petrol station and narrowly missed hitting a newspaper stand as my careful braking didn't account for the overloaded rear end. Mike and I looked at each other and I laughed nervously before reversing level to the pumps.

'I think my shock absorbers are in shock.'

'I'm not surprised,' Mike said. Being used to a male passenger whose reproofs ranged from patronising to imperious, I cast him a withering look and he frowned.

'Because of the heavy load,' he explained, his thin frame shivering as he got out and started to fill the tank.

I really must endeavour to be less cynical.

'Just put £20's-worth in, please.' I had a horrible feeling this was all I had in my purse, and began to panic when I saw the price zooming way past my limit.

'Mike! You're going over!' I said urgently.

He smiled. He has a nice smile. 'No worries – I'll fill it up: this is business, and the business will pay.'

Wow! A whole week's worth of petrol.

I shrugged as though I was used to such generous gestures. 'OK. Thanks.'

On the slow drive to the village I discovered Mike is not the run-of-the-mill gofer I first thought. He is, of course, Ethan's manager/right-hand-man, and has been for the past three years, but I was surprised to learn he is actually a trained lawyer and has worked with various high-profile personalities in the States. I was dying to ask him who, but he was obviously being discreet and doesn't seem the sort to name-drop. Apparently his work is mainly to do with contractual agreements, but he did hint that some of his clients occasionally needed his services to extricate them from tricky situations. I couldn't help wondering how that tied up with Ethan's escapades with secretaries and the like – but I kept quiet about that: hopefully I shall learn all the graphic details in the not too distant future. Anyhow, I also learned that Mike was born in California, is divorced and has a daughter of thirteen, Caroline, who he doesn't see as often as he'd like as she lives in York, her mother's home-town. He's also fanatical about scuba diving when he has time.

I was just debating how to ask him about Ethan's current love-life (the Sunday papers said he was seeing Aveline, a well-known "glamour model") when we came up behind the Porsche, stationary in front of high wooden gates half hidden in a very tall laurel hedge. I parked behind it and was confronted by an archetypal, whitewashed cottage, complete with thatched roof and a garden now covered in inches of snow. It looked quite beautiful, as if it had been painted for a Christmas card.

It wasn't small either – at least, not by my standards. I counted four gables and as I followed Mike up the path to the open front door, noticed the ornate Victorian ironwork of a conservatory to one side. I later discovered it spanned the entire back of the building and opened out on to a sprawling lawn. This spread to a high wall bordered by a variety of shrubs and to the side, behind another high hedge peeked a dome-shaped structure that I was told housed a heated swimming pool and sauna.

As we walked in I looked around in awe: this was my idea of perfection, my dream home.

The entrance hall, which was paved in parquet with walls panelled in a gorgeous cherry-coloured wood, led to a long, beamed, living room with more of the same, and an inglenook fireplace that stretched across the back wall. Pale yellow and cream sofas surrounded a large, rustic coffee table sitting on a thick cream rug. Apparently there were seven bedrooms if you counted the housekeeper's annexe.

We followed Ethan into the kitchen and he filled a kettle and set it on a stove that looked like an old, solid-fuel range but was cunningly electric. This room was large and tastefully restored with a quarry-tiled floor and real wood fitted cupboards, some with leaded-glass doors that match the Georgian-leaded windows. It was cleverly lit by concealed spotlights shining on worktops like granite (they probably are), and a hanging rack of gleaming stainless steel pans above a huge rough-hewn, farmhouse table with legs as solid as tree-trunks.

As I sat on an unpainted wheelback chair to drink the coffee my boss had made, I had never felt more at home, and for one dreamy moment allowed myself to imagine what it would be like to be mistress of this gorgeous house...

...Thankfully I wasn't allowed to complete my fantasy as I was dragged back to the real world by an entreaty to view a small but attractive room the other side of the entrance hall that was to be Ethan's office and my work area.

I've slaved in shabbier surroundings.

By 3.30pm it was almost dark – and snowing again. Since lunchtime (cheese and ham rolls from the local general store), I'd been rattling off Ethan's tape, stopping only briefly to question him over some minor point, and gradually became aware of the fast encroaching gloom and deepening snow. My boss had his eyes closed and was listening intently on his headphones, stopping every now and again to rewind a state-of-the-art tape deck, and seemingly unaware of my growing agitation.

Having to navigate unfamiliar, ungritted country lanes in freezing conditions was never my favourite pastime, and the longer I left it, the worse they were likely to become. I knew I must leave very shortly.

'Ethan?'

No reply. I got up and tapped his arm and his eyes opened with a start. His initial look of irritation immediately changed to a rueful grin.

'God, Rosie, you made me jump. I was miles away. What's the problem?'

'I'm sorry, but I'm going to have to go home now.'

His sleepy green eyes widened. 'Have you finished that tape already, then?'

I shook my head. 'No. I'm afraid not, but it's still snowing and it's getting dark.'

He looked out the window. 'So it is. I was hoping you'd finish it today as I wanted to start dictating tomorrow morning…But hey! When you've gotta go, you've gotta go. See you tomorrow then.' He replaced his headphones and closed his eyes. I was dismissed.

I slid out to my car and began to sweep the snow from it with my coat sleeve. It was freezing - and I was disconcerted. Surely my request to leave early wasn't unreasonable, given the circumstances? Yet somehow I felt I'd just lost half-a-dozen brownie points.

The journey home was nerve-wracking. Once I'd negotiated the slippery back roads the by-pass, though well-gritted, was covered in inches of grey slush that splattered the windscreen making it more opaque with every sluggish sweep of the wipers. In the middle lane I was crawling along, the victim of an unbroken line of ten-wheelers on one side and suicidal sales reps on the other.

So when I got indoors the last thing I wanted was to be greeted by a suspiciously cold house and a letter from my bank.

Throwing the letter on the hall table I checked the central heating thermostat: it was set on 20C but the thermometer next to it read 12C, and the hall radiator was stone cold. Without taking off my coat I raced out the back door and scrutinized the oil tank gauge. It said Low, and as I stared at it balefully I recalled Simon complaining that the needle wasn't accurate, especially when the level was down. The tank was almost certainly empty. And given the spell of freezing weather we were experiencing, I judged my chances of getting a delivery within a week to be less than nil. To add insult to injury, my budget hadn't accounted for this expensive commodity: as we normally buy oil in the summer I assumed I had sufficient to last until Spring. Bloody Simon.

Despondently I went back indoors where Geoffrey gave

me a reproachful look and miaowed piteously. He hates being cold at the best of times, and at present has a bald patch where I'd had to resort to shaving the wax mishap: it hadn't helped that he'd managed to rub his sticky head in next door's compost heap.

Still in my coat – it was either that or a duvet – I filled the kettle, plugged it in…and the lights went out.

I looked out onto the street convinced I was the target of some sick conspiracy, but it was pitch black apart from a couple of flickering lights as my neighbours dug out the emergency candles. I knew without looking I had none. I remembered using them early last summer for our first (and last) family barbecue. Then I recalled the table-decoration Linda next door got me from the WI Christmas Bazaar. I also had a torch by the back door.

I carefully felt my way and located the torch. The batteries were so weak it was almost useless, but held out long enough for me to rummage through the dining room cupboard and find the festive table centre. Then all I needed was a match. Being a smoker-free and non-gas house, this was also a major challenge and eventually I had to knock next door and beg a box of matches.

Linda was out and Ron brandished a box of Swan Vestas and offered to "come and light my fire". I was wary of his turn of phrase and have no wish to alienate Linda, so told him no thanks, I could manage. I'm sure he didn't mean anything underhand, but since I've become a divorcee, almost every male I know speaks to me as if I've lost half my brain cells and found two vaginas. Even the milkman accompanied his words with a sly grin when he asked if I'd "be wanting anything extra for the weekend as he was sure he could supply it". Maybe I'm just ultra-sensitive, but I think not.

Geoffrey followed me until I took the hint to feed him. Unfortunately, no longer enjoying my lunchtime shopping fix, I'd forgotten to buy his favourite tins and ended up opening a can of tuna. He purred ecstatically as I stabbed at it with my standby can-opener, and jumped up on the worktop trying to butt my hand out of the way so he could get to this manna from heaven. Aiming to prevent him from further disfigurement, I brushed my own hand on the jagged edge and yelped as the blood dripped profusely. I grabbed a tea-towel to stem the flow, forgetting I'd hung one of my good white blouses on the towel-rail to dry.

I eventually ate half a cheese sandwich and at 8.30pm, cold and miserable, went upstairs to bed. With incredibly bad timing I spotted the letter from the bank on the hall table, ripped it open and squinted at it in the remains of my candlelight.

The manager is concerned that I am over my overdraft and wants me to make an appointment to see him as soon as possible. How can I be over my overdraft? I didn't even know I had one.

I got into bed and hid under the covers.

I was freezing. I was starving. I'd upset my new boss. I was probably on the point of bankruptcy. And my palm was throbbing like hell. It was all Simon's fault.

At this point self-pity overcame optimism, and I sobbed myself to sleep.

After a restless night I woke just as it was becoming light, and the futile flashing of my radio alarm told me the power was back on. Not that it made much difference as I would still have to leave the warmth of my duvet and step into the refrigerator that was my home to get ready for work. Though at least I could have a cup of coffee and some hot buttered toast. The phone interrupted my moment of euphoria.

'Rose? Where the hell are you?'

It was Ethan.

'I'm here…at home. Is there a problem?'

'Of course there's a bloody problem – you should have been here half an hour ago.'

Oh my god - what was the time? Sod! It was gone nine.

'I'm so sorry Ethan – we had a power cut here last night and my alarm didn't go off…'

'Humphh.'

'I really am sorry. I'll be there in half an hour.'

Before he had a chance to say "don't bother" or something equally final I slammed down the receiver and was half dressed before my feet hit the floor.

Damn. Damn. DAMN! (Not the actual four-letter words I used, but since I was forced to scrub it off the wall of a school toilet with a toothbrush, I have great difficulty in writing the F-word.)

I almost cried with relief when the car started, and though the snow was deeper the by-pass was clear, and through the back roads I followed in the wake of a large lorry which made the journey relatively easy - though my nice white vehicle now looked like a dirty Dalmatian.

I pulled up outside Lime Cottage exactly half an hour after Ethan's phone call, and took a deep breath as I made my way up the path. The door opened and my boss leaned against the frame. For one awful moment I thought he was going to send me packing, but he said, almost jovially 'Hello sleepyhead! Glad you made it.'

Expecting to have to make up for lost time I was taken aback when he insisted we have coffee first in the kitchen. Though I'd had little time to make myself presentable, I felt I hadn't done too poor a job in disguising the effects of my collapsing lifestyle, but Ethan was more perceptive than I'd credited.

'What's bothering you, Rosie? You look shagged out – but I bet it's not that. And what have you done to your hand?'

My hackles rose at the sexual overtone, but his expression seemed one of genuine concern. Anyhow, what made him so sure my washed-out air wasn't the result of a sex marathon?

I explained about my cut palm, which was much sorer than I admitted, and made him laugh when I went on to tell him about Geoffrey's bald patch. I also told him about the central heating oil and he insisted I ring the supplier there and then. I had intended to check my finances first, but had no desire to let him know I was on the verge of insolvency, so I rang.

As I suspected, delivery was delayed – up to ten days. When I repeated this in an incredulous tone, Ethan snatched the receiver.

He purred and cajoled and promised the surly creature on the end of the line a signed photo and tickets to his gig at the Carlton Rooms, and my liquid gold is now scheduled for delivery before the weekend. I just hope my credit card is still in credit.

Fame and potent sex appeal may count for nothing at the gates of heaven, but I'd take my chances for a sliver of it.

We worked solidly then until about 2pm when Ethan decided to visit the general store. He said he needed to get some goodies as he was expecting a visitor that evening.

'Aveline called this morning,' he said, as if I knew her. 'So I'll be needing some high-octane fuel!' He grinned lasciviously as he strolled to the front door.

Aveline! The rumour that she's his latest squeeze is obviously true. Well you never know, she could have a brain to match her enormous boobs.

Though my new boss sometimes displays the temperament of a spoiled child, which I suppose is not too surprising as he's been surrounded by yes-men and willing women for years, as his life story unfolds I detect a vulnerability, a wistfulness almost. And as I get to know the man behind the sexy, snake-hipped singer, I sometimes find myself feeling quite sorry for him.

I believe part of him is still the sad little boy who was shunted from one foster home to another before being adopted at four years old – he's certainly obsessive about tracing his biological parents now his adoptive ones have passed away. He was ecstatic the other morning as he thinks he has a new lead to his mother. I'm not sure that I'd want to meet a woman who was too selfish to look after me, yet waited so long before allowing me to be adopted.

I'm reading between the lines and surmising, of course: there could be any number of legitimate reasons why this happened. Maybe she was terminally ill and wanted to be sure her son went to a loving family; maybe she was a drug addict or incapable of looking after him for some other reason – or perhaps she was going to marry someone who didn't want another man's child.

Whatever the reason, there may be no stigma now, but fifty years ago things were very different, and I can't help feeling Ethan could open a can of worms. He seems to be pinning an awful lot on his quest to discover his roots, not least as the *pièce de résistance* for his autobiography. The fact is, he's rich and famous and may find himself lumbered with a retinue of relatives that come crawling out of the woodwork. Or the mother who rejected him once could reject him again. I wonder if he's considered this? I wonder if I ought to mention it?

Perhaps it would be better to say something to Mike.

I forgot to say that Ethan found the first message I wrote about Allegra's abusive phone call as I'd screwed it up and carelessly missed the wastebasket. He apologised profusely and said he was tearing his hair out over her. He confided that her mother makes things twice as bad by constantly "slagging him off" and allowing Allegra to run wild. And she (the mother) has a drink problem.

Given my present circumstances, I find it difficult to sympathise with anyone who can afford to overindulge on stimulants, be it alcohol, uppers or downers. If the bank manager has his way, soon I'll be lucky to afford a cup of cocoa to put me to sleep or an aspirin in a can of coke to pep me up - and I haven't tried that since I was a student. I wonder if it still works.

Anyhow, back to the day before yesterday when Ethan was expecting Aveline.

He returned from the store with champagne and caviar (it's a well-heeled area so has a very sophisticated village shop), and a couple of rolls for our belated lunch - and was covered in snow. My heart sank when I looked out of the window and saw a blizzard raging.

I tried not to think about it as things were going really well and we'd made a great deal of progress with the manuscript: also I dare not ask to leave early again after my late start. In the end I didn't have to as he dismissed me at 4pm. But that was just the beginning of my problems.

My car refused to start and I ran the battery down trying, so had no alternative – other than sitting in my vehicle and waiting for hypothermia to set in – but to bang on the front door and ask to be readmitted.

Ethan frowned. 'You'd better come in. God, you look frozen.'

'Yeah, there's a blizzard.'

My sarcasm wasn't lost on him and he grinned ruefully. 'Sorry. I'll run you home.'

'In the Porsche? You're joking! It won't negotiate the ruts on those country lanes. You'll ruin your axle or suspension or something.'

'OK, OK I'll ring Mike – he's got the 4x4 – in fact he's meeting Aveline at Stansted and bringing her over so he can take you home.'

He rang Mike's mobile and it was agreed, so I spent a cosy hour with my boss in the kitchen watching as he expertly seasoned steaks and prepared hors d'oeuvres for his evening's entertainment.

While he showered in readiness, I sipped a glass of wine and contemplated returning to my three-bed freezer. As I was about to meet my first glamour model, I also wondered about her: would she turn up in a fur coat and very little else?

She turned up an hour late (the plane had been delayed) wearing an expression that could halt a charging rhino and enough make-up to keep Max Factor in business single-handedly.

'Who's she?' she spat sulkily as she noticed me in the living room.

Ethan, who'd greeted her eagerly, shrugged apologetically at me, and Mike frowned.

'Rose-Anne Grant, my secretary. Rosie, meet Aveline...

she's a model.'

Not a model nice person, that was for sure. I raised a pleasant look and offered my hand. She touched it briefly and then flung herself at my boss.

'Oh babe,' she crooned. 'What I really need is an 'ot barf… would you care to join me?' Her accent was unadulterated East End, her body language pure sex.

Completely ignoring Mike and me she took his hand and tugged him towards the stairs.

We looked at one another and raised our brows.

'I'm just going to have a coffee, then we'll be going,' Mike called after the retreating lovebirds. 'If that's OK with you, Rose?'

Having had a coffee, he insisted I stay indoors until he'd run the motor of his Range Rover and warmed the vehicle's interior. On the drive home – the sturdy vehicle made mincemeat of the conditions - he said he'd get a battery from the garage when he picked me up for work in the morning, and fit it in my car; however, if the roads were still bad, he'd take me home again. I turned to look at him as he spoke; no wonder Ethan relied on him so heavily – his laid back manner hid a strong, capable character I suspect would remain unfazed in the craziest situation. And in his line of work he must have faced a few.

I was taken aback. 'Thanks, Mike. But you really don't have to go to all that trouble.'

'It's no trouble: Ethan will expect you to turn up for work, and it's my job to make sure you do.'

Right. Just duty then.

I wanted to ask him what he thought of Aveline, but thought better of it. I'm sure his loyalty is unquestionable.

In the morning the snow had stopped but it was still freezing and the ruts in the back roads were ever deeper, making them impassable unless you had anything other than a rugged vehicle, but true to his word, Mike was there on my doorstep at 7.40am and got me to the cottage on time. He wouldn't hear of me paying for the new battery.

Although I was ready to roll, my boss was still in bed, so his night had obviously been a success. He eventually came down, made two mugs of black coffee, gave me some correspondence to sort out, and lurched back upstairs where he remained for another two hours. I tried to ignore the thumps and groans coming from somewhere above me.

Just before noon, Ethan emerged, washed and showered, and made himself some breakfast, not looking any the worse for his night of passion, but it was after lunch before his partner in crime made an appearance and I was gratified to see she looked ruff (no, it's not a spelling mistake). Gone was the plastered makeup revealing a very young, unspectacular face – though her figure could not be described as the latter: it had more curves than a clock-spring. And more silicone too, if I'm not mistaken.

Her disposition, however, had not been affected by her romp with a superstar. She ignored me, couldn't keep her hands off Ethan (I saw him unhook them more than once), and spoke to Mike as if he were a menial.

'Stop at Boots before we get to the station,' she ordered when they were just about to leave. Perhaps she'll buy some Bad Attitude Antidote I thought as I saw Mike's jaw twitch, but he nodded and picked up her bag.

'We'd better leave now or you'll miss your train.'

She gave Ethan a sulky look. 'I don't see why 'e can't drive me all the way 'ome. I 'ate trains– I get pestered 'cos people recognise me.'

Not without the face-paint, dearie.

Ethan looked irritated. 'Because I need Mike here. And he may have to take Rosie home too. Besides, you've a First Class ticket, so what's the problem, babe?'

Aveline shrugged, causing her mighty breasts to wobble dangerously over the top of a deep V-neck. She deserved to catch a chill.

'Promise me you'll ring later, Ethee baby?' she cooed up at him, and he took her in his arms. I returned to my desk: I didn't think my stomach was up to the farewell scene.

Leah came home on Saturday as she planned to go to an old school friend's hen night. At least, I think it was Leah. I almost collapsed with shock when this vision with softly curled hair, a short skirt and high boots walked in. The last time I saw her in a skirt – indeed, looking anything other than a tomboy – was when she was forced to play a fairy in her junior school's Christmas pantomime, and even then she managed to sneak on stage in her Doc Martens.

The new-look Leah was also wearing makeup, and she looked gorgeous. Before I could open my mouth (or close it and speak coherently) she said 'Don't say a word, Mum. I just decided to change my image, OK?'

Her expression was familiar, and dared me to pry. I think she's in love!

'All right, love. Keep your hair on. But I have to say – you look stunning.'

She shrugged nonchalantly, but seemed pleased. She was only home for a couple of hours before she went out and we spent the time talking about her skiing trip with her friend Dawn's family. Had she met someone there, I wondered? Or was it someone from Uni? Anyone I knew?

I had to keep these questions to myself. Leah, I know, will tell me what she wants, when she is ready. For the first time in ages I was sitting chatting normally (almost) to my daughter, and I wasn't about to risk this breakthrough.

Ethan is in the recording studio every morning this week: he seems very excited about the new album He's installed a synthesiser and some recording equipment in one of the smaller reception rooms and has been up until the early hours perfecting new songs, according to Mike – who, by the way, I am becoming increasingly comfortable with. I voiced my concerns about Ethan's search for his mother, and Mike said that when he first had the idea of tracing her, he was given counselling and told not to expect too much as not all cases turn out to have a "happy ever after" ending. So I needn't have worried because at least he's been warned, but Mike seemed pleased that I'd asked. He's very easy to talk to, whereas I am always slightly wary with Ethan. But that's probably because he is a sexy superstar and I still haven't relinquished my teenage dreams. Ha! Who am I kidding?

Anyhow, as I'm almost up-to-date with the tapes, I've been given leave to see my bank manager on Tuesday morning. Ethan's story, by the way, is hotting up nicely and some of the names popping up in connection with his misspent youth are so controversial I wouldn't be surprised if they have to be cut. Though undoubtedly there are some long forgotten celebrities and one-hit wonders who will be pleased to get a mention, albeit as fleeting as Ethan's connection with them. I hope Mike knows his Media Law – or someone that does - or Ethan's profits could be eaten up fighting libel suits!

When I'd made the appointment with my bank manager (actually one of his po-faced deputies) he asked me to bring copies of my mortgage statements, and a list of outgoings. It sounded ominous and I was right to be worried.

'Sit down Mrs Grant,' he said, unsmiling, and I complied, handing him a folder with the documentation he'd requested. As he studied it, he shook his head and blew out his cheeks. Ultimately he looked up and said 'This won't do, Mrs Grant. This won't do at all.'

Already feeling intimidated, I became more wretched by the minute as he catalogued my bad housekeeping. I felt like I had when my mother railed at me for spending a whole month's pocket-money (plus lunch-money) on a signed poster of Ethan and a piece of black silk shirt ripped from his very back. (I'd completely forgotten about that – I must tell Ethan – particularly as the "silk shirt" came from Woolworth's and was bought by a classmate's brother!)

Amusing as that might sound now, the bottom line is anything but: I have three choices; I can increase my overdraft – which will ultimately cost me more and prolong the problem; I can use the meagre remains of my redundancy payment and take out a loan to consolidate my debts, and in the process lose my credit cards (unthinkable); or I can sell my house and move somewhere smaller.

I've never really had to manage money: Simon always sorted out the bills and told me what we had left to spend (that sounds so pathetic now I see it in black and white), but I can't understand how I've managed to get into trouble so quickly… except that I gave Jamie the cash to buy an old banger…and paid the deposit for Leah's new house-share when Simon pleaded poverty (and has not fulfilled his promise to pay me back)…and I had to buy a new washer/dryer…and the alarm system I had fitted was essential after a spate of daytime burglaries…not to mention that tankful of heating oil…and the MOT on my car is due next month…

But as the bank manager pointed out, my home was costing almost as much in outgoings with just me in it as it did when the whole family were there.

Following my chastening, nay depressing, interview I returned to my desk in Great Ashley in a daze and was still sitting immobile when I heard Ethan's car on the driveway.

The recording session had obviously gone well as he was buoyant.

'Hey, Rosie! We laid down a couple of really hot tracks today – and I aim to celebrate. Let's break out the brandy, girl, and we'll party!' As he spoke he did a shimmy and moon-walked to the drinks cabinet. I think the party was already under way.

I raised a wan smile but hadn't yet uttered a word, and this must have registered as he suddenly turned to me. 'I meant you and me Rosie…hey – what's up?'

'I had to see my bank manager this morning.'

'Oh, yeah…well, I've been there and done that more times than I care to remember. Bloody divorces! I tell you, I'll never get married again. What's the problem? Can't manage on the alimony?'

A cynical laugh escaped my pinched lips. 'Alimony? That's what rich people get isn't it?'

'How d'you mean?'

'I don't get alimony, Ethan. I have the house – in lieu of everything. I used to earn…' I pulled the reins, '…a good wage, so it was deemed I could support myself. Now I can't, and the only real choice is to sell my…h-home.' I desperately blinked back the tears smarting my eyelids. I really hadn't intended to inflict my doom and gloom on anyone else, particularly as I hadn't yet sorted it in my own mind.

'Hell Rosie, that's tough shit. Come here, babe.'

Before I could stop him – or myself - Ethan had pulled me from my chair and was hugging me to him. Despite my despair I could feel every inch of his sinewy body and the heat from his hands burned into my back. And slowly slid downwards. Right then it would have been the easiest thing in the world to lose myself in the moment, to just let instinct take over and move my hips as his hands were urging me to…He smelled of alcohol and spicy aftershave as he laid his cheek, slightly rough, against mine. Then our lips were almost touching…

As suddenly as the embrace began, it was over as we both stepped away. I had been in a place I used to dream of, but somewhere in my brain a red light was flashing: call it survival instinct, whatever.

Ethan, too, realised it was a bad idea. 'Work and play don't mix, Rosie,' he said with a harsh laugh. 'And it's much easier to find a good shag than a good secretary.'

If I'd been in any doubt that my boss would have taken full advantage of me, given half a chance, he'd just confirmed it in the most unflattering terms.

'Ethan! Am I supposed to take that as a compliment?' The incident had thrown me off balance and I probably sounded angrier than I felt.

He looked surprised. 'Of course. What did you think it was?'

'It was sexist. And insulting. To assume that I would…' Oh god! Talk about digging yourself into a hole. 'Forget it. It's really not important.'

I was amazed to find my words left him with an almost penitent expression: he reminded me of Jamie as a little boy.

'Sorry, Rosie. I know I can be a crass idiot at times. And I should have learned my lesson after the last time'. (So it was true about his previous secretary, then). He went back to the drinks cabinet and withdrew a bottle of brandy. 'You can still join me for a drink, though – it sounds as if you need one.'

'OK, just one, then. Brandy's good for shock, isn't it?'

'Yeah, and you know what they say - a trouble shared is a trouble halved. Or some such shite - sorry Rosie - stuff.'

APRIL

My relationship with my boss seems to have entered a different plane since then. I now feel much more relaxed with him, and I'm sure he feels the same. It's as if we've got the sex thing out of the way and can now function as equals. Not that I kid myself he found me anything other than a passable convenience: he's so inured to women throwing their knickers at him I suppose it's second nature for him to try his luck. And despite my youthful and not-so-youthful fantasies, I don't find it that hard to resist him because, although there's a spark, actually, he doesn't light my fire. Wow! Now there's an admission – or maybe I really have gone frigid (thanks, Simon).

Ethan was very sympathetic about my financial situation, and said if I needed a small loan or an advance on my wages, he'd be happy to oblige. He's not poor by normal standards, but I think it's true he's being hammered by the ex Mrs Hammers, so I was touched by his offer but turned it down as I realised I'd simply be perpetuating my problem.

If I'm realistic I know the sensible thing is to sell the house, and the more I think of it the less traumatic it seems. Yes, I've lived here since my marriage (so?). Yes, my children were born and brought up here - but someday in the not too distant future, they will set up their own homes and leave permanently.

If I bought a two-bedroom flat or a small terraced place, they'd still have a place to call home. And they've also got their father and some grandparents, not to mention aunts and uncles and cousins…

I know it wouldn't be the same (I'm anticipating the twin's objections), but they're adults. They've had their 18th birthday and are just coming up for their 21st. I was almost married at their age. At least that's how it seemed as Simon was always very controlling and possessive. To think I was flattered by his jealousy.

I decided to call my girlfriends to a Summit Meeting. They're all coming round tomorrow evening with wine, and I'm providing food. Or rather Pizza Express is.

Many years ago, when one of us had a problem we decided to set up a "Summit Meeting" and run it in an orderly manner, like an authentic meeting of world leaders. The difference is that their representatives are provided with soft drinks, speak when they are invited to, and tend to remain dignified no matter how traumatic the subject under discussion. Actually not like us at all.

Anyhow, my problem was first on the agenda: To sell or not to sell? That was the question.

Heidi, who couldn't afford to buy her ex-husband's share of the marital home, was uncharacteristically fervent. 'Sell it, Rosie. It's only bricks and mortar.'

'But it's been my home for 21 years. There's all the memories.'

'You can take the memories with you. They'll be in your head for ever.'

Madeleine (who was looking decidedly peaky) nodded. 'She's right, Rose. Better to live in a hovel and have some cash than struggle to pay a mortgage.'

I glared at her. 'That's all right for you to say. When did you last live in a hovel or struggle to pay a mortgage?'

She lifted her shoulders but didn't bother arguing the point, which is very unlike her.

'I can see what a wrench it would be for you Rosie,' Gina said. 'But I think they're right. The twins will leave home – they virtually have already - and you could be struggling for years to keep the house, just in case they ever want to stay there.'

'Sell it, Rosie. Pay off your debts, buy a small, easy-to-run place and bank the spare cash for a rainy day.' Heidi was resolute.

'What changed your mind, Heidi? You were devastated at having to sell your place.' I really wanted to know.

She shrugged. 'Well, my new place may be compact and off the beaten track, but it's *mine.* Apart from Martin's room I've got my choice of colours, my pictures, my ornaments, and not one single, sodding beer mat!'

We all laughed knowing her ex collected them and insisted on sticking them all over the walls.

'What about that awful stuffed stoat with the snake wrapped round it?' Maddy asked.

Heidi looked hurt. 'It was a mongoose - and I burned the bloody thing!'

I looked round the familiar living room and remembered when, prior to their divorce my dad had left my mother and was living in a grotty flat. "Home is where the heart is, Rosie," he told me. "It's wherever your loved ones are. The surroundings aren't important."

I nodded slowly. 'I think you're right, girls. I'm going to sell.'

We toasted my decision with another bottle of wine and the discussion then proceeded to where I should go. I don't really fancy a flat or maisonette, and besides, there aren't many available in our area. There are lots of new buildings optimistically labelled Starter Homes, which are clean and modern, and the size of a shoebox, but I had already decided I wanted two bedrooms, minimum.

Anyhow, I plan to start the rounds of estate agents tomorrow. Gina says I should agree a percentage of the sale before I put it in their hands, or I could end up paying through the nose. Having never sold property before, I didn't know what she was talking about. I always imagined the buyer paid for everything, but apparently not: I have to pay the agents for finding a buyer and it could run into a few thousands, depending on the selling price. I think I'm in the wrong business.

By the time our meeting proceeded to Any Other Business it had degenerated into a free-for-all. Heidi was about to start her new job, and we toasted that. Gina and Lloyd's dialogue was warming up nicely: in fact it had become so hot Gina had to cancel her first two clients the previous morning, so we toasted that too. And then we looked to Madeleine, who had been unusually reticent, and more than usually cynical, and seeing one of the bottles she'd brought empty beside her, realised she was well and truly rat-faced.

'So?' she slurred belligerently when we teased. 'Aren't I allowed to get pissed every now and again?'

'Of course you are – it's just that you're usually so…anal these days,' Gina said.

'Anal? I'm not anal. I've never been anal in my entire life… I'm not anal…I'm…'

Without warning she burst into tears, slumping on the arm of her chair.

We all rushed to her side, stroking her hair, wiping her tears and hugging her.

'Maddy – what's happened?'

'What's wrong?'

'I'm sorry Maddy, I didn't mean it.'

'He's d-d-dumped me,' she snivelled.

We three exchanged knowing looks.

'You mean Ross Gibson, the soap star?'

'Star!' Maddy's nostrils flared. 'He's not a star! He's a poxy little bit-part player who'll never amount to anything.'

'Are you sure it's over?' I said soothingly. 'Maybe…'

'How sure do you want? I went to his dressing room to surprise him and he was screwing that scrawny little ginger thing who plays his sister. Incestuous bastard!'

'Beth Madison?' Heidi was impressed. 'Her song is number five in the charts and climbing - Martin told me. She's really pretty – in fact she reminds me of you as a teenager, Maddy…' her voice trailed off.

Wrong!

Maddy now slithered into a quivering heap and began wailing piteously.

This continued until she fell asleep on my sofa. I covered

her up and left her snoring like a freight train.

'She thinks she's got problems!' I said, trying not to sound bitter. 'She'll have no problem finding another man – or boy, if she so chooses. She has five homes and I have to sell my only one.'

'Whatever happened to family values?' Heidi asked inconsequentially.

Gina and I looked at one another.

'Ask that horny young pup who's screwing his scrawny ginger sister,' Gina quipped, and we collapsed, giggling inanely.

So much for our Summit Meeting. I think world leaders should run them on the same lines: you all get your say, each problem is dealt with sympathetically, and in the end you're still friends.

Of course, it would only work if they were all women.

Decision made, first thing this morning I went to town and started with the estate agent at top end of the High Street. I hadn't been able to get hold of Ethan, but asked Mike to let him know I'd be happy to work late tonight to make up for the time I was taking off: as he was still in the recording studio, I knew it wasn't essential for me to be there early in the morning.

At Allcock & Avis, I explained to the obligatory spotty youth what I required of his company i.e. to sell my property and buy another, smaller one.

'And how much do you want to spend on the smaller property, Mrs Grant?'

'That rather depends on how much I get for my house.'

'And how much is your house worth, Mrs Grant?'

I stared at him. 'I thought it was your job to tell me that.'

'So you'd like us to value it for you, Mrs Grant?'

'I imagine that's essential if you're to sell it,' I couldn't prevent the sarcasm.

'So you'd like us to sell it for you, would you Mrs Grant?'

'Isn't that what you do, *Marvin*?' I stressed the name on his badge.

'Of course, Mrs Grant, but we have to take some details, get an estimator and surveyor out, and you must sign a contract.'

'*I* sign a contract?'

'Yes, Mrs Grant. Giving us a percentage of the sale price.'

Before I could ask he added 'That's two per cent.'

Though maths wasn't my favourite subject, I was pretty astute at on-the-spot calculations. 'Two per cent? So if you sold my house for £100,000, I have to give you two thousand pounds?'

He picked up a calculator, and after many minutes of frowning and jabbing it with his finger, said in a surprised tone 'Yes, that's correct, Mrs Grant. £2,000.'

I wanted to pick him up and shake him. In fact, I didn't care if they were the most successful estate agents in the county – as their advertising claimed – I wasn't going to use them.

'Thank you very much, Marvin. But no thanks,' I said as I rose and stalked to the door.

'Mrs Grant…we can negotiate…I can work out a deal…'

'Sorry, I need it now, not next year.'

As I closed the door he was staring after me with a puzzled expression.

After that, disheartened as I was, I tried another five agents, and they were all very much the same, though none quite so up front with their extortionate charges. I found one who said they'd agree to a straight fee, once the house had been valued, which they were all more than happy to do, so I agreed to let all five of them come and do their worst. They all mentioned the "benefits" of employing them as "sole agent". I'm not entirely sure what that means, but if their lackadaisical attitude is any guide I'm sure it will take more than one of them to find me a buyer before I am due to collect my pension - and then the only home I shall need to purchase is a pine box.

Anyhow, I said I'd phone them with a time that was convenient.

'Convenient to us, I hope?' said one misguided young madam.

'No, convenient to me,' I told her. 'If you want my business, that is.'

If some undeserving firm is going to get the commission on two sales from me, the least I expect is good service.

One decision I have to make, and was therefore unable to tell the agents, is the area I'd like to live. As a general rule it appears the closer to town, the more expensive the property, though there are many very high-priced places in the villages – like Lime Cottage, for example, from which I'm sure you'd get no change from a million, if not two.

I discussed it with Ethan who was once again on a high when he returned from the studio. I'm sure he's on something chemical. He said I should just look at places within my price range and go with my gut feeling. He's probably right. Anyhow, he's going up to London with Mike on Friday and suggested it might be a good day to have off so I can get the estimators round. God knows I can't afford to lose the money, but needs must. It seems I'm already paying for a service not yet provided.

Leah rang me last night, closely followed by Jamie. Apparently their father has set the date of the wedding to his "Angel". It is in three weeks time, and they're honeymooning in Disneyland. I was so shocked I couldn't articulate, not even to remark on the pertinence of the destination.

Despite everything, I'm sad - and mad: I'm having to sell my house, and he's swanning towards his second childhood. It's so unjust. And so final. This really will mark the end of an era and I spent a sleepless night mourning the past and contemplating my future. A year ago, my job was my only problem: now, my job is the only thing in my life that's going well. Then I remembered that it too was temporary. Even Geoffrey couldn't stand my tossing and turning and jumped off the bed in disgust. I thought I'd already hit rock bottom, but by 4am I wasn't so sure.

My insomnia wasn't helped by the knowledge that the Angel child is broadcasting her life story (and therefore Simon's) to her hundreds of contacts on Facebook. I discovered this when Gina rang to ask if I'd heard the news: apparently the Bimbo is one of her contacts. Gina hadn't realised she was sleeping with the enemy as she rarely uses the site, but added all her clients so she could broadcast special offers in her salons – and *she* was on her client list. Gina assured me she is now blacklisted. Nevertheless, we decided it would be prudent not to "unfriend" her as it could be interesting to be one step ahead of any developments. Like Simon ditching her at the altar, haha – or "lol" as they say nowadays (for many months I thought it meant "lots of love", but it's "laugh out loud"). Of course.

I made appointments, at two-hour intervals, for four estate agents to come and value the house. The fifth had said it was impossible to send anyone today, so I told them to forget it. I needn't have bothered with the two-hour intervals either, as none of them were there for more than 45 minutes – one only stayed for 15. Talk about money for old rope!

Their valuations differed by as much as £20,000, and apart from the one who stayed longest, an amenable young man called Darren, were actually rude about my home. I never imagined when I chose a pink bathroom suite that fifteen years later white would be the *only* colour acceptable, or that carpet tiles in the kitchen were *terribly* outdated, or that strip lights were *all* being replaced by spotlights - inset in a false ceiling, of course. I felt as if someone had criticised my cat, or my children.

The good news is that the house is worth quite a bit more than I imagined; the bad news, that I'll be paying the estate agents even more. And which one to choose? Darren was the nicest – but his lot want two per cent, no deals.

It came to me in the middle of another sleepless night.

I've been in advertising and marketing for years; I've persuaded people to buy all sorts of rubbish at inflated prices: surely I was capable of selling my own house?

I vowed I'd launch my own website, with photos and graphics. Sod giving my hard-earned cash to the property vultures.

Having learned from TV property shows that buyers expect a pristine, unlived-in look, I stuffed everything in cupboards, tidied each room and made them look as impersonal as possible. By the time I'd finished putting paraphernalia from the twin's rooms into bin liners, the garage was bursting at the seams – but I wasn't going to take pictures of that as everyone knows what a garage looks like. I know the plundering of their possessions will cause wounded complaints from my offspring, but if the rooms don't look good in the photos, I'll never get the price I want. Anyway, I had just set up the first shot when the phone interrupted my artistic flow. I was surprised to hear my boss on the line.

'Rosie, I know it's Saturday, and I'm sure you're busy, but I desperately need you to do me a favour…'

Oh-oh, what now? 'If I can Ethan, of course.'

'I've got a gig in Leeds tonight, and I've got my daughter coming for the weekend. The thing is, I promised to take her shopping this afternoon - and I have to leave at lunchtime.'

Oh, no! Not the teenager from hell. 'And you'd like me to take her shopping?'

'Oh, please Rosie, if you would. I'll pay you of course. I-er-won't be back until the early hours though, so do you think you could possibly stay at the cottage with her? I'll be forever in your debt.'

Great. Babysitting the brat, too.

'Well, er, I had plans tonight, Ethan…' For an aromatherapy bath, a Brad Pitt video, and a minor session with the man from Cadbury's.

'Oh, god. Now what am I supposed to do? She'll throw a wobbly if I get in a professional babysitter – if I can find one - and I daren't leave her on her own.'

By the sound of it Allegra was more in need of a professional minder.

'I'll pay you double, Rosie, I'm desperate. It's the first time I've seen her for four months, and you've no idea what I had to agree to. If I let her down now, it will be years before her mother lets me see her again.'

I sighed. The money would be good, and besides, I have no time for selfish, twisted women who use their children as weapons on the post-divorce battleground. Even if I understand their sentiments.

'All right, Ethan. Do you want me to come over?'

'Rosie, you're a doll. No, I'll drop her off at your house. You've got a key to the cottage, haven't you?'

'I have. You know where I live?'

'No, but Mike does and he'll be with me. See you about 1.30pm. And thanks Rosie, I won't forget this.'

I don't expect I will either.

It's over six years since I've had to cope with a stroppy fourteen year old, and I can't say it's an experience I ever thought I'd repeat. (At least, not until I am a grandmother when I will be a wise and patient mentor, of course). However, it seemed Allegra liked shopping, and I assumed her father would provide the wherewithal, so that should take care of the afternoon. And then what? Her choice of supper and a DVD? Or mindless hours of MTV and continuous teen-soaps? Or perhaps she'd want to play on Ethan's X-Box? Oh, hell, I'd know soon enough, and the sooner she was here, the sooner the ordeal would be over. I'd take the Brad Pitt movie anyhow, and maybe I could watch it when she'd gone to bed. Though I had a feeling I'd be worn out long before she was.

I was looking out as Mike's Range Rover stopped, and was taken aback to see Ethan, followed six steps behind, by a sullen faced blonde who looked at least 18.

I opened the door, and he smiled tautly.

'Rosie, this is my daughter, Allegra. Allie – this is Rose.'

Allie gave me a scathing look and didn't speak.

Ethan laughed nervously. 'She's always been a bit shy.'

His daughter muttered something that sounded distinctly like "bollocks".

Ethan laughed again and handed me a wad of notes. 'There you go. Half each - treat yourself, and if you spend any more, within reason, of course, I'll repay you tomorrow, OK Rosie?'

He was almost hopping from one foot to the other, desperate to be off. He put an arm round his daughter's shoulders and hugged her unyielding body to him briefly, planting a kiss on her cheek. She immediately rubbed at it.

'Bye then darlin' – I'll see you in the morning. Have a good time, girls.' And he was down the path and in the Range Rover quicker than a rat up a drainpipe.

'Well,' I said mustering a bright expression. 'You'd better come in.'

For a moment I thought she was going to bolt, then she shrugged and pushed past me. As she did I noticed the depth of her makeup: it was not unlike Aveline's.

'God this is a dump,' she said bitingly as she stood in the living room.

I valiantly ignored her discourtesy, sure she was baiting me deliberately.

'Would you like something to drink, or a snack?'

'I haven't come here to dine – I thought my father had bribed you to take me shopping.'

Ouch! 'He hasn't bribed me, Allegra. I'm an employee and he pays me to do things for him.'

'I bet!' she retorted ambiguously. 'And don't call me Allegra, I'm Allie. Only a stupid bloody musician would stick a kid with a name like that.'

I shrugged and picked up my car keys. 'Whatever you say. OK, let's go. Do you need the loo or anything first?'

Her rolling eyes told me I'd made another faux pas.

'I'm fourteen years old, not four – and it's a long time since I needed anyone to wipe my arse.'

Had she been mine, she'd have received a clip round the ear, politically correct or not; instead the house rattled as I slammed the front door after her.

We drove to town in silence, until she attempted to light a cigarette.

'Please, don't do that in the car, Alleg…Allie.'

'For god's sake! I'll open the window.'

I almost stamped on the brake but restrained myself as we were in a line of heavy traffic, and said through clenched teeth 'No you won't. Now put the cigarette away, and wait until you're out of my car.' Even Leah knew not to mess with me when I used that tone.

There was hesitation, and I thought she was going to carry on regardless, then she put the cigarette back into the packet and stuffed it in her bag.

'Thank you. You know, if you have to…'

'Oh for chrissakes, don't start lecturing me. I *know* it causes lung cancer. I *know* it makes your hair stink, but I like the smell – and I don't give a shit if I get cancer – everybody dies someday.'

I was shocked. Not by her language but by her slant on life, convinced her attitude owed more to wretchedness than rebellion. Underneath that ugly, petulant manner was a very unhappy young woman, unless I am very much mistaken. Either that or she's the epitome of an obnoxious, spoiled brat.

'I wasn't going to lecture you. I was simply going to tell you if you're looking for clothes, there's a new boutique in the High Street that opened just before Christmas. I believe it's very good.'

'As if you'd know.'

'Do you practise being unpleasant, or does it come naturally?' I couldn't take much more, and my duties had only just begun.

She glared my way. 'Do you practise being an uptight bitch, or does that come naturally?'

I dug my teeth into my bottom lip so hard I tasted blood. I didn't slam the brakes on, but with knuckles white on the steering wheel, signalled and pulled into a bus stop, then leaned across and opened her door. 'Right – out! Now!'

She turned to me and for a second seemed surprised, then the sneer returned and she unbuckled her seatbelt. She got out and held out her hand.

'Give us the dosh then.'

I shook my head. 'No way. If you want to act like a monster, you're on your own. I'll pick you up at 5pm.'

I made to close the door, but she still had hold of the handle.

'But I haven't got any cash. And I don't know this place.'

'Then I suggest you get back in and apologise.'

At that point my senses started to return, and I prayed my bluff worked or I'd be in grave danger of child abuse – not to mention losing my job.

Just as a double-decker touched my bumper and hooted loudly, she slumped back into the passenger seat, and despite more hooting I glared at her, not moving.

'All right. I'm sorry,' she said sullenly, and with a silent sigh I inched the car back into the traffic.

'I'll be telling my father. It's his money. You have no right to keep it from me.'

'Allie, I don't care. Tell him what you like.'

She was very quiet and, I hoped, just slightly contrite: certainly she was disconcerted. She's clearly used to being humoured by everyone.

The town was busy and we eventually parked, and she got out and lit a cigarette. I refrained from commenting; after all, apart from the next few hours, she really wasn't my problem. But I walked ahead of her mentally telling Leah that all was forgiven. Compared to this little beast, she had been the perfect teenager.

I waited until she stood on the half-smoked cigarette. 'OK, where would you like to go? How about Top Shop?'

'Top Shop? You can't be serious. That's for paupers. We'll start at Karen Millen – if there is one in this god-awful town.'

While she was browsing, I checked the cash Ethan had given me. There was £300, and he'd said half was mine. It wouldn't go very far if his daughter insisted on shopping in places like this.

We went from one expensive boutique to another, and Allegra tried on a variety of tops and trousers. I have to say, if she ever stops applying makeup with a trowel, stops slouching and starts smiling, she'll be stunning: she's about five-ten and slim and shapely with it.

Then she found a pair of leather jeans; they were £230 – in the sale.

'That's rather a lot, Allie. Your father has only given you £150.' Only!

The pout appeared instantly. 'He said we could spend more. You heard him say he'd pay you back.'

'I'll tell you what. We'll look at a few more shops, and if that's all you want, then we'll come back and get them, OK?'

'It'll have to be, seeing as you've got all the money.'

Right.

On our way to yet another row of over-priced outfitters, we had to pass Debenhams's, and I was determined to browse in my favourite store. On this detour she was half-a-dozen steps behind, and scowling darkly.

'I'm going to get some underwear for my son, and then go up to the fashion floor,' I told her. 'If you want to go off on your own, I'll meet you in the Coffee Shop in half an hour.'

She shrugged. 'I might as well stay. I didn't know you had a son – how old is he?'

This was the first time she'd shown any interest in anything other than herself.

'Jamie's almost 21. He has a twin sister, Leah. He's at Art College and plays in a band. And Leah's…'

'He plays in a band? What sort of band?' She obviously had no interest in my daughter.

'I've only seen them once, but they're pretty good I think. They play all sorts and do gigs all round the area.' I was picking out underpants.

'God I bet he hates wearing those awful jockeys. Everyone wears Calvin Klein's or silk boxers now.'

I stared at her as a fleeting image of Minnie Mouse crossed my mind. 'And how would you know?'

She flushed. 'Well, all the pop stars do – and – well, everyone does.'

Come to think of it, Jamie had mentioned them. I hesitated

then remembered I had £150 to spend, and picked up three pairs.

Allie gave a nod of approval. What's the world coming to when you're judged by the label in your underpants? I'll get a waiver at the heavenly gates – mine are St Michael (OK, M&S, but I'm sure St Peter will see through the disguise).

Upstairs I found a gorgeous silky dress in my favourite shade of sea green that had been reduced to £50, and battled with my conscience: I know I have money troubles, but the cash I had today was a bonus. I went to try it on, leaving my reluctant charge to wander round the rails.

When I emerged from the cubicle knowing I had to have the green dress, Allie was standing there holding an armful of clothes, and looking uncomfortable.

'Are you going to try them on?'

She shrugged, on the defence again. 'Might as well. It might not be crap.'

I shook my head. How had one so young become so cynical? I decided to wait and see if she wanted to buy any of her selection.

When she came out her expression was almost animated.

'These trousers look all right – and they're not too short either. I can't believe they're only £40 – and all three tops are OK too.'

I lifted the price tag and saw they were all under £25.

'If you forego the leather trousers, you can have all of these – and still have change.'

'Yeah. That's cool. For cheap gear they're not too bad.'

'Just because they're not expensive doesn't necessarily mean they're rubbish,' I said, and I could tell by her blank look that she'd retreated into deaf-mode. 'Anyway, with a figure like yours, a dish-rag would look good.'

Her eyes widened, and she seemed to be about to speak; she didn't, but there was the hint of a smile on her lips. Hallelujah!

We paid for our purchases and then went for a coffee; at least, I had a black coffee and she had a milkshake and two iced doughnuts. She'll be fighting the flab at forty if there's any justice in this world, but I wasn't about to tell her.

There's no way the rest of my sentence could be described as pleasant, but once my charge had been allowed to have McDonald's from the drive-thru for supper, plus a large bag of cheese and onion crisps, two Snickers and a Jolly Bag, followed by an overdose of MTV, she was no longer totally hostile.

Nevertheless, all attempts at social intercourse, particularly regarding her home life and her father, were met with a shrug. She did, however, ask if "that ugly retard with the big tits" had gone to Leeds with Ethan. I answered quite honestly that I had no idea, but I don't think she believed me.

I wouldn't be over the moon if my father were dating the likes of Aveline either.

I managed to sneak the Cadbury's under cover of Allegra's junk food binge and despite the fact that I had to forego Brad Pitt, and notwithstanding her less than charming disposition, my sympathy for her deepened. She's the result of a totally dysfunctional family, a perfect illustration that material wealth is no substitute for good parenting.

I know that sounds cheesy, and there's no such thing as a perfect parent (ask any teenager), but an absent father with his own pubescent problems and an alcoholic mother do not add up to a stable environment. Perhaps she has reason to be angry.

In the early hours I was woken briefly by the triumphant return of my boss. I say triumphant as he was obviously high about something (or probably *on* something) but the only other voice I heard was low and male, and I thought it sounded like Mike, so even if Aveline had been at the gig as suspected by Allie, at least he'd had the decency not to flaunt her under his daughter's nose.

The next morning I waited in vain for Ethan to rise so that I could leave and salvage some of my weekend, but by 10.30am only Mike made an appearance. He insisted on cooking me breakfast, the aroma of which drew Allie, and then Ethan to the kitchen.

Allie had washed off her makeup to reveal a very pretty fourteen-year-old, but any headway we'd made the previous day was negated when she glared at me and snapped 'You're still here then?'

'Don't talk like that, babe,' her father said with an irritated frown. They looked very alike.

'Why the hell not?' she muttered, now glowering.

'Because it's bloody rude, Allie, and well you know it.' This came from Mike, and amazingly the girl looked shamefaced.

'I'm off now, anyway,' I stood up.

'Thanks a lot, Rosie. I owe you,' Ethan said.

That reminded me, and I dug in my bag. 'Here's your change. Allie got some great things, and she has change too.'

She gave me a look that would sour vinegar.

Ethan looked surprised and turned to his daughter smiling.

'Good girl, Allie. That's great.' The girl visibly melted under his approval. 'Now thank Rose for putting up with you.'

Ouch again! My boss certainly has a talent for opening his mouth and putting his foot in it: if he were in the Diplomatic Corps a nuclear crisis would be the least of their worries.

'I didn't have to put up with her, it was a pleasure,' I lied because I saw the hurt in her eyes, and the retort she was about to give remained unuttered.

Mike saw me to the door. 'She's a good kid,' he said. 'Unfortunately for her she has two parents who either ignore her or overindulge her. It doesn't strike a happy balance.'

'I gathered that. It's a shame. I get the impression that underneath her thorny image is a very unhappy and confused teenager.'

'You're right about that. I keep hoping something will happen to make her father grow up. Maybe when he comes to terms with his own parentage...'

He stopped, perhaps because he didn't want to be seen to be criticising.

'In my experience, most teenagers are confused, and most men never grow up,' I said, hoping to lighten the atmosphere with my home-grown homily.

Mike raised his eyebrows and smiled. (Have I mentioned he looks not at all anxious and skeletal when he smiles? Quite appealing in a lean sort of way.)

'And some women, Rose, have to learn that not all men are immoral idiots with their brains in their trousers.'

That put *me* straight!

MAY

My house advert was in the local paper last night; it will be in the weekly, which comes out on Friday, too. I have also put it on the Internet, and constructed a For Sale board, which I planted by the front gate. At least, Ron planted it after he watched me struggling as my first attempt toppled and almost axed a passing child.

'I think you need a good man to *erect* that, Rosie,' he said as he noticed my dilemma and swaggered towards me. I'd never noticed him swaggering before. 'You shouldn't get too used to doing without, you know. I'm always happy to help out.' He accompanied this second *double entendre* with a theatrical wink.

Perhaps there's a disease known as Divorcée Induced Dementia. There must be some explanation because until my Decree Absolute Ron was happily married Mr Nice Guy from next door. Linda will kill him if he displays the symptoms in her presence.

Come to think of it, I don't think it was just Minty Mike who had hands like an octopus during our New Year's Eve Twister fest. No wonder wives regard divorcées with suspicion. I must be more watchful - though according to Mike I'm already bordering on the paranoid as far as men are concerned. I'll discuss it with Gina at the weekend.

I have just had two phone calls from interested buyers – I knew this would be a doddle! They're both viewing on Saturday.

I've also had five emails. Two were adverts for Viagra, two for get-rich-quick investments, and one from a person who wondered if I'd rent him a room, and said he had his own tools and would be happy to service my appliances.

Is he winding me up or do divorces come with their own

telepathically transmitted DNA?

It's as though I've descended to a different plain. This time last year I was still a blissful innocent, naïve in the face of such sexual innuendo – or certainly sufficiently inured to it to be immune.

And if I'm truthful, bored. And probably boring.

There's food for thought.

The house smelled of brewing coffee and baking bread, as advised by the TV house sale experts and I had just showered and changed after a manic burst of cleaning when my first buyers turned up.

I'm not a snob by any means, but I have to confess I was surprised by their appearance. To put it kindly they looked – and smelled - as if they'd been on the road for a fortnight, and when I glanced out onto the street I saw a rust-coloured Ford Granada parked outside with a Rottweiler's head jammed in the partly-closed passenger window. As I watched, someone walked by and the dog started barking with malicious intent, saliva dripping from its jaws.

My initial optimism faded further as it became apparent my viewers were the Weekend Rubberneckers Heidi warned me about – in other words, their hobby is nosing around houses for sale with no intention whatsoever of buying.

I was quite relieved when they said it wasn't really what they were looking for and left. My neighbours will be sticking pins in my effigy if I sell to the likes of them.

My second viewers arrived late which was just as well as I'd forgotten about the baking bread and the house now smelled throughout of blackened toast. Apparently part-baked batons need only 15 minutes, not 50, as I'd misread.

Anyhow, the viewers were a young couple with three of the rowdiest little boys I've ever come across. After they'd knocked over a vase of flowers (also bought specially for the occasion) and Geoffrey had fled in terror, I suggested they play in the garden while their parents looked around. They were only out there for two minutes before one of them had thrown a missile that crashed resoundingly through Linda's prized greenhouse. When I went to pacify her, and naturally offered to pay for the broken pane, she handed back the missile – a stone duckling that had stood beside my back door for over twenty years and now had a missing beak. Little ruffians.

The couple liked the house and said they'd be in touch but I don't think I'd dare sell to them - I'd have to emigrate.

I've had further response from my web-page: two more ads for Viagra. I never knew it was so readily available. Perhaps this is what causes husbands to stray and virtuous fathers to behave like sex-mad morons - a secret network of Viagra pushers. Maybe it's channelled through barbers' shops - that would bring a new concept to "anything *extra* for the weekend, sir?" But I digress…

I also had one inquiry that seems genuine, from a woman whose husband is being transferred to this area and would like to see the house. Unfortunately they can't make it until next month, so want me to let them know if it is sold. I said I would, but I hope to goodness I sell long before then as I'm already sick of strangers invading my home and pulling it to pieces.

I can't believe how quickly time flies. I'm already two-thirds of the way through my contract with Ethan and have just realised I'll soon be back on the job market. I'd better start ringing the agencies again and buying the evening paper.

I know one thing – I've been spoiled by this opportunity and will sorely miss being on the fringes of the rock 'n' roll lifestyle, and being privy to Ethan's roller-coaster existence. Not to mention the man himself and my cosy chats with Mike over coffee in that totally gorgeous kitchen. (That's the first time in my life I've used a hyperbole for a room with a cooker!)

It was during one of these coffee-break chats that I learned they've finished recording Ethan's new album. He had abandoned his autobiography for the day after a call from an agency who was trying to trace his mother, and Mike had prepared coffee and insisted I join him. As my only task was to make a few phone calls, I didn't need much persuading.

Anyway, word is the album is a good one, and the record company is convinced it's going to make mega-bucks, which is great news for them all. Ethan is talking about buying a place in the sun. He used to own a villa in Marbella, but had to relinquish it to the second Mrs Hammer. Mike is trying to persuade him not to spend the cash before it's in the bank - so far, successfully.

Apparently he's still seeing Aveline, but Mike says her days are numbered as she hinted at the M word. (Marriage, that is.)

'What Ethan needs is a woman nearer his own age who has her feet firmly on the ground,' he said. 'But he's always been a bloody idiot with women. Especially when it comes to marrying them.'

'Well I'm sure we all get married with good intentions,' I told him. 'I mean when you love someone enough to marry them you imagine it's going to last for ever. You don't think "oh well, if it doesn't work out we can get a divorce", do you?'

Mike raised his brows. 'Don't you? Judging by the divorce rate I'd say that's exactly what too many think. But I have a feeling Ethan will be a bit more careful now he's been twice bitten.'

'Has it had the same effect on you?' I don't know where that came from and mentally kicked myself: Mike tends to be very guarded about his personal life. I tried to make a joke of it. 'Once is more than enough for me! I've no intention of getting bitten twice, let alone a third time!'

He looked at me with a mixture of surprise and, I think, empathy. 'I think everyone should have a second chance. Even if a broken marriage doesn't teach you exactly what you want, it shows you what you don't need in your life. The problem is, as people mature and broaden their lives, they often grow apart. It doesn't necessarily mean you've made a bad choice. Sometimes it's the right person but the wrong time.'

I wondered if the latter remark showed he was still in love with his ex, though reading between the lines he appeared to have no regrets about his situation. I wasn't sure how to respond and for a few seconds we regarded one another in silence, but his answer had disconcerted me with its insight. He understood my messed up emotions, and seemed to have been there himself. However, unlike me, he didn't come across as being bitter. There again he's had longer to come to terms with his circumstances, and perhaps, in a few years, I will also be able to think of this time without rancour.

I'm not holding my breath.

I changed the subject.

'What's Mrs Hammer Mark II like?' I asked, though I already knew she was an actress, and much younger than her ex-husband.

'Marnie is a bitch.' Mike was uncharacteristically blunt.

It was my turn to raise my brows. 'That good, huh?'

He nodded. 'Believe it or not, he married her because she was pregnant with Fender.'

'Poor kid. Allegra's a pretty name, but why call your son after a guitar?'

'Well at least he didn't use Stratocaster as a middle name!'

We both laughed, though it wasn't really funny, and Fen, as the six-year-old was known, was a sweet kid, according to Mike. 'Yeah, I did joke about that at the Christening – I'm his godfather, by the way.'

I was surprised when I realised Mike and Ethan must have known one another for longer than I'd imagined.

He noticed my quizzical look. 'We met way back in the States when I was a student and did a tour as a roadie, and we kept in touch over the years. When I needed a job over here, he offered to help me out.'

'I see.' I nodded, wondering what had caused him to leave his apparently lucrative practice in California.

'My wife became homesick, and I needed to come over for my daughter's sake,' he stated as if he'd read my mind. Was I really that transparent?

If his trip across the Atlantic had been an effort to save his marriage, it obviously hadn't worked. But I was still left wondering about his feelings for the ex-Mrs Robbins.

'I go and see Fen as often as I can,' he continued, obviously not about to disclose anything further on the subject of his move to England, or his marriage. 'Marnie doesn't make it easy for Ethan. Though as long as he keeps paying through the nose, she has no option but to give him access. Anyhow, the little fella's seven next Tuesday week and Ethan's applying to have him for weekends and school holidays occasionally. He goes to court the Thursday after next.'

It was obvious Mike was very fond of his godson, and of Allie, though he predicted she'd soon be completely off the rails unless someone woke up and took responsibility for her. Like one of her parents.

'Damn! That reminds me, Bianca – that's Mrs Hammer Mark I - called to say she wants a meeting with Ethan. If she's hitting the bottle again that could signal the beginning of World War III. I'll set it up for tomorrow or Wednesday, and you and I had better be on Red Alert in case she goes for him.'

He grinned when he saw the horror on my face: I know my duties are unspecified, but I hadn't envisaged fending off psychotic ex-wives.

'Don't worry – I'm sure she'll be sober.'

That was a great comfort.

Gina came round last night. She thinks I've lost weight and suggested I go to the gym with her a couple of times a week to tone up. I'm thinking about it, seriously. I'm a bit worried as that's the second hint I've had about toning up in as many weeks: Ethan has installed a multi-gym in his conservatory and offered me use of it. Are they trying to tell me something?

Of course, the purpose of my friend's visit wasn't to talk about exercise, not the conventional sort, anyway. She was full of her renewed relationship with Lloyd, and is certain he's on the verge of proposing (again). They're going away next weekend - which came as a blow for me as it's the day Simon marries his Angel child, and I was hoping we'd go on an out-of-town girlie trip as a diversion.

I don't know why it should bother me but it's a really weird feeling when your children are about to attend the wedding of the man with whom you've spent 25 years of your life, to a woman who is half your age.

Leah's presence will be under duress, and she says she has no intention of making polite conversation with her future stepmother. I think her father probably bribed her, yet he still hasn't repaid me the deposit on her house-share. Typical!

Jamie says they want to start a family right away. That made me feel sort of surreal – especially when Gina, confirmed Jamie's words: apparently it's all over Facebook. She has to be joking: Simon was stressed out for years when the twins were growing up. Love has obviously induced amnesia. Or Alzheimer's. Gina, who remembers how freaked out Simon was, thinks it's definitely the latter.

I obviously don't know him as well as I thought I did, but even so I can't believe he bargained for a new family when he embarked on his fling. I bet it never entered his head. But I doubt he was being guided by his head.

I know not everyone has parental urges: Gina is the first to admit she's never had a maternal bone in her body. She begged her doctor for a hysterectomy when she was twenty-seven. He refused, so she went private and paid to be sterilised. I used to think she'd change her mind, but I've never seen a sign that she's regretted her decision.

I've never really understood her attitude because she has three Persian cats that are only allowed outside in a specially constructed run, and therefore do their business indoors. I would rather change ten babies' nappies than one tray of cat poo.

But it takes all sorts, and she's always been a great friend. I think I might go to the gym with her. I'd rather not shake my cellulite in front of Ethan - though watching him would surely help me forget my protesting muscles.

Bianca Hammer-Crossland was still tall, blonde and beautiful – until you got up close and saw the ravages of drink tugging at her once flawless skin.

I admitted her to Lime Cottage for her appointment with her ex-husband and was amazed to find she was charm personified. Unlike her daughter, she accepted my presence without hostility and thanked me for my offer of coffee.

Ethan entered the room, almost creeping through the door with none of his customary exuberance, and seemed to flinch when she rose and approached him, kissed his cheek and greeted him pleasantly.

'Hello Ethan, darling. You're looking well. Thanks for seeing me. I know how busy you are.'

I closed the living room door, and went to the kitchen to make the coffee, convinced this wasn't the woman whose visit Ethan – and Mike – had been dreading.

Mike came into the kitchen as I put the cups on a tray, and I told him so.

He lifted his shoulders. 'It always starts off that way.'

When I took the coffee in, Ethan was hunched in a chair as far away from his first wife as the room would allow, but Bianca smiled pleasantly and thanked me.

'Why does she still keep Ethan's name?' I asked Mike.

'She says it's for Allie's sake. And Crossland, her second husband, was a minor aristocrat, but penniless. She thought he had money, and he thought she had, so that was another non-starter. I think she likes the kudos the names bring. Anyhow, you can guarantee she's here to try and get more money out of him and she's got no chance: last time Ethan raised her alimony so Allie could have a larger allowance, she didn't pass it on. Her alcohol bill alone is astronomic – she blames him so expects him to keep paying for her addiction.'

As I was absorbing the circumstances of Allegra's mother, still convinced Mike was exaggerating and Ethan paranoid, I nearly jumped out of my skin as a crash emanated from the living room, and something shattered against the wooden door behind me.

'You never change, do you, you tight-fisted scumbag!'

Crash!

'I wouldn't have a freaking drink problem if it wasn't for you...'

Crash!

This screaming and crashing was interspersed with Ethan's pleas for her to calm down. His voice was beginning to sound panicky and I looked at Mike

Though alert, he didn't seem unduly worried. 'He'll shout for me when she gets dangerous,' he said with a twisted grin. Hopefully that would be before she rendered him unconscious.

Crash!

'If you won't give me any more money, *you* can look after your daughter. Have a taste of what it's like to live under the same roof as an ungrateful teenager...'

'Now come on, babe...'

'Don't you babe me! Save it for that blow-up Barbie doll you're shagging...'

Crash!

Ethan yowled. 'Now stop that you mad cow...Mike!'

'That's it,' muttered Mike, and strode through the door. I stood in the doorway and surveyed the chaos as he grabbed Bianca whose face was now red and blotchy, her hair in disarray. She was also shoeless so I guessed she'd used them as missiles. My boss was clutching the side of his head, and blood seeped through his fingers.

When I was certain Mike had a good grip on the raving ex, I went over to Ethan to inspect his wound.

'Oh, I should have guessed,' Bianca grated, her face contorted with contempt as I bent over the wounded man. 'Have you ever had a secretary you didn't screw?' She turned her laser glare on me. 'He always employs slappers, you know! Ha!'

'Come on, Bianca – I'll drive you home,' Mike said, still gripping her arms which had all but stopped flailing; she was suddenly as floppy as a rag doll.

'Not without my flashk...' her words were slurring and she was pointing to the floor where I noticed a large silver hip flask lying on the parquet, alcohol already dulling the polished surface. I picked it up.

'Fill it up, you...cut-price pussy.'

I clenched my jaw.

'For chrissakes give her some scotch and get rid of her,' Ethan said. He'd removed his hand and I could see the cut on his forehead was superficial as it had practically stopped bleeding.

Mike nodded and rolled his eyes, and I went to the drinks cabinet and dutifully filled the outsize flask. No wonder Allegra was such a pain.

Eventually Mike manoeuvred Bianca into her BMW and got behind the steering wheel.

I wanted to ask how he was going to get back, but decided it was prudent not to put myself in the firing line: he'd probably ring anyway.

Back indoors, Ethan was inspecting his wound in the hall mirror.

'How could I ever have fancied that demented wino? She's probably scarred me for life.'

I inspected the cut closely. 'You'll live. I mean it's not deep. It certainly doesn't need stitches. Go and clean it then…' it was as if I was talking to my son, and the pathetic look he gave me was identical. 'Oh, all right, I'll do it. Do you have any antiseptic?'

I was following him upstairs and he turned to look at me in horror. 'You're not going to put neat Dettol on it are you? I'll need anaesthesia for that…'

'Don't be such a wimp,' I said. 'I'll dilute it.'

He really was a bit of a wuss, wincing theatrically as I bathed the small cut, and insisting on a plaster. I marvelled that this was the source of so many female fantasies. He was just a man, after all. Quite a nice one when he dropped the showbiz persona; he just needed to grow up a bit, and face his responsibilities. And thinking of that…

'What are you going to do if she brings Allegra to live with you?' I asked, emboldened by his vulnerability.

'Huh! She was just bluffing! It's one of her regular threats.

She won't let Allie come to me, she'd lose too much bread.'

'I see.' Poor kid. She really was a pawn in her parents' power struggle.

'I wanted to have custody of her, you know.' My boss must have read my thoughts. 'I know I'm not perfect, but even I can see she's ruining the kid.'

It was on the tip of my tongue to tell him he was also doing his share of that, but caution won. Instead I said 'There's no such thing as a perfect parent – we all learn as we go along. But have you tried suggesting Bianca has treatment for her… condition?'

'*Condition?* You talk as if she's got some kind of illness.'

'Alcoholism is an illness, Ethan.'

He frowned. 'Yeah…well…whatever.'

Conversation over.

An hour later Mike rang on his mobile. He was almost at Bianca's place and wanted me to drive over and pick him up.

'She's out for the count now,' he explained. 'I'll stay just long enough to make sure she's out of harm's way. I don't like asking you Rose, but it wouldn't be very clever if Ethan was here when she comes round.'

'No problem. Just give me the directions.' I was quite happy to go for a drive as it was a beautiful early summer afternoon.

'Use the Range Rover if you like.'

'I don't know, Mike. I know it will be more comfortable for you, but I've never driven an automatic – or anything that big.'

'I wasn't thinking of my comfort – more of your convenience. You'll be fine, Rose. It's like driving a dodgem – one foot for the accelerator and brake, and no clutch. Just take it slowly until you're used to the size. It's a doddle.''What about insurance?'

'Rose, it's insured for any driver – and you're not going to have an accident. If you do happen to do the woman thing and put a dent or two in it…'

I bit immediately. 'I'll have you know I'm a very good driver – and I've never put so much as a scratch on any car I've driven.'

Mike laughed. 'OK, OK, I was just winding you up! I've already sampled your driving. I wouldn't be offering it to you if I thought you couldn't handle it.'

I came to the conclusion that after today's eye-opening pantomime, anything would be a doddle.

When I reached Bianca's home, a smart detached house in Woodford Green, Mike was watching from the front window. He came quickly to the door and said she was, thankfully, snoring her head off on the sofa.

I was already in love with the big 4x4 and Mike was happy to let me drive it back to Great Ashley. It was an interesting journey. He filled in the gaps in Ethan and Bianca's stormy relationship. It wasn't quite the same version he had in his autobiography.

Apparently, though they were crazy for each other they were a lethal combination. While it was true Ethan introduced Bianca to booze, she had encouraged him to try the hard drugs that once almost killed him. Luckily for him, the close call opened his eyes - eventually - and after three incarcerations in rehabilitation clinics, he'd managed to remain drug free apart from the occasional spliff, for which Mike was on constant alert.

Bianca had also succeeded in beating her drug habit, but seemed to spend most of her life in an alcoholic haze, by which time the marriage had broken down.

'Why doesn't Ethan threaten to use it as proof she's an unfit mother?' I asked. Not that I wish to deprive any mother of her child, but hoped the warning might bring her to her senses. And I think Allie deserves a better deal.

'A whole mix of reasons. He doesn't want Allie to suffer: the press would have a ball if it came out that Bianca's an alcoholic, even though it's often been hinted at. Also, his lifestyle isn't conducive to raising a child, let alone an impressionable teenager. Can you imagine how bad Allie would be if she used his conduct as a moral guide?'

I felt my hackles rising again.

'Then he ought to do something to change it. Let's be honest, Mike, Ethan is a bit old for acting like a horny teenager. He's a father. His children deserve better than that. Bianca is sick and should have treatment, and Ethan should take responsibility for Allegra. No wonder she's such a little mare – can't they see how she's hurting?'

Forgetting I was driving an automatic I tried to change gear and Mike laid a hand on my arm.

'Take it easy, Rose.'

'Sorry. Bad for the gearbox.'

'Forget the gearbox. I meant don't stress out. I agree with you. Absolutely. And I have to say that after today's little show, I think Bianca's hit the bottom of the barrel. I intend having some serious dialogue with Ethan – before it's too late.'

I was slightly mollified. When I think of people like Heidi who's struggled for years to bring up her family and always been there for them despite having to work full-time and cope with a loser of a husband, it makes me so angry to hear the way these pampered individuals carry on.

'I'm glad to hear that. If he'll listen to anyone, it's you.'

When we returned to Lime Cottage so I could pick up my car, Ethan was flat out on the sofa, an empty brandy bottle beside him. Mike shook his head, and his expression was not sympathetic. 'Stupid bozo.'

I collected my things and he walked to the door with me, glowering.

'We're just on the verge of turning his finances round…the occasional toke is bad enough, but if he starts hitting the bottle again he can kiss his backside – and me - goodbye.'

'Not in that particular order, I hope.' I intended the quip to bring a smile to his angry features, and it did.

'Sorry Rose. You've been brilliant today. As usual. Don't worry, I'm going to have strong words with him. In fact I intend spelling it out plain and simple about his behaviour and his parental responsibilities. Mark my words, things are going to change around here.'

As I drove home I reflected on the vagaries of life at Lime

Cottage and once again I was reminded of how much I would miss not working there. I now had only three weeks of my contract to run though it could be extended by a week or so as the manuscript was slightly behind schedule, but after that Ethan was due on tour and my services would no longer be required. I felt quite low.

Then I started thinking about the necessity of getting another job, fast, and of having to move house; and of the coming Saturday when Simon is getting married, with the twins in attendance. I felt as though I didn't belong anywhere. Gina would be away, and Heidi was working, and Maddy was recuperating from her jilting in Mauritius, so that left me and my faithful Geoffrey, home alone. I felt very low.

When I got home, I had a phone call. It was Mike.

'Rose, with all the carry on today I completely forgot – Ethan wanted me to ask if you'd like to come to the gig on Saturday?'

Is the Pope Catholic? 'This Saturday?' I asked coolly. 'Is that the one at the Regency Club in Norwich?' As if I didn't know.

'That's the one. We're staying there overnight and normally eat after the show. We'll make a weekend of it - do something on Sunday, perhaps.'

Thank you, god. 'That sounds nice. Yes, I'd love to.'

'Great. I'll give you the details tomorrow.'

Leah rang to assure me she'd never accept Angelica as part of her family, and predicted she would turn up at the Register Office looking like a meringue. It was only because she'd promised her father (or spent the bribe) she was going at all.

Jamie rang to ensure I was OK and wouldn't be sitting at home alone. Thanks to Ethan, I was able to put his mind at rest on that score. Actually I'm so looking forward to tomorrow night I doubt I'll give the wedding a thought.

Of course, when the ceremony was due to take place at 11.30am, despite my uplifted spirits and busy schedule (hair wash, face-pack, pedicure etc), my mind found time to stray, and instantly regressed to the day more than 22 years previously when I was marrying Simon.

As I have done so many times before, I lurched through the full spectrum of emotions from sad to angry, resentful, nostalgic...but this time ultimately accepted Simon and I were no longer a couple, would never be anything other than joint parents. There was now another Mrs Simon Grant.

Perhaps I should revert to my maiden name? I always thought Keeling had a much classier ring to it.

The Regency Club was very smart, a top cabaret venue. Ethan's show was sold out and I felt a bit special being introduced as his Personal Assistant and being allowed to watch the lighting being set up, and the sound checks, and having coffee and doughnuts with the band.

I'd never met any of them of course, but they were in fact the musicians featured on Ethan's new album, and shortly would be touring with him to promote it. He and Mike, however, knew them of old, and they reminisced and joked about previous gigs and tours. It seems all the rumours pertaining to the decadence of the rock scene are unexaggerated and the phrase "No turn unstoned" was more than a spoonerism. Anyhow, my minimal education in these matters was greatly enhanced.

Later a trio of girl singers arrived, and it was apparent Ethan was very familiar with them, particularly a pert little brunette whom he couldn't seem to keep his hands off. I wondered what would happen if Aveline was expected. She'd certainly been at the last gig (as Allie had surmised).

We were staying at the Royal Court Hotel, and I'd been given a very nice room that overlooked the city's beautiful cathedral. As I luxuriated in my fine surroundings I couldn't help but dwell on my change in circumstances. Whoever would have believed I'd be here, at the request of my boss, who just happened to be the idol of my adolescent years?

Later as I watched Ethan performing, I recalled exactly why

I'd been so smitten by him. As soon as he stepped on stage he came alive, emanating a charisma that seemed to flow over his audience, at least, so it seemed to me, and judging by the frenzied welcome he received and the screams when he stood in his tight leather trousers and moved his hips (and this was before he'd sung a note), I was not alone in my perception.

He rocked, he crooned, he joked, he pulled an excited young woman onto the stage and had her melting in his arms as he sang to her alone. He was fantastic: a star most definitely on the rise again. Basking in the afterglow, for the next few hours I forgot about him being a dysfunctional parent and dissolute person, and I fantasized about him just as I had when I was fifteen.

I was still spellbound when much later, having escaped the clutches of some over-zealous fans intent on besieging the hotel, we dined and then continued drinking in the bar, which they'd closed to the public. Aveline had not made an appearance, and Mike told me the relationship had run its course, so I wasn't surprised when the dark-haired singer announced she was going to bed and gave Ethan a meaningful look. He, however, didn't follow her, but slung his arm round me: we were all pretty wasted by this time.

'Women!' he slurred. 'Who needs 'em? I'm better off with a good secretary than a good shag, eh Rosie? Mind you – the two could go together. You're not like the others Rosie…you're sort of clean and…pure…'

I have to say my feelings at that moment were anything but…

'…and…motherly…'

Passion plummeted.

'You're lovely Rosie. I wish I knew who my mother was. I'll find her y'know…'

As Ethan rambled on, I caught Mike eyeing us, shaking his head with a rueful grin. He got up and came over.

'Come on Ethan, you don't pay Rose enough to sit up half the night listening to your burbling.'

Docilely Ethan allowed Mike to lead him towards the lift, and he lurched amicably between us.

'Don't want to screw up this time. Mike talks a lot of crap, Rosie, but it's not all crap,' he squinted up at me drunkenly. 'You're lovely, you know...'

I left Mike to sort out the boss and went to my room, my head so full of the evening that I never even thought about Simon's wedding. That has to be progress.

The next morning I was lying in bed still mildly amazed at being part of this talented crowd when the phone rang.

'Good morning, Rosie!' It was Ethan, sounding much chirpier than he deserved. 'I thought we might go to Great Yarmouth for the day – have a bit of good old English seaside fun. You know, go on the roller coaster, suck a bit of rock – I said *rock,* Rosie...'

'Ethan! Behave!'

'OK, OK. Are you game?'

'For the rock-sucking, yes... '

'Oooh Rosie, you are awful!'

'I was about to say I'm not too sure about the roller coaster.'

'Don't you worry, honey, Uncle Ethan will look after you.'

Last night I was his mother, this morning he's my uncle – no wonder his kids are confused. 'That sounds great. I'll be down in 30 minutes.'

'Fifteen.'

'Good god, Ethan, I'm still in bed. Give a girl a chance!'

'Still in bed, huh? Mmm, perhaps I could come over...'

'See you in 20 minutes, Ethan. In the lobby.' I replaced the receiver before my mind even went there: though he was an idol with feet of Play-Doh, my senses were still buzzing from last night's reawakening, and I wasn't sufficiently acclimatised to be totally immune.

It was lunchtime before we made it to Yarmouth, and it was much as I remembered it. Simon and I had taken the twins there a couple of times on holiday, staying at one of the large static caravan parks at the end of North Beach. As we drove along the seafront looking for somewhere to park I thought fleetingly of Jamie and Leah staring in rapt amazement at a

Punch and Judy Show: many years later Jamie said he thought it was 3D television!

'Penny for your thoughts,' Mike said. I was sitting next to him as he drove, and Ethan was sitting in the back seat between the brunette and one of her partners. Obviously he'd forgotten his previous night's denunciation of womankind.

Anyhow, it was a beautiful day and the carefree company and fun location were just the diversion I needed. I even went on the roller coaster and despite good intentions, ended up clinging to Ethan and screaming with the best of them. It was very liberating.

We had fish and chips for lunch, then strolled along one of the piers eating ice cream, and Ethan presented me with a huge stick of suggestively-shaped rock. It was too big to go in my bag and caused me no end of embarrassment as I had to carry it everywhere we went.

Then we spotted a clairvoyant's kiosk and I knew I had to go in: I'm a sucker for "astrological mumbo-jumbo" as Simon calls it. As the thought came, I realised, joyfully, that it no longer mattered what Simon thought, or said: I could do as I pleased without feeling guilty, or stupid, or intimidated. This was the freedom I'd been given, and it was heady stuff.

The clairvoyant was a young man, and he immediately latched on to the fact I am divorced. A cynic would have said he saw the mark where my wedding ring had worn a telltale track. However, he went on to tell me I'd have a change of career (very likely), a change of house (undoubtedly – though not the mansion he foresaw), a new husband (never), and there would be at least one more baby (when Hell freezes over).

Buoyed by the thoughts of this fantasy future, I fairly bounced through the town, happy to be part of this sparkling group – which included a couple of very large minders. Ethan was trying to keep a low profile by wearing a baseball cap and large dark glasses, but even so we were frequently pointed at when people recognised him - though he claimed it was my stick of rock drawing their attention.

Then WHAM!

Outside a newsagent's a billboard advertising a popular Sunday rag announced *"Aveline: Why I dumped Ethan Hammer"*.

Ethan had turned pale, and Mike grabbed a paper from the rack and flipped quickly to an inside page. Under the advertised headline, it quoted *"He loved drink and drugs more than me, says heartbroken glamour model"*.

'That lying slapper!' Ethan's words were hardly a curse. He sounded resigned.

Mike's face was serious. 'Come on, let's get back. I need to make some phone calls.'

On the drive to Great Ashley, there was silence until after we'd dropped off the girls at Ipswich station.

'I knew she was trouble,' Ethan said dully.

'Did you do drugs in her company?' Mike's tone was sharp.

'No. Well, maybe a spliff – nothing more. And that bitch could drink me under the table.'

'We're going to have to move fast to control the damage – though most is already done. It's not going to do the album, or the tour much good. Perhaps we should extend it, and use a nice clean youth band as support.'

'Perhaps if you gave a percentage of your profits to an anti-drug campaign...' my voice trailed off as they both turned to look at me with expressions of shock.

'Sorry. It's none of my business.'

Neither responded. Then Mike looked at me thoughtfully through the mirror. 'That's not such a shabby idea, Rose.'

Back at Lime Cottage, things moved fast. The phone lines were red hot with calls to and from lawyers, publicity agents, the media, and the occasional concerned venue manager. Mike handled it all with cool assurance, while Ethan paced up and down wearing a hangdog expression. I made myself useful answering calls when Mike was on the other line, sent emails and faxes, and brewed numerous cups of tea.

After a couple of hours the pace slowed and we realised we hadn't eaten. As it was late, Mike suggested I stayed and Ethan's gloom lessened as he busied himself creating a curry.

'I think we've done all the damage limitation we can,' Mike summarised as we ate. (Ethan is a very good cook.) 'That was a great idea of yours, Rose. I've got the publicity machine working on Ethan's generous cut to the "Just Say No" scheme, and the logo is being included in all the tour and album material, with bumf available at every venue. No mean task as it's due out next week. Also there'll be a full denial in tomorrow's dailies. So I'm warning you Ethan – not even one single spliff. Jeez! Have you got any gear in the house?'

Ethan looked as if he was about to deny it, but Mike's expression was menacing.

'Couple of ounces. In my bedroom.'

'Go and get it and I'll flush it. I'm serious, Ethan. All of it. It's a wonder the cops aren't here already.'

Ethan put down his fork and left the room.

Mike shook his head as he stared after him but made no comment.

I contemplated yet another bizarre experience and came to the conclusion the word *mundane* can be erased from my vocabulary.

JUNE

Leah and Jamie both rang to report on The Wedding, and amazingly I barely felt a twinge of anything; they could have been talking about a stranger. But their accounts were a graphic illustration of the chasm separating the sexes.

According to Jamie the bride "looked really pretty in a tight white dress that had a low-cut top and a skirt that was quite short at the front and long at the back, and very sparkly high heels".

According to Leah, the bride "looked like a hooker with her boobs hanging out, a pussy-pelmet and tart's trotters".

She said her father now wore a wedding band so wide his finger looked as if it were in a splint, and a thick gold neck-chain – a wedding gift from his new wife. And to cap it all he'd had an ear pierced. What next? Tattoos? A ponytail?

Leah said she left immediately after the meal as it was totally nauseating to see him all over the Bimbo like a rash. And the new in-laws were just as awful, especially the acne-ridden, no-brain cousin they tried to pair her off with. In fact my daughter is of the opinion that Simon is on the verge of a mental breakdown as no middle-aged man in his right mind could behave in such a puerile manner. She has a lot to learn, bless her. But it will be a very long time, if ever, before the rift with her father is healed. Which I find infinitely sadder than the demise of my marriage.

I slept well in the comfortable room allotted me at Lime Cottage: too well, as it was 8.30am before I woke to the sound of raised voices. I hurriedly got out of bed and went to the window that overlooked the front garden. There was no car in the driveway, but the front gates were open and swinging, and I thought I could see a vehicle parked beyond the laurel hedge.

Dressing in record time, I went downstairs and stopped dead as I came eyeball to eyeball with a very aggressive looking Bianca. Ethan, standing with his arm around Allegra's shoulders, and Mike, all stared up at me from the hallway.

Bianca snorted 'I knew it! I knew you'd got your boots under his bed, you brainless cow! Well make the most of it, sweetie, because as soon as he's used you, he'll chuck you out! You've no more nous than mega-tits Aveline.' She swung towards Ethan. 'And you, you tosser, if you can support another woman, you can certainly look after your daughter - how convenient she's so...*mumsy*...'

Without waiting to gauge the effectiveness of her onslaught, she slammed the door and was gone.

What a way to start the day.

Ethan lifted his shoulders and Allie shrugged off his arm as he turned to guide her into the living room.

'Sorry about that, Rosie. Come on Allie, don't start sulking – I've got enough on my plate without that.'

Allie's customary scowl deepened. 'She's right. You *are* a tosser. You don't want me any more than she does.'

Poor, poor kid. Obviously Bianca had carried out her threat, and Allie was now Ethan's unwelcome burden.

'Of course he wants you, Allie,' Mike said. 'It's just a bit of a shock, and I don't have to tell you about the power of the press and the trouble they can cause.'

He spoke as if to an equal, and the girl's green eyes, so like her father's, widened as she regarded him.

'Have you eaten, Allie?' I asked. 'I'm about to make some coffee and toast.'

Her gaze narrowed again as it swept over me.

'I'd love some, Rose.' Mike said. 'Come on, Allie.'

We trooped through to the kitchen. Ethan was already sitting at the table and the kettle was coming up to the boil. He half-smiled at his daughter and looked hopefully towards Mike as if he'd miraculously found the solution to the situation.

After an uncomfortable silence, he said 'Looks like it's good we got the house. At least we've got plenty of room. Did your mum say anything about how long you're staying?'

Tact was not Ethan's forte.

'Don't be so bloody dense,' Allie snapped. 'She said *permanently* – that means you're stuck with me for good.'

'She can't do that! Can she Mike?'

'I think Allie's old enough to make up her own mind who she wants to live with, aren't you?' Mike turned to the girl.

'S'ppose so. Can you get me my own place?'

Ethan's expression lifted, until Mike cut in 'Not until you're 16, minimum. Until then, you have to live with a parent, or a responsible adult.'

'That let's the pair of them out then.'

She was right about that.

I found two pairs of male eyes resting on me expectantly.

'Perhaps…you could stay here while you decide…?' I said lamely.

'That's great,' said Ethan. 'Except that I'm out a lot. And I'm on tour in a few weeks. What's going to happen to her then?'

'Look. Stay here for now, Allie, we don't have to rush into anything, and every problem has a solution, so we'll work something out if you decide you want to live with your dad permanently,' Mike's tone was decisive. He turned to Ethan and glared meaningfully. 'I'm sure that's what your dad means.'

'Course it is, sweetheart,' Ethan reached across the table and took Allie's hand. 'I've always wanted you to live with me. I shouldn't have let you stay with that demented dame.'

She snatched her hand away. He couldn't be diplomatic if his life depended on it.

Ethan has a housekeeper, Betty Morgan, who comes in every weekday morning and does the washing and ironing as well as the cleaning, but that was the least of Ethan's worries as far as his daughter was concerned.

Two days later the matter came to a head. At fourteen Allie was too young to stay on her own overnight, and she needed to go to school. The solicitor who handled Ethan's domestic affairs was of the opinion that Bianca was an unfit mother, and if it ever came to court, she could lose custody. But although Ethan seemed to be the better bet as a parent (disregarding last week's tabloid scandal), his lifestyle was hardly propitious to having residential custody of a teenager.

The solicitor suggested that if Allie chose to live with her father, if only while her mother was receiving treatment for her alcoholism (for which it appears she's volunteered), a guardian must be appointed to care for her while he was away. Perhaps boarding school was the answer.

Whilst I could see the wisdom in this, both from a practical and inter-personal viewpoint, it was hardly likely to mend any bridges between father and daughter, or reduce the resentment causing Allie's anti-social behaviour.

However, it was not my decision, nor my business. So I was shocked when I arrived the following morning to be ambushed by Mike and Ethan who'd ganged up to ask me if I would consider becoming Allegra's temporary guardian.

'You could live here while I'm away, Rosie,' Ethan said. 'We would extend your contract.'

'And give you a hefty pay rise,' Mike put in. 'Betty will still do the housework, and some cooking. All you'd have to do is take Allie to school and collect her.'

And act as taxi service, phone monitor, homework police, and the voice of reason to someone who doesn't want to listen and knows it all anyway. The Teenage Experience was something I had no wish to repeat. But the salary, not having to worry about another job in the immediate future, and having somewhere to live if my house is sold made it an attractive proposition. Nevertheless...

'This is totally unexpected. Something I hadn't even considered, so I hope you don't mind if I take some time to think it over?'

'That's fair enough,' Mike agreed quickly, and then in a quieter tone. 'I know she's not the easiest kid in the world, Rose, but she's basically all right. You'll be good for her. She needs someone with their feet firmly on the ground, someone...'

'Mumsy,' I finished with only a tinge of vinegar.

'I was going to say kind, patient and understanding. Not that there's anything wrong with being maternal.'

'Yeah, it beats self-centred alcoholic any day,' said Ethan acridly. 'And you may be maternal, Rosie, but in my book you're definitely a MILF.'

'Ethan!' Mike frowned and glanced at me as if to gauge my reaction. Perhaps he thought I wouldn't understand the acronym, but that's one of the joys of having had teenagers – I asked Leah: it means a Mother who Is Luscious and Fanciable. That's what she told me anyway, and I pretended to believe her.

And flattery, as they say, will get you anywhere. As will a pay rise and a roof over my head.

Before I committed myself to what could be months of purgatory, I decided to consult The Coven – as Simon once derogatorily referred to my female friends (according to the Oxford Dictionary one of the meanings of "witch" is "fascinating woman" so we decided to keep the name). Anyhow, just as I was about to call Gina, the phone rang.

It was the girl herself. 'Rosie! Where have you been? I've been trying to get you since the weekend. Can I come round? I've loads to tell you.'

'Sure. That would be great,' I said, and before I could think the line went dead. I knew that tone. What was the betting her engagement to Lloyd was back on? Ah well, one thing was for sure – I wasn't going to get much packing done tonight.

I tried Maddy's mobile. As far as I knew she was still in Mauritius and I was just about to give up when she answered, somewhat agitated.

'Yes?'

'Maddy – it's me, Rose.'

'Hi darling – sorry you've caught me with my pants down…'she giggled, then gasped.

Obviously she wasn't exaggerating. 'I won't keep you then. It's just that…' I went on, briefly, to explain about the situation with Ethan. I had the distinct feeling she wasn't really concentrating on my dilemma.

'Darling, if the money's good – and up front, go for it. You can handle a stroppy kid – you managed fine with Leah, after all. Just make sure that being Ethan's bed-mate isn't part of the deal…Ooh Jean-Claude!'

'Maddy, I know how to say no!'

'I wish I did,' she said breathlessly. 'Must go…Ooh yes, yes…'

I felt like a voyeur.

I had to ring Heidi's mobile as she now worked most evenings. Apparently the wealthy invalid in Dedham was not only doubly incontinent, but a demanding, bad tempered insomniac. Heidi had only survived for two weeks and was afraid she'd made a major mistake in leaving the care home. But now she was much happier, and spent her nights with a nice old widower in Frinton who was suffering from crippling arthritis yet managed to stay cheerful and tried hard not to disturb her sleep.

'I tell you, he's so sweet and considerate – if he was a few years younger I'd propose to him! By the way, have you spoken to Gina yet? No? I'm not allowed to tell, but you'll never guess her news!'

Bless. Is there something different about a re-engagement?

When I'd explained about Ethan and Allie, Heidi was all sympathy.

'Oh you've got to do it, Rosie. That poor girl. Imagine having an alcoholic for a mother. Still, she has Ethan Hammer for a father…' Her voice turned dreamy: in her mind his teen-idol image was unsullied, so I was hardly going to get an unbiased opinion.

The doorbell rang, so I said goodbye and greeted a starry-eyed Gina.

She hugged me and then shoved her left hand under my nose, fluttering it so the large jewel on her third finger glittered in the hall light. I held it still to admire the diamond claw, trying to remember if it was the same one she'd had the first time round – and then I saw the wedding ring.

I looked up at her and she smiled and nodded and hugged me again.

'We got married,' she said. 'You are looking at Mrs Lloyd Parkinson!'

Heidi was right: I never would have guessed.

'It wasn't commitment he was afraid of, he just didn't want a big wedding, so he booked the hotel and got a special licence. Oh Rosie, it was so romantic – I just wish you could have been there – but we're going to have a party for all our friends and relatives next month, then a honeymoon in the Caribbean.'

It was an hour and a bottle of wine later when we got round to discussing the Ethan-Allie situation.

'It's a challenge, Rosie. But you're up to it – and it will certainly solve your more immediate problems, won't it? I mean the money, the job. And even a home if yours gets sold.'

When Gina had left to return to her husband I rang Lime Cottage to confirm I was willing to be responsible for Allie for the three months until Ethan's tour ended. Mike said that was more than fair, and he was sure I wouldn't regret it. I'm not.

This morning I accompanied Ethan to his bank to open an account in my name for household and Allie's expenses into which he paid the first monthly allowance. It was very generous, as is my pay rise. In fact I can now seriously consider taking the house off the market.

On that front I've had a couple who came back twice then decided on something else, more unhelpful emails, and a further message from the woman whose husband is transferring to the area. She made an appointment for them to view on Sunday afternoon, and though I'm now in two minds whether or not I want to sell, I suppose that decision is immaterial until I actually receive an offer.

In the meantime I am installed in a spacious suite at Lime Cottage. The bedroom has a sofa, a small writing desk and a flat-screen TV as well as a luxurious bathroom, so living here is certainly no hardship. My workload, however, has increased. I actually think it will be simpler when Ethan starts his tour, though having sole responsibility for his daughter is never going to be a walk in the park.

Allie has been enrolled at St Hilda's Convent and starts on Monday. I didn't realise Ethan was Catholic, though he admitted the last time he went to church voluntarily (almost) was when Allie was baptised.

Knowing the amount of time and effort teenage girls put into seeking the company of teenage boys, if only to humiliate them, I can't help doubting the wisdom of the single sex school. That there are fewer distractions on the doorstep does not counteract raging hormones, supreme curiosity, and the imaginative powers of a Hollywood scriptwriter. The fact that where there's a will, there's a way, just means pupils spend more time hatching devious strategies to put their will into practise. Call me cynical, but a convent is not the environment I'd have chosen for a rebellious 14-year-old.

Before Allie starts at the school I have the joys of another shopping trip to look forward to, this time for school uniform. On Sunday Ethan is off to join Mike in London for the album launch, then they have promotional appearances and gigs, and the following week they'll be away on tour. Things have happened so fast I don't know where I am half the time, and it doesn't help that everything I need is 13 miles down the road in my wardrobe or at the back of my airing cupboard. Or so it seems.

Allie has informed me she's become a vegetarian, which means I've had to dig out my veggie cookbook. (Leah was also one at that age - until she decided she couldn't live without Kentucky Fried Chicken.) Not that I've had to do much cooking, thank goodness, as Betty has been serving gargantuan platefuls before she leaves at six – which is the latest she's agreed to stay as her Horace has to be fed. At first we thought Horace was her son, but he's her cat, so I understand perfectly.

Geoffrey, of course, is my biggest problem. Linda's always fed him while I am away, but three months would not only be pushing the bounds of friendship, it wouldn't be fair on the cat. And despite his hair-shedding and that he snores like an asthmatic hog, I miss him sleeping on my bed. However, as any cat person knows, you don't own the cat, the cat owns you – and cats will only go where they want, when they want.

Geoffrey loves his own home; nevertheless, as it's likely to be sold from under him it was agreed he'd come to Lime Cottage. I think Ethan would let me keep a pet buffalo in the bedroom as long as I took charge of Allie, which may be only slightly less harrowing. Anyhow, the vet advised he'd be fine as long as he was confined indoors for a couple of weeks, when he'd be ready to explore his new territory, so I planned to put him in his travel basket for the short journey. (Geoffrey, that is - though I wouldn't reject the vet).

This was the theory. In fact it would have worked splendidly if he hadn't legged it the moment I brought his basket in from the garage. I suppose it was a bit thoughtless of me not to recall that last time he'd entered it he'd been traumatised by a massive syringeful of antibiotics, an even bigger one to take a blood sample, and a thermometer like a number four knitting needle stuck up his bum.

I searched high and low, calling his name and rattling a container full of crispy bacon and cubes of best cheddar, but even the scent of his favourite treats didn't tempt him from his hiding place and eventually, as I'd promised to return to Lime Cottage before Betty left, I had to go without him. I just know he was watching me – and probably gleeful at having had his revenge for that last visit to the vet. Cats are like that.

At the end of the uniform shopping torture I was still sane but decidedly ragged. St Hilda's has a strict code of uniform which must be purchased from a pricy outfitter and includes a list as long as your arm. They even "suggest" the style of underwear the girls should wear, and I have to admit to commiserating with Allie when knickers like barrage balloons were produced for inspection.

'No way!' she said, her lip curling. 'If you buy them, I won't wear any.'

I wouldn't put it past her, but decided to compromise anyway.

She also curled her lip at the length of the skirt, the sack-like blouses, the geriatric shoes, and the summer dresses designed for four-year-old African refugees.

When we eventually left the shop I felt as if I'd done ten rounds in the ring with King Kong (and so will Ethan when he sees the dent in the new bank account). Then we had to get a new bag, notebooks, pens and all the other paraphernalia. I let Allie wander round WH Smith's with a basket and tried to unwind among the Humorous Cards.

On the way home she suggested McDonald's and I pointed out it was hardly the place for a vegetarian. For once she was unable to come up with a suitably scathing riposte.

'You could have a salad, I suppose.'

'I hate salad.'

'Then I'll make you a nice plate of roast vegetables when we get home.'

'I hate…vegetables…'

I cast a sidelong glance at her and raised my eyebrows. She had the grace to look discomfited.

McDonald's golden arches loomed ahead.

'I want a Big Mac,' she said sounding like a normal child. 'Please.'

I slowed and headed for the car park. It looks like the veggie-phase is over for the time being.

Before we returned to Lime Cottage we made a detour to the house in the hope Geoffrey had recovered from his strop and could be enticed into his basket. And there he was, waiting nonchalantly on the windowsill.

His ears pricked up as the car rolled into the driveway, but as soon as I walked into the sitting room he disdainfully turned his back, letting me know in no uncertain terms I was beneath his contempt. I was just thinking of a foolproof way to lure him to me when Allie squatted down, called him, and contrary as ever, he trotted eagerly towards her, tail erect.

'Quick, let me have him and I'll get him in his basket.'

Two pairs of eyes glared at me. 'It's OK, I'll hold him.'

Geoffrey snuggled his head under her arm: he's always had the notion that if he can't see you, you can't see him.

'I don't think that's a very good idea Allie. He doesn't like going in the car.'

'I'll keep hold of him. He'll be fine.'

I couldn't face another altercation.

For the first two minutes of the journey my feline friend fooled me into thinking that perhaps, after all, he'd overcome his dislike of motorised travel. But just as we hit the by-pass he dug his claws into Allie. She loosened her grip, allowing him to shoot over her shoulder and throw himself dramatically against the back window.

He then proceeded to race up and down the parcel shelf until his frenzied efforts caused it to tilt, thus tipping him into the boot-space. The ensuing yowls and frantic scrabbling would have done a wild-cat justice, and I knew I had to stop before he either did himself a mischief, shredded Allie's new school clothes, or scored an escape hole in the vehicle's shell - which sounded like a distinct possibility.

I pulled onto the hard shoulder.

'Don't open the door!' I screamed as I saw Allie's hand on the handle. 'We've got to manage this from inside – if he gets half a chance he'll be away – and I don't fancy his chances against...that...' an articulated lorry sped by, rocking my small car and almost sucking us up in its wake.

Without another word, Allie unbuckled herself and climbed over, kneeling on the back seat and trying to ease the parcel shelf back into position. Meanwhile Geoffrey's furore had dissolved into pitiful mews. And the parcel shelf was jammed.

I also climbed into the back, and between us we were able to dislodge it. But we weren't quick enough, and Geoffrey, no longer pathetic, streaked past us both and burrowed under the driving seat. Just as I was about to make the ungainly manoeuvre to return to the front, another sound caught my attention – along with a flashing blue light.

A burly, grim-faced policeman strode towards the car,

walked round it, peered in and stopped by the front passenger door, indicating we should wind down the window. I leaned forward to comply and caught my sleeve on the handbrake. As I struggled to extricate myself it disengaged, only for a split second, but long enough to catch the policeman's foot – as I realised when he pulled back and hopped about clutching at it.

With Allie and I both still ensconced in the back – the car having only two doors – Geoffrey saw his chance and leapt towards the open window just as the policeman hobbled towards it again. I don't know who was the more surprised as the cat landed directly on the policeman's chest, front claws just nicking his now florid neck which, as I watched in horror, started to ooze blood onto his snowy white collar.

It was like a Tom and Jerry cartoon.

Allie, with great presence of mind, folded down the front seat, opened the door, and extricated Geoffrey from the hapless policeman's jacket. I grabbed him, shoved him unceremoniously into his basket, and turned to face the wrath of the law.

For a moment he didn't speak, and I tentatively handed him a tissue to staunch the bright red trickle under his chin.

'Can I see your driving licence, madam?'

I didn't have it on me, and he handed me a ticket telling me to produce my documents at the police station within five days.

'I stopped to see what the problem was,' he said heavily. 'But obviously it was the cat. It's an offence and extremely dangerous to have a wild animal loose in the car, madam. Next time, make sure you cage him.'

'Yes, Officer. I'm very sorry. It won't happen again. He's a bit traumatised, you see.'

'I know how he feels, madam,' the policeman said without a glimmer of humour. 'And I'd get that handbrake seen to as well.'

With that he limped back to his vehicle, and proceeded to follow us to the Great Ashley turning. When he'd disappeared

Allie started sniggering, and soon we were in convulsions. Geoffrey joined in with a loud wail. I'm seriously considering that cage. And it's lucky for him he's already been castrated.

My appointment with the house-viewers went very well: they loved it and I'm almost certain they're going to make me an offer. I'm still not sure how I'll feel if they do, though when I discussed it with Mike, he pointed out that the level of wage I'm currently receiving cannot be guaranteed, so do I really want to struggle with a mortgage for the next ten years?

The couple wants to come round again with their children, but as they're based in Yorkshire, it will have to be next weekend. I promised not to sell it to anyone else without giving them first option – though I think there's little chance of another offer unless it's from one of those stiffy-pill pushers.

With the added pressure of Allie's unscheduled arrival at Lime Cottage, Ethan suddenly realised it was Fen's birthday. Not only was he supposed to be taking his son out, he hadn't even remembered to buy a present, though I know Mike reminded him before he left.

Panicking and blaming everyone, he directed me to go to the village store for a card and gift. The choice was limited, and I returned with a couple of books, some felt-tips and a tipper lorry.

'For god's sake! Is that the best you could do?' My boss wasn't happy.

'It's a village store, Ethan, not Toys R Us.'

He flashed me a black look then half smiled. 'I suppose I could take him there after the movies. Anyway, you wrap them while I go and get him – I'm late already and I'll be in for a mouthful of abuse from Marnie as it is.'

I didn't blame her: keeping a seven-year-old waiting, especially on his birthday, is guaranteed to cause strife.

I wrapped three parcels and got down to some work. It was more than an hour's drive to Ethan's ex-home, so I wasn't expecting him back for a while. I scanned the diary and was reminded he's due in court the day after tomorrow, to ask for increased access to Fen.

Allie had gone riding at a farm on the outskirts of the village. Word had got out that Ethan was living in Lime Cottage and the farmer's wife, who claimed to be an avid devotee, had called by to offer him a ride.

In Ethan's experience, there was only one sort of ride worth talking about, and as he was patently not into horses or hale and hearty middle-aged women, he'd already turned down her offer when Mike hastily explained Ethan had an equine allergy, but that his daughter, Allegra, would be happy to take up her kind offer. Obviously disappointed yet happy to be able to retain some contact with her celebrity neighbour, Arabella Smythe left an open invitation to her stables.

She was to give Allie a lift home at midday, and Ethan was hoping his daughter would join him and Fen for lunch and the cinema - plus Toys R Us - though she hadn't yet been informed of her father's strategy for her to get to know her half-brother. Sadly, with all the animosity between husband and ex-wives, the two children were virtually strangers.

My peace was shattered exactly two hours later when the Porsche screeched to a halt, scattering gravel and knocking over a large earthenware pot as the rear end slewed. I was contemplating the wisdom of this display with a child in the car when I saw him wrench himself from the driver's seat and stride to the front door. There was no sign of Fen.

The door bounced off the ancient wall, which shuddered as it slammed.

'Frigging bitch!' He said as he saw me. 'I got there on time and she wasn't there. She left a note saying she was taking Fen somewhere special for his birthday – and I'd be seeing a lot less of him, not more, if I don't increase her alimony. Frigging bitch!'

His anger was tangible, but so was his pain: there's no doubt he genuinely cares for his children, in his way.

'Did you keep the note?'

'What? No of course I frigging didn't; I tore it to shreds and stuffed it through her letterbox. I should have set fire to it.'

'Arson wouldn't help your case,' I pointed out. 'But that note might have: it's blackmail and would have shown her for the gold-digger she is.'

'Oh. Bollocks. What am I going to do, Rosie?'

'Let's have a coffee and think about it. Allie's due back shortly and you were going to ask her to go with you and Fen so why don't you take the opportunity to have some time on your own with her? After all, you won't be around much when you start your tour.'

Thankfully Ethan calmed down a tad and agreed. 'Yeah. Nice idea, Rosie.'

When Mrs Smythe ("do call me Bella – all my closest friends do") dropped Allie, she wondered how Ethan would feel about opening the Village Fete. Without pausing to ask her the date, Ethan was told her he'd be away on tour.

Allie readily agreed to spend the rest of the day with her father especially when she was told she could choose where to go, and her mood which, understandably had been downcast and very dispirited, seemed to alter perceptibly. Though she was careful not to appear too eager, after her nonchalant shrug of acceptance I saw the smile as she turned to run upstairs to change. If only her parents realised how little it took to make her happy.

It was evening before Ethan and his daughter returned, and the atmosphere between them was noticeably relaxed. So the day was not a total disaster. I just hoped that little Fen enjoyed the birthday he should have spent with his father and half-sister.

As Mike was delayed in York, he asked if I would make sure Ethan got to his solicitor's office in readiness for his application to be heard, so I offered to accompany him.

When we arrived it was to be told the case had been postponed and Marnie had successfully had his access to Fen suspended in view of his immoral conduct and irresponsible behaviour (i.e. having the fictional version of his affair with

Aveline splashed over the tabloids) which was deemed not to be compatible with his responsibility as a father. Or words to that effect.

I thought Ethan was going to drag the lawyer over his desk.

'She doesn't give a flying fuck about my conduct – she knows about the new album and the tour and just wants more cash. It's blackmail – she can't stop me seeing my boy…'

'I'm afraid a judge says she can, Mr Hammer. We'll have to see what we can do.'

There would be no instant solution and Ethan was silent and morose as we drove home where he stomped into the sitting room and slammed the door. Just like his daughter. Talk about the apple not falling far from the tree!

Betty had left a casserole in the oven and I was overcome by a rare urge to make cheesy scones to complement it. Actually, despite my antipathy to kitchens, there was something about the one at Lime Cottage that drew me, and soon I found myself happily singing along to the radio and up to my elbows in flour. Yes, I know making scones doesn't necessitate coating yourself in flour, but I was *cooking* -voluntarily. Perhaps that Naked Chef guy has the right idea.

Allie had been persuaded to go to the cinema with Bella's (or Horse-face, as Ethan referred to her) daughter, Zara, who was about the same age and was also a pupil at St Hilda's, so a while later I set a couple of places at the kitchen table and prepared to dish out the casserole and savoury scones. (Amazingly they seemed to have turned out well – at least I assumed they were OK as the tiles didn't crack when one fell on the floor.) So I wandered through to the sitting room to let Ethan know supper was about ready, and there he was, slumped on a sofa with a half-empty bottle of best malt whisky on the table in front of him, and a half-full glass in his hand.

He gave me a lop-sided grin and patted the sofa. 'Come and sit down next to me, and have a drink, Roshie.'

Yes, he was six sheets to the wind, probably seven.

'Not just now, thanks Ethan. I just came to tell you that supper's ready.'

'Oh, *shupper*,' he said. 'We called it dinner in our house.'

I shrugged. 'Well, it will be on the table shortly and if you don't come it will get cold.'

'Shtuff dinner, Roshie, I want you to talk to me.'

I thought quickly. 'Well come and sit with me in the kitchen while I eat mine – I'm starving.'

I went back to the kitchen and sat down, but my appetite had diminished. As Mike wasn't here I would have to cope with the boss's binge – in addition to his demon daughter. Perhaps it hadn't been such a good idea to move in.

Two minutes later, Ethan lurched through the door, and Geoffrey, who had ventured downstairs for the first time and was tentatively nibbling his food, shot out into the hallway and up the stairs, back to the safety of my room.

'What the fuck was that?' Ethan bellowed.

'Geoffrey – my cat. Remember you said I could bring him to stay with me?'

'I thought it was a fucking rat.' He dragged out a chair and sat down.

'Ethan, you'll have to mind your language when Allie is about. She'll be back soon.'

He was picking at his plate with a fork. 'I'm shorry, Roshie. I'm a fucking failure – shorry - a failure as a father. And it's all down to cash, Roshie. Bianca wants it, fucking Marnie – shorry Roshie - Marnie wants it, even Allie only wants me for it…'

He slurped another mouthful of straight malt.

'You're wrong about Allie. All she really wants is a stable home and a father who loves her and spends some time with her.'

'But I have to tour, Roshie – otherwishe there *is* no cash.'

'It's all about quality time. You enjoyed taking her out the other day, didn't you?'

'It was great – we went to the bowling alley ya know – and you know what? She bloody beat me! Can you believe that?' He shook his head, grinning lopsidedly.

'She'll remember that day. And when you're on tour, make

sure you ring her regularly and visit whenever you can.'

'I will...but what about poor little Fen? That f... - shorry - that bitch probably won't even let me talk to him.'

'Maybe it will be sorted out sooner than you think. Hopefully your lawyer will be able to persuade the opposition that the tabloid story was grossly unfair.'

'It's not fair, Roshie. I love that little boy. And Allie too. I wanted them to have a proper family. I never had one, Roshie. Did you know I was adopted? They were good to me, my mum and dad – but it wasn't the same. I need to find my real mum...I thought I had, ya know...but it was someone else with the same name...'

He was slipping down the chair, his chin in his hand, and his eyes glistened.

He was also in danger of dropping his glass and falling into his casserole, so I removed the glass – on which he had a vice-like grip – and managed to persuade him to let me help him up the stairs, telling him it wasn't a good idea for his daughter to see him in that state.

'I'm not drunk, Roshie, jus' very, very upshet...' he argued, but nevertheless allowed me to pull him up and drape his arm around my shoulders.

With great difficulty I got him upstairs and onto his bed. I bent to take off his shoes and he took the opportunity to grab hold of me and pull me towards him. For a nanosecond I was practically lying on top of him, and despite alcohol fumes strong enough to cause a sub-nuclear explosion, looking into those darkly-fringed, somewhat glazed green eyes, I felt a distinct frisson (as they say in romantic novels). Anyway, at that moment he was still the stuff fantasies are made of.

'D'ya fancy a shag, Roshie?'

I yanked myself off him, went out and closed the door just as the front door opened and Allie appeared. The look she gave me was distinctly suspicious.

'Where's my dad?'

'He's...just gone to bed. He's had an upsetting day.'

'What were you doing in there then?'

'Just taking him a drink, Allie. How was the film?'

Her expression changed to outrage.

'Don't think I'm going anywhere with that uptight little twat, ever again. She's fucking unbelievable!'

'Allie, please don't use that language.'

And I was worried about her father.

Sunday was yet another round of yo-yoing emotions. The Browns want to buy my house – and they didn't even quibble over the price. Of course I said yes as I'd have looked a complete idiot telling them I'd changed my mind, particularly as they've spent the past two weekends travelling back and forth from North Yorkshire. They're a very nice family and she even brought me a home-made cake, which was delicious. If this is any gauge of her standard of cooking, the nice shiny oven I sold them will be in shock: it's eight years old and only used to occasional work.

They want to move in as soon as possible, and they've been advised this could take less than eight weeks if the legal people get their fingers out. I felt quite emotional when they left – almost like apologising for my disloyalty to the bricks and mortar that have succoured me for the past 20 years.

Reading what I've just written I think I must be cracking up.

While the house business was a mixture of highs and lows, getting Allie prepared for her new school was definitely a trough of despair, especially as she was sulking theatrically over her father's imminent departure. She couldn't see the point in starting at all when there were only four weeks of the term left. And he didn't help matters by slamming round the house with equal drama, shouting "where's this, and where's that, and what the frig had Betty done with his lucky T-shirt?" (At least he'd moderated his use of the F-word.)

When it was time for him to leave, he hugged Allie and told her to make sure she took good care of herself. 'Love ya, Babe,' he mumbled gruffly.

As he turned to say goodbye to me she raced upstairs, her eyes moist. The drama was not really called for: as the tour was in the UK and many of the venues were less than 100 miles from Lime Cottage, he had promised to come back whenever time allowed, and Mike had assured me he'd make sure the promise was carried out.

'Bye Rosie,' Ethan said. 'I owe you for all this. You won't regret it.' Famous last words, I thought as he pulled me to him and deliberately kissed me on the lips. There are quite a few things he could make me regret.

Alone for the first time with Allie, I woke on Monday morning overcome with anxiety, not least because Geoffrey hadn't roused me with his customary yowling.

Allie was very upset over Ethan's departure – though she'd originally tried to mask her unhappiness by being obnoxious.

'How typical that I'm left with one of his hired hands,' she spat cuttingly when I tried to console her. 'At least I'm *someone* not just someone's gofer. And I suppose you've slept with him too.'

Knowing her tirade stemmed from misery, and recalling I was being well paid for my forbearance, I valiantly ignored her until she'd cussed herself into floods of tears. Later, when Geoffrey came to investigate where his human had gone, he settled on her bed, and that was where I'd last seen him.

Dragging myself reluctantly from under the duvet I assumed my cat had been shut in with his new friend, and imagined him gazing beseechingly at the closed door, so the first thing I did was rush to release him. But Allie's door was ajar, and His Lordship was stretched out with his head on her pillow, her blonde hair splayed over his cream body. As I watched he looked at me and blinked. I was once told a cat's blink is like a kiss: how typically male to think he'd be forgiven his infidelity with a single snog.

Getting Allie geared up and into the car in time for school was like pulling teeth without anaesthetic. I walked with her to the school office where she would wait until collected by her class tutor.

As we made our way across the grassy expanse between gates and school, groups of similarly clad girls whispered and pointed, and scattered among them, crow-like in their black habits, nuns silently watched our progress. Allie, tall as she was, marched in front with her head up and an expression that would have frozen alcohol (and believe me, it doesn't freeze easily – I know as I once tried to make vodka lollies). But I saw her hand tremble slightly as she lifted it to smooth her already sleek hair, and admired her courage. Being the new girl was bad enough; being the new girl with a father who was not only famous, but the subject of a Sunday rag exposé must be twice as difficult. Taking my cue from her I said a casual goodbye and told her to wait for me to pick her up at four.

When I returned to the cottage I had other unpleasant tasks to attend to – like telling my children their home was about to be sold. And then begging them to come and start sorting through their belongings.

You'd have thought I was suggesting they heaped their most treasured possessions in the garden and lit a bonfire under them. But undoubtedly, Jamie took it hardest and made me promise he could keep his sledge. I told him I have no idea where it will fit if all I can afford is an apartment with no attic.

'Perhaps you could turn it upside down and store some of your shoes in it, as I'm sure you won't be throwing any of *them* out,' he said with more than a tinge of sarcasm.

'That's most unfair, Jamie. I've just donated half-a-dozen pairs to *Help the Aged*.'

'Yeah. I bet some granny is searching high and low for a pair of sequinned canvas mules that are two different sizes.'

'Whatever happened to respect for your elders?' I asked in a foolish attempt to deflect his line of reason.

'As you're likely to be the cause of some old lady's broken hip, I fail to see how you can ask, Mother,' he retorted reproachfully.

'OK, you can keep your sledge.' I quickly brought the conversation to a close before he started on my photographic collection.

Leah was unusually calm and understanding – which made me very wary. Then she said she'd be coming home next weekend and would I mind if she brought someone? She then hinted she had something important to tell me. Naturally I am now dancing with frustration, though I'm sure her guest must be her new man. But surely she's not thinking of getting engaged already? Oh my god! Perhaps she's pregnant. No, She can't be. She's much too sensible and career minded... though mistakes happen...Oh hell! I'm too young to be a grandmother.

When I collected Allie she almost looked pleased to see me.

'So how was it?'

Her expression clouded instantly. She shrugged, made some unintelligible sound and stared moodily ahead.

I should have known better than to question a teenager about school. They seem to lapse into amnesia the moment they walk out of the gates. This can last any amount of time from five minutes to infinity, depending on whether they (a) require money, (b) urgently need to contact a classmate re homework (an excuse for a phone call/visit completely unrelated to work of any kind), or (c) recall some imagined slight by a teacher or an incident where a teacher is made to look like a social outcast with the brainpower of a Brussels sprout.

Snippets of what they actually learn are dispensed in minute morsels, usually at inopportune moments (e.g.: Leah, age 13, at an elderly aunt's table: "Did you know that elephants only crap once a month and it can weigh up to twenty eight pounds?") and the like.

So I turned on Radio 2.

After five minutes of a listener's dire choice of Golden Oldies, the presenter announced the launch of Ethan Hammer's new album. Allie and I glanced excitedly at one another. Then he went on to mention "the Old Rocker's steamy sex-life and penchant for buxom blondes". As Allie snarled unprintable invective I reached to switch it off, then the disembodied recipient of her wrath was saying that *Flashback* was destined for the very top of the charts, and the familiar chords of the single were filling the air.

It sounded great, undoubtedly a hit. Ethan definitely has the old magic - and I still found it hard to believe I was so closely acquainted to this idol of the masses.

'For god's sake stop drooling,' Allie said, and I realised I'd been singing along happily.

'Don't be ridiculous,' I retorted a tad too quickly. 'I was just enjoying the song. It may not be your scene, but it's very good and your dad has lots of fans.'

'Including you,' his daughter's tone was caustic.

'Yes, I suppose I am, if that means I like his music.'

'Huh, pull the other one. You like more than his music – I've seen the way you look at him.'

'Allie, stop this. Of course I like your dad; he's my boss and he's a nice man.'

'Yeah, right.'

The conversation ended as did Ethan's song, and she lapsed into moody silence.

Teenagers!

And she was completely wrong. Ethan is unreliable, dissolute and incapable of fidelity – all the things I despise in a man. The fact that he's also delectable to behold and oozes sex appeal doesn't sway me at all. Not one iota.

As I tossed and turned that night with one thought racing into another, I recalled my self-assurances about him, and had to acknowledge that, despite his blatant appeal, Ethan really didn't light my fire. Yes, there was a spark, but there was something I couldn't quite put my finger on that seemed to hold me back. Self-preservation, I expect.

I don't recall where this thought lead. I only know I had some very peculiar dreams.

Madeleine turned up at Lime Cottage last night. I was stunned when I opened the door and she stood there. She was tanned and tarted up as usual – well not exactly tarted up as she was wearing jeans and a designer T-shirt, but on her they looked a million dollars – and she was carrying an Oddbins bag that clinked ominously.

'Hi, darling,' she said, air-kissing me on both cheeks. 'I was passing so I thought I'd pop in.'

Passing? People only pass here on the way to the crematorium that happens to be at the end of the lane. It was on the tip of my tongue to ask her if she was going to a funeral, but then I recognised the drawn look underneath the bright smile. Besides Ethan and Mike were away, and I'd been told to treat Lime Cottage as my home.

'Come in, Maddy. It'll be great to have some sensible adult company.' Maybe.

I got out the glasses and a bowl of low-fat nibbles and we decided to stay in the kitchen as Allie was watching MTV (I'm getting worried – I've spent more time in this kitchen than is natural).

Anyhow, it didn't take more than half a glass of Sauvignon and my perfectly natural enquiry into her trip to Paradise Island to open the floodgates. Though Maddy can cry at the drop of a hat.

She'd been dumped again. This time by Jean-Claude, the tennis coach she was leading astray during our phone call.

'Oh, Maddy,' I said after the usual commiserations. 'Everyone knows Tennis Coach is a euphemism for Gigolo. What did you expect?'

She regarded me with an exasperated expression. 'I expect adoration, Rosie. It's what I'm used to. I don't expect to be dumped for…skinny little teenagers who look as if they should still be wearing gym-slips…'

I stared at her with raised brows.

'I know, I know. None of us are getting any younger. I suppose what I need is a more mature male.'

I nodded. 'It might be better for your self esteem to go for someone who's at least potty trained. There again, when it comes to men, older doesn't necessarily mean more mature.'

'You're right there Rosie.' She dabbed her eyes and took out a gold compact to inspect her barely disturbed make-up. (I don't know how she does it: when I cry my face looks like a crumpled, post-party balloon with panda eyes.)

I poured the final drop of wine from the second bottle she'd bought.

'Men! Who needs 'em?'

'We do!' we chorused, a relic of our teenage years, and clinked our glasses together giggling.

Allie chose that moment to wander in, and gave us a withering look.

'Are all adults pissheads?' she asked, rudely staring at Maddy. 'I suppose you're one of my father's old tarts too?'

'Allie, don't be so obnoxious. This is Madeleine. She's a friend of mine. Maddy, meet Allie, Ethan's daughter.' The teenager from hell.

'I need some money for school tomorrow. We've got to make some yucky spaghetti dish with spinach in Home Economics.'

'What happened to the money you had today? That was supposed to last all week; surely you can't have spent it already?'

Allie dropped her head and shrugged, then shot daggers at me. 'It's none of your business what I spend *my father's* money on. Do I have to ring and ask him for money for cookery?'

'Jeez!' Maddy hissed.

'Allie, I'm your guardian at present, and I have every right to know what you're doing – including how you managed to spend a whole week's allowance in one day without even going out of the school gates. And if you don't ask properly, you can go to school without your cookery money. And *I'll* be ringing your father.'

She was silent for a moment, and I registered the looks of surprise, defiance, and confusion.

'I lent a girl some money to buy a card for her mobile. And I bought a few bars of chocolate at lunch time.'

Buying friends? I wondered, though it didn't seem to be Allie's way.

'Well I hope the girl's going to pay you back,' I said. 'It

doesn't grow on trees, you know.' I could have super-glued my lips when I saw her eyes roll. I sounded just like my mother.

Suffice to say I gave her what she asked for and she went off to bed, assuring me she'd done her homework.

'Jesus! You're a glutton for punishment, Rosie. I hope Ethan's paying you a fortune to look after that brat.'

Contrarily I found myself defending Allie. 'She's really not that bad. It's not her fault she's got useless parents – she's been alternately spoiled then neglected by a drunken mother and philandering father. It doesn't make for a well-balanced child – without the added burden of puberty.'

'I'm so glad Andreas is normal,' Maddy looked wistful as she spoke of her son. 'Mind you, every time he comes back from visits to his father's family in Cyprus he thinks he can boss me about like he does his aunts and grandmother. Out there man is still king. He was telling me the local boys shag as many tourists as they can and then marry local girls – who will be virgins and treat them with respect. I can see I shall have to disavow him of that illusion.'

'Sooner rather than later, Maddy,' I agreed. 'There's enough male chauvinists in the world.'

'Not that I mind a smidgeon of macho…especially in the bedroom. You can get a bit fed up with New Man: it's one thing to have them please you, and another to have to direct a sex session as if it were a sleazy porno movie. There's a lot to be said for spontaneity.'

'You mean a quickie in the broom cupboard.' I was feeling no pain. Maddy giggled. At least I'd managed to cheer her up. But I was more worried about Allie than I cared to admit.

Maddy stayed the night as I could hardly let her drive, and all the taxi firms seemed to be on strike or simply didn't want to come all the way out to the village. "Great Ashley?" they said as if it were in another galaxy. "Sorry love, we're busy for the next couple of hours…you should have booked." Spontaneity *is* dead.

Allie seemed even more reluctant to get to school and we only just made it to the gates as the Duty Nun closed them.

'Come along, Allegra,' she tutted. 'Or you'll be getting a hundred lines.'

Lines? Was this the 21st century? I watched as she walked up the path, her usual arrogant stride faltering slightly. I suppose she'll be all right when she settles in.

When I got home (goodness! I'm starting to think of Lime Cottage as Home), Ethan's car was in the driveway. He'd called to say he would be here, but I'd been expecting him later. Maybe he was getting some early nights. He greeted me buoyantly.

'Rosie! How're ya doing, babe?' he slung a careless arm around my shoulders and planted a kiss on my cheek. I have to confess his appearance had lifted my spirits.

'We've done it, Rosie. *Flashback*'s racing up the charts already. They say it will make number one.'

'Yes, we heard it on Radio 2 – Allie and I.'

He frowned. 'Where is she?'

'At school, Ethan. I've just dropped her off She started at St Hilda's this week.'

'Is she doing OK?'

'It's early days yet but I'm sure she'll be all right when she gets used to it.'

'Yeah, poor kid. It's not much fun starting a new school.'

'I don't suppose you've heard anything from her mother?'

He shrugged. 'No – but I wouldn't, would I? Bianca would stay in rehab for a year if she thought it would needle me. But you know what? I like looking after Allie. Bloody women! Except for you, Rosie, and … Madeleine!'

He stared towards the stairs where Maddy (the mare!) was making a Grand Entrance. She could have been on a Paris catwalk as she posed then descended – wearing my best silk robe – and glided towards Ethan who was virtually drooling. Maybe I'm exaggerating, but his admiration was transparent.

'Hello Ethan.' I'd never heard her voice more husky.

'Wow, babe, you look *fantastic*. Haven't changed a bit.' As he spoke she proffered her cheek for his kiss, which he gave eagerly.

'What are you doing here, babe? Not that I'm not pleased to see you.'

'Rosie, asked me to stay. We've been friends for years.'

'Good for Rosie,' he said, still not taking his eyes off the vision before him. I could cheerfully have strangled her. 'How long are you going to be here?'

'Just last night,' I put in before she could say I'd offered her bed and board for a fortnight. 'We'd had a bit to drink. I hope you don't mind.'

'Of course I don't mind,' Ethan dragged his eyes from her at last. 'Any friend of yours is a friend of mine, Rosie.' That didn't please Maddy half as much as it did me.

Honestly, when I said she needed a more mature man, I didn't mean my boss. An entanglement with a woman perceived to be a friend of mine would only serve to further antagonize his daughter. Besides, hadn't he dumped Maddy once already?

Whether or not my supposition was correct, he now seemed quite happy to spend time in her company, and I don't mind admitting I felt quite miffed as they sat at the kitchen table exchanging gossip about mutual acquaintances. After a while I left them to it and grudgingly settled in front of my computer. And I didn't mean to slam the door.

Eventually hunger forced me back. They were sitting closer together, laughing, and the table was littered with dirty cups and an overflowing ashtray. Maddy didn't deserve to look that good on 40 a day.

'It's lunch time,' I announced opening a window to clear the blue haze. For added effect I flicked on the extractor hood above the cooker. It sounded like a Sea King helicopter taking off. 'This atmosphere won't do your voice much good, Ethan,' I said when they both looked quizzically at me.

'Rosie's quite the little mother, isn't she?'

Another nail in the coffin of our friendship, Madeleine.

'Yeah, isn't she brilliant? She really looks after us, don't you

Rosie? Are you going to make us a snack then, or shall we go to the pub for lunch?'

'Oh we don't want to trouble Rosie – she's obviously busy. Let's go to the pub,' my soon-to-be-ex friend said.

'You come too, Rosie,' Ethan urged. 'It won't hurt to have a few hours off.'

No way was I going to play gooseberry. 'No thanks. You go,' I managed to say without actually gritting my teeth. 'I've got to collect Allie. Unless you'd like to?'

Ethan's face lit up. 'Great idea, Rosie. I'll come with you.'

By the look on Maddy's face I knew I'd scuppered her plans for the afternoon.

'See you later then,' I said sweetly. 'Be back by 3.30pm, won't you?'

I'd intended to persuade Ethan to collect Allie on his own, then to spend some time with her, but when he and Maddy returned from the pub at 3.25pm he was in no condition to drive.

I had by then conditioned myself to speak civilly to my treacherous friend, and in front of Ethan managed to say goodbye to her without spitting in her eye as she got into the cab I had bribed to collect her, though I couldn't resist an ambiguous comment.

'Bye Maddy. And don't worry about Jean-Claude – I'm sure the rash will soon clear up.'

She looked at me as if I'd gone mad, and Ethan frowned at her, but I think she got the message. Who am I kidding? In a straight contest for his affections she'd win hands down. In any case, that's not what I want. *He's* not what I want. So why did I feel so resentful? Why did I want to claw the sultry look from the face of one of my oldest friends?

You know, I swear I feel sort of protective of him. Really, I do. In his head he's not much more than a boy. Though I appreciate his sensuality, it's not jealousy. God forbid! I feel almost…maternal about him. Yes, that's what it is.

He was voluble on the drive to the school, and I cautioned

him not to breathe over his daughter. I didn't want her to know he'd been drinking, or to remind her of the family penchant for alcohol that had already taken her mother away from her.

I told him of my impending house sale. 'And that reminds me – I have to ring storage companies for quotes.'

'What for?' my boss asked.

'I have to store my furniture and most of my belongings until I buy another place.'

'Oh, I see.'

I shook my head ruefully. It was obvious Ethan hadn't had much experience of the real world. I suppose being surrounded by an entourage, one didn't have to worry about the minutiae of life.

'Why do you have to use a storage company?'

'Because it takes up quite a bit of room. And where else would I put it?'

'How about one of the garages at Lime Cottage? If you don't mind leaving your car outside, that is?'

I tried not to show my surprise. 'Well – I suppose that's possible. If you're sure it wouldn't be a problem. They're certainly well maintained so it should be weatherproof.'

'It's yours if you can use it.'

'Thanks Ethan. That's very thoughtful and will save me a few bob.'

See, he really is a nice guy.

'So, tell me about your friendship with Madeleine. How long have you known her?'

My feelings of bonhomie faded somewhat.

As predicted, the sight of her father quickly turned Allie's hang-dog expression to one of delight. Or as near as a teenager comes to expressing pleasure. Asked what she wanted to do she decided on the shopping precinct to buy some DVDs, followed by the inevitable visit to McDonald's.

As the designated driver I was forced to tag along and followed them to the Music Superstore in the High Street, more aware than they were of the attention Ethan's presence was causing. Gradually, at a distance, a retinue began to build up behind us, and as we entered the store, what should be blasting out of the speakers but Flashback, complete with raunchy video of my writhing, leather-clad boss and a posse of barely clad dancers.

Suddenly conscious of his highly magnified image, Ethan did a double take and an about-turn – only to be confronted by the gathering crowd who were now in no doubt as to their quarry. He was trapped.

The fans started to shout and clap and wave pieces of paper under his nose, edging him deeper into the store where curious customers now swelled the crowd.

A suited man with a badge declaring him Store Manager pushed his way to Ethan's side and tried to introduce some restraint. Meanwhile, intrigued by the commotion within the megastore's doors, more people came in, and soon the islands of CDs and DVDs were acting as crush barriers, and harassed staff were urging people to wait outside. Even so, they were repeating Flashback I noticed as I was jostled, my arm tightly round Allie whose expression had changed from angry to anxious.

Ethan looked round and catching my eye gave us a crooked smile then mouthed "Call the cops!"

At first I thought he'd been robbed, but then it occurred to me he'd been in this situation before, and it was becoming scary.

I scrabbled in my bag, only to realise I'd left my mobile at home.

I grabbed the manager's arm. 'You'll have to call the police,' I said. 'This is getting dangerous. Someone will get hurt.'

'Who are you?' the manager asked.

'Mr Hammer's personal assistant,' I told him with a calmness I wasn't feeling. I'm a bit claustrophobic at the best of times. 'Please do as I ask immediately.'

Seeing one of his CD stands beginning to topple, the manager whipped out a mobile and thumbed the keypad. As he turned away and pushed his way through the crowd,

I distinctly heard him say "Evening Gazette?" and my heart starting pumping violently.

Allie and I clung together and we managed to ease our way towards a doorway at the back of the store, just as a cacophony of sirens and blue lights announced the arrival of the police.

When they reached Ethan he indicated Allie and me, and we were all escorted outside – but not before an eager press photographer's flash illuminated us half a dozen times, not to mention a host of camera phones held by eager fans. Ethan and Allie were hustled into a police car amid another eruption of lights.

The crowd lost interest and I made my way back to my car.

No wonder famous people are neurotic

Even though Allie had been wearing her school uniform (admittedly, she'd discarded her blazer and tie) next day's national newspapers had copied the lead from the local evening edition (and no doubt copiously rewarded its photographer), and printed photos of Ethan with his arm around "another stunning young blonde". What these scandal sheets failed to point out, nay, failed to be concerned about, was the fact the blonde was his fourteen year old daughter.

One or two tabloids even had a very unflattering shot of me. But it was barely recognisable, and they didn't know my name, thank goodness.

Mike returned that evening and pointed out that though they'd got the facts wrong, no real harm was done – and in showbiz there was no such thing as bad publicity. However, he agreed with the police spokesperson who said Ethan was irresponsible to seek publicity in this manner. Not that Ethan had been seeking publicity, but it seems he'll have to resume his Big Star lifestyle as his popularity waxes, and not appear in crowded places without protection. Mike sent a donation to the Police Benevolent Fund on his behalf.

Was I the only one concerned about how it affected Allie? Perhaps. But it didn't seem to do her any harm at school – until the following day when the local weekly named her, hinted she was living with her father in a nearby village, and that she was enrolled at an exclusive convent. As there is only one, it wasn't difficult for anyone to pinpoint it, if they had a mind to.

It didn't take long: a day later a creepy note was hand-delivered to Lime Cottage. Mike was the only one who saw it and would only say it pertained to vile accusations including incest. Nevertheless it worried him sufficiently to insist Allie has a bodyguard while her father is away.

As said bodyguard is to live-in and accompany Allie everywhere, I prayed he wouldn't be a muscle-bound no-brain with disgusting personal habits - though in the movie "Bodyguard" the heroine had Kevin Costner on duty 24/7, which seems like a pretty good deal to me, so I live in hope.

I didn't have time to digest this latest turn of events before I heard raised voices.

'It's not fair! You've only just come back – and now you're going away again.'

Oh, dear. Allie had discovered her father was off first thing in the morning to appear live on Britain's Best Bands.

'All right, babe, calm down. Tell you what – why don't you come with us? You can be in the audience.'

There was a short silence. Followed by a shriek.

'Lady Gaga! Lady Gaga's going to be on – I saw the trailer last week…oh yes, *please,* Dad.'

Unlike me at her age, she was drooling over a female singer: hopefully this indicated she was still at the stage of despising the opposite sex. That would be one less thing for me to worry about.

But who was going to explain to Reverend Mother that her newest pupil was going to miss at least one day of her third week at the convent?

That's right, me. Perhaps I could take the bodyguard?

In readiness for her trip to see her idol, Allie tried on every item of clothing in her wardrobe – as well as full makeup and an array of hairstyles. She even asked for my opinion when she was down to the final six guises, and though most were rather outlandish, my conviction that she was going to be one of life's true beauties was reaffirmed. In fact she was already gorgeous, and with the sort of alabaster skinned, innocent air envied by women and irresistible to men, she'll undoubtedly be a heartbreaker.

She eventually paraded before me in tight, low-waisted jeans that flared into a sequinned panel, matching belly-button ring, and a cropped top; her hair was twisted into a spikey fan on top of her head, and I was delighted she'd taken my advice and toned down the makeup. Nevertheless, she'd have passed for 18 any day, which was a bit worrying. I never had that problem with Leah – it was all I could do to get her to put soap on her face, let alone anything else. Perhaps I should have been grateful.

I hope I manage to maintain a compassionate demeanour if my daughter tells me she's pregnant.

Allie was so thrilled by the forthcoming trip I decided to take some photos while she was so unaffectedly animated. I persuaded her to cooperate by telling her she could send copies to her mum, and they would be a keepsake for her. Also I wanted to practise with my new digital SLR camera. I still love photography. I might begin classes again and take it up more seriously.

Simon wasn't happy about my Evening Class after he found some black and white prints of a nude youth in my portfolio. They were very tasteful (no dangly bits exposed) yet he took offence. Yet while I was innocently looking in the name of art, he was most definitely handling the goods. Adulterous hypocrite.

That's the first time I've thought of him in weeks, well days, maybe. Leah told me he had to wear a surgical collar for most of his honeymoon in Disneyland after his Angel persuaded him to go on one of those rides that loops upside down. As he used to refuse to take his children on the Big Wheel "in case they were scared" it serves him right. He once came off a kiddy ride with buses and fire-engines looking a peculiar shade of green and had to sit on a bench for the rest of the afternoon. The twins were mortified. Or maybe that was just me.

Anyway, he'll now have to settle down to life with another child. She's over 21, but according to Leah, the new Mrs Grant is demanding, sulky and always asking for new toys. They've just bought roller-blades and have booked to go snowboarding at Christmas. I foresee disaster. Or at least another surgical appliance. Hopefully a truss.

That's not spiteful, simply realistic.

I was in the office about to download the photos onto my computer when Allie reappeared. Her hair was loose and shiny and she wore an outsize T-shirt with a teddy bear motif. Gone was the makeup, and she looked the antithesis of her earlier self.

I was so struck by the contrast I lifted the camera to my eye and snapped away as she sat on the chair opposite me and drew her knees up to her chin. She seemed almost ethereal in the diffused light from my desk lamp, silently regarding me with almond-shaped green eyes and a pout.

'You OK Allie?' I asked casually. I didn't want to spook her – there was definitely something on her mind.

She shrugged. 'Yeah.'

'Shall I make some hot chocolate?'

She shrugged again. 'Nope. Thanks.'

'Are you worried about school or anything?'

Her eyes lowered. 'I'll feel stupid having a bodyguard. They all think I'm flash as it is.'

So, it was school.

'He'll only be there to escort you to and from the gates. With me, if you like.'

'Oh.'

'I know it's early days, Allie, but starting a new school is always difficult – and if anyone's being nasty it's only that they're jealous.'

She gave a snort. 'Just wait until they find out I'm going to see Lady Gaga! That'll give them something to be jealous about!'

The thought seemed to brighten her and she uncurled herself and made for the door.

'G'night, Rose.'

Discussion over. At least for now: I'm sure we've only scratched the surface of her problems, but it's a start.

'Night, Allie.'

While Ethan, Mike and Allie were at rehearsals for Britain's Best Bands, I met Jamie at the house which had been his home since birth.

He'd phoned out of the blue and said he was taking a couple of days off to sort out his stuff.

I wasn't kidding myself it was for my benefit: Jamie is a hoarder and he just wanted to be sure I didn't get the opportunity to throw out something precious to him. I'd hoped to persuade him to discard some of them: his collection of beer bottle tops for a start – I'm sure he must have gone off the idea of creating a modern mural by setting them in plaster on his bedroom wall. Also the pieces of driftwood and lengths of metal he was saving for a sculpture. Goodness knows what he intended to make, but along with the rusty sheets of corrugated iron he had in the garage, he could build his own shanty town.

When I let myself into the house I heard voices. Maybe the lovely Joshua was with him – brazen, but a sight for sore eyes.

'Jamie?'

My son appeared, and the person with him was indeed very attractive – and most definitely female.

'Hi Mum,' he smiled and kissed me (I love that he's never been ashamed to do that no matter who's watching: Heidi's Martin would cross the street rather than acknowledge her in front of his friends).

'Mum, this is Kirsten. She's going to help me sort my things out.'

'Hello, Kirsten,' she was even prettier when she smiled. 'Does that mean you don't need my help?' I asked lightly, fingers crossed behind my back.

'No thanks, I'm sure we'll manage just fine,' my son said, giving the girl a sidelong glance.

I think it's going to be a long job.

'I've put some boxes in the garage, and there's a roll of rubbish bags in the kitchen. I'm going to sort out a few cupboards while I'm here, and then I'll leave you to it. But first I'm going to have some coffee. Would you like some?'

'Have you got any mineral water, Mum? Kirsten and I are into macrobiotics -you know.'

Yes, I knew. A vegetarian variation with no chemical additives, if I remember correctly. Well, I expect they'll grow out of it.

'You won't be wanting any of these Jaffa Cakes then?' I said slyly, and watched my son's face drop.

'By the way,' I said as they made their way upstairs with two glasses of water and some dry crispbread. 'Did you know Leah's coming home at the weekend? She says she's got something important to tell me. And she's bringing someone with her.'

Jamie and Kirsten paused in their ascent and I didn't miss the look they exchanged before Jamie replied.

'Yeah – she did mention it, Mum.'

'Jamie, is she pregnant?' I know it was mean, but I'd been conjecturing every possible scenario for days, and I didn't want to wait any longer.

'Er, not that I know of, Mum. We haven't really spoken much lately.'

'But she's OK?'

'Yes, Mum. She's fine.'

'So I can set my mind to rest, then?'

He hesitated a split second too long. 'Er, yes, Mum. Got to get on now. See you before you go,' he pulled Kirsten onto the landing and his bedroom door slammed as I stared after him.

He hadn't told me the truth, of that I'm sure. And I was equally sure I'd get no more out of him: twins can be irritatingly loyal to one another when it suits them.

But at least it seems my daughter isn't pregnant, and I can't think of anything worse than that. Yes I can; she might be seriously ill. Oh, my god! No, don't be stupid – Jamie said she's fine and I'm sure he wouldn't be able to keep it to himself if it were serious.

I sat on the bed I'd shared with Simon and began sorting through boxes of papers from the loft. Naturally I had to keep stopping to read and reminisce, and my heart was heavy with nostalgia.

There were so many memories: Christmas and Mother's Day cards the children had made with wads of cotton wool and eggbox cups painted to look like tulips; Easter cards with fluffy chicks and eggbox cups painted to look like daffodils; their first Swimming Certificates; the story Leah had written for her Writer's Badge at Brownies…

And then there were the letters from Simon; the gaudily padded birthday cards he'd sent in the early days The swizzle sticks from our first holiday in Spain, the silk Valentine's rose…

Uninvited, the tears gathered and fell as I recalled how besotted we were with each other, with the twins. The carefree family outings…the fun (and sex) we had decorating this very room (and every other room, come to think of it). How excited we were when we found a piece of furniture we could afford…

I blew my nose. Yes, they were happy days, and if I were the philosophical sort I'd count myself lucky as some people never have times like those. I only had to look as far as poor Heidi. But sitting there amongst the ruins of my home, I found it hard to be philosophical.

Not that I still love Simon. I don't. He's hurt me far too much – and he's no longer the man I married with his trendy clothes and earring. I *am* lucky: I'll have the cash from this house and I have a job that will never be boring, albeit temporary. And I'm no longer petrified of the future. So I've something to thank Simon's betrayal for.

As long as Leah's all right.

To take my mind off my anxieties, and because I needed some girl-talk, I invited Gina and Heidi round to watch BBB (Heidi's elderly employer had his son staying and had given her a couple of nights off).

It took us back a few years as the familiar signature tune blared and we sat with our wine and Pringles (though originally it was cider and supermarket crisps). I hadn't invited Maddy, but told the others of her predatory behaviour with Ethan.

'Predatory's the right word,' Gina agreed. 'When she decides to go for it there's no stopping her. I bet she's already made arrangements for a private performance.'

'Maybe he'll fall in love with her,' Heidi said. Bless her.

'He's an alleycat, Heidi,' I said kindly. 'He doesn't want commitment.'

'He'll probably hump her and dump her again,' Gina said.

At that moment *Flashback* was announced and there was the man himself, sex on two legs, poured into leathers that left little to the imagination, and astride a throbbing Harley Davidson.

I felt the familiar excitement.

'Jeez…' said Gina. 'He could put his boots under my bed any day…'

'Gina!!' chorused Heidi and I, not taking our eyes from the hypnotic thrusting on screen. 'You've only been married a month!'

'There's Allie!' The camera had panned the audience and rested on her as she swayed, her slim body almost echoing her father's movements. It panned away and came back again. What I'd give to be her age and look like that! Or even my age and look like that with wrinkles.

The music faded and we grinned approvingly at one another.

'Don't tell me you'd turn him down if he gave you half a chance,' Gina said.

I shrugged nonchalantly, heady with the wine. 'I already have. More than once.'

My friends' eyes widened. 'What, you've had Ethan?'

'No! But I've had the chance and turned it down.'

They looked at me, aghast.

'You wouldn't!'

'Why would you do that?'

Why, indeed?

I was now wishing I'd kept my mouth shut. I shrugged again. 'It would be difficult to work for him if I did. Anyhow, it just didn't feel right.'

Gina was beside herself. 'I can't believe you gave up the chance to make all our teenage fantasies come true. It's...it's sacrilege!'

'I dunno,' Heidi said dreamily. 'I can understand where Rosie's coming from.'

'I can't,' said Gina vehemently. 'But I know where she should be going – to the funny farm.' She continued to shake her head in disbelief.

I was now certain I should have kept quiet as they wanted to know all the details of Ethan's propositions, so I may have exaggerated the incidents. Now I have an awful feeling my friends think my working life is a series of erotic encounters with my boss, which I have humiliated myself (and by association, them) by refusing.

At least they hadn't recognised that awful picture of me in the paper – now *that* would have been humiliating.

I forgot to record my conversation with the Reverend Mother at St Hilda's.

I had every intention of telling the truth about Allie's day off school, more or less: that she was spending time with her father who was about to go away for months.

But that wasn't good enough for the Head Crow.

'Ms Grant, this will not do at all. The child is about to start preparation for her GCSE's. She cannot have time off on so flimsy a pretext.'

Knowing how important it was for Allie to spend time with Ethan, my hackles rose instantly - though I'd heard that parents of State school students could be fined for taking their offspring out of school during term time, I reasoned Ethan was paying a fortune for his daughter to attend this outdated institute, so there had to be some privileges. I kept my cool.

'I'm sorry, Reverend Mother, I fully understand your viewpoint, but Allegra's family circumstances have been extremely distressing for her, and it's important she regains confidence in at least one of her parents.'

'Humph. And why particularly must she spend time with her father today? Why not the weekend?'

'Mr Hammer leaves at the weekend.' Though not until Sunday evening.

'Harrumph. Well I cannot prevent him taking her out of school. But please warn him, Ms Grant, that I will not countenance another absence of this kind. Does he intend taking her on an educational visit? Or a religious one, perhaps?'

'Oh I'm sure, Reverend Mother. In fact he mentioned something about worship.'

It wasn't entirely untrue. Allie would be worshipping her pop idol - and being educated in a few choice phrases, if I knew Ethan.

I just pray the Head Crow isn't a devotee of BBB.

The Reverend Mother may not have been a pop music fan, but apparently at least one of her underlings was. How else would it have come to her attention that Allegra Hammer was spotted "gyrating in an unseemly manner on the TV"?

It's highly unlikely that BBB was seen within the cloistered walls of the convent, so I surmise Allie's appearance was reported by an envious pupil. Whatever, she was called upon to answer her accusers, whereupon she shrugged and admitted her sin.

'*I* never said I wasn't going there,' she said carelessly, still buoyed by her meeting with Lady Gaga. Which may have been the truth – but it left me with egg on my face. And probably a veto from St Peter.

I was subsequently phoned by the school administrator: she wanted to speak to Ethan, but he was still in bed and asked me to deal with it. I was told, in no uncertain terms, that *"if there were any repetition of this sort of irresponsible behaviour"* (it sounded as if she meant mine) *"Allegra would no longer be welcome at St Hilda's. She was already considered to be an unsettling influence on some of the girls. Also her behaviour tended to be unbecoming. And she had a very lax attitude towards her religion."*

As I replaced the receiver, my sympathy was entirely with Allie. Sure she had problems, but underneath it all she was just a normal teenager, and I was even more convinced St Hilda's was not the best place for her. If she were ever to have her faith in adults restored, it wasn't likely to be achieved by clicking rosary beads and reciting a dozen Hail Mary's.

There is only one week to go before the school summer holidays begin; time enough to rethink this whole situation.

JULY

On Sunday I was meeting Leah at the house, and Allie was to spend her last day with Ethan. The bodyguard was due to arrive later in the afternoon, and Mike asked if I could be back in time to meet him and discuss the arrangements for my charge's safety.

While I was waiting for my daughter, still uneasy over her important news, I busied myself with more clearing and packing. I'd had a big stack of boxes delivered and they were gradually filling up.

I'm amazed at the amount of junk we'd accumulated. I say *we* because it certainly wasn't me who saved pieces of flex, rusty screws and a set of chimney sweeping brushes - even though we hadn't had an open fire for more than ten years. Jamie obviously inherited the hoarding gene from his father.

I can't imagine why Simon didn't take his rubbish with him when he moved out, though I don't suppose the child-bride wants a pair of particularly ugly Victorian china bulldogs any more than I do. They were a present from his mother – and a very good caricature, if you ask me.

Well, the charity shops will benefit, but I suppose I'd better give Simon one final chance to rescue anything he doesn't want dumped or donated. I must be going soft in the head.

Leah arrived. She looked tired and drawn, and she was alone.

'Hi, Mum.'

'Hello darling. I thought you were bringing a friend.'

She gave a sharp laugh. 'I was, but we're no longer an item. So that's it.'

I held out my arms as her eyes, most uncharacteristically, filled with tears. I don't think I've seen her cry since she dislocated her shoulder playing rugby.

Briefly she allowed me to hug her.

'Don't cry, darling. There are plenty more fish in the sea. I know that sounds trite, but it's true, believe me.'

She sniffled and blew her nose.

'Er…and have you anything else to tell me? You mentioned something important?'

'And you think this isn't?' she snapped. This was my daughter. 'What else do you want to know?'

'Nothing, sweetie, nothing at all. I was worried in case you were ill or something.'

'Ha! You mean pregnant, don't you? Well, set your mind at rest, Mother, as that will never happen. Never!'

I wanted to tell her that someday, in the distant future, I'd probably like it to happen, but I could see my aspirations to grandparenthood were unlikely to ease the situation.

'All right, darling. That's fine by me.'

'Is it?' she asked, her tone cynical. 'Most mothers can't wait to have squalling grandchildren.'

She needed to take her hurt out on someone, so I didn't bite.

'Not me. I've only just got over you two – and now I've been lumbered with another teenage ingrate. I must be a glutton for punishment. Anyhow, shall we go to the pub for lunch?'

Leah brightened a tad. 'You mean roast beef and Yorkshire pudding like cannonballs, cooked by Minty Mike?'

'I don't think he actually does the cooking. Please god.'

'I don't give a toss, anyway,' my daughter said. 'Salmonella would be a happy release.'

I know we all have to go through it at some time or other, but I'd love to get my hands on the dirtbag who's hurt my daughter.

Kevin Costner he is not, but this is not necessarily a bad thing. I'm talking about the bodyguard, of course.

Shortly after I arrived back at Lime Cottage – to find Ethan and Allie lying on the floor in front of the TV playing Mortal Combat, and Mike doing his nut (well, slightly put out) because

Ethan hadn't even started his packing - the doorknocker was rapped so loudly it made the solid oak frame shake.

The figure that entered as Mike opened it had to stoop to get in, and when he straightened up his head was almost touching the beams. And he was as wide as he was tall.

He was greeted warmly by both Mike then Ethan, obviously an old and trusted acquaintance.

My first thought was whether he'd fit into the bed we'd allocated him; my second was gratitude that it was downstairs. I don't think 400-year-old ceilings were intended for man-mountains.

He was coffee-coloured and fearsome looking, but when I was introduced to him, though his hand shrouded mine completely, he smiled broadly and his tone was gentle.

His name is Timothy Adams and his father was born in Trinidad. I wonder if Mrs Adams would have called her son Tim if she'd known he was going to grow into such a Goliath – who'd be known as Tiny.

Even Allie seemed awed when she met him, and I swear there was a smug grin on her face as she turned back to the TV. I'm not surprised: if you have to have a bodyguard, make it one the size of a house with more beef than a Mr Universe final.

Mike showed Tiny his room and I offered to make coffee.

'No coffee for me, Ma'am,' said the giant with another wide grin . 'I only ever drink water or green tea.'

Not another health freak! He was a genuine Jolly Green Giant. (Ho, ho, ho!) Still, if he was going to frighten the weirdoes away, we'd better humour him. As long as he didn't expect steak and eggs for breakfast. He'd be sorely disappointed with Coco Pops and a slice of toast.

Mike and I were dwarfed by him at the kitchen table as his duties were discussed.

Normally he was to have Mondays off, when he'd be relieved by Tony who'd also worked with Ethan before and lived locally. The bodyguard would accompany Allie wherever she went, except when she was in school where she was not to leave the grounds without express permission.

Thank goodness Mike had taken it upon himself to ring St Hilda's to inform them of the arrangement. He didn't say a lot, so I can only surmise the reaction from the Head Crow, but I can't wait to see the response to Tiny's appearance. I hope he wears a dark suit and shades.

Mike had already lectured Allie on the necessity for the bodyguard's presence, and though he tried not to alarm her, despite her bravado she seemed to take the advice to heart. Though once again I found myself sympathising with her. On the one hand she might enjoy the prestige of having her own minder, but it placed her apart from her compatriots, and in teen language, different equals distrust, which in turn equals envy. From the very few remarks she'd made about her new school, I had already detected a massive element of that in the air.

Tiny went to his room to unpack. Mike grinned when I whispered that I hoped he hadn't got more than one suit as I didn't think the wardrobe would hold them.

'Yes he's a big'un all right – but a gentle giant. Until someone steps out of line and then he can move like the wind. He's very self- sufficient too: spends most of his time reading. And he'll be responsible for his own food.'

'Thank goodness for that!' I breathed a sigh of relief – it was bad enough catering for a fussy teenager. I couldn't cope with an organic, seaweed-eating mammoth.

'By the way, you've got a new vehicle – Tiny's driven it down – do you want to have a look?'

'A new car?' I was about to ask why, but the image of Tiny in my economical hatchback was too risible to contemplate. An articulated lorry was more his size.

'Come on.' Mike grabbed my hand and pulled me to the back door.

Standing in the driveway behind Mike's Range Rover was another large 4x4. This one had smoked windows all round and Mike opened the door and urged me to sit in the driving seat. After we'd adjusted it he pointed out some other unusual features. There was a concealed switch that activated the lights and a siren, and a telephone that tuned directly to the nearest police station. And then he showed me the thickness of the window glass. It was bullet-proof.

It was at this point I had serious doubts as to my decision to take on this teenager, who, it seemed, was even more troubled than I could ever have imagined.

Mike saw the look on my face. 'Rose, it's only a precaution,' he said gently, a reassuring hand on my shoulder. 'You get a lot of nutters when you're in the public eye. Ethan feels bad enough about Allie – if anything happened to her he'd never forgive himself. You don't have to worry. Tiny will look out for you both. You just get on with your life – and keep persevering with Allie. She's already noticeably more civilised.'

My instinct for immediate flight faded. Firstly, Mike was making sense, and secondly, I didn't have much choice. My home was dismantled and all but sold, and jobs of any kind were not that easy to come by. I would have to bite the bullet.

Not a good analogy.

Later that evening there were hugs and kisses and tears as Allie said goodbye to her father.

'You be a good girl and do as Rosie tells you,' he bade her, then turned to me. 'And you, Ms Grant, don't do anything I wouldn't do.'

He pulled me roughly to him and kissed me hard on the lips. As he pulled away he whispered gruffly 'Thanks for everything, Rosie. I owe you one.' He winked theatrically and added 'And that's a promise!'

Even knowing he had the morals of a tomcat couldn't prevent a quiver as his green eyes burned into mine, yet emotions instantly catapulted from sensual to solicitous. I've never had a relationship with anyone that is so confusing: one minute I see a tantalizing man, the next a troubled boy.

Standing immobile by the door, Mike scowled and shook his head. His arms hovered as if he was about to hug me too, but he obviously thought better of it.

'Look after yourself, Rose. And don't hesitate to ring if

there's anything you need.' He got into the driver's seat, gunned the motor and they were gone.

Heidi is coming round this evening. Her nice old patient's son has insisted on a relief carer twice a week. I think I'll let Tiny answer the door!

I'm worried about Allie. I drove her to school with Tiny – who didn't disappoint re the dark suit and shades - but the flashy new car and heavily tinted windows drew looks that were more cynical than covetous, though it was hard to tell the difference. Allie hopped out so quickly she was already at the gates before I realised she'd left her packed lunch on the back seat.

Without a word, Tiny grabbed it, jumped out of the vehicle and caught up with her in two strides.

All action in the vicinity stopped to form a tableau of wide-eyed, open-mouthed girls – not to mention a nun or two - as the massive male thrust the package into Allie's hand.

'See you later, Miss Allie,' he said, and as he sprinted towards me I heard catcalls and wolf-whistles. The last thing I saw as I pulled away were the duty nuns, their heads swivelling accusingly as they aimed to root out such unladylike behaviour.

I glanced across at Tiny. He was still grinning.

When we went to collect her at 4pm, rather late because of traffic, Allie was by the entrance and surrounded by a group of four girls. Though she stood head and shoulders above the rest she appeared to be cowed, hunching her shoulders in a manner that could only be described as defensive.

When she spotted us her shoulders straightened and she pushed through the clique as Tiny rolled down the window and glared towards them. Before she reached the car her look of relief had changed to her usual sullen countenance.

'Everything OK, Allie?' I asked glancing at her through the mirror.

The normal shrug. 'Yeah. Why shouldn't it be?'

'No reason. You can invite some of your new friends home

if you like, you know.'

'Of course I know,' she replied with heavy cynicism. 'When I want to, I will. And I don't need your permission.'

'Miss Allie. It is not clever to be rude to your elders. Ms Rosie is just trying to help. I think you owe her an apology.' Tiny's deep voice filled the interior. I was surprised, and for a moment Allie was stunned into silence. But only for a moment.

Then I, too, was stunned when she said in a small voice 'Sorry.'

After dinner and just before Heidi was due, I went up to her room.

'No homework?'

She was lying on her bed with headphones on staring at a signed photo of Lady Gaga. Irritably she pushed them off. 'What?'

'I said haven't you any homework?'

The inevitable shrug. 'Done it.'

I wasn't going to ask to see it. This time. 'Allie, you will tell me if there's anything bothering you, won't you?'

She stared at me. 'I want to see my mother.'

'OK,' I said thinking fast. 'I can't see why we shouldn't visit her. I'll ring the clinic tomorrow. Perhaps we can arrange something for the weekend.'

She nodded and replaced the headphones.

This was my first day in full charge and I was already teed off by her hostile behaviour; it made me glad, briefly, that my own daughter was past that wearisome phase. Then I was reminded of Leah's delicate emotional state and decided to ring her.

'Mum? Hi! Is everything Ok?' she sounded almost elated.

'Yes, dear, everything's fine. I just wondered how you were – you know…'

'Me? Oh I'm great. Everything's great. Did the old dog get off all right?'

She was, of course, referring to my boss. 'Yes, he did. Well, that's all right then. As long as you're OK.' I could hear voices in the background, and I don't mind admitting that whilst

I was glad she seemed to have made a miraculous recovery from her broken heart, I was a bit put out.

'Must go, Mum – I'll go round to the house at the weekend and sort the rest of my stuff…Bye.'

Kids!!

And now it's the summer holidays to contend with.

AUGUST

'Bloody kids!' said Heidi as I let her in the front door. 'Martin's been in trouble with the police again. He smashed a window in the High Street and they kept him in a cell all night. I had to bail him out this morning.'

'Oh Heidi, you can do without that,'

'Tell me about it!' She sighed as I reached for the corkscrew. 'Where have I gone wrong, Rosie? And he's doing really well at work, Lloyd says. By the way, I saw Gina yesterday – they're having their wedding party at the Knutsford Park Hotel on the 15th. She said you can book a room at a special rate if you like.'

'Will you be able to make it? I'm sure I can leave Allie with the minder for one night.'

'Minder? You mean a babysitter?'

I laughed. 'Hardly that. Since Ethan's become so high-profile again we've had a few threats against Allie, so he's hired a bodyguard.'

'A bodyguard? Does he live in?'

I nodded.

'Where is he now then?'

'He has the en-suite in the annexe beyond the kitchen.'

'What's he like?'

As she spoke I heard movement in the kitchen, then Tiny's huge smiling face appeared round the door.

'Everything OK, Ms Rosie?' As he spoke he caught sight of Heidi who is almost his complete opposite, being a ridiculously petite blonde.

'Everything's fine, Tiny. Tiny this is my friend, Heidi Fox.'

Heidi rose to her full five feet one and held out her hand with a stunned look on her eternally childlike face. Tiny grasped her hand in his. Talk about Little and Large!

'Please to meet you, Tiny.'

'Pleased to meet you…Mrs Fox.'

'Heidi.' Heidi's hand was still enveloped in his.

'Heidi.' They were staring deep into one another's eyes.

I was waiting for the violins to start. I coughed. 'Would you like to join us, Tiny?'

'No, ma'am. I wouldn't dream of intruding. But maybe I could have the pleasure of your company some other time? I'll wish you both goodnight.'

He may have been speaking to us both, but he didn't even glance my way.

'Wow!' said Heidi as the door closed behind him.

'Stop slobbering!' I said.

'But he's gorgeous!'

It was my turn to do the Allie shrug. 'I suppose so, if you like them big and beefy. He's very nice and well-mannered, for sure.'

'Nice! You want your eyes testing, Rosie. Is he available?'

'I've no idea. I'll find out, OK? Now, what are you going to do about Martin?'

'I'd strangle him - if I could get my hands round his neck. Seriously though, Rosie, I've tried. He treats me with the same contempt his father did. Since he left it's as if Martin thinks he has to replace him.'

'What he needs is a short, sharp, shock. Or guidance from an adult male he respects. One with sensitivity as well as strength. Or a mixture of both…'

We looked at one another, and I can't vouch for Heidi's vision, but I pictured Martin being confronted by Tiny. Whether he was giving gentle advice or pinning someone against the wall with one massive mitt, I couldn't imagine anyone even trying to argue the toss with him. Anyhow, we both giggled like schoolgirls.

'Tiny doesn't like alcohol,' I said. 'But I believe he enjoys a game of Scrabble or Monopoly. Perhaps we should arrange one on your next night off?'

'Rosie, you are an angel.'

'No, that's the second Mrs Grant.'

Heidi looked devastated. 'I'm sorry Rosie – you know I didn't mean anything.'

'I know. But you know what? I really don't care. I'm over Simon. Completely.'

And I mean that most sincerely, folks.

At ten 'o'clock this morning I had a phone call.

'Simon! What's the matter – is it one of the twins?' My instant guilt at not knowing if something had happened to one of my children was negated very quickly.

'No – it's Angelica.'

'Good! I mean good god, Simon, how can that possibly be of interest to me?'

'She's pregnant.'

Zip-a-dee-doo-dah!

'I thought you ought to hear it from the horse's mouth.'

He sounded so smug he might as well have referred to himself as The Stud.

'What do you want me to say, Simon? Congratulations and can you remember how much you hated the twins when they were babies?'

'That's not true, Rose-Anne. I've always loved my children.'

'As long as you didn't have to get up in the night to them, or feed them or change a nappy or they didn't throw up on you.'

'It's different nowadays. I'm a New Man.'

'Yes, Simon. With a new woman. Well you never know, perhaps babies have changed too. For your sake I hope so because I can't believe you've changed *that* much.'

'Rosie, there's no need to be so bitter.'

I couldn't help it; I slammed down the receiver. And then I burst into tears. I don't know why.

I'm NOT bitter. OK?

I rang Gina and she confirmed the glad tidings were posted all over Facebook, so I expect I was the last person to know.

I don't know whether or not Ethan will approve, but I've had no instructions regarding Allie visiting her mother, so I made an executive decision and rang the rehab centre. In any case, if Allie wants to see her mother, I could see no good reason why she shouldn't be allowed to: she's obviously seen her in some pretty unsavoury states before now, and at least Bianca would be under supervision.

'We don't normally encourage visitors, Ms Grant,' Sister Marriott, the head warder (or whatever she's called) said, and I could picture her pinched mouth.

'I appreciate that, but her daughter is 14 years old, and she's missing her mother. I can't see how keeping them apart will achieve anything.'

'Are you a doctor, Ms Grant?'

'Obviously not. But it doesn't take seven years' medical training to understand the bond between mother and child.'

'Well really! This is too much!'

'And so are your fees, Sister Marriott. Perhaps Mr Hammer will see fit to place Mrs Hammer elsewhere.'

I only knew about the fees and that Ethan was paying them because he'd instructed me to transfer the funds. Of course I was pleased to think he had taken my advice, but while I made this not-too-veiled threat to the dragon on the other end of the line, I was aware it could be my job at risk if he took against the notion of Allie visiting Bianca.

'Very well, Ms Grant. When would it be convenient to come?'

My, how money talks!

'Allegra will be free on Saturday. We could make it for 10am.'

'Thank you, Ms Grant. We'll look forward to seeing you both.'

As we'd have to be accompanied by Tiny who would doubtless report back to his boss, I realised it would be better to mention the visit myself. I rang Ethan's mobile number and felt a twinge of disappointment as I was switched directly to his voicemail. I couldn't help wondering what he was up to. Something decadent, no doubt.

I didn't leave a message, and tried Mike's number.

'Hello Rose. Is everything OK?' His familiar tone was reassuring. I can't imagine him being part of the promiscuous pop tour scene. Not that I disapprove. Or I certainly wouldn't if I'd had the chance to give it a whirl - when I was younger, of course. I can think of worse ways of misspending youth.

Anyhow, I explained the situation to Mike and he thought it an excellent idea that Allie should have contact with her mother.

'Take some chocolate marzipan. It's Bianca's favourite – and give her my regards. How are things going, Rose? Is Allie OK?'

'Yes, on the surface. But I'm still not sure that St Hilda's is right for her. I just can't believe old fashioned rules and regulations, not to mention an overdose of religion, are the answer to her problems. Not that she isn't in need of some discipline.'

'I'm inclined to agree with you. But Ethan wanted her to go to the most expensive school in the area and St Hilda's certainly fits the bill. But give it a few weeks when the new term begins, Rose, and if you still think it's not working out I'll get him to rethink the situation.'

'Fine.'

'You getting on all right with Tiny?'

'Absolutely,' I said. 'He's a great guy – he doesn't talk much about himself though. Tell me, Mike, is he married or otherwise encumbered?'

There was a brief pause. 'No. Neither, as far as I know. Um, I know it's none of my business, but are you thinking…I mean do you …um…'

Somehow I saw what he was getting at. 'No! Though he's a lovely man. But it's not me, it's Heidi.'

Mike laughed. 'I see. Well, come to think of it, she'd be his type. He's into very small blondes. Tell her to offer him a Terry's Chocolate Orange and he'll be putty in her hands!'

'If only all men were so easy to please,' I quipped. Not that Ethan's intentions were complex – it was obvious what he wanted. The only difference between chocolate and gratuitous sex is that you still fancied the chocolate afterwards.

Which is bad news if you're dieting.

'Is Ethan all right? I rang him but his mobile's off.'

'It would be; he's still in bed. I'll tell him you were asking.' He sounded rather terse.

Ah, well. Mike seems to be an expert on his acquaintances' tastes in chocolate: I'd better let him know I am partial to Thornton's Viennese. As gratuitous sex seems to be off the menu perhaps I'd better stick to chocolate.

Talking of chocolate – or lack of it - reminds me, I've lost weight in the past few months. And now Tiny has persuaded me that a spell on Ethan's gym equipment, at least every other day, will do me the world of good.

As I have more spare time than I've had for years, I was unable to manufacture a feasible excuse when he offered to work out a fitness programme for me, and before I knew it I'd donned shorts and trainers and was being professionally assessed.

Tiny is an expert, as his huge, well-muscled body proclaims, and he occupied himself lifting ten-tonne weights while encouraging me as I struggled to push against a pathetic wedge of iron, and strained my stomach muscles doing leg raises and reverse crunchies. Don't ask.

The day after the first session I could hardly move, but he insisted I persevere, and I have to confess it has started to become easier. I feel quite self-satisfied when I've completed my programme.

I shall buy one of those two-piece Lycra outfits at the weekend. Tiny says if you wear the right clothes, you take your exercise more seriously.

So now I know why I never achieved my target doing aerobics in pyjamas and fluffy slippers.

Ethan has really made an effort to keep in touch with Allie and though she tries to act cool, it's obvious she loves his calls. She's trying to persuade him to start a Facebook page, but I think that might be a bit too ambitious as he's only just mastered text messaging.

An increasing amount of correspondence is arriving daily, so it seems a number of fans have discovered Ethan lives at Lime Cottage. Also there are sometimes clusters of people hanging around the gates. Tiny had to chase off a couple who'd come in and were nosing round the garden picking roses! Cheeky monkeys – they're probably intending to sell them on eBay.

I'd have probably been naive enough to buy one when I was a besotted would-be groupie, and to be honest, since I started opening some of the fan letters, I realise how very unworldly I was. Still am, if some of those sickos are any gauge – and that's just the women. They must sit with a copy of the Kama Sutra or porn mags with titles such as "Bondage and Bestiality" or "Masochist Monthly" while they're composing their letters of lust and undying servitude. And dissolute as he may be, I can't imagine Ethan being tempted by a pair of handcuffs, a large jar of mayonnaise and a bucketful of tuna fish.

Maybe I'm just not the adventurous type.

But I digress. Among the pile of soft porn and marriage proposals came a missive that really turned my stomach. Just like in the movies, it was created with letters cut from newspapers, and spelled out a very nasty threat to Allegra. It suggested she would be kidnapped and disfigured if her father did not cancel his "devil worshipping, licentious performances which corrupted young people and incurred the wrath of God".

It was quite obviously from a religious nut, but Tiny and I decided the police should be aware of it.

Chief Inspector Andrews was sympathetic, but didn't hold out much hope of tracing the writer. Nevertheless, after we'd explained about the nuisance caused by some fans, he agreed to regular patrols past Lime Cottage.

'And if there's any trouble, call us. I don't want any have-a-go heroics,' he said, his beady eyes fixed on Tiny.

'Of course, not, sir,' Tiny responded respectfully. 'My

job is to ensure the safety of Miss Allegra, not harass over-enthusiastic fans.'

I think the Chief Inspector was taken aback by his articulate response.

I thanked him and he grunted his dismissal. I had to smile to myself, picturing Tiny's reaction if anyone laid a finger on Allie – I could just see him saying "Hang on a minute, old chap, I'll just ring the police".

I'm really proud of the photos I took of Allie. She is exceptionally photogenic, but there's one pose of her sitting on the chair with her legs curled up and her eyes looking huge and sad, which is positively haunting. Anyhow, I've printed off some copies for her, and suggested she take some to Bianca, and maybe send one to her dad. She was quite surprised when I told her we'd be going to visit her mother on Saturday. I hope she won't be disappointed.

Leah rang, primarily to heap scorn and repugnance on her father's wife being with child.

'It's disgusting!' she said. 'He's too old to be a father. People will think he's a pervert!'

Though in my heart of hearts I felt much the same, as a supposedly responsible adult I had to offer a slightly less biased viewpoint.

'He's not that old, darling. Many people of his age have second families.'

'Don't give me that crap, Mother. Don't tell me you're not as shocked as I am. Angelica is an unadulterated airhead, and the child she bears will be my half-sibling. How would you like to be related to the product of such an ill-matched union?'

No words of reassurance were going to give comfort or hope to my aggrieved daughter, and though I tried to hide my empathy, she wasn't fooled. Our reasons were not the same, and I was loath to admit it, but we were both still suffering from Simon's defection.

Even though I was sure I didn't want him, I abhorred the fact someone else was carrying his child. And Leah hated that she would never again be the apple of her father's eye.

Only Jamie seemed unaffected by the forthcoming event. He quite liked the idea of having a baby brother or sister. Leah commented, with sisterly affection, that he'd always been a saddo.

I am just depressed.

I don't know why.

We started off early on Saturday morning loaded with chocolate marzipan, the photos of Allie, and an armful of those magazines that show the homes and families of a few movie stars plus legions of z-list "celebrities".

Sister Marriott herself greeted us. As I predicted, she was a hard-faced sergeant major with steely hair and a manner to match.

'Ms Grant, Miss Hammer, and…?' she grimaced at Tiny.

'Good morning, ma'am. Timothy Adams, Miss Hammer's protector.'

'Protector? This is a medical clinic, Mr Adams, I hardly think Miss Hammer will need your protection in here.'

'Probably not, ma'am. But it's my job to accompany her everywhere. I'll wait outside her mother's door.'

Grudgingly the battleaxe conceded, but told us we'd have to wait a few minutes as Bianca wasn't quite ready.

I had no intention of going in to see her, but Tiny and I sat in the plush waiting room with Allie as she fidgeted and paced.

When the door opened, it wasn't one of the American-style white suited nurses who appeared, but Bianca herself. She wore no makeup, and her blonde hair was showing half an inch of dark roots. I barely recognised her until Allie jumped up and threw herself into her arms.

'Mum!'

'Darling.' Though she hugged her daughter there was little joy in the gesture. In fact very little emotion at all.

'Shall we go to your room?' Allie took her mother's arm.

Bianca shrugged and affected a small smile. 'If you like, darling.'

They went through the door where I noticed a couple of nurses watching their progress, and Tiny stood up to follow them.

The nurses fell in behind and through the glass door I watched the procession as it made its way down the carpeted corridor and out of sight.

Less than an hour later, on the way back to Lime Cottage, Allie was even less communicative than usual, but when I caught sight of her in the mirror, her eyes were noticeably brighter.

I have only two more weeks until I sign the contract for the sale of the house. I know I shall have to buy somewhere else eventually, but for a while I shall be rich and I have a terrible urge to splash out on a holiday villa in the Mediterranean, or take a cruise around the world, and stuff the consequences. I was taught you have to speculate to accumulate – and I could meet a wealthy old widower and become a wealthy widow, which would be money well spent. Ah, but I dream. The reality is more likely to be a functional two-up, two-down on some faceless estate.

I am forcing myself to concentrate on the future as it's still pretty painful to dwell on the past. As I sift through the clutter of twenty-plus years, all sorts of memories have been stirred up, but I am becoming more ruthless as the pile of belongings for storage reaches ridiculous heights, literally. One stack of carefully packed boxes toppled over and took out the (mock) Tiffany shade on the landing. Mind you, it was fortuitous as they revealed Jamie's bottle-top collection which he'd sworn to relinquish. By the time I'd retrieved them all I had no compunction about chucking the lot out with the kitchen garbage. He's welcome to retrieve them if he's a mind to.

He'd left a note to say he and Kirsten would come round a couple of evenings next week to finish packing his things. Linda next door tells me they've been round almost every evening for the past fortnight, and as far as I can tell, the only thing that's moved in his bedroom are the sheets.

When Ron saw me over the fence as I struggled to heave yet more rubbish into the rusty brazier Simon set up to contain his bonfires, he said, quite sadly, 'I suppose there'll be no more games of Twister now you're mixing with the rich and famous. Linda says no one could live under the same roof as Ethan Hammer and not...you know…'

'Well I can,' I retorted sharply. 'Mixing business and pleasure doesn't work, Ron.'

'It did for Simon,' Ron said. 'Sorry Rosie, but he's the lucky bugger with a wife young enough to be his daughter.'

'Who happens to be pregnant.'

Ron gaped. 'My god! That's not so hot. Ooh, no – I don't think I'd want to cope with all that again.'

'Cope with what?' Linda had come out and caught the tail end of the conversation. Lucky for Ron it was only the tail end.

'A young pregnant wife,' I said. 'Simon's wife.'

'No? Ha! That'll teach him!' Linda laughed. 'Remember how useless he was with the twins?'

I nodded. 'He says he's a New Man now.'

'Yeah, right. And I'm a born-again virgin!' Linda came closer to the fence as Ron headed back indoors. 'So tell me all about Ethan then.'

'Oh, you know…he's basically a nice bloke. I've had much worse bosses. Allegra's a bit of a pain, but it's really not her fault, she's been shoved from pillar to post and screwed up by her mother and Ethan.'

Linda shook her head impatiently. 'Never mind the daughter being screwed – what about you? What's Ethan like – you know...?'

'Oh for god's sake, Linda, I don't know. And I'm not about to find out. I'd be stupid to mix business with pleasure.'

'Who are you trying to kid?' Linda's tone was dripping with disbelief. 'You were always a big fan! I don't believe you'd turn down the chance of a session with that sex machine – I know I wouldn't.'

'Well I would. I'd probably lose my job. And my place to live. It wouldn't be worth it. And besides, I don't even fancy him.'

'Jeez, Rosie. Keep trying to convince yourself – it might work.' Linda was shaking her head as she walked back up her garden.

What is the matter with everyone? Why can't they understand that things are different now I'm working for my one-time idol. Also, I am a mature woman, not a star-struck teeny-bopper. Ethan might have been able to cajole me into becoming his daughter's guardian, but as for anything else...

Linda is *so* wrong.

Leah came round while I was scrabbling deep into kitchen cupboards.

I've never been fanatical about sell-by dates, but even I was surprised to find tins that should have been discarded ten years ago, though the *coup de grâce* was a packet of banana-flavoured milkshake mix the twins had rejected over fifteen years ago.

I'll never forget it because having seen it advertised on TV, they gave a command performance in the middle of Tesco's when I refused to buy it. Leah flung herself on the floor and started screaming and Jamie obligingly followed suit, and yes, I allowed myself to be blackmailed: it was a case of give in, or get thrown out. And any modern mother who imagines a mild reprimand (e.g. "Don't do that, darling, you'll get a sore throat") would have worked equally well has not had the pleasure of stereo screeching, nor been the target of multiple do-gooders poised to ring the NSPCC.

I reminded Leah of this as I sat on the floor surrounded by dusty cans and packets.

'Oh. Yeah. I remember. It was vile stuff, too. Probably tastes better now it's matured a bit...Mum?'

I looked up, taking in her clean jeans and pretty top, thinking how great it was that she'd at last overcome her aversion to looking feminine.

'Mum, I need to talk to you.'

I stood up. It sounded serious, but she'd been so light-hearted on the phone, I was sure it was nothing awful...

'What is it, love? Shall I make coffee?'

'No, Mum. Let's just sit at the table.'

I sat, with a vague feeling of unease.

She sat opposite me and regarded me seriously with her beautiful hazel eyes.

'Mum, you know what you said the other day about not wanting any grandchildren?'

So, she was pregnant after all. I gripped her hand. 'It doesn't matter, darling. I didn't mean never ever…'

'Mum. *I* meant never ever…you see…'

Oh god, she was going to tell me there was something incurable. How could I cope with that? I willed my features to remain serene.

'You see, Mum, I don't like men. Not in that way. I'm gay.'

I don't know whether or not I actually gasped, but if I did I like to think it was with relief. Rather a lesbian than an incurable disease. Though part of me, at that moment, was unsure of the difference.

I gulped. 'Darling, are you sure?'

Leah gave a harsh laugh. 'It's not something you mistake, Mother. I'm sorry if you're shocked, but it's something I've been struggling with for quite a few years.'

'But – what about the other weekend – the guy who dumped you…oh!'

'No, it wasn't a guy, Mum. It was Dawn. My girlfriend. And we're back together now. We're living together and I want you to meet her.'

I didn't know if I was quite ready for this. But my daughter was very understanding.

'Maybe next weekend, Mum, when you've had time to think about it all?'

'Yes. Yes darling. That would be great.'

'I'm sorry to disappoint you, Mum.'

I took both her hands in mine and looked at my beautiful little girl, my daughter, contending with a jumble of emotions, yet mostly glad that she was fit and healthy, and happy. I knew there would be moments of self-recrimination and of regret.

But Leah is my child, and I would always love her, regardless. She had been struggling, she said, with the knowledge, for a long time. Years probably. It must have taken so much courage for her to admit her persuasion to me.

'I'm not disappointed, my darling,' I said. 'A bit surprised, perhaps, but it doesn't make any difference. I love you and I want you to know you'll always have my support.'

'Thanks, Mum. I knew you'd understand.'

What bigger compliment could any child pay?

Then it struck me. 'Leah. Does Jamie know?'

'Yes, Mum, he's known for ages.'

'And your father?'

'No – but I can't wait to tell him.' It was the malevolent tone of a woman scorned. Or whatever it is a displaced daughter feels.

Though I'm sure I reacted as well as could be expected, and said all the right things, back at Lime Cottage I walked round in a daze for the rest of the day. Allie had gone bowling with Tiny so at least there was no one to notice my preoccupation.

And, of course, the guilt escalated until I was certain Leah's orientation was all my fault, and that I'd failed her by not noticing the signs and channelling her back onto the right path.

The truth is, if anything it was Jamie's feminine side I worried about. It never occurred to me Leah was anything other than a tomboy, and she'd never been any other way. From birth she'd been the aggressor, the boss, the strong one. It was the way she was. Not that those characteristics necessarily had an underlying meaning: Leah hadn't changed, she was as nature made her. That was it. Nature made her the way she is, and nothing I could have said or done would have changed her. Nor would I have wanted to.

As I sat at my desk staring blankly at the wall with thoughts cascading through my brain, the phone startled me from my stupor.

'Is that you, Rose?'

'Yes. Oh, hello Mike.'

'You OK?'

'Er, yes. Sure.'

'I just rang to see how the visit went?'

'Visit?'

'Allie's visit to Bianca?'

'Of course. Sorry. Well, she didn't say a lot, but I thought she seemed happier afterwards.'

'Rose, are you sure you're all right? You sound a bit – strange.'

'Oh, it's nothing. A bit of a family thing, that's all.' Mortified I found myself choking up. I've no idea why because I wasn't unhappy. Just emotional.

'Rose, you know what they say – a trouble shared and all that.'

I shook my head and swallowed, deliberately brightening my tone before I replied. 'It's just something I've got to come to terms with. It's been one of those weeks…' It's not every week you discover your husband has impregnated a woman half your age, and that your only daughter is a lesbian (There, I've said it. My daughter is a lesbian).

'How are you getting on with your packing?'

'Oh, I'm getting there. You know.'

'We're in Cambridge tomorrow and Ethan has a hot date, so I was thinking of driving over to give you a hand to start moving some stuff into the garage, if you're ready.?'

'That's very kind of you Mike. I was beginning to wonder exactly how I'd manage.'

'Right, then. See you tomorrow.'

The phone was dead before I had a chance to say goodbye. Fancy him thinking about that! Mike was one of those rare guys who never ceased to surprise me. Unlike Ethan. I wondered if his hot date was with Madeleine.

Mike's concern had awakened my need to share my turmoil, so I rang Gina. As I imparted the latest episode in my family saga, I was half afraid of her reaction.

'Are you telling me you never suspected?' Gina said, surprised.

'Of course not. Why? Did you?'

'Darling Rosie. I think we've all had our suspicions. And I can understand you being upset – you know, about the grandchildren thing – but what does it matter? Besides, she can have a child if she really wants one, and she's still Leah, the same as she's always been. It doesn't really change anything.'

'I know that, Gina. I'll always love her no matter what.'

'And I bet Jamie will give you your grandkids – sooner than you might want them.'

'What do you mean?'

'Only that he's all man, Rosie, or did you think he was gay, too?'

I know she meant it in jest, but it was too close for comfort, and I rebuffed her huffily.

'Sorry Rosie, I shouldn't have joked about it. So when are you going to meet the girlfriend then?'

'Kirsten – I've told you about her. She's nice. Very pretty.'

'No – Leah's.'

'Oh. Yes. Her name's Dawn. Next weekend, I think. Christ, Gina, I hope she's not one of those big butch ones with a crewcut, like you see on Cell Block H.'

'They're not all like that: I've got a couple of gay clients who are totally feminine and gorgeous. And they never have to worry about contraception. I tell you Rosie, if I had to sleep with some of the minging blokes you see about, I'd think about batting for the other side myself.'

You could always trust Gina to bring things into perspective, even if it did lower the tone, and as I said goodbye I could feel the gloom beginning to lift. While I was in lighter spirits, I rang my son.

I know it was irrational, but I was aggrieved that Jamie had kept Leah's secret. I shouldn't have been in the least surprised as they'd always shared everything, but I'd imagined they'd grown apart in recent years, and no longer harboured confidences. Obviously I was wrong.

It was not difficult to stem my aggression when I heard Jamie's sheepish tone. I felt sorry for him: he'd been so worried that I'd be devastated by his sister's confession, poor lad.

He had no hang-ups about it, so that was one worry off my mind.

'Have you met Leah's…partner?' I couldn't resist asking.

'Dawn? Yeah, she's great. Waste of a good woman.'

'Jamie!' Well, I had to pay lip service to motherhood. 'Does that mean she's...er...nice and feminine?'

'She's a cracker, Mum. Really fit. Not butch, if that's what you're worried about.'

If I'd had any hopes that this was all one big, wicked wind-up or that Leah had fallen for this Dawn because she was very masculine, they dimmed at my son's candid words.

I had another sleepless night, and pitiable as it sounds, my biggest torment was the effect of Leah's revelation on her father. Not that I cared if he was hurt/mortified/suicidal. If there was anyone to blame it was him, encouraging her to act like the son he wanted, buying her Man United kits and football boots, teaching her how to bait a fishing line. He was never sympathetic to Jamie's "arty-farty ways" as he called them.

When my mother bought Leah Barbie and Ken instead of another Action Man, she made Action Man garrotte Ken and had Barbie shacked up with a long hidden Sindy doll. Obviously I am guilty of dereliction of duty in not recognising the message my child was conveying all those years ago.

My brain was doing gymnastics, trying to distinguish fact from fantasy. Common sense and reading Cosmopolitan told me no one was at fault, and that being gay was a perfectly acceptable way of life.

I eventually drifted off to sleep having determined I will neither hang my head in shame, nor deny Leah's lesbianism. So there.

Mike arrived at 11am just as I was making my weekly concession to cooking – Sunday brunch - better known in my circle as a Motorway Special.

Tiny had already breakfasted on muesli and prunes or

something equally vile, and had accompanied Allie out riding. He didn't ride, which was a bonus as I don't think Bella's stables contain any carthorses, but he followed in the 4x4.

Anyhow, Mike and I sat down at the kitchen table with cholesterol laden plates. It's Murphy's Law, isn't it? The higher the calories, the better the taste. (That Murphy will be a eunuch if the cellulite-harbouring women of the world ever manage to get hold of him.)

After a while, during which my thoughts had once again returned to Leah's revelation, Mike interrupted them.

'Rose. I know something's worrying you. Are you going to let me help?'

He was regarding me with clear blue eyes, his expression perturbed.

'It's not a problem, just something I've got to learn to live with.'

\ 'You're not ill, are you?'

'No, nothing like that.' He was worried about me, and even if it was only that he was afraid there'd be no one to care for Allie, I felt I could trust him. He's that sort of guy. And anyway, I wanted to gauge an outsider's reaction to my disclosure.

I took a deep breath. 'My daughter, Leah, told me yesterday that she's gay.'

I waited for the look of distaste, but it didn't come. Instead he reached for my hand. 'So?'

'So…that's it.'

'Was it a shock?'

'Absolutely. Until I started thinking back.'

'And blaming yourself, I guess?'

I nodded. He still held my hand in his. It was large and just a little rough.

'You shouldn't. It's nobody's fault. She's still the same person.'

'Of course she is,' I said quickly taking my hand away. 'I'll love and support her no matter what. It's just a lot to think about. Her father will be devastated and I'm very afraid he may reject her altogether. It would destroy her, and I don't think I can bear that. She's only just heard his new wife is expecting and she's already upset about that...' I knew I was gabbling.

'Ssh, calm down Rose'

'She wants me to meet her new partner.'

'Rose. If she has a partner, hopefully she will support her, and if her father can't accept the way things are, it's his loss. Tell me, how long did it take you to realise you were married to a self-centred asshole?' He looked and sounded a bit like Clint Eastwood as he said that. When he was younger, of course.

My eyes flew to his face to see a quirky grin.

'A lot longer than it should have done,' I said sheepishly. 'But he hasn't always been one – I think it came with age.'

'Senile dementia, then.'

'Something like that.'

'He'd have to be going senile to prefer some airhead to a woman like you, Rose.'

My eyes flew to his face, but before I could even think of a reply he stood up and turned towards the sink with his plate.

'I'll just put these to soak, and then we should get over to your place. I can only stay a few hours.'

The remainder of the day was spent heaving boxes and transferring them to one of the garages at Lime Cottage. Despite his slim frame, Mike had an amazing amount of strength and stamina and I was grateful indeed for his help. Nevertheless there was still a lot to do, and time was running short.

'We're in Southampton next weekend, and then we've a day before the gig in Bournemouth, so I'll come next weekend to help you finish the job' Mike said as we ate some of the service-station sandwiches I'd stuck in my fridge.

Regardless of his reasons, I was glad of the offer as it would save me having to hire a man with a van. And he's good company. My big furniture is being collected and packed for storage the following week.

'Thank you, Mike. If you're sure you can spare the time, that would be great.'

He nodded and chewed on his sandwiches.

'Sorry they're a bit dry, but they're only just past the sell-by date.'

He looked with mock horror at the small portion left on his plate. 'I know men are out of favour in your life, but I think poisoning's a bit extreme.'

I couldn't help grinning. 'Idiot!'

It's a shame there aren't more men like him about.

SEPTEMBER

I've received a rare missive from my mother that Linda thoughtfully redirected to Lime Cottage. She's threatening to come over for a holiday. Somehow she's latched on to the fact I am Ethan Hammer's assistant, and imagines I am living in the lap of luxury and part of the showbiz 'A' List. "Naturally, she always supported my decision to leave Simon, and besides, she hasn't seen her grandchildren in ages."

I've always been under the impression the less time she spent with the twins, the better, and that she infinitely prefers the company of my brother's un-mannerly brats. And I know the twins can't stand her constant fussing and whingeing. She was apoplectic when Jamie said he wanted to go to art school and possibly become a fashion designer – apparently all the designers she knows are as "bent as a butcher's hook, and she didn't want her grandson associated with their kind". (I didn't even hint the thought had occurred to me, and I never tried to dissuade him.)

But we both got it wrong. Whatever will she have to say about Leah?

Bingo! I'll write and tell her – that will put a stop to her gallop! I'll also let her know Ethan is away and unlikely to return for months, if at all. I hope she doesn't discover I am also his daughter's guardian or she'll be telling everyone she's related to him.

The one thing this circus does not need is my mother.

The circus continues. Yesterday's Call of the Day was from Simon. Leah had obviously rung him.

'I don't believe it!' He could do a voice-over for Victor Meldrew.

'Hello Simon, what's the matter now?' I was icy calm,

knowing I could predict every moment of this conversation.

'Don't give me that innocent tone. Leah – *your* daughter – she's…she's a…she's a…'

'Lesbian.'

'I knew you were in on it!'

'How's that, Simon? Do you imagine I persuaded her not to bother with men after your faithlessness? In which case it would be your behaviour to blame, not mine.'

'But she was always perfectly normal as a child. She was my little girl, for Christ's sake.'

'She's still your little girl, Simon. The only thing that's changed is that you're now married to one.'

'And she was vile about the baby. Angel asked her if she'd like to be a godmother, and she said "not to anything you two could produce". It's probably sour grapes if she's determined to be a dyke…Oh god, I can't stand it. I'll never be able to hold my head up again at the Golf Club…'

'I fail to see why not. Half the members are chasing each others' teenage daughters, and the rest are rogering that camp barman. Get real, Simon. Our daughter is gay. And for all your denigrating remarks, our son is not. Live with it, or lose them both.'

I replaced the receiver with great deliberation.

How could I ever have thought I loved that shallow, self-centred bigot?

The good news is that Allie is getting on famously with Tiny. The bad news, she's not getting on at all at school since the new term started.

I've had the mealy mouthed school assistant on the phone again complaining she'd forgotten her PE kit even though I packed it in her bag myself. Also there was uncompleted homework, and an incident in the toilets that ended with accusations of Allie picking on Zara Smythe.

Back home I questioned her about the missing kit. There was the usual shrug.

'Dunno.'

'Where is it, then? You left home with it this morning.'

'I must have dropped it somewhere.'

'Don't be ridiculous, Allie. You couldn't possibly lose anything that big and not notice.'

Another shrug.

'I want to search your bag. I can't believe it's not there.'

'Am I to have no privacy at all? I'm not a child, you know.'

'Then act your age.' I held out my hand for her schoolbag. She slung it gracelessly onto the table.

The PE kit was certainly not there.

'Allie.' The light disappeared from the kitchen door as Tiny loomed in the frame.

She looked at the big man warily. 'I gave it away.'

'You gave it away?' I couldn't disguise my annoyance. 'For god's sake, why? Those trainers alone cost £90.'

Again the shrug. I wanted to throttle her.

'Allie. Are you being bullied?' Though he spoke quietly, Tiny's words brooked no prevarication.

Allie hung her head, and I could have slapped myself.

'What about the homework you haven't been doing?' I prodded more gently.

'I did do it.'

'Then why does the school say you didn't?'

A shrug.

'And why have you been picking on Zara?'

'I didn't.'

I knew we'd get nothing more from her. The problem seemed likely to be bullying in one form or other, and I suspected she was being set up to take the fall. Undoubtedly jealousy was at the centre of it all.

But though the problem may have been identified, the solution will not be so straightforward. I told Tiny I would run it past Mike.

Next weekend it's Gina and Lloyd's wedding party and Tiny is quite happy for me to stay over at the Knutsford Park Hotel. I went to a reception there once before, but have never stayed so am looking forward to a dollop of five-star luxury and a good night out.

I had a satisfying day shopping in honour of the occasion, achieving the purchase of a wonderful new dress (size 12!?) which I'd feel inordinately guilty about if it weren't for the mega-bucks that will be filling my bank account next week when the house is sold – not to mention keeping that wretched bank manager off my back. I was also fortunate enough to obtain perfectly matching shoes which cost almost as much as the frock, and have booked to have my hair done on Saturday morning.

I'll worry about the credit card bill when it arrives. I'd pay it outright except it would go against all my most dearly held principles and take away the entire essence of plastic power.

Yes, this is a fundamental example of female logic.

I've invited Heidi over for a game of Scrabble. There was a definite gleam in Tiny's eye when I asked him if he'd be interested in joining us and I can't help feeling I'll soon become surplus to requirements. Nevertheless, Tiny seems to be a really genuine, gentle guy, and I'd love to see Heidi with someone who will treat her well, so if it works out no one will be more pleased than me. Though his lifestyle must be rather erratic, given the nature of his job…and Heidi has only just settled in her new home. Now I'm really jumping the gun.

I suddenly remembered Mike's coming over at the weekend – I'd completely forgotten about the clash of dates when he offered to come and help me finish packing, so I rang to explain and he flippantly said he wouldn't mind accompanying me to Gina's do. When I realised he was half serious I thought, why not? The invitation gave me the option to bring a partner, so I asked him (with matching flippancy) if he'd like me to ring and book him a room. His next revelation left me speechless when he stated that Ethan was also coming, as Madeleine's guest, so he'd see to the bookings himself.

That subversive she-wolf! It's bad enough making a play for

my boss right under my nose, but to bring him into our inner circle is really pushing it. Not that I was really that surprised: Maddy has always been totally self-absorbed.

I rang Gina.

'It'll be great to have Ethan as a guest,' she said, still sounding as if she were on Cloud Nine. 'I knew she was bringing someone but didn't know it was him. I expect she'll steal my thunder with a Grand Entrance - but that's her all over. As far as she's concerned I guess we'll just have to bite the bullet.'

Or fire it at the underhanded, thick-skinned witch.

Allie was looking so drawn and miserable when we picked her up from school I suggested a trip to McDonald's. Though she agreed as if she was doing me a favour, it did little to lighten her spirits, but that evening, miracle of miracles, Ethan rang to ask her if she'd like to go somewhere on Sunday. I have no idea if he mentioned he'd be in the area because of the wedding party and his hot date with You-Know-Who, but Allie was happier than I'd seen her for days, so I wasn't about to say anything to suggest her treat was merely a by-product of her father's sex-life.

I don't know why I feel so nettled about the whole affair. Even if pigs flew and I was the sole target of Ethan's lust, I couldn't cope with the constant barrage of adoration he faces whichever way he turns. It must be very wearing. And very hard to resist. I've had one experience of being a cuckold (or whatever the female equivalent may be) and have no intention of lining myself up for another.

On a day to day basis I don't find it in the least difficult to ignore his boyish appeal, and the red hot flame of unrequited passion I felt for him in my teenage years has long since cooled.

I just wish he wouldn't keep trying to re-ignite it with his sexy looks and stirring suggestions, as I know seduction is simply second nature to him.

So I have to remember to keep my feet firmly on the ground

at all times when dealing with him. Though even a literal interpretation of this is no guarantee of a safe passage. Ha! No pun intended. Or was it a Freudian slip?

Yesterday Allie came home with felt-tip writing over the back of her white blouse announcing "My ma's an alkie slut", and a black eye.

Having dragged the facts from Allie under threat of every dire consequence I could think of, before St Hilda's had a chance to call and complain about her behaviour, I was sufficiently incensed to drive over to the convent and demand to see the Reverend Mother.

She was apparently au fait with the incident and had the grace to apologise "for the damage to Allegra's clothing."

'Never mind her clothing, what about the mental damage? What about the anguish this sort of malice and bullying causes?' I seethed.

'Come, come, Ms Grant, I'd hardly call it malice. You're imagining things. It's just high spirits. And Allegra is not the easiest of pupils.'

'I'm aware she can be difficult, but that's no excuse for standing by and allowing bullying and spitefulness. She has a black eye – or am I imagining that too?'

The RM now took on even more crow-like characteristics, looking down her beaky nose at me with beady eyes.

'As I understand it, she slipped in the lavatories and knocked herself on a wash basin. I'd hardly call that spiteful.'

Allie's version detailed being cornered and thumped by four other girls – led by Zara Smythe – and I was aghast at the naivety of the woman in charge of her wellbeing.

'I cannot believe anyone who knows teenagers could be taken in by such utter…hogwash.'

She rose and drew herself up to her full height.

'*Ms* Grant, you have questioned my authority, my veracity, and my competence. I therefore question, under the circumstances, whether or not your - ward – should be entrusted to the care of St Hilda's. It seems you have very little faith in us. Perhaps if Allegra had a little more faith and humility she would not arouse such hostility. Faith is the key, Ms Grant.'

I stood up too. I could see my confrontation was pointless in the face of such an ostrich-like attitude. I also felt desperately sorry for Allie having to endure it on a daily basis. And I was seething.

'Faith may move mountains, Reverend Mother, but it takes patience and understanding to win the trust of a troubled teenager, and you're right, I have no faith in St Hilda's, or it's outdated practices. And as far as I am concerned, Allegra Hammer is no longer a pupil. Good afternoon.'

Before I reached my car, breathless with righteous indignation, I started to regret my diatribe. Unless Ethan agreed to withdraw Allie from St Hilda's, I'd made things ten times worse for her. Not to mention demeaning myself if I was forced to apologise.

Oh dear. Be that as it may, I still think I was right. St Hilda's may well have a brilliant academic record, but for Allie I believe there are more important and long-reaching issues than ten shining GCSEs and a set of well-worn rosary beads.

I haven't told Allie the entire transcript of my confrontation with the RM (i.e. she's no longer a pupil) but have kept her home from school. It's not that I'm putting off breaking the news to Ethan, but I've decided it might be prudent to discuss the situation with Mike first to see where his sympathies lie, and hopefully gain some support for my case.

Of course, I shall have to come up with a viable alternative school so am checking out the possibilities. Leah and Jamie went to the local comprehensive and both did very well, but I think somewhere smaller would better suit Allie. I know of a private school, Michaelmas, where Roman Doyle's children are pupils, and I believe it now has some of the best facilities in the county. Also there is no uniform – not that I'd normally advocate this, but it would certainly save the hassle and cost (both mental and physical) of having to buy another. The drawback is that it's further away. Though this may not be my problem if Ethan takes exception to my wrangle with the Reverend Mother.

I should have let Allie know she didn't have to return to St Hilda's. Even though I'd let her stay home, she was skulking in her room with her TV continually tuned to MTV, and refused to eat anything except the occasional bag of crisps. I could understand why she was despondent, but as I told Tiny when he queried her frame of mind, I thought it best to leave her to come round in her own time.

Tiny not only agreed that I'd done the right thing in telling the Reverend Mother where to stick her school, but proposed to go round and reiterate our point of view. As I didn't know him sufficiently to be sure he wasn't threatening violence, I refused his offer.

Anyhow, I was expecting a call from Michaelmas and then planned to break the news to Mike, and hope he agreed with my actions: and of course, as he knew how to handle Ethan, that he would then relay the whole incident to him. Rather him than me.

The call I was expecting came. Deciding it was pointless to try to pull the wool over anyone's eyes, I'd already explained Allegra's circumstances in an email to Michaelmas, and a very pleasant-sounding woman said yes, they had a vacancy, and that subject to Allegra visiting the school and deciding if she liked it (that was an eye-opener!) they would be happy to take her immediately.

To me it sounded just what Allie needed and I couldn't wait to tell her that her sentence at St Hilda's was over.

Although it was 9.30am she hadn't made an appearance, so I knocked on her door, and receiving no response, pushed it open, calling her name.

The smell hit me immediately: stale alcohol and vomit.

The thick curtains were closed and fighting down panic I turned on the lights. Allie was sprawled across her bed, her face white and vomit everywhere. Beside the bed was a bottle of whisky on its side, what was left of its contents soaking into the rug.

I stood over her, calling her name, shaking her thin shoulders.

She moaned and opened her eyes and I could have cried with relief. At least she was alive.

Tiny must have heard the commotion as he suddenly appeared beside me and leaned over her, immediately appreciating the situation, but his suspicions put me on the verge of hysteria.

'Ms Allie,' he said, his big face close to hers. 'Have you taken anything else apart from the whisky?'

Her eyes were closed again and she tried to shake her head and winced.

'Nothing else at all? No weed or coke? No pills?'

'No!' she ground out the word, then wretched. She eased herself onto her elbows. 'My head hurts so-oo'. Now there were tears in her eyes.

I was angry, not at Allie, but at myself for not preventing this, for not telling her she didn't have to return to the convent. I felt only pity for her: spoiled she may have been, but she was still a child, and obviously very unhappy.

'Come on,' I said gently, trying to ignore the vomit in her hair. 'Let's get you cleaned up. A nice hot bath and some paracetamol will do the trick.'

I guided her into the bathroom and made her sit on the loo seat while the bath ran. Meanwhile I went back into the bedroom to change her sheets, only to find Tiny had already stripped the bed. He returned with clean sheets as I was clearing the remains of the teenager's binge.

'Do you think we should call a doctor?' I asked him.

He shook his head. 'I don't think so. If she'd got alcoholic poisoning she'd be a lot worse. I have some rehydration salts – they should help her – and a good sleep.'

I went back and ensured Allie was safely in the bath then returned to help Tiny with the bed. Not that he needed much help – his reach was so long he could tuck in both sides at the same time.

'I feel terrible. I should have watched her more closely. I should have told her she didn't have to go back to that bloody school!' I was close to tears myself.

In one stride Tiny was beside me and I felt myself enfolded by massive arms. 'Don't worry Ms Rosie, it's not your fault. Miss Allie has many problems and that school was no good for her.'

'I know,' I said when he let me go. 'But I think there might be more to it – and I intend to get to the bottom of it. She told me she hates the taste of alcohol. Getting drunk was a cry for help.'

'You are right, I'm sure, Ms Rosie. Are you going to tell Ethan?'

His question caught me off guard: I thought he would tell his boss anyway, but it seemed he was leaving it to my discretion.

'If it's just about the school, then perhaps not. If there's any other reason, then I'll probably have to. But I still have to tell him about the school situation. Anyhow, I'll have to discuss it with Allie first.'

'Discuss what with me?' Allie said as she emerged from the bathroom looking clean but pale.

'Get into bed, Allie, and we'll talk.'

Without hesitation Allie complied with my request, and Tiny turned to go.

'I'll bring the rehydration salts – and some dry toast,' he said, not waiting for a reply.

I regarded my charge who looked so young and vulnerable with her damp hair and pallid face, and she regarded me with big eyes, for once not wearing an expression of defiance. She almost looked scared and I could have wept for her.

'Oh Allie,' I said and took her limp hand. 'You must feel awful. There's nothing much worse than a hangover. Are you going to tell me why you did it?'

'I'm not going back to that school, you know, ever.' The defiant look was back.

'Allie, you don't have to. I should have told you yesterday, but I haven't discussed it with your father yet...'

'I don't care what he says, I'm not going back.'

'Actually, you won't be able to, no matter he says. I'm afraid I had a bit of an... altercation with the Reverend Mother.'

Her face brightened. 'Did you hit her?'

'No, of course not Allie. But suffice to say you wouldn't be welcomed back. There is another school, Michaelmas, much nicer,' the frown returned, but I plodded on. 'Boys and girls and no uniforms. If your father agrees, you might be able to go there – if you like it.'

The latter sentence seemed to mollify her. Then she changed the subject completely.

'Can I get a new mobile phone number?'

'Yes, I suppose so. What's wrong with the old one?'

'Nothing – except I gave it to... some people and I don't want them to have my number any longer. And I might need a new Facebook account.'

The penny dropped: 'Have they been sending you nasty messages?'

She nodded. I'd heard about cyber-bullying.

'Do you want to tell me about it?'

She shook her head, then winced again and closed her eyes.

'No. It's no big deal. I'm used to thickos saying things about my parents.'

'OK Allie. Go to sleep now. You'll feel better when you wake up.'

I think she was asleep before I reached the door, and Tiny was standing there with the rehydration drink and toast. I placed it on her bedside table and crept out.

Now I just had to break the news to her father. I was about to ring Mike, but still traumatised by Allie's whisky binge (that could have been so much worse) I chickened out and decided to save it for the weekend and tell them both face to face.

Heidi came round for her game of Scrabble dressed to kill – and bearing a Chocolate Orange which I thought was rather forward, the flighty madam. Seriously though, we had a pleasant evening even though, as predicted, I felt like a spare whatsit at a wedding after the first five minutes.

Tiny is a charmer, always smiling and courteous. He is also very clever at placing his words and won quite a few games. It transpires he's been taking a distance learning course and is awaiting the results of his final exam to become an accountant. When he joked he'd be going from people crunching to number crunching, Heidi laughed her best tinkling laugh. She had listened in rapt attention to every sound he uttered, jumping up to refill his glass (non-alcoholic grape juice) and fluttering her eyelashes so hard I could feel the draught from across the table.

However, her feminine wiles won the day, and they're going out on Monday, and if Tony, the relief minder, agrees to do Saturday night as well, Tiny may come to the wedding party as Heidi's guest.

I'm getting quite good at playing cupid: first I line up Maddy for Ethan – albeit inadvertently - and now I've set Heidi up with Tiny.

What a shame my gift only works in the third person. No, strike that. I like being single. I really do.

Not having to face St Hilda's, Allie has been almost human, though the bruising round her eye is so many colours it would make a macaw jealous. This morning she offered to go to the shop for the newspapers and some bread. She bought herself a teen mag and we had a cup of coffee and settled down to our respective reading matter.

I was a more than halfway through my Daily Mail when my attention was caught by the face of a small boy with tears running down his face, in the arms of a stylish blonde who was holding him like an accessory, smiling brilliantly, and seemingly unaware of his distress. The blonde was leaning into a dark-eyed, fit-looking youth.

Though I hadn't met Fen I recognised him immediately from the framed photos Ethan keeps in the sitting room, and the accompanying report confirmed it was indeed his son. He'd been snapped at Heathrow "saying goodbye to his mother, actress Marnie Mitchell, as she left for the Bahamas with her latest squeeze Antonio Berretta Junior, 27, heir to the Berretta Recycling fortune...The beautiful divorcee, is the former wife of born-again pop idol Ethan Hammer, father of Fender, 6."

They always say a picture paints a thousand words, and my heart went out to Fen (7!). He looked so miserable and his mother might have been posing with a stuffed toy for all the attention she was paying him.

God, these self-obsessed people make me sick!

I must have said it aloud because Allie looked up from her reading and asked me what was wrong. I passed her the paper and she stared at it for a long time before thrusting it back to me.

'Yeah, well,' she said in her usual careless tone. 'He'll soon get used to it.'

But I saw the surreptitious movement as she wiped her eye with the back of her hand.

What a night! I haven't laughed so much since I heard about Simon's Disneyland whiplash.

Gina and Lloyd's party was brilliant. The hotel was gorgeous, the food delicious, the booze flowed, and there was a decibel-controlled disco, a live band, and an up and coming comedian as cabaret.

Further entertainment was provided by Maddy endeavouring to keep a rein on Ethan as he flirted and danced with almost every female in the room, including Gina's granny. She (Maddy) looked ravishing, of course, and soon drew her own circle of admirers, though in her partner's absence she kept latching on to Mike. I have to say he looked very elegant in his dinner jacket, but I was irritated to hell at the way she acted the coquette with him every time Ethan spun past with another female, though he didn't seem to mind.

Mind you, she did precisely the same to Tiny (Ethan had been quite happy for Tony to mind Allie for the evening) - or at least she tried to. Heidi was having none of it and I don't know what she whispered to him, but he left Maddy's side like a rocket and avoided her like the plague for the rest of the evening. Knowing he's a health freak, I wouldn't be surprised if Heidi hadn't labelled Maddy as the carrier of some highly contagious infection. (Probably Jean-Claude's rash.)

I also had my share of being in the spotlight – more than once, actually, when Ethan grabbed me for a couple of dances. There was one particular slow number during which I was singularly aware of his body welded to mine, and given the party atmosphere and alcohol intake, it was very difficult to ignore his whispered pledges that he was going to have my body before much longer. I reminded him what he'd said about good secretaries being hard to find, and he replied that I was now a personal assistant, and that was a different matter altogether as I was supposed to assist him in any way he chose.

I guess it's way too late to ask for a job description.

Anyway, his carnal plans for me certainly didn't prevent him from lurching towards the lift with his tongue halfway down Maddy's throat, and his hands not visible at all.

For all that, Mike was a lovely escort – and a very good dancer. He saw me to my room and I have to confess to an alcohol-fuelled snog, which was rather enjoyable. In fact, very enjoyable. Though now I recall Mike actually unhooking my hands from round his neck and saying he'd see me at breakfast. How embarrassing!

The demon drink has a lot to answer for. Though in my own defence, however inebriated, goodnight gropes normally have the tendency to sober me up pretty quickly.

We all had breakfast at the hotel; my head was filled with cotton wool, but you can't beat a Full English to soak up the alcohol. Anyway, Mike didn't treat me like a pariah, and came to sit with me, which was provident as I needed to speak to him about Allie and St Hilda's.

He was one hundred per cent behind my action, especially as I could offer a viable alternative in Michaelmas, and said he'd back me up when I broke the news to Ethan - which I would have to do there and then as he was driving back to Cambridge after his outing with Allie. So fortified with yet another high dosage of cholesterol, (and probably still a tot or two of vodka) I girded my loins (or should that be guarded?) and made my way over to Ethan's table. He'd been primed by Mike and sent Maddy on her way in readiness for our "business discussion".

Though I'd allowed Maddy's behaviour to get under my skin, I felt quite sorry for her when I saw the bleak look on her face as she left the table. It was there for only a second before she'd lifted her chest, flicked her hair, set her supermodel smile, then glided cat-like across the room, blowing goodbye kisses to all her new admirers.

She'd been with Ethan last night, and maybe she'd have him for a few more, but judging by the way he still flirted shamelessly with anyone who'd let him, I wouldn't want to be in her shoes for all the tea in Tesco's. Well, maybe a small spoonful.

Ethan, at first angered by my tale of woe regarding St Hilda's, did an about-face when I described her unhappiness and injury.

'Bloody Catholics!' he said unreasonably. 'You find out who did it, Mike.'

'Why? So you can set Tiny on a bunch of silly schoolgirls? Don't you think we've got enough PR problems?' Mike was unusually ruffled.

'Never mind the PR problems – it would just make things worse for Allie,' I said.

'So what are we going to do about her? I don't want her going to the local comprehensive.'

'There's nothing wrong with the local comprehensive.' Now *I* was ruffled. 'My twins went there – and they're both at university. However, I agree it's not the right place for Allie.'

I went on to describe Michaelmas and the enquiries I'd made, and Ethan agreed we should give it a try. I thought it prudent not to mention that, in line with the school's policy, the decision would ultimately be Allie's. Nevertheless, as we made our way to the car park he was still chuntering about his daughter's treatment at St Hilda's and vowing to sue the convent.

'For god's sake, give it a rest,' Mike said. 'Let the poor kid put it behind her. Let's just go and break the good news to her. Besides we already know who the ringleader was.' I glared at him but he continued. 'And you'll find out as Allie's no longer going riding.'

'You mean it was Horse-features' kid? I'll sue the little mare...'

Mike and I looked at each other and grinned.

'Ignore him,' Mike said rolling his eyes at Ethan. 'After he's had a skinful he's not happy unless he has someone to have a pop at.'

Ethan got in the Porsche and spun out of the hotel entrance, and Mike and I followed at a more leisurely pace.

'Bloody idiot,' Mike said mildly. 'But he thinks the world of Allie – and Fen, of course.'

That reminded me of the picture in the paper and I told Mike about it.

'I told you Marnie's a bitch.'

'I wonder who'll be looking after the poor little chap while she's away?' I was musing out loud. 'I suppose there are grandparents?'

'She doesn't have parents. She was created in a test-tube in a lab researching beauty without soul or sensitivity.'

I couldn't help grinning.

'Seriously, Marnie hasn't any family, except a sister who refuses to have anything to do with her. So I expect he's with a nanny.'

'*A* nanny? Doesn't he have a permanent one?'

'Well, put it like this, the nanny will be full-time, but hardly permanent as they seem to change every few months.'

Poor little kid.

We were about halfway back to Great Ashley when my mobile rang.

It was Tony, the minder, and he sounded panic-stricken.

'It's Miss Allie,' he said. 'She's disappeared. I went in to call her this morning and – she was gone, Mrs – what am I going to do?'

'Oh god!' Stiff with fear, I relayed the message to Mike who grabbed the phone.

'Stay put. We'll be back in 15.'

'Ethan will be there first,' I reminded him.

'Get his number, will you?'

With trembling fingers I dialled Ethan's mobile.

After an age he answered it in his usual mid-Atlantic manner. 'Yo?'

Mike signalled me to hand him the phone, which I did - praying there were no stray police patrol cars about.

'Ethan, I'm sure there's no cause for panic, but Tony's just called to say Allie's missing. Don't do anything until I get there. See you in ten.'

Not giving the boss a chance to reply he cut the line, and we drove in silence the rest of the way.

I say silence, but with my brain in overdrive and my heart hammering hard, I'm sure it could be heard above the roaring of the diesel engine.

Naturally, my first feeling was guilt. I should have been there. I shouldn't have suggested Tiny come to Gina's party. I shouldn't have introduced him to Heidi. I should have been there...

Of course, if she'd been kidnapped, would it have made any difference if I had been? Tony obviously didn't hear anything...Oh god! What if the psycho who'd written those sick letters had hold of her? I'd never forgive myself.

All too soon we were back at Lime Cottage. Tiny and Ethan were there ahead of us: Tony was distraught and Ethan incensed.

'I never heard a thing, Boss,' Tony was saying. 'We watched Ancient Aliens on TV and she went to bed about 10.30pm. I knocked on her door to see if she was OK and said goodnight about 11pm, and she sounded fine.'

'Had you been drinking?' Ethan glowered suspiciously at the stockily built man.

'No, Mr Hammer. I never touch alcohol. I take good care of my body.'

'It's true, Boss,' Tiny affirmed.

'Right,' said Mike, immediately taking charge. 'We'll search the grounds thoroughly, make some calls to see if she's with a friend - and if there's still no joy, we call in the police.'

Less than an hour later the police arrived headed by Detective Chief Inspector Andrews himself.

We'd searched high and low, opened all manner of unlikely cupboards, and phoned practically everyone she'd spoken to in the past few weeks, even the horse-faced Smythes. Nothing. I was sick with worry. We all were. Ethan looked pale and shaky (though I'm sure his condition was partly due to the massive amount of alcohol he'd consumed the previous night). No that's unfair. We were all hung over – and it was his daughter who was missing.

'Are any of her things gone?' DCI Andrews asked. 'Such as her toothbrush? Extra clothes? Cash?'

None of us had thought to look.

'I'll look,' I said, glad of something to do.

'Try not to touch anything,' the policeman warned me. 'It already looks as if an army has marched over the crime scene.'

'Crime scene?' I heard Ethan exclaim as I went up the stairs, careful not to touch the bannister unless I put fingerprints on it. 'Do you really think that?'

I was unnerved by the seriousness of the implication too. Not that I hadn't already considered it, but to hear my fears being expressed so openly was horrifying.

Two minutes later there was a chink in the black cloud. Allie's toothbrush was missing. And so were the ripped jeans she wore with pride, also her favourite hooded fleece, and the small backpack she kept her purse and makeup in.

I double-checked before I told anyone. And then I looked on her bed, and Piglet was missing. She'd told me, rather shame-faced, that she'd had the stuffed character since her father bought it when she was two. And she never went anywhere without it.

I broke the news.

'Well, that puts a different aspect on it,' the policeman said. 'At least we know she hasn't been kidnapped. She's run away.'

'So? My daughter's still missing.' Ethan glowered

'Yes, Mr Hammer. And as she's a minor we'll put the wheels in motion to find her. But as she appears to have gone of her own accord, we no longer have to organise immediate search parties, and road blocks and the like.'

'What do I pay my taxes for?' Ethan exploded. 'For you lot to sit around in your Noddy cars eating fish 'n' chips while you wait for some poor bugger to do over 70mph?'

Mike reached and put a heavy hand on Ethan's shoulder. 'Shut up!' he hissed grimly. 'I'm sorry Chief Inspector, I'm afraid Mr Hammer is overwrought. I'm sure he'll be making another donation to the Police Benevolent Fund...'

The policeman nodded curtly and turned to the door. 'That's his prerogative, sir. Well, I'll leave you in the capable hands of my sergeant. Try not to worry. I'm sure she'll turn up safe and sound. Fourteen's a difficult age – you'll probably find there's some boy involved. Good day to you.'

Ethan muttered 'Wanker!' but if the sergeant heard him, thankfully he ignored it. Though I'm sure he smirked.

Sergeant Owen and his sidekick, a very attractive policewoman called Sandra, were very efficient and dealt with everything in a sympathetic manner that had even the distraught father calming down and trying to be helpful.

I felt dreadful. Perhaps Allie was afraid that Michaelmas would be just as awful as St Hilda's. I couldn't believe that she was still being bullied over the airwaves as we'd been out the very next day and bought her a new SIM card for her phone, and set up a new Facebook account. And I really believed we were making progress in other directions: she was no longer constantly hostile.

What she'd done was thoughtless and selfish...but she'd so been looking forward to going out with Ethan that afternoon, it didn't make sense. Had something else happened in the past few days to upset her enough to run off? I wracked my brain to recall everything she'd said, to pick up on something significant I may have missed, but it was useless.

My emotions swung between anger and anxiety, censure and sympathy, and most of all I felt totally impotent. Which was more than I can say for Ethan. He was being given the third degree (quite unnecessarily, I felt) by PC Sandra, and despite the circumstances, seemed to be enjoying every minute of it. I think she must be a fan as I'm sure the police don't normally dribble when conducting an interview. I tell you, the man just can't help it - he must have been born with a sycophancy inducing gene that turns sensible women into simpering idiots.

Unable to sit still any longer, I went into the kitchen to make some coffee.

Tiny had gone with Tony who knew the local area and they were driving around in the hope of spotting Allie. I think they just couldn't bear sitting and doing nothing. I knew how they felt.

Mike followed me out and gave me a sympathetic grimace. 'Try not to worry, Rose. I'm sure she'll turn up. Allie's never had to rough it. I bet she comes home with her tail between her legs before nightfall.'

'I hope you're right.' I didn't add that whatever happened I knew my time here would soon be over, because I'd tried to file that unpleasant fact at the back of my mind. Ethan was bound to make other arrangements for his daughter after this, and I'd be down at the Job Centre.

As I turned with a newly opened jar of coffee in my hand, a movement caught my eye and what I saw from the front window caused the jar to slip from my hand and coffee granules to fly in a million different directions.

Up the path came a slightly bedraggled Allie – hand in hand with a small blond boy. It was Fen. They were followed by Tiny and Tony sporting grins that would have daunted a Harley Street dentist.

'Allie!' I managed to croak, and Mike and I rushed to the front door collecting Ethan and the policewoman in our wake.

Ethan, uncharacteristically uncool, held out his arms and rushed to greet his children.

It transpired that Allie had been haunted by the newspaper picture of her unhappy half-brother, and it bothered her so much she decided to rescue him and look after him herself. She knew where he lived, having once been a regular visitor, and had astutely checked the address on my computer. Then in the wee small hours of Sunday morning she put her plan into action, catching the early train to London, taking a taxi to Marnie's house, and waiting for an opportunity to get Fen away.

It hadn't been difficult. The little boy was wandering round in his pyjamas, with no sign of the current nanny who, as it happened, was having a Sunday morning love in with her boyfriend. This was the reason Fen's disappearance hadn't been noted for hours, or reported for more hours, which was borne out by the fact that Ethan had only just received a phone call informing him of his son's disappearance.

I hope the nanny is disbarred, or struck off, or whatever they do to so-called professionals who fail so abominably in their duty.

Anyhow, once Allie had Fen, she realised she'd have to bring him home with her and throw herself on her father's mercy. He was so pleased to see her safe and sound, he would have forgiven her anything. He was also livid at the careless way Marnie had treated the little boy, who was overjoyed to see his dad.

'Jeez,' said Ethan shaking his head, sitting on the sofa with an arm round Allie and Fen on his knee. 'What am I going to do with you?'

'Well you certainly can't send him back home to be neglected by that nanny,' I said without thinking.

'Perhaps I should try to get his mother to come back for him?'

'No! I want to stay with Allie,' said Fen, his face crumpling.

Allie hid a triumphant grin.

'Jeez,' said Ethan looking helplessly from Mike to me.

Mike raised his eyebrows questioningly at me, and it didn't take a genius to know what he wanted me to say. So because I'm a soft touch, I obliged.

'Perhaps Fen could stay here for a while…I wouldn't mind looking after him until his mother comes home. Assuming I still have a job, of course.'

Ethan looked wide-eyed at me. 'Why wouldn't you have a job, Rosie? Oh, I see – well don't give it another thought, none of this is your fault.' He gave me one of his meaningful stares and the sexy twisted smile, 'Besides, I told you – I've got plans for you.'

See? It doesn't matter what the situation, he's programmed to beguile.

'Oh please, Dad,' Allie fluttered her lashes at him adoringly. I expect she's got the gene too.

'Oh please, Dad,' Fen copied her almost exactly.

'Can we do that, Mike?' Ethan deferred to his right-hand man.

Mike signalled him and me to come out to the kitchen.

'Under the circumstances, I can't see it causing too much bother. You're his father and the nanny his mother left him with wants shaking. But don't forget there's the small matter of the Court Order suspending your access. That could be a problem, though it would mean Marnie having to admit to leaving Fen in the care of a dangerously incompetent person, and she won't want bad publicity. So let's say he can stay for a few days, and in the mean time, we'll have to contact Marnie. OK?'

Ethan nodded. 'Is that OK with you Rosie? I'll pay you extra.'

'Yes it's fine, but I don't want any more money, Ethan.' Was I going gaga? 'Not for such a short time, anyway.' Rationality was restored.

We didn't have to tell Allie and Fen of the decision; they were already whooping.

Did I say soft touch? Soft in the head, more like.

OCTOBER

What a week! I've been so busy I haven't had time to think, let alone put pen to paper.

Ethan's solicitor wasn't too happy about the situation with Fen, but when Marnie was contacted and told of her son's neglect, she grudgingly permitted Ethan to take care of him rather than return early from her Caribbean love-fest. It wasn't mentioned that Ethan himself would not actually be at home, though I was described as Allie's guardian.

Fen's a very sweet little boy, and idolises Allie. She's great with him: she reads him stories and helps him write emails to Ethan (I suggested he got a Hotmail address as I thought it the ideal way for him to keep in touch with them). Despite everything, I think they're good for one another.

Allie certainly needs some affection after her horrendous experiences at St Hilda's. Apparently, right from day one she was intimidated, then blackmailed, robbed of her trainers, and finally beaten up. So much for "being educated to a high standard in the company of other young ladies" as the blurb went. It was akin to a guerrilla training camp.

Allie is starting at Michaelmas on Monday and I took her on a preliminary visit. I found it a bit on the lax side as the students, who lounged around the premises as if it were the Costa del Sol, were very casually dressed and sported more piercings and tattoos than a roomful of football hooligans. But when Allie was introduced to these "study groups" they appeared articulate and amiable and seemed to accept her, so I think she liked it. Perhaps it's something to do with one particular tall, dark, gypsy-like youth whose eyes followed her everywhere. And I daresay that will be my next problem. But she's said she'll give it a try, for which I am thankful.

As Fen may be with us for at least three weeks, I've enrolled him at the village primary school. I shall now have to run Allie over to Michaelmas, then be back in time for Fen to start. I can't believe I'm back on the school run and all the malarkey that accompanies it. Before long I'll be making cakes for the PTA and going to coffee mornings.

Somehow, while at the crossroads my destiny seems to have taken a wrong turn. This is not how I imagined life as a singleton. Whatever happened to all that freedom?

And now I'm truly at the crossroads as yesterday I signed the contract giving my house to the Browns. It was a strange occasion to say the least. I'd hired a small furniture van to deliver the remainder of my things to Lime Cottage, and when the men had loaded up and driven off I walked round the empty rooms for the final time, not really surprised to find my throat constricted and my eyes pricking. As I reached the bedroom that overlooked the front garden, Leah and Jamie walked slowly up the path, side by side, and the years rolled back.

Seeing me at the window they came up and we stood hugging one another in the empty room where, if they did but know it, they were most likely conceived.

That poignant memory started a chain of thoughts that stirred me in a way I never expected.

As I began writing this for posterity and can therefore expect it to be read at some stage in the very distant future by my descendants, I have no intention of penning any graphic sex scenes à la Jackie Collins. So there won't be much more than meaningful looks, heaving breasts, and the closing of the bedroom door – more your Barbara Cartland.

That is providing I have any descendants as the chances have probably been halved by Leah's revelation. Though I think this tome may survive, given my son's hoarding instinct.

Once again I digress. I just wanted to record, without sounding like a she-wolf on heat, that all of a sudden I realise I'm missing sex. Not that I had much in the closing stages of my marriage as I now admit it wasn't just Simon whose appetite had diminished, but mine too. Though to be fair, he was being well sated elsewhere. However, as far as I was concerned it was there if I wanted it. So occasionally, after a glass of wine or two, Simon and I would go through the familiar motions, as you do after more than twenty years together, and that would suffice until the next blue moon.

But just lately I have to admit to the odd frisson or two that's reminded me it's now over a year since I have indulged in pleasures of the flesh. Probably more like ten years since my marital relations could be described with that degree of enthusiasm. And my imagination has begun working overtime, especially when I mull over Ethan's threats to have my body.

This is a problem as I know, under certain conditions, I would find it very difficult to say no to a romp with someone who, let's face it, I've fantasised about most of my adult life. It could be exactly what I need...

...But who am I kidding? I've never been the type who can separate lust and love, or indulge in one-night stands. Though there's always a first time. However, I'm very aware I mustn't get myself into a dubious position with Ethan (Freudian slip?) as (a) I want to keep my job for a while longer, and (b) I don't want to be just another notch on his bedpost.

So. I have now re-convinced myself that any carnal contact between me and my boss is a non-starter. Right?

Mind you, it's not just him I've been having lascivious thoughts about. Ever since my post-party snog with Mike, I seem to be looking at him in an impure light too. Though I don't think I've ever had such a great friendship with a male, and have no intention of spoiling it.

Of course these erotic reveries have inevitably brought me to the question of how I will cope if I ever get to a situation where losing my post-divorce virginity is a possibility. I am over forty-five (well, almost 47 but you'll never hear it from these lips) with stretch-marks, cellulite, thread veins, crows' feet and hair that now must be coloured out of necessity rather than choice. And I haven't even started to go through the "change" yet...what an insipid pseudonym for such a pivotal event. Having read that list of defects, I wouldn't even give myself a second look!

Undressing in front of Simon, who witnessed my body's southerly decline, was one thing; exposing my imperfections to another man is daunting in the extreme. I would certainly demand all lights to be extinguished, and Gina warned me never to go on top once you're over forty. (She's right – put a mirror on the floor and look into it if you don't believe me).

This is ridiculous, especially as it's all hypothetical.

Allie, Fen and I have been invited to Ethan's concert in Ipswich next weekend so I must get a tight rein on my debauched deliberations before then. Besides, doubtless he will pick himself a pubescent peach from the audience, and Mike, should he interpret my licentious looks, would probably run a mile.

I wonder if you can buy bromide over the counter at Boots? If not there's always the Internet – there must surely be an antidote to Viagra?

Having just read through my last lot of ramblings, I hardly like to begin on today's as the association is too inconceivable (no pun intended). I've just met Leah's partner.

I invited them over for lunch and excelled myself cooking the full traditional Sunday roast - though I cheated with Aunt Bessie's Yorkshire puddings as mine always have to be chiselled from the pan. And the beef was only slightly leathery.

Leah looked gorgeous and very feminine. (I've realised I keep referring to my daughter's feminism, but I'm not being anti-Sapphic – if that's the right word – I'm just so pleased to see her making the most of her considerable assets).

Anyhow, Dawn is stunning, in every way. She's not only tall, slim and beautiful, she's also very bright and funny and compassionate, and obviously thinks the sun shines out of Leah. Not that they touched or gave any physical display of their affection – which I must admit I'd been rather concerned about, but their affection was obvious in the way they looked at one another and the rapport between them.

My biggest pang came when I watched them with Allie and Fen. Allie was treated as one of them (I mean a fellow girl of their age) and bloomed, looking happier and more confident than she's been for ages. And they were so sweet with Fen, making him scream with delight as they gave him piggyback rides and played Hungry Hippos and Snap.

Naturally I pondered on my daughter never becoming a mother, and felt very sad – but mostly for her, I think. In any case, it's not at all unusual nowadays for same sex couples to adopt children, or use a donor. Indeed, who's to say a male/female couple make better parents? I didn't have to look very far to see two perfect examples of children who'd suffered as a result of their conventional parents' inadequate relationships.

By the time they left I felt I was coming to terms with my daughter's orientation, though I don't know if I ever will completely. The problem is that when you have a daughter, from babyhood you imagine preparing a white wedding, then going on to become a big part of their lives as they raise their children. Having said that, not having to endure Simon as father-of-the-bride accompanied by the burgeoning Bimbo is some compensation for not having a big wedding. There again, Leah has never wanted that.

But the old adage is true when it says "a daughter is yours for all of your life, but a son is yours until he takes a wife" – because his wife tends to spend more time with her mother than her mother-in-law, so now I'm no longer sure what to expect. But who does? Mothers always have dreams for their children, but expecting them to fit in with your fantasies is only for control freaks. So I'll just hope that I've given mine the qualities to live happy and fulfilling lives, and be content with the outcome – no matter what.

Anyway, I really like Dawn and can see she's making my daughter happy. She's also a science graduate and is therefore very supportive of Leah's ambitions to work in space technology.

Next weekend they've invited us round for lunch, so I'll see them in their own environment. This will certainly test my liberality.

In just over a month it's the twin's 21st and I always envisaged a big celebration. If word about Leah gets round this could instigate a family feud as Simon's mother is even more narrow-minded than mine, and just as likely to say something insensitive and embarrassing. If I told my mother Leah was coming out she'd think it was an invitation to a white frock bash at the Savoy (à la 1950s' debutantes, for the uninitiated).

I don't think the twins are bothered about a party, so I'll have to think of an excuse as to why there'll be no major carousing. I have a feeling it will be easier said than done. Unless I spirit them out of the country. Now there's an idea!

I wonder if they'd like a holiday as a 21st present? With the house money in the bank I think I can afford to treat them (and their partners, of course). It's worth a thought.

Heidi is smitten with Tiny, and it seems her feelings are returned. She came round to see him the other evening, but Allie had an unexpected invitation to go to a new friend's house after school, so Tiny had to accompany her and remain on guard outside. After the fiasco of her disappearance, Ethan was even more adamant his daughter would be constantly shadowed, and Tiny did his duty diligently, much to Allie's chagrin.

Naturally I offered Heidi a drink while she was waiting, and after a couple of glasses (Fen was already asleep) we decided to call Gina to come out to play. Serendipitously (I just love that word) it was Lloyd's night for coaching a local football team, and Gina jumped at the chance of some girl talk.

She'd just arrived in a taxi (obviously preparing for a serious session) when there was another knock at the door. I opened it and there, looking ever-so-slightly sheepish, stood Madeleine.

My first instinct was to slam the door in her face, but something about her stopped me.

'This is a surprise,' I said tightly.

'Hello, Rosie. May I come in?'

I opened the door and waved her through. 'You might as well join the party.'

Maddy went through to the sitting room and hesitated. 'Oh. You're all here.'

'Well, come in,' Gina said. 'Don't hang about in the doorway – you look as if you're touting for business.'

'Thanks, Gina,' Maddy said sardonically, her normal high-handed tone returning. 'There's no need to be vindictive.'

'Oh really? You're like a door-knob – everyone's had a turn.' Gina wasn't in the mood to pull punches. 'Are you so desperate that you can't survive for a week without a new man?'

'My, my, that sounds like the green eyed monster to me, Gina.'

'Not me – I have a husband I love to bits, but did you have to make a play for Ethan right under Rosie's nose?'

'Gina!' Now I was uncomfortable. 'Ethan's my boss, nothing more…'

'Pull the other one,' Gina said. 'And I'd say he was pretty fond of you too, the way he was dancing with you at the party.'

'He dances like that with every woman,' I said, secretly pleased she'd noticed.

'Exactly!' Maddy jumped at the excuse. 'Look Rosie, I'm sorry if I've upset you – but you must know what Ethan's like. He's just a crass, over-sexed tosspot.'

'Dumped you again, did he?' Gina's voice dripped with sarcasm.

Maddy glared at her. 'As a matter of fact it was the other way round.' Then she turned to me and Heidi, and her features dropped. 'I suppose I should have known better. I'm sorry girls. I just seem to be losing it… everything…nothing's going right – I even lost out on a crummy TV ad because they said I was "too mature". Well we all know that's just a euphemism for "too bloody old"… ' The tears were falling, and I think we all recognised in that moment how very unhappy she was.

'Come on, Maddy,' I soothed. 'It doesn't matter. We still love you. And if you're losing it, what hope is there for the rest of us?'

'But I'm finished…my looks are going…I can't keep a man…'

'Oh for god's sake! You still look great – the Botox makes sure of that,' Gina was still disgruntled. 'Plus you're loaded. You just need to be a bit more choosy. You should knock the toyboys and old tarts on the head and wait for a decent bloke to come along.'

'Like I did,' said Heidi dreamily. We regarded her fondly. I just pray Tiny is the paragon she thinks he is.

Maddy dabbed at her eyes. 'I know you're right, it's just that I need the…intimacy.'

'You mean you can't do without sex?' Gina said.

'No! You couldn't be more wrong. I don't really want the sex. In fact I've never rated it highly.'

'Jeez!'

'Maddy!'

'You could have fooled me!'

Maddy looked uncomfortable. 'It's true, I swear it. It wouldn't bother me if I never had it again. It's the closeness, I miss.'

'Well perhaps you should stop coming on to every Tom, Harry and Willing Dick who takes your fancy.'

'Thank you Gina, I'll try.' Maddy's tone was taut. There's always been a love-hate relationship between the two of them. In some ways I think it's because they're too alike, though I'd lose both of them as friends if I voiced my opinion.

We continued with our favourite subject but eventually got round to other things, so I brought up the question of the twin's birthday celebration, and my idea for giving them a holiday instead.

'Why not use my villa in Cyprus?' Maddy suggested. 'In fact why don't we all go? We could have a party and a holiday at the same time.'

'Wow!' Heidi's eyes were shining. 'I've never been to

Cyprus. I haven't even been abroad since we went to Lloret del Mar just after we left High School. Do you remember those Spanish waiters…?'

I giggled. 'Yeah – yours was Manuel – and that hotel was a dead ringer for Fawlty Towers.'

'I shall never forget his castanets,' Heidi said.

'No, I bet you won't – especially when he was displaying them in his bright red Speedos!' Gina successfully lowered the tone.

Once again the evening degenerated into a nostalgia-fest, and by the end of it we were all extremely cheerful and looking forward to a holiday which may or may not come up to expectations, or even materialise. But it was good therapy.

It was time for our trip to see Ethan perform in Ipswich, so I had my lowlights done and bought a trendy outfit – skinny jeans and a sparkly top that cost me an arm and a leg. So I felt pretty good when I called in at Tesco's on the way home. And then I saw Simon.

My first shock was the trolley he was pushing. When we were married he didn't know which end the handle was and imagined there was a special section in the Driving Test that women had to pass to steer them. (Sad thing is, I think he actually believed it). The second was that despite his spiky haircut, earring and youthful clothes, he looked thin and jaded. And he seemed to be on his own.

He hadn't spotted me, and I watched, fascinated as he browsed the greengrocery department, poking tomatoes and squeezing aubergines. When we were together he was amazed when I told him not all vegetables came out of tins. And I once caught him trying to eat an avocado with the skin on after telling him it was a pear.

I sauntered up to him. 'Hello Simon.'

His mouth hung open for a second and I was gratified to note the appreciative gleam in his eye: it's not a look you misread after living with someone for years.

'Just doing a little shopping,' he said, sheepishly.

'I see. And where's your *wife*?' It felt very strange.

'Oh, Angel's not too well – she's not having a good –er-pregnancy.'

'Well, some suffer more than others,' I said airily. 'But she's young – a little younger than I was when I had the twins.'

He looked at me sadly. 'I know. It seems a very long time ago'

'Well, I must be getting on…'

'You're looking good, Rosie. I like your hair – and you've lost weight too.'

'Yes – I think the single life suits me,' I said, somehow knowing it would dismay him. Bloody good job.

But as I walked away, feeling him staring after me, I couldn't suppress the wave of sadness that swamped me. I suppose you can't spend so many years of your life with someone and feel nothing for them. Even if it's only pity. I have a feeling he may regret making the bed on which he's now committed to lie: together we had some comfortable and carefree years to anticipate; with a young wife and a new family it's probably starting to feel like Ground Hog Day for Simon.

Mike booked us into a hotel on Saturday night, and Allie and Fen's excitement was tangible as Tiny drove us to Suffolk's county town. It was an unseasonably warm day, and boded well for the open air concert being held at Ipswich Town's football ground. Ethan personally met us in the foyer and told us it was a sell-out - as were all the other venues on the tour, which was extremely good news.

Mike, who accompanied him greeted us warmly. He said Ethan would normally be sleeping at this time of day in preparation for the show, but he was obviously making an extra effort for his children, giving them promotional T-shirts and baseball caps, chatting to them about their new schools, and playing video games.

Mike also told me Ethan was considering a film script – which reminded me his publisher was getting twitchy about the finished manuscript. I'd fielded several phone calls that week.

'He wants to finish it with finding his birth mother,' Mike reminded me. 'But he hasn't had any new leads for a while, though they seem to think there's an American connection and his father may have been a GI. That must narrow it down to a couple of million.' I love his dry sense of humour.

'Shoot!' I delved in my handbag. 'That reminds me – I brought some mail – there's one from Family Searchers enclosing a letter from the States. Perhaps this will be good news.'

I handed Mike the envelopes and he glanced at them and put them on the side. We sipped our iced Pepsi's.

'Is everything going OK at home, Rose?'

'Absolutely fine. The schools seem to be working out and Allie and Fen adore each other. It's a shame it can't last – I mean eventually they'll go back to their respective mothers.'

Mike nodded grimly. 'More's the pity. Mind you, Bianca's great when she's on the wagon, but Marnie's a different ballgame. She was born mean. Ethan's worried about the way she treats Fen – he spends most of his time with a succession of nannies while she careens all over the place. She says her absences are necessary as she's pursuing her career. What career? To my knowledge she's only had one bit-part in the past year. What she's pursuing is her next rich husband – and the poor kid comes a long way down her list of priorities. But with Ethan's lifestyle – not to mention all the bad publicity – he's got naff all chance of getting custody.'

It was rare for Mike to get so steamed up.

'You're Fen's godfather – can't you speak up for Ethan?'

'Yes, sure I can, but you know what? I think the bottom line is all down to money. Marnie would soon change her tune if she was offered a sufficiently large incentive.'

'She'd give up her son if the price was right? She sounds like a complete cow.'

'That's an understatement. But now Ethan's bank account is looking healthy again, I think he might just go for it.'

'That's all very well in principle, but in reality what Fen needs is stability, not another absent parent.'

Mike's frown deepened. 'It's possible to maintain a relationship without being there all the time. My daughter and I have a great one.'

Whoops. Foot in mouth. I'd forgotten about Caroline, Mike's thirteen-year-old.

'I'm sorry, I know it's possible but it requires both parents to put the child's interests before their disputes – which you and your ex obviously do. Have you seen your daughter recently, by the way?'

I knew Mike drove up to Yorkshire every few weeks to spend the weekend with her.

He nodded then suddenly reached out and put his hand on my arm. 'We've got a couple of days off the week after next, and I was…er… wondering if…'

'Hey Mike!' Ethan came bounding through to the tiny kitchen area followed by a beaming Fen and Allie. 'What say we send out for some Big Macs?'

Mike lifted his shoulders and gave me a rueful look.

'Great idea,' he said, looking at his watch. 'And then we'll have to get over to the stadium.'

We watched the concert from the very front of the stage, protected from the masses by Tiny and another burly bodyguard. But despite the electric atmosphere, and Ethan's energetic, charismatic, talented performance, every now and again my mind returned to Mike, and speculation on what he'd been about to ask me. Instinctively I felt it had been something significant.

After the show, having put an exhausted Fen to bed, we ate in the hotel restaurant where Ethan had laid on a bit of a party. The champagne flowed, and eventually Allie, who seemed to have had a relaxed and happy day, went over to say goodnight to her father who, it happened, had wandered over to the bar where I'd been chatting to Tiny.

Of one thing I was reassured: the big man is deadly serious about Heidi – more smitten than she is, if that's possible. He dutifully followed Allie towards the lifts and as I watched, out of the corner of my eye I saw Mike dancing very intimately with the dark-haired beauty from the band, Lisa - who I'd discovered, was very popular with the whole entourage. As they smooched past me it was obvious they were entirely in a world of their own, and inexplicably my insides knotted. I don't know what came over me, but I knocked back two flutes of champagne in quick succession.

Ethan, who'd been chatting to the barman turned and gave me one of his sexy, heavy-eyed smiles.

'Tiny's serious about Heidi,' I said conversationally to my boss, covering my confusion – though to be honest I think I was slurring as I stumbled over the words. 'I'm really glad about that. As I introduced them I'd have felt personally responsible if he let her down…she's such a nice person. I couldn't bear to see her hurt...'

I knew I was rabbiting and all of a sudden Ethan grabbed my shoulders, pulled me towards him and kissed me hard on the lips; then his lips softened and just as I found myself getting over the shock and (almost) responding, he pulled away.

'Shut up, Rosie,' he said. 'You know what your trouble is? You care too much about other people.' All the time he was sweeping me with those hypnotic green eyes. Then he lifted a hand to my face and cupped my chin, his face inches from mine. Weakened by the demon alcohol, at that moment I didn't care that we were surrounded by dozens of curious spectators.

'What would I do without you?' he murmured as my eyes closed and my lips puckered in readiness. The kiss was sensuous, but very brief. He took my hand and pulled me toward the lift. 'Come on, Rosie. There's something I want to show you.'

Like a lamb to the slaughter I went to his suite.

I don't really remember much about the journey in the lift, just an onslaught of sensations I hadn't experienced for a very long time, and an elderly lady tutting and shaking her head.

But once he urged me through the bedroom door, slammed

it behind us and pulled me onto the bed, my sanity kicked in. What was I *doing*? I'd sworn to avoid this situation at all costs…Remember? I didn't want my first sexual encounter to be a notch on anyone's bedpost. Especially not the man who was paying me handsomely for doing a very pleasant job.

Oh god - how was I going to get myself out of this now? I'd be damned if I did, and damned if I didn't.

As I stared at the ceiling above Ethan's bed, desperately trying to ignore his lips, now dangerously close to my breasts, I was suddenly aware he'd become still. And then came the sound of gentle snoring. I lifted my head and confirmed he had fallen asleep.

And then, of course, I was incensed. Quite irrationally, I know. It didn't matter that two minutes ago I'd changed my mind. What if I hadn't? It was a gross insult. I pushed him off me and lay watching him, my senses swinging between anger and relief.

The next thing I knew, I awoke fully clothed, next to my fully clothed boss, and it was 6am.

With throbbing head, a huge dent in my self-esteem, and mortified by my ignominious conduct, I picked up my shoes and crept back to my own room down the corridor.

As I inserted the keycard in the slot, Mike appeared from his room next door. He gave me a peculiar look, went to speak, changed his mind, shook his head sadly and hurried off down the corridor.

I haven't felt so ashamed and humiliated since I lost my bikini bottom diving into a swimming pool. And that was when I was six years old.

You know the expression "running through the gamut of emotions"? Well that's been me this week. One minute I'm despising myself for getting drunk enough to be seduced (theoretically) by Ethan, and next I'm reliving the sensual moments we shared.

Then again I feel deeply uncomfortable every time I think of it, and even more so when I recall the look Mike gave me when he caught me sneaking back to my room: it was undoubtedly contemptuous. And that was unfair, because I didn't sleep with Ethan (well I did, of course, but not in the accepted sense) and why should I care so much anyway?

Except that I do. I care about Mike's opinion of me, and judging by the way he studiously avoided me for the rest of the day, I know I have descended several echelons in his estimation.

As for the boyo himself, I don't think Ethan actually remembers what happened. He certainly didn't refer to it, or act as if anything had changed between us.

Writing this down has demonstrated graphically that if I had given in to my hopping hormones (and Ethan hadn't fallen asleep), he probably wouldn't have remembered it anyway. Which would be ultra-humiliating. So I must reiterate – *I must not have sexual relations with that man* (now I sound like Bill Clinton – with a degree of sincerity, I hope).

There are so many things I like about Ethan. Underneath the Jack-the-lad exterior I believe lies a genuine warm-hearted human being. But as far as the opposite sex is concerned, forget it. If I want to continue working for him I must accept he'll probably keep trying to seduce me. And I apologise to all you feminists who think I should have him hauled over the coals for Sexual Harassment, but I quite enjoy the game. If he ever started touching me inappropriately or forcing himself on me, that would be a very different story. But I wouldn't have lasted very long in the advertising world if I'd grassed up every male guilty of sexual innuendo. I actually feel sorry for youngsters nowadays: when I was a student, if I'd passed a building site without a host of wolf-whistles, I'd have been disappointed. Now appreciative workers risk getting the sack. It's laughable.

But back to what's really bugging me…

Mike. He, on the other hand *is* a very different story. He's a much more complex character, one of the most thoughtful, caring, astute guys I've met in a long time. I feel dreadful that he thinks I slept with Ethan. I don't know why. And I don't know what to do about it.

'I don't know what to do about it!' Gina wailed.

If I thought I had problems, Gina's are ten times worse, in her estimation. But knowing her as I do, I both understand and sympathise with her plight. She's just discovered she's pregnant.

I'm sure I've mentioned she's so anti-baby she had her tubes tied in her twenties? Well, apparently one of them came untied, and her frenzied, newly-wed shenanigans with the lovely Lloyd have resulted in her being with child.

'When I was single – you know – there was never any question, any doubt at all,' she whimpered when she came to share her secret. 'I'd have gone straight to the clinic, paid my money, and that would have been that…but now I'm having *doubts…*'

'How does Lloyd feel about it?'

'I haven't told him, Rosie. He agreed he didn't want any more children - you know he's got two from his first marriage. The thing is, his daughter Jane – the one who got married just before us – is pregnant, and Lloyd's over the moon. He just keeps talking about how brilliant kids are.'

Poor Gina was really torn. She was pale and her baggy eyes told of sleepless nights.

'Gina, you're the one who has to carry the child, and give birth to it, and take care of it most of its life. It's no good having it just to please Lloyd. And I'm saying this only because I know how you've always felt about it, not because I believe it's right. I suppose what I mean is, if you decide to go ahead and have a termination without telling your husband, I'll back you, no question. Only you have to be sure it's what you really want. And that you can live with the consequences.'

'I know. That's the problem,' she said miserably.

'On the other hand, children are a great joy,' I said, crossing my fingers behind my back. 'Childbirth nowadays isn't painful as you can have an epidural – or if you're too posh to push, a designer Caesarean. You don't lose your figure if you watch your diet and do suitable exercise. And as Lloyd's not exactly on the breadline, I'm sure he'd agree to a home help or an au pair.'

Gina listened gloomily.

'But in the end, love, no one else can make the decision for you.'

She nodded, then wailed again. 'What about my cats? They don't mix with babies.'

'Of course they do. You just have to be sensible, like not letting one into the same room as the baby when you're not there. And oh, yes – you mustn't handle the litter when you're pregnant. You can catch a virus or something that could be transmitted to the baby. And you mustn't eat soft cheese as it contains listeria.'

'Jesus Christ, Rosie, I'd have to change my entire lifestyle.'

'But it's worth it in the end,' I said, only half-believing it.

No really, of course it's worth it. I wouldn't be without Leah and Jamie for anything. But anyone who says child-rearing is a wonderful experience should have their tongue cut out.

Mike rang this evening. It was the first time I'd spoken to him since Ipswich, and though I was pleased to hear from him, his tone was decidedly chilly. Anyhow, he hadn't rung to revile me, but to tell me Family Search had given Ethan an address in America to contact the woman they thought was his mother. He'd written and was now awaiting a reply, so it was possible we could soon finish the final chapter of his autobiography.

I'd had a phone call from the publisher just that morning, saying the book was now being put back until their Autumn List next year as the deadline had long since passed and he was lucky they hadn't decided to sue for the return of the advance they'd paid. Privately, the Editorial Assistant (who I'd once worked with at The Company) told me they were very impressed with the copy, and thought being reunited with his mother was an ending worth waiting for.

As my conversation with Mike drew to a stilted close, I wracked my brain to find something pertinent to say vis à vis the fiasco at Ipswich. And somehow, in my desperation I blurted 'I didn't sleep with Ethan, you know'.

Instantly numbed by my crassness I almost dropped the

receiver, but was aware of a pregnant pause before Mike replied.

'Rose, it's none of my business who you choose to sleep with.'

He didn't believe me. I'd debased myself for nothing.

The line went dead and he hadn't even said goodbye.

We took Allie to visit Bianca again, and were amazed at her progress. She was smartly dressed with full makeup and perfectly quaffed hair, though her skin had a yellowish tinge. She also insisted we all (Tiny, Fen and I) come to her room and have coffee.

When we were settled and had finished talking about the weather she announced 'They're letting me out next week – providing I go to regular AA meetings, and behave myself! So you'll be able to come home too, Allie.'

Allie tried to look pleased, but the expression of disappointment on her face was unmistakable.

'I'm glad you're better, Mum, but what about Fen?'

Bianca also tried to hide her dismay. 'Well. I expect he wants to get back to his mummy…'

'No I don't,' shouted Fen. 'I want to stay with Allie. And I like my new school and my dad. And Rosie. And Tiny. And Geoffrey.' His lip quivered.

I put my arm round him. 'I'm sure we can work something out.' God knows what.

'Why can't we both stay at Lime Cottage with Dad – and just visit our mothers – instead of the other way round?' Allie said, reasonably.

Out of the mouths of babes…

'Is that what you want, Allie?' Bianca spoke quietly.

Allie nodded then hung her head.

'It's all right, darling. I can understand why you feel like that. I know I've been horrible to live with, but I'm getting better now. I won't let you down again. OK?'

'But I'll have to go back to my old school and I hated it. I like Michaelmas and I've got loads of new friends…'

Poor Allie. My heart went out to her. Puberty was punishment in itself without being pushed from pillar to post.

'Perhaps Allie could stay at Lime Cottage just until Fen's mother comes back?' I suggested. 'It would only be an extra week, and it'd give you time to settle in, Bianca.'

I thought for a moment she was going to bawl me out, but she just smiled and lifted her thin shoulders acquiescently. 'All right. Just until then. Meanwhile I'll talk to your father about the situation.'

Before we left she thanked me for taking care of her daughter, and I decided Mike was right: Bianca is actually a very nice person – when she's on the wagon. The question is, will she stay on it? For Allie's sake, I sincerely hope so.

Marnie, on the other hand, doesn't require alcohol to be a selfish, uncaring she-devil. She's left her son with a stranger for three weeks and hasn't even bothered ringing him, though she's certainly been alive and well as she's been pictured frequently with her toyboy in the press, and there have been hints they're getting engaged.

The telling thing is, Fen hasn't mentioned her either, other than to ask how long it was before she returned, and expressing his desire to stay at Lime Cottage.

Eventually the call came. Not from Marnie, but some lackey who apparently worked for the marital heir presumptive. They would be over to pick him up the following Tuesday, and would I kindly ensure his things were ready. I was not happy.

'If Fen's mother wants to pick him up, I suggest she rings his father and makes suitable arrangements,' I said as calmly as I could, after all, it wasn't the lackey's fault.

For the hundredth time I wondered just how heartless this woman could be – and also that Fen was such a nice little boy. He reminds me of Jamie at that age.

Just after the first call, a second one came. It was the She-devil herself.

'Mrs Grant? It's Marnie Mitchell. I am unable to get through to my ex-husband. He knew when I was due back, so there will be no problem about *when* I pick up *my son*. I just wanted to make sure you have Fender suitably dressed when my fiancé and I arrive. We're taking him to Be-erwick He-ouse to meet his new in-laws and I don't want him letting the side down. So jacket, trousers and a tie, I think, and the lemon shirt to match my outfit. Oh, and don't forget to polish his shoes.'

Not a word about her son's welfare, not a glimmer of remorse, not a syllable of appreciation. I owed this monster nothing. I could not contain myself.

'Mrs Mitchell, I've been taking care of *your son* as a favour to his father - since the trollop in whose care you left him will be charged with neglect. I am Mr Hammer's assistant, not some skivvy at your beck and call. Fen has no such clothes here, so if you want to dress him like Little Lord Fauntleroy to show him off to some nouveau riche scrap merchant, I suggest you get over here and do it yourself.'

I heard her gasp and try to speak but I wasn't finished.

'Women like you are not fit to breed. You don't deserve a lovely little boy like Fen. You've been away a month and never once rang to check if he was all right, let alone bother to speak to him,' I had to draw breath and she cut in, quick as Flynn, cold as ice.

'My capability as a mother is absolutely nothing to do with you, and you have no right to criticise me in this slanderous manner. I shall be speaking to my lawyer about your allegations.'

'You do that, Mrs Mitchell. Because I've already made a statement to Mr Hammer's lawyer for use in his custody case – which I've no doubt he'll win. Goodbye!'

I lied. Big time. But I was so disgusted by that awful woman's attitude.

I just hope Ethan doesn't think I went too far. I'm still so riled if she was standing in front of me right now, I'd punch her on the nose. And I'm a pacifist.

As I slammed down the receiver I turned and was chastened to find myself regarded by Allie's large green eyes. I was still forming a credible excuse for my outburst when she turned wordlessly and went upstairs.

NOVEMBER

On Monday morning when I went to wake Allie for school, she wasn't there. And nor was Fen.

Tiny was perturbed and I was panic-stricken. While Tiny rang Mike I looked for the obvious clues praying they hadn't been abducted from under our noses. And then I found the note.

Dear Rose,

Please don't worry, I will look after Fen. He doesn't want to go back to his mother, but they will make him so we have gone away. Please tell Dad not to worry, and tell Tiny I am sorry.

Love Allie

At least they'd gone of their own accord. We broke the news to Mike who told us to hang fire for an hour before ringing the police because he had contacts who could check out railway and bus stations etc. Meanwhile I was to ring Allie's new school-friends to see if she'd given them any hints as to her destination (she'd spent time with them at the weekend).

Tiny, once again with the help of Tony and a couple of acquaintances who would scare you in a dark ally but seemed to have hearts of gold, scoured the surrounding area in their cars, hoping to pick up the runaways' trail.

I manned the phones, using my mobile for outgoing calls so the landline was free for important ones.

Our hour's grace was almost up when it rang and I grabbed it, my hand shaking.

'Rose, is that you?'

'Yes. Yes it is, who's this?' I recognised the voice but couldn't put a name to it.

'It's Bianca. Allie's mother.'

I blanched, wondering how I was going to break the news to her.

'They're here. Allie and Fen.'

'Oh, thank god.'

'I need to discuss this with Ethan, but I thought you'd be worried so I rang you first. Does he still have the same mobile number?'

'I think so. Bianca, I don't know what you and Ethan want to do about this, but give me five minutes to call off the search, will you? And thank you so much for letting me know. I can't tell you how relieved I am…they all will be.'

One crisis over, and another one about to begin for me, because with no children to oversee and no manuscript to work on I would soon be redundant.

But I was impressed Bianca rang and "ratted on her own daughter" (as Allie later put it): it served to prove she really is a caring mother, and basically a good person. And Ethan surprised me by hiring a helicopter and flying (with Mike) directly to his ex's home in response to Bianca's request for a meeting to discuss the matter.

Of course I wasn't party to the finer details of the meeting, but it emerged Bianca had to go into hospital for tests on her liver. She'd had an MRI scan as part of her check-up before leaving rehab, and hinted it was quite serious and may require prolonged treatment, so asked Ethan if Allie could stay with him (or me, more accurately) as she was obviously happy at Lime Cottage and Michaelmas.

Ethan was more than happy to agree, and apparently is paying for his ex-wife's hospitalisation.

When they brought the children back, they landed the helicopter on one of Smythe's fields, incurring the wrath of Horseface Bella who stalked over ready to tear a strip off the intruders.

Ethan, I'm reliably informed by his children, told her if she didn't shut up and go away, he'd be pressing charges against her evil daughter for assaulting Allie. Upon which Horseface went away quietly. (I'm quite sure the version I heard had the four-letter words edited out).

Of course, the catalyst of the entire episode had been Fen's reluctance to go back to his mother, or rather his mother's jurisdiction as he seemed to get precious little maternal love. It was therefore necessary for me to voice my concern over Marnie's total lack of care and consideration toward her son while she'd been away. I also deemed it prudent to repeat the telephone conversation I'd had with her, leaving out nothing and confessing my comment re the custody case.

I noticed both Mike and Ethan hiding a smirk halfway through my diatribe (it wound me up again just in the retelling), but they both expressed serious concern. Ethan, without hesitation, went to the phone and dialled. Seconds later he was talking to his other ex-wife.

'Marnie, where are you? I need to speak to you about our son. I don't care. I'll be with you in…twenty minutes.'

He slammed the receiver and grinned. 'She probably thinks I'm coming by car – I just hope they've got a lot of fields at Berwick He-ouse!' Ethan's parody of Marrnie's affected tone was perfect.

Mike followed him, and minutes later we heard the helicopter taking off.

What was actually said at Berwick House, I can only guess, but suffice to say for the time being Fen is to remain in his father's custody.

Officially this is because his mother and new stepfather-to-be are travelling a great deal, and also Marnie has a part in a Hollywood musical. I couldn't resist speculating that she was playing the Wicked Witch of the West in The Wizard of Oz, out to steal a poor child's ruby slippers. Ethan said if she ever wore ruby slippers they'd be round some stud's neck in a low budget porn movie.

Unofficially, she's agreed to Fen staying because Ethan has threatened to tell the press of her abominable treatment of her son, and declare she's an unfit mother. He also embellished my claim of a custody case with numerous damning sworn affidavits.

With a new (very wealthy) husband in the offing, not to

mention potential Hollywood stardom, and because she really is a heartless shrew, Marnie capitulated. Though she will be allowed access to Fen, so can still use him as an accessory when it suits her purpose. I don't know why she doesn't just get herself a poodle and dye it to match her ensembles.

So, Allie and Fen are happy, and as I still have a job I suppose I am too.

During the crisis Mike stopped treating me like a pariah, though we still haven't regained our former intimacy (*close acquaintance, familiarity*, according to The Oxford Dictionary, nothing more).

I had a phone call from Lloyd today that put me in a real quandary. Apparently he's worried sick about Gina's strange behaviour and wondered if I had any explanation for it.

What could I say? There was no way I could tell him my best friend's secret, but I felt very sorry for her husband and said I'd speak to her and see what I could do.

I rang Gina immediately and arranged to meet her at her salon at lunchtime. She offered to give me a pedicure, but suspecting the rendezvous could become emotional, I was wary of allowing her near my feet with a sharp object, so declined. (Once she almost took a layer of skin off my leg whilst waxing in a fervid state over some man).

Anyhow, I walked in as her last client of the morning walked out, and was shocked at her haggard appearance.

'I know I look like shite,' she said bluntly.

'Not exactly. But if you carry on like this you'll be needing Polyfiller, not collagen.'

She grinned wryly at my attempt at humour. Then I told her about Lloyd's call and she burst into tears.

'Oh my poor baby,' she sobbed. (I think she meant her husband).

'You're not being fair, Gina. Not to him or yourself – and least of all to your baby.'

'I know, I know. But every time I go to tell him, something stops me. I mean – I'm almost forty-six. What sort of mother will I make? And Lloyd will be a granddad before this one's even born. We'll be ancient by the time he's a teenager…Is that fair to a child?'

Thinking of Marnie, and even Bianca and Ethan, I knew that, corny as it might sound, there was something much more important to a child than the age of its parents.

'All a child needs is love, and a sense of security. You can't give them anything more important than that.'

Gina looked at me with wide, anxious eyes. 'But…what if I can't love it? What if I have it and feel nothing but resentment? I can hardly send it back and ask for a refund.'

I considered this deeply. She had a valid point, if only because of her lifelong aversion to pregnancy (and I believe it is pregnancy rather than children). My gut feeling was that it would be the making of her.

'I truly believe you're worrying unnecessarily. Though you may not realise it, you already feel something for this baby – you referred to it as "he" not "it" just now. Lloyd is devastated because he thinks you regret marrying him. All he wants is for you to be happy, and if that means a termination, then I'm sure he'll go along with it because he loves you.'

Gina drew a shuddering breath. 'I don't. I don't want a termination, Rosie. I'm just scared of screwing up.'

I hugged her. 'We all have to learn to be parents. Unfortunately babies don't come with a set of instructions. And if they did we'd probably ignore them…'

'…then turn to the manual when things go wrong and discover we've had them upside down or something.' Gina laughed through her tears. 'Oh Rosie, I feel strange – sort of excited and frightened at the same time. But I've had a weight lifted from my shoulders.'

'Don't' worry – you'll soon get it back – all round your middle.' Perhaps it was too soon for that joke.

'Oh don't Rosie. Oh, god! Lloyd might hate me fat. What if he really doesn't want another child?

'There's only one way to find out, love. Tell him. Tonight.'

'Better get my talking underwear out then,' Gina said, smiling.

I rose to leave, sure she'd made the right decision. Equally sure her husband would be delighted.

'Thanks Rosie,' my friend said. 'Can I give you a pedicure – or how about a manicure?'

I shook my head. 'No thanks, Gina. Another time. You're still a bit twitchy and I'd prefer to leave the salon with all digits intact, if you don't mind.'

'Oh ye of little faith.'

I grimaced at an incoming client as I left. 'Watch her with the scissors,' I said.

Through the window Gina mouthed something that ended in "off".

She'll survive.

I'm not so sure about me.

I'm having weird dreams, most of which involve sex and just about every male I'm acquainted with including Minty Mike at the Queens Head.

Perhaps I need therapy.

Before I returned to Lime Cottage and my duties with Ethan's children, I had an impulse to go shopping. Apart from a complete set of luxury lingerie that put Gina's talking gear to shame and almost melted my credit card, I acquired a giant bottle of body oil and a tub of chocolate spread. It was only after I left the premises I realised it was a sex shop, and the chocolate was of the body-paint variety, to be licked off at leisure. It doesn't say you can't put it on toast.

I was just settling down to some correspondence when a car skidded to a halt in the driveway. It was Ethan.

'Hi, Rosie. How ya doing? How's it going? Kids at school?' He leaned over and pecked me on the cheek.

'Hi. Fine. Fine. And yes.' I was caught off guard by his presence. 'What are you doing here?'

'I live here, remember?' he grinned and then looked more sober. 'I've got to be in Cardiff by six this evening for the gig, but I'm on my way to visit Bianca. She's not too good, Rosie.'

'I'm sorry to hear that. I like her.'

'Yeah. She's one of the best.' for a second his eyes glistened and he hesitated. 'They think it's the Big C.'

Cancer! Poor Bianca. Poor, poor Allie.

'There's a lot they can do nowadays, Ethan. People live for years with it – or they cure it and you'd never know they'd had it. And there are liver transplants.' I was feverishly trying to think of all the positive things to balance this dreadful news.

'Yeah. I know, Rosie. And she'll have whatever it takes. I don't care what it costs. Thank god I'm making a bit of dosh now. That reminds me, the book could be finished soon – I've had a letter from my biological mother.'

So it wasn't all bad news. 'I'm so pleased for you. When are you going to meet her? Where does she live?'

'In Florida. At first she wasn't over the moon to hear that I wanted to get in touch, but she talked to the agency and they told her my name, and now she wants to meet me. There's a bit of a problem though as she hasn't told her husband and family about me yet, so I can't meet her right away.' He looked gloomy again.

I struggled to make a positive reply as I already had a niggling doubt concerning this woman's sincerity. It seemed strange that she only agreed to contact him after she was told his name: if she recognized it, there was a possibility that her motives were less than altruistic.

My feelings were purely protective. I really didn't want to see Ethan get hurt, but nor did I wish to rain on his parade.

'Well that sounds perfectly reasonable. You were warned about the possibility she'd kept your birth a secret. The main thing is she's accepting you, which is great.'

'S'pose so. Anyway – I only called by to collect some stuff for the accountants. Bloody Inland Revenue. Now I'm making a bit of bread they want to take it off me.'

'Have you got time for a coffee?' I asked.

He looked at his watch, and then gave me one of his loaded grins. 'Yeah. But I'd rather have another shag.'

My chin almost hit the floor. Even concern for his ex-wife

didn't stop him: he was incorrigible. And totally incorrect.

'What do you mean *another*?'

He lifted an eyebrow. 'Don't tell me you've forgotten? If I remember rightly, we were getting *very* horny in the lift on the way up to my suite at your mate's wedding party.'

'Yes, and that's all you remember rightly,' I said, indignity hiding my discomfort – and realised that his alcohol-fuelled amnesia might save me from further humiliation. 'I…just wanted to make sure you got to your room all right. You fell asleep. Fully clothed. And besides I was very drunk or I'd never have gone anywhere near your suite.'

He looked sheepish then grinned. 'Are you saying you don't fancy me, Rosie?'

This stopped me in my tracks and in the few seconds I stalled, a million images flitted through my mind.

'You're very fanciable – as you well know. And yes, it would be easy to succumb to your many charms…'

'...and massive dick…' he interjected, intent on making me squirm. And if Maddy was to be believed, he wasn't joking. Anyhow I didn't allow myself to dwell on his juvenile claim and continued as if I hadn't heard it.

'…but for me, sex has to be something both of us can remember. Something that makes me feel special. For you it's as habitual as a…a post prandial brandy – and about as predictable.'

'*Post prandial…*' he mocked. 'I'll take that as a no then?'

I laughed despite myself. 'Ethan, you're a great boss, and a genuinely likeable person. But I'd hate myself in the morning.'

He laughed. 'Yeah, so would I.'

I wasn't sure if he meant himself or me.

We had to rummage through some files to find the paperwork he needed, by which time he hadn't even time for a coffee.

'That's it then Rosie, I'm off.'

We walked to the door.

'Give my best wishes to Bianca. And if there's anything I can do to help, just ask. Perhaps I could bring Allie to visit?'

'Thanks Rosie. You know I really appreciate what you're doing for my kids and everything. Even if you won't succumb to my many charms. Maybe one day…'

I shook my head decisively, knowing that this time I really meant it. The hotel episode had taught me what I definitely *didn't* want. 'Don't hold your breath.'

He got in the car and regarded me speculatively. 'In that case, perhaps I'd better put Mike straight. He's been really pissed off about me sleeping with you. See ya!'

He roared off, leaving me once again open mouthed and perplexed.

I was just settling down to work again after my erratic interlude (which could so easily have been erotic) when another vehicle scattered the gravel on the driveway, and Maddy emerged from her silver Audi.

Don't tell me she's still on Ethan's trail. Doesn't she ever learn? (I can now afford to say this, as I have.)

But no, she was bearing two cream doughnuts and a wonderful, freshly baked lardy cake. It had to be a special occasion as she would normally be bearing gifts such as a box of oranges and a crate of Evian water.

I know I'm watching my diet, but willpower flew out the window as the aroma assaulted my nostrils. And as far as I was concerned Maddy could have Ethan and every single one of his charms. Just give me the cake.

Maddy was buoyant because she'd just been signed up for a TV advert for low-fat yoghurt.

I pointed out that cream doughnuts and lardy cake were not suitable fare for the face of Lutz Light and offered to save her from herself by eating her share. She was scathing in her refusal saying she'd already negated the calorie intake by spending two hours at the gym.

We were just sitting down with a nicely softened dish of butter ready to spread on our hunks of lardy cake, when there was yet another knock on the door. I got up to answer it.

'I've spat on mine,' I warned Maddy, sure she was eyeing

my portion. (How childish habits die hard!)

Heidi stood on the step next to a very suave, smartly dressed man with a fine head of silver hair. I glanced over to the gateway and clocked a pale blue Rolls Royce.

'Hello Rosie. This is Bernard Landseer – it's his father I'm nursing.'

'How do you do?' He held out his hand and shook mine firmly. 'Heidi's told me so much about you…'

Before I could actually invite them in, Bernard Landseer's eyes slid from my face and were mesmerised by something in the hallway.

Yes, that's right…

'Madeleine!'

Was there any personable male she didn't bewitch?

Heidi grimaced at me as her patient's son followed the sweep of my hand and entered, not taking his gaze from the vision before him

'I do beg your pardon.' Good breeding kicked in. 'You must think me very rude. Heidi mentioned you were a friend of hers. I'm Bernard Landseer. How absolutely delighted I am to meet you.'

Maddy inclined her head graciously and allowed him to take her hand.

Another one bites the dust.

Please just hurry up with the niceties so I can eat my lardy cake. And now I'd probably have to share it. As much as I love my friends, this could sorely test my loyalty.

I offered Bernard a seat in the sitting room and went to make some more coffee, leaving Maddy chatting to him. I signalled Heidi to follow me, intrigued by her reason for being with the middle-aged charmer.

'Oh bloody bollocks!'

As you know, I'm not prone to bad language, but this was just cause. Geoffrey was on the kitchen table licking the butter dish as if there were no tomorrow. There was also evidence of suspicious gouges in the doughnut cream, and ragged edges to my lardy cake.

I've never approved of cruelty to animals, but at that moment he was lucky there wasn't a bucket of water handy as I'd have cheerfully held his thieving head in it. Not that he hung around to determine the extent of my wrath; he flew off the table so fast he skidded into the back door and head-butted it. Serves him right.

I wasn't going to waste the goodies. I scraped the top of the butter, removed the indents in the cream, and trimmed the edges of the lardy cake before covering them with Clingfilm and secreting it all in a high cupboard. I didn't imagine Maddy would be too worried about cake when she was in the thrall of a new admirer - and she certainly was that. Heidi and I had one ear each cocked to the sycophantic conversation taking place in the room beyond.

'Is that Landseer Property Development?' Maddy was asking, her voice croaking with the effort to keep her excitement from surfacing. 'I thought I read something about them buying out the Chatsworth Hotel chain?'

'That's right, my dear. How very astute of you. Yes, we believe they'll be a great asset to us – when we've refurbished them to a higher standard, of course.'

'I believe there's one in the Bahamas?'

'That's right, my dear. And Kuala Lumpur, Hong Kong, Sydney to name but a few.'

'Mm,' said Maddy thoughtfully and we didn't have to see her face to know what was going through her mind.

'By the way,' I asked Heidi, 'what are you doing out with Prince Charming? I take it he's not married?'

'Divorced. My car broke down, so he took me to Tesco's and mentioned how he was looking forward to meeting Tiny, so while we were in the area, I got him to make a detour on the off chance.'

'But you've obviously spoken to him about Maddy?'

'Yes – and you and Gina. It's a shame Tiny's not here – but what a coincidence that Maddy is.'

'Fate. That's what it is. They could be made for each other: she's beautiful and greedy, and he's rich and gullible. It's a match made in heaven.'

I took the coffee into the sitting room and felt entirely superfluous, so returned to the kitchen with Heidi and we demolished the cake.

A short while later, as we stared guiltily at the crumbs, Heidi realised she had frozen food in the back of the Rolls and we went into the sitting room to remind Bernard.

It was like the balcony scene from Romeo and Juliet. Madeleine was standing by the fireplace posing and pontificating on the rigours of filming her forthcoming TV "production" and Bernard was sitting on the edge of the sofa, one knee almost touching the floor, gazing awestruck and hanging on her every word. Real pass-the-bucket stuff.

Anyhow, we eventually managed to get Bernard's attention and after a protracted farewell, he went off with Heidi, having reiterated his intention to pick Maddy up that evening.

After we waved them off we returned to the kitchen and I asked Maddy if she wanted more coffee. She froze in the doorway, eyeing the empty cake plates.

'You greedy cows! You've eaten my cake!'

And I thought she wouldn't notice. I shrugged, unashamed. 'Count it as payment for matchmaking services, Maddy. Besides, you should save up your calories for tonight.'

'I shan't be sleeping with him!' she shot back, affronted.

'Did I say you were? I simply meant you wouldn't need to calorie count.'

'Oh.'

'Seems like a nice guy, though.'

'Yes, I really like him.' Maddy said, almost dreamily. 'And not only that but he's a multi-millionaire. Rosie, I feel this is going to be special…'

Her eyes were shining and I could almost see the dollar signs in them.

'…something just clicked…'

Like a fruit machine when the jackpot comes up.

Gracious, I'm becoming cynical. Maybe Bernard will turn out to be the love of her life.

'Oh Rosie, I almost forgot,' she delved in her Gucci bag and handed me a business card.

'Give this woman a call. I showed her Allegra's photo, and she wants to see more of her. She was very excited…'

'Hold on a minute! What photo?'

'The one Ethan had of her – curled up on a chair in a big T-shirt…'

'I took that,' I said inconsequentially, trying to assimilate the facts and failing. 'What woman?'

'Freya Deauville – she's the head of the agency I work for – she thinks Allegra's got what it takes and wants to speak to her parents about assessing her. And you're her guardian, so…'''

'She thinks Allie's model material?'

Maddy nodded impatiently. 'Of course. Did you think I was trying to sell her into slavery? Though modelling can feel like that sometimes.'

'She's not even fifteen years old.'

'So? Many of them start at her age – the younger the better. Look at Kate Moss.'

'Yes, look at her – the cause of more anorexia than Nestlé and Hershey combined.'

'It doesn't have to be that way. If her face fits she could make a fortune.'

'I'll talk to Ethan about it. By the way, her mother's very ill, you know. It's cancer. Ethan's visiting her as we speak.'

Maddy looked shocked then surprised. 'You don't say?' I mean it's terrible. But he's never lost his soft spot for Bianca, you know. Or should I say hard-on? In fact I think he still loves her.'

It strikes me she could be right. He's certainly going to a lot of trouble for an ex-wife. But a few miracles will have to occur before there could be a happy ending to this sorry tale. Perhaps Allie could do with something to take her mind off her parental problems.

Having been extended because of its popularity, Ethan's tour finishes in just under two weeks and he's asked me to stay on, particularly in my role as foster-mother. He's coming back to Lime Cottage with the intention of working on his new album. Other than that he has only a few TV shows to do between then and the New Year.

At the end of the tour, Mike's going to Yorkshire for a few days to see his daughter, then will also be joining us at Lime Cottage. So it will be one big happy family. Ha!

I haven't yet approached Ethan about Allie's modelling possibility as Bianca has just had an operation to remove part of her liver. The doctors' prognosis is optimistic as they found no evidence of secondary tumours, though she now has to undergo a gruelling course of chemotherapy. Ethan's arranged for her to go to a private rest home for two weeks where she'll be nursed while she recovers from her op, then he's hiring a nurse to care for her at home.

I'm taking Allie to visit her mother next weekend. I'm amazed at her resilience, and how this crisis – and having a small brother - has matured her mentally. She certainly doesn't need any further physical ripening.

Fen also is coming along in leaps and bounds. The only time he's shown signs of stress and become clingy was before Marnie came to collect him to display him to his new in-laws. Apparently she's not giving the scrap dealer a chance to change his mind, and the wedding is next week, so it won't be long before she's Lady Muck. The ceremony is at a local Register Office, very low key, but they're planning a "he-uge" party at a later date in the US for "hundreds" of friends. I hope Lord Muck has some as I'm sure hers are few and far between.

In view of my protracted employment, the holiday in Cyprus is off for me, so now I have to think of another way in which to celebrate the twin's 21st. As that's in just over two weeks' time, and with Christmas also to consider, I should start to panic shortly.

I'm panicking.

It's been another supercharged week. We took Allie to visit her mother at the rest home, a beautiful old stone-built pile in acres of Kent countryside. She looked thin and pale but was overjoyed to see her daughter and seemed optimistic. She was very sweet to Fen who had refused to leave his sister's side.

Nevertheless, Allie was quiet on the journey home. The seriousness of Bianca's illness had not missed her anymore than it had Tiny and I.

'You OK?' I asked.

'S'pose so. I told Mum I thought I should move back and be with her while she recovers, but she said she didn't need me as Dad has got her a nurse, and I was better off with Dad and you for the time being.'

'Well I'm sure she only means while she's recovering. It might be very difficult for you both while she's coping with the chemotherapy.'

'But I'm her daughter!'

'I know, sweetie. But she's going to be feeling pretty ropey, and it will be easier for her with a professional nurse who's used to dealing with these things. She probably doesn't want you to see her like that and be upset.'

'I wouldn't mind. I'm not some sort of wimp.'

'Of course you're not. But she'd be getting stressed out if you were upset, and it'd only make things worse for her.'

'S'spose so.' She said sulkily. She is her father's daughter, no doubt.

Fen, god help him, now has a new stepfather. Mr and Mrs Antonio Berretta came to visit him to say goodbye before they left for their honeymoon in Bali and various South Pacific islands. Even though the weather was pretty mild for late November, Mrs Berretta was swathed in a fur jacket gaping sufficiently to display her magnificent breasts spilling from a cerise satin bustier. She also wore a tight cream mini, long leather boots, and ostentatious diamonds glittering from her hands and ears. She'd have looked more at home sitting in a window in Amsterdam. And I'm not talking about the jewels.

Fen at first refused to leave his bedroom, certain they'd come to take him away with them, and it took me an embarrassingly long time to convince him to leave his sanctuary.

Meanwhile, Marnie, who'd got my back up by sneering at the "bijou" Lime Cottage (I didn't think anyone used that word nowadays) wore tracks in the carpet pacing back and forth and scattering cigarette ash over everything. It was obvious by her clamped jaw she was seething, but was doing her best to hide it from "her darling Tone". He looks like a cross between Elvis and Al Capone, chews gum and speaks with a phoney American accent which he said was the result of a prolonged stay in California (a year at college when he was nineteen – some people are easily swayed).

Fen grudgingly accepted the new PlayStation and a box of games his stepfather produced from the boot of his flashy, white Cadillac, and equally grudgingly responded to his mother's request for a big hug accompanied by a storm of kisses, which he immediately wiped off with his sleeve. Her lip gloss was so thick he looked as if he'd been caught in an oil slick.

You'd have thought she'd at least offer to take him out somewhere, or spend a few hours playing with him, wouldn't you? But no, less than an hour after they arrived, they were off to begin their honeymoon in the South Seas.

I believe they still have cannibals in some of those places, so you never know. Mind you, as she's as tough as old boots they'd have to stew her for a year before she was edible.

You'll probably think I'm at best imprudent, at worst, stupid, but as neither Leah nor Jamie are bothered about celebrating their birthday with anything other than a small gathering for close family and friends, I've decided to give them £5K each.

I made much more than I expected on the house and will eventually be buying somewhere smaller, and as I've virtually thrown them out of the nest, feel it's only right to give them a helping hand.

They can, naturally, save it or spend it as they wish, but I will be giving them the proviso that if they fritter it away… Well, what can I do? They'll be absolute adults, not like eighteen when they're old enough to drink, vote and marry, but still revert to child-status when it suits them. So I'll hand it over with my dearest love, and pray that sudden wealth doesn't corrupt them.

It will be interesting to see what happens, but I guess I feel confident it'll be used wisely or I wouldn't be doing this.

I don't know what came over me, but I thought I'd ring Simon and mention what I was intending for his children's coming of age.

I couldn't believe it when, having told them about the money he suggested it should be from us both as he had paid for the house in the first place. So all the years I have spent working, caring for the family, cleaning and wrestling in the kitchen have all been worthless in his eyes.

I felt compelled to itemize my contribution to our marriage and send him a bill, and tell him to buy his own gifts, but decided it wasn't worth the bother. It certainly wouldn't change him – or anything else. And I didn't want my children to realise the extent of their father's parsimony.

Having asked them who they want to invite, I have booked the Millbank near Chelmsford as the young people want to go clubbing after us oldies have tottered off to bed. They begged me to tell my mother they'd left the country and were travelling incommunicado, or she'd be flying over and organising a ball at the Dorchester and putting an announcement in The Times. It wasn't a complete lie as they intend going on the ferry to France to avail themselves of vast quantities of duty free booze.

I braced myself to make the duplicitous call and was amazed to hear my mother accepting my lies without a murmur, saying only that she'd send her grandchildren a cheque they could bank when they came home. I almost felt guilty. And then she announced she'd be coming over at Christmas, and I reverted to defence mode and frantically tried to think of a plausible excuse: I'd be abroad. In hospital. Working...Of course!

'I'm not sure about that, Mother. You know I've sold the

house and I'm still working for Ethan Hammer.'

'I know. It doesn't matter. I'll work something out. I'll stay at a hotel. Goodbye dear.'

Dear! What was she up to? I smell something fishy. My mother never calls me anything but Rose-Anne.

My spirits sank as I envisaged having to spend the festive season with Attila and her adoring sidekick. I'm sorry, I know you're not supposed to feel so negative about your own mother, but believe me, she's only a couple of steps up from Marnie. Well maybe that's an exaggeration because at least she was about when we were growing up. And as I advised Gina, babies don't come with instructions; no one tells you how to be a parent, you just learn it as you go along, and do what you think is right at the time. Maybe one day my children will think back and judge me a terrible mother. So perhaps I'd better not judge mine too harshly.

Nevertheless, Christmas will be even more stressful than usual. I will practise yoga and try to maintain my karma.

DECEMBER

The tour is over and Ethan has returned triumphant.

Mike, as arranged, has gone to Yorkshire to visit Caroline. Things aren't quite so strained between us, but unhappily we are not back on our former friendly footing, and I really miss that.

Ethan is giving his children his undivided attention, and Allie and Fen are lapping it up. He really is pretty good with them when he has a mind to be, and he suggested I took a few days off.

My first instinct was to refuse – mainly because I didn't know where to go. I still wasn't used to the notion of being free to roam wherever I chose, within reason, of course. Or within budget. Now I'd earmarked a sizeable chunk of my spare cash for the twins, I had to revert to prudence.

The twins have their own lives at uni and I was sure they didn't want me intruding; in any case I think I'm past the stage of sleeping on someone's floor. And my friends would think I'd lost it if I invited myself to stay for a few days. Except Maddy who is always very generous with her properties and would probably have been quite happy for me to slum it in one of them. But what was the point in being in luxury if you were all alone?

Eventually I took the opportunity and went to visit my dad and Edna. I didn't realise how much I missed them. It's a long drive, but the Lake District is beautiful and I spent many tranquil hours being fattened up by Edna's wonderful cooking and burning off the calories hill-walking with Dad, often accompanied by sleety rain. As much as I love being at Lime Cottage, despite the dramas, it was a welcome break not having to worry about them. Besides, my time here would soon come to an end, and they will all have to manage without me.

This realisation immediately made me think about the diverse occupants, and wonder what *would* become of them all.

I was especially worried about the children. Although Allie seemed to improve by the day and obviously loved both her parents, I couldn't envisage how she would react if, god forbid, Bianca had a relapse – either of her cancer or her addiction to alcohol.

And what was going to happen to Fen if his mother kept custody of him? I truly believe he should live with his father as it has become increasingly obvious to me that Ethan has the makings of a good one. And surely anything would be better than leaving him with the heartless woman who gave birth to him, and a series of nannies.

I just hope Ethan's birth mother is nothing like Marnie. In any case, the planned reunion, if it happens, will undoubtedly be sensational.

And then there is Mike. It saddens me greatly that we are no longer good friends, and every time I picture the look on his face when he saw me coming out of Ethan's hotel room, I want to kick myself. But what's done is done.

Anyhow, I no longer feel guilty that I've seen so little of Dad and Edna this year. They have agreed to travel down for the twin's birthday meal, but Dad was relieved to know my mother won't be gracing us with her presence. It wouldn't bother Edna – in fact, genial as she generally is, she's not averse to giving my mother a few home truths if she starts to belittle my father. It wouldn't be the first time, so probably best that they're kept apart.

I didn't mention the subterfuge in keeping my mother away, though I'm still mystified that she acquiesced so easily. Still, we have her Christmas visit to look forward to. I haven't mentioned this to her grandchildren, nor will I until it's too late for them to make alternative arrangements or they'll surely find a long lost friend who desperately needs them, or some urgent project to attend to. Like poking themselves in the eye with a sharp stick.

Children have much more perception than they are credited with: I've never actively condemned my mother, yet they have grown up instinctively aware that her priorities in life are entirely shallow – herself and the pursuit of money. And not necessarily in that order.

Unfortunately, though my sister is coming to the celebration, her husband can't leave the farm, so she's using it as an opportunity to pop up to London for some Christmas shopping. I'm hoping to join her.

My brother, of course, sponges off my mother in the US, and even if he lived next door I wouldn't want him and his gargantuan family embarrassing me with their penchant for plates piled so high you need a ladder to eat off them. Last time I saw them, they were also loud-mouthed and ill mannered, and of course I can't invite them without alerting my mother to my duplicity in telling her the celebrants were skipping the country.

Also my mother hasn't mentioned offering to pay for their flights over at Christmas, so I doubt we'll have to order extra food. Perhaps the apron strings are being severed at long last.

Sad really, I know, but it's not just wealthy show-biz families that are dysfunctional

Though there are some people, however undesirable, who have to be invited regardless of sensitivities – Simon, naturally – and Angelica.

Jamie tells me Simon is now coming home from work and doing most of the housework including the washing and ironing, and that Angel has had to cease working as she's so sick. No wonder Simon looks haggard. The way he used to stare in wonder at my constantly humming washing machine, I thought he imagined it was another TV channel. Where did I go wrong?

As Ethan is going to be here I've also invited him: Jamie really likes him and Ethan thinks he's a very talented musician. In fact he's coming round tomorrow for a promised jam session, and to show Ethan some of the songs he's written.

Mike will be back on the morning of the birthday, and

Tiny's employment will be ending. This is not as tragic as it sounds: he's just heard he's passed his accountancy exams and is taking Heidi to visit his family in Trinidad. He'll then try to get a permanent job either in this area or in London.

Bernard Landseer, Heidi's patient's son, is getting in a temporary carer while she's away. He (Bernard) is spending more and more time with Maddy; there have even been pictures in the press and comments on their "budding romance". Not all of them have pleased Maddy – particularly the one saying it was "about time she found someone of her own age". As Bernard is ten years older than her, this went down like a lead balloon.

I'll have to invite Mike, but don't know if he'll want to come. Anyhow, I've booked a couple of spare places.

For most of the week I've spent quiet evenings with Ethan, talking about anything and everything, with no sexual overtones, and not a hint of innuendo.

The truth is he's very anxious about Bianca and has been visiting her regularly. Apart from the distressing effects of the chemotherapy, he says she's in wonderful spirits - definitely no pun intended as he believes she's truly determined, if she survives this ordeal, to swear off alcohol for good. I really hope so.

He says he's also seen the light, and is going to lay off the booze and spliffs.

'I think my days of sex and drugs are over, Rosie. And though I'll always love rock, I was pretty wrecked on the tour. It's a young man's game and I've a mind to go into producing. Maybe just do the occasional album – but quit the circus while I'm ahead.'

We also discussed his childhood (in much more detail than he went into in his autobiography), and his obsession with finding his birth mother. His adoptive parents were quite elderly, very good to him but didn't really understand him. (Where have I heard that before?) His father died when he was fifteen and he rebelled, leaving school on his sixteenth birthday and joining his first semi-professional band. Then his adoptive mother died and the rest is history.

He said he still felt guilty about not being there for his adoptive mum and I assured him we all do selfish things when we're young, and was certain she wouldn't have held it against him.

But it's his birth mother that troubles him most. He thinks he remembers her. Certainly he remembers being in many different foster homes, and being angry and unhappy – which is hardly surprising. I think she sounds like a selfish mare. But who am I to judge? She must have had her reasons.

I almost forgot – I asked him how he feels about the modelling thing, explaining that I hadn't yet mentioned it to Allie. He said he'd ask her mother!

I feel I've learned a lot about him this week. Boss, former heart-throb, former would-be lover. Anyway, I can't help but like him, much more so since our relationship has been strictly platonic. Seriously.

That last sentence makes it look as if I'm still trying to convince myself I no longer see him as a sex object. Maybe I am, but it's like trying to douse the Olympic Flame – only possible when the fuel fails to ignite. And at the moment there are still pockets of combustible gases that could rekindle - under certain circumstances. I just know the resulting explosion would be a big mistake.

I felt really proud listening to Jamie jamming with Ethan. My son is also a talented musician and singer, and Allie was almost awestruck! She thinks he's "awesome", the best thing since jelly babies. I hope this won't develop into a problem – especially as Jamie's relationship with Kirsten is off. I think macrobiotics were just a phase whereas Jaffa Cakes are a lifelong passion.

The good news is Ethan thinks Jamie's songs are great and wants his record producer to hear them. The bad news, having listened to a recording, he's not too impressed by the rest of Jamie's band.

This is inevitably a problem for my soft-hearted son, who thinks he should be loyal to his mates – even though this particular line-up has only been together for six months.

'If you love your music and believe in it, you owe it to yourself to do what's right for it, Jamie. If you wanna be in with a chance of making it, you have to leave the dross behind,' Ethan told him. 'Make no mistake, they'd do it to you.'

'Yeah, right,' said Jamie disconsolately. 'I'll think about what you've said.'

Later I had words with Ethan. I wasn't happy about him filling my son's head with dreams. Jamie is a brilliant artist and could have a great career in the world of graphic design, and I didn't want him side-tracked on the off chance of pop stardom.

'Rosie, the lad's good. He's really got something. A real feel for the music – not to mention charisma. You only had to look at Allie to imagine the girls throwing their knickers at him.'

'Well, you'd know all about that,' I said. 'I don't know if it's what I want for my son.'

'Come on, Rosie. He's almost 21 – it's about what *he* wants, not you. Let him decide. And I'm not filling his head with dreams. I can't guarantee his success, but I'd put money on it.'

I nodded

'In fact…I could produce him myself. Mike could manage him…' he spoke almost to himself. 'Yeah…'

Bianca has reluctantly agreed to Allie being approached by the model agency, but has made it clear her daughter's schoolwork must not suffer if anything comes of it. I say reluctant because she knows the pitfalls, having started out as a model herself, and is not keen for her daughter to follow in her footsteps. However, she is also aware Allie's resentment could be far-reaching if she were kept in the dark about the offer. So I've been given leave to ring Freya Whatsit and see how the land lies. But first I had to tell Allie.

She blushed to the roots of her golden hair. 'They want *me* to model? Oh my god! I can't – I mean I'm not sure…'

'Allie, nothing may come of it. There are no guarantees, and I've told you what your parents say.'

She nodded, bemused.

I rang Freya the next day, and another prodigious event occurred – she requested a portfolio. I was just about to argue the toss as to the prudence of outlaying what could amount to hundreds of pounds, when she asked me if I could use the same photographer who did the original shots!

Thinking with the speed of light I told her the photographer was new to the game, so she probably wouldn't know her by name.

I thought she was going to insist, but she just commanded me to have it done as soon as possible and have them despatched by express courier.

Of course, I immediately had doubts as to whether or not I could do justice to Allie artistically. My knowledge of photography is improving all the time, especially since I've been perfecting my efforts with the help of Ethan's state-of-the-art computer programme. Though I say it myself, my shots end up looking pretty professional, even when they don't start out that way. It's not cheating: airbrushing a model's blemishes has been done for decades: the only people with skin that's magazine cover perfect are newborn babies – though some of the models are now so young you can't tell if they're suffering from acne or milk spots.

I talked myself into splashing out on some more sophisticated equipment: a new printer, a scanner, a couple of decent lights.

My next home is likely to be a caravan. If I'm lucky.

But I think I am. I can't believe just over a year ago I was ensconced in the security of suburbia. Now, not only do I work for one of the most successful singers of the era, I have a son on the fringes of showbiz, am surrogate mother to a teenager on the verge of becoming a top model, and have a chance to establish myself as a photographer. Life is full of surprises.

They also say pride comes before a fall, and it does. I've been so full of my latest project, I forgot my intended appointment at Gina's new tanning booth, so last night decided to make use of a bottle of fake tan I've had for…a very long time. I should have discarded it when I moved, but old habits etc…

Anyhow, to cut a very long and harrowing tale short, I woke this morning, my children's 21st birthday, looking like someone from that weird TV advert where you drink fizzy orange and end up looking like one. Plus extra tangerine patches on my knees, ankles and elbows, and hands that looked as if they were encased in grubby Marigold gloves.

At least I had the sense not to put it on my face, because by the time I'd finished exfoliating, and scrubbing my joints with toothpaste (Gina's advice), I looked like a Red Indian (sorry, Native American, but you get the picture). I had to cover myself in salve to allay the effects.

At least Geoffrey wasn't involved in this DIY beauty disaster: *he* learned his lesson last time. It takes some of us a bit longer.

Mike arrived back just as I was about to embark on my third remedial bath. He seemed markedly more friendly and laughed when I confessed my faux pas with the faux tan. He also accepted my invitation for this evening's meal.

My children were actually speechless when they received my most generous birthday gifts. As will I be when my bank statement arrives. But they're worth it.

Their grandmother succeeded in astounding us all by not only matching my cheques, but not lecturing the twins in her amazingly brief birthday message. I can't help wondering if she's had a brainstorm that has provoked a personality change. Perhaps she's simply mellowing with age? For a moment I felt guilty she was missing our celebration, but even a head and body transplant wouldn't ratify her presence in my dear old dad's mind. He still cringes when her name's mentioned.

It was a lovely occasion. I handled the Simon and Angelica situation quite well, I think. She looked as pale and drawn as her husband, and I almost felt pity for her: she was out of place and subdued by the exuberant family ambience, though everyone was kind to her, even Leah. The trick was to treat her like a sick child, yet she rallied sufficiently to lick her glossy lips and pout prettily when Ethan complimented her, though after his first few forays, Simon's proud glow simmered to a narrow-eyed sulk.

He was also distinctly uncomfortable when he recognised the relationship between Leah and Dawn; not that they flaunted it, but they spoke about "their" flat, and I watched his face as he assimilated the facts and put two and two together. The sad thing is, I don't think he'll ever accept his daughter for what she is. It's his loss.

I'm sure I detected a fleeting expression of regret as he observed the merriment, unable to join in as he pandered to his wife's constant needs. She ate two helpings of burger and chips washed down by glasses of chilled Diet Coke, and had to have her back massaged in between. That pudgy chin owes more to pie-munching than pregnancy cravings.

I am so proud of my children – who are now no longer children but fully fledged adults. They are decent human beings. What can be more important than that?

It was great to spend time with my sister. She also thinks Mother is acting strangely. We've concluded she's having marriage problems and is being nice to us in case she needs moral support. I guess we'll have to wait until Christmas to get to the nitty gritty. I'm glad she's going to stay in a hotel; apparently she's booked into Knutsford Park. If Mike brings his daughter, and Ethan still has Allie and Fen, it's going to be a full house. Thank goodness Leah and Dawn are giving Jamie a room when he's back from college. In the New Year I'm going to have to seriously look for somewhere to buy. I know they're both officially adults, but I feel bad that I haven't anywhere for them to live, should they need it.

My day Christmas shopping in London with Lizzie turned into two, and both were as frenetic and magical as ever. I just love the lights in Oxford Street, and the splendour of Harrods.

And why is it you can get things in Central London branches of M&S that you never see in the provinces?

We came home as usual with aching feet, smouldering credit cards and a great sense of satisfaction.

Parked outside Lime Cottage was a smart black transit with blacked out windows. I thought the ''A Team'' had arrived, but inside was my son, grinning like the proverbial Cheshire cat.

'D'you like my new wheels, Mum?'

Please, please don't tell me he's blown his entire nest-egg…

'Don't look so worried, Ma – it's secondhand, and I'll need a decent vehicle to cart my stuff to the recording studios.' His face told me how badly he wanted my approval. I melted.

'Are you saying you're going to make a record?'

'No Mum, I'm going to cut an album. I've got a contract with Ethan and Mike's new company! Your boy is going to be a star!'

I hugged him. My sister hugged him. Allie looked on enviously.

'What about college?'

'I'm taking a year out, Mum, and if I don't make it, I can go back and finish my degree.'

'But he's going to make it – he's going to make the fortunes of Hammer Sounds!' said Ethan appearing and slinging an arm round Jamie's shoulders. 'Aren't you pleased, Rosie?'

'Of course I am,' I said with more confidence than I felt. Not that I doubt my son's talent, nor Ethan's judgement: one thing he does know is the music business, but it was yet another change to take on board. 'Your new car's nice,' I added.

'Nice?' said my excited son. 'It's fecking brilliant!'

(I excused his bad language – one of his best friends is Irish, and he seems to think replacing a *u* with an *e* annuls the profanity.)

I can't believe how much I've enjoyed doing Allie's portfolio, not to mention how much I've learned. And even though I struggle on the technical side, I had lots of ideas that worked out astonishingly well. Gina did her makeup and despite Allie's lack of experience, once we started she was a natural – and the camera loves her. So does Geoffrey who managed to wheedle himself into a couple of shots.

Allie thinks we should get him on the books of one of those animal agencies that supply film and TV companies with talented pets. I pointed out that the number one qualification for this is Obedience, plus a malleable, placid personality, which instantly nullifies Geoffrey as a candidate.

Did you ever see that TV ad where a dog, a cat and a mouse sat in front of the fire together? I always used to picture Geoffrey as that cat: the only part of the mouse in sight was its tail – hanging out of Geoffrey's mouth. He regularly used to come home with algae round his mouth, always about the time a neighbour was complaining his goldfish were disappearing. No, I'm afraid the thespian audition circuit is a non-starter for Geoffrey. Though if they ever need an obstinate, contrary, imperious moggy, he could be in with a chance.

But I'm rambling: Maddy gave me the lowdown on what's expected from a portfolio and we just used the house and garden as background and Allie's own clothes. The only time she was uneasy was over the swimsuit shots, which doesn't surprise me as she's certainly not in the market for underwear modelling. We compromised, and got some very nice shots with the aid of a couple of chiffon wraps. The culmination of our labours is now winging its way to Freya in London, having been approved by Maddy, and I have to confess I'm very happy with the result.

I just hope, if the agency likes Allie, that it turns out to be a good move. The situation will certainly need careful monitoring: she's had enough to contend with in her short life and can do without being exploited because she happens to be beautiful.

With a bit of luck, by the time the real problems start Bianca will be back in the driving seat.

Ethan and Mike have been out of sight for most of the week.

They're negotiating a unit on an industrial estate they think is suitable for use as a studio. They're all on a high as it seems they have backing for their latest business venture, and have also just signed another young band, and a girl singer whose first album flopped but they believe has untapped potential.

I am happy for them and sincerely wish them the best of luck, particularly for my son's sake. And with Jamie being under contract to Hammer, I'll be able to keep in touch with them all when I leave Lime Cottage, or at least follow their extraordinary lives. I know how much I will miss being part of it all.

I am also happy to report that Bianca seems to be coping well with the chemo, though she has a while to go yet before they can tell her how successful it has been. I took Allie over to see her last weekend as Ethan had a TV appearance, and she's a completely different person when she's off the booze; also this illness has certainly sobered her up both physically and mentally. I really like her and have nothing but admiration for the way she's coping with the sickness, not to mention her beautiful hair falling out. Allie insisted we bought her a selection of bright scarves which she now wears with great panache.

I am happy for Leah as she is altogether a sunnier person since she came out and met Dawn, though I still get pulled up sharply sometimes when I find my mind drifting to images of my daughter's wedding, or imagining her with children. I daresay there'll come a day when it will no longer disturb me, because I really don't mind, as long as she's happy. And she's elated at present as Dawn, who is studying some sort of biology has just heard she's got a placement in Florida too, so they'll be able to stay together while Leah's interning at NASA. I will miss her, though.

So I am happy for everyone. Except me. And I don't know why. I've been lying awake for hours at night trying to analyse my discontent. Perhaps if I write down the pros and cons I might get closer to an answer.

The question is, why do I feel so down when everything's going so well?

I have a job I'm enjoying – but it's still temporary. In any case I am not short of money. (Though I will be if I keep thinking like that.)

I live in a gorgeous house – also temporary. (I need to buy somewhere soon).

I may have a future as a photographer, which has always been my dream.

My children are healthy and happy. And not children anymore.

I don't miss Simon. Though I suppose I miss being half of a partnership – even if I was less than half of ours.

I'm happier about the way I look – I've lost over a stone this year, and everyone says I look years younger with my new hairstyle. Maddy also says I've gained in confidence, which has improved my posture, but I think that's exercise and yoga. I feel good physically, anyway.

I have lots of good friends (who are less available since they all seem to have found Mr Right – or Mr All Right for Now in Maddy's case).

Mm.

Reading this list I think I'll feel better when I'm more settled.

So next year's priorities are: my own home, a permanent job – and a definite goal to aim for career-wise. I would make these my New Year Resolutions except it will give them the kiss of death as I've never managed to stick to one yet.

OK. Now that's sorted, perhaps I'll get a good night's sleep.

My mother rang again to tell me she's definitely coming over for Christmas and is staying at the Knutsford Park Hotel, but hopes to see her grandchildren on Christmas Day. She also said she'll be on her own, so I guess Lizzie and I were correct in our forecast of marital disaster. God, I hope she doesn't decide to move back here to live.

Ethan had a letter to say his birth mother was visiting relatives in England, and would love to meet him, and possibly spend some time with him over Christmas. Naturally he was very excited and wanted to invite her to stay.

We were all in the kitchen and Mike and I looked at one

another and raised anxious brows.

'Perhaps you could just invite her for Christmas dinner?' I ventured.

My boss gave me a searching look.

'Rose is right, Ethan,' Mike said. 'I know she's your mother, but it could be a bit tricky. You may find you don't have anything in common with her.'

'Yes. Look at me and my mine! If her name wasn't in black and white on my Birth Certificate I'd never have believed I came from her loins.' My comment was heartfelt.

'I'm not stupid,' Ethan retorted hotly. 'I don't expect to fall in her arms and forgive her for giving me away. I just want to meet her and discover my roots. Do you know what it's like not to have one single picture of an ancestor? I don't care if my great grandfather was deported for sheep shagging or if he was knighted for licking the King's arse. I just want to know...'

'Could be either with your proclivities.' Mike aimed to ease the tension, and it worked.

Ethan grinned. 'OK, OK, just making a point. I'll invite her for dinner – if I like her. But I want a meeting first. I don't want to bugger up Christmas Day for the kids. By the way, I've invited Bianca too. Have we heard anything from That Bitch?'

I shook my head, unthinking. 'No, Marnie's still incommunicado.'

'Let's hope she stays that way: every day she's out of touch with Fen gives me a stronger case for custody.'

Amen to that.

Ethan disappeared to work on his manuscript. I hope it's going to be an ending worth waiting for.

'Rose, there's going to be a hell of a houseful on Christmas Day. Are you sure you don't mind me having Caroline down here?'

I flashed Mike a surprised look. Fancy him asking me! 'I don't mind the crowd, but we'll need extra help with the cooking. Let's see now, there's Ethan, Allie, Fen, Bianca, you, Caroline, Leah, Jamie, Dawn, my mother, and possibly Ethan's mother. And me. Twelve. Perhaps we could go to a restaurant...'

'We can if you really want to, Rose, but I can cook, so don't look so worried,' Mike laid a gentle hand on my arm. 'We can do ninety per cent of it beforehand, though we can buy everything ready prepared – even the vegetables.'

Thank god for Tesco's Finest. 'That doesn't sound much like good old American home cooking to me - and if that's the royal "We" I've heard it all before.'

Mike's hand moved up to push a stray hair from my face (god, that sounds *so* Mills & Boon – but that's what he did, and it disconcerted me no end).

'Not from me, Rose. If I say I'm going to do something, you'd better believe it. Now, shall we make a list? We can leave Allie and Fen finishing off the tree and then we'll go to the big Tesco and empty their freezers. You know I have to leave later this afternoon to go and collect Caroline?'

I just nodded – because I was experiencing a quiver of seasonal anticipation I hadn't felt since the twins stopped believing in Santa.

At least I thought that's what it was. When I really allowed myself to think about it, I knew it was Mike. Our feud was over and I was so happy and relieved that we seemed to be back to our former relationship.

I hate shopping. Well, you know that's not true, but like millions of other women, I detest shopping for food and household necessities – a fact that never ceases to surprise most men who regard the weekly supermarket dash as a form of female recreation. I'm glad to see more and more men now participate in this thankless, wearisome task, and am gratified to note they don't look as if they're enjoying it much either.

But I'm wandering again. I'm afraid my mind is away with the fairies.

All I was going to say was I *usually* hate shopping. But today in Tesco's, something wonderful happened.

From the moment I wheeled the trolley (handpicked by Mike who ensured it hadn't a mind of its own) into the heaving hypermarket, aware of his hand on my back guiding me through the throng towards the fruit and veg, a warm, tingling sensation swept over me. I swear it started at my feet and oozed through me until it reached the parts no man has reached before. Well, not for a very long time.

It was more than sexual attraction, though undoubtedly my body's reaction was pure unadulterated lust. And all at once I saw in Mike not just a friend but a kindred spirit. I think what stunned me most was that it had never struck me before: he was lean, attractive, considerate, intelligent…kind to animals and children…

Or maybe I just hadn't allowed myself to think of him in that way. If I am honest, I had been deeply affected by the withdrawal of his goodwill after the hotel incident, and it upset me way more than I was prepared to admit that he should think ill of me. Also while I'm baring my soul, I suppose part of me felt safer fantasizing about Ethan – knowing that whatever ensued, it wouldn't end in heartbreak. It would just have been a short fling or a one night stand, and my eyes were wide open to this. Which is obviously why it was fated never to happen.

But Mike, my relationship with him, had always been on an entirely different plane; one that was based on friendship and (until that incident) mutual respect. I think. But I'm becoming over-analytical, and the truth is, there's no logical explanation about how I am feeling now.

I don't remember too much about the shopping except that I enjoyed every minute of it, even the forty we had to wait at the checkout. All I know is that I just wanted to look at Mike, and touch him, and was ridiculously happy just to be in his company. He seemed happy too and we were still laughing when we paid the astronomic bill. Hey, it was only money!

Nothing specific was said, but I'm sure he feels the same. The whole fabric of our relationship seems to have changed.

And when he left to collect Caroline, I knew I wasn't

imagining it when he pulled me to him, kissed me, very gently and whispered. 'I'll be back. Wait for me.'

The sensuousness of his touch and the promise his words implied, quite literally made my knees go weak.

Just recalling it sends shivers down my spine, or more accurately, daggers of desire (more M&B?). Forget the frills, I'm horny as hell. The erotic encounters I've had with Ethan were lustful, playful, but what I was feeling now was something altogether different, something real that spread through my body like wildfire. Something I thought I'd never experience again.

I hardly slept a wink, but have concluded that my long-standing fantasising over Ethan blinded me to Mike's much more desirable attributes.

Mike. Michael Robbins…Michael J Robbins…I wonder what the J stands for…

What a Christmas present! Freya rang. She *adores* Allie and wants to talk business. They definitely want to sign her, though I know Bianca and Ethan will want to have their say on every aspect of the contract, with school coming first, so her work will be limited, which can only be a good thing. Anyhow, I'm sure Mike will oversee any contract.

I was thrilled for Allie, of course, but nevertheless a little disappointed that the quality of the photography hadn't been mentioned. Then just as she was saying goodbye, Freya said (in her very languid tone), 'By the way, darling, great photos – who did you say took them?'

'Rose-Anne Grant.'

'Never heard of her. She's good though. Tell her to give me a ring. I may be able to use her.'

Before I had a chance to reply, she'd rung off. I forestalled my first instinct to ring her right back. Stupid woman. She knows my name is Grant – you'd think she'd put two and two together…

I'll ring her in the New Year.

Allie was delighted – for us both.

'Great! I'll insist you are my personal photographer,' she said.

Bless her. It's a nice dream, but I'm not sure I'd want to be hustling round studios, or standing on freezing street corners for hours. I'm not sure how I want to use my newly recognised talent. And where would Mike fit into this Utopia? Now I really am fast-forwarding. But I can't stop thinking about him.

Mike came back at lunchtime with his daughter. She's gorgeous. A year younger than Allie, quite petite, with long shiny dark hair and blue, blue eyes. Like Mike's. She's also very polite and seems to have inherited her father's good nature.

Allie, buoyed by the prospect of working for a top modelling agency, was instantly friendly and generous towards her, and Fen won her heart by looking up from under long dark lashes and saying, 'You are very, very pretty – like Dannii Minogue'.

He is undoubtedly his father's son.

As the youngsters got to know one another, Mike and I sat at a corner of the large kitchen table, our knees touching, neither of us bothering to excuse ourselves or shift back a tad. And oh, I wanted so much more.

'Caroline is lovely,' I said, not willing to risk anything more intimate.

But that did it. He reached for my hand, and the tingle intensified.

'So are you, Rose...Rose…you must know how I feel about you…'

All at once we were kissing, gently at first, and then with intent…but there is a time and a place, and it was not right then.

With an effort I pulled away.

'How *do* you feel about me, Mike?'

His eyes spoke volumes. 'I think you're the woman I've been looking for for a very long time.'

We were almost on the point of devouring one another again when Fen appeared at the door. 'Caroline's hungry,' he announced.

Mike groaned. 'She can't be – she ate like a horse at the motorway services. But I guess that was a couple of hours ago.'

'Allie says perhaps she'd like a McDonald's…'

'I bet she did,' said Mike, ruffling the little fella's hair. 'What do you say, Rose? Shall we indulge them? It's the day before Christmas Eve – and you know who's coming then, don't you Fen?'

By this time Fen was nearly jumping out of his shoes, shrieking with excitement. As if a seven year old needs winding up at this time of year!

'Well it will save on the cooking,' I said, picturing the mountain I'd be doing over the next couple of days. And you know what? Even that didn't cast a shadow on my euphoria.

My heart flipped as Mike gave me a lingering look, hoisted Fen on his shoulder and went to round up the others.

That night I waited in fevered anticipation for him to come to my room and claim me for his own. (I know, it's getting really soppy now). But when he eventually appeared, it was only with the intention of kissing me goodnight.

'Rose, I feel there's something really special between us and when I make love to you I want it to *be* something really special, in a wonderful place…I want to take you to a romantic tropical paradise, and…'

Men! Sod the romance. I'd waited long enough, and I wanted paradise *now*…So I persuaded him to change his mind.

And he didn't seem to mind too much.

It's Christmas Eve, and this afternoon I am to meet my mother at the Knutsford Park Hotel. Goodness knows why as I'll be going to collect her on Christmas morning, but she was most insistent. As if I haven't got enough to do! I resisted the urge to ask her about the state of her marriage as I hadn't time to listen to a catalogue of complaints, but she certainly sounded rather odd on the phone.

By coincidence, Ethan's birth mother is also signing in to the Knutsford Park, and he has been decidedly jumpy about his forthcoming meeting, which is hardly surprising.

Can you imagine if the two mothers bump into one another? It could be the Clash of the Gorgons. But I'm being wicked. I mustn't judge as I don't even know the other woman. And it *is* Christmas, after all: goodwill towards all men, and all that.

Very goodwill towards one man in particular.

The day started early, mainly because Fen was tearing round the house at 5.30am. God only knows what time he'll wake up tomorrow. Anyhow, Mike had returned to his own room (we thought it politic not to flaunt our relationship just yet, particularly with his daughter staying), so I got up and started the preparations for the annual pig-out (Jamie's expression, and it's very apt considering we all eat way too much).

By 7.30am I'd cooked two batches of mince pies, and another couple of sausage rolls: I say cooked, not made or baked as they were frozen ones and much nicer than my pastry, I assure you. The turkey, which was the only part of the meal that had to be specially prepared, had already been defrosting for two days, so I constructed some Pigs in a Blanket (bacon wrapped round a mini sausage), checked that all the vegetables were handy at the top of the freezer, and peeled ten tonnes of potatoes.

And where was my fellow chef? Still in bed. I sent Fen to wake him, and told him to make sure he didn't leave until Mike was standing up. I'd have gone to wake him myself but knew I couldn't be trusted not to take advantage of him.

I was so contented, the morning flew by. Even with constant interruptions from an over-excited little boy and two abnormally uncool teenagers Mike and I worked side by side, using every opportunity to brush against one another, grabbing the occasional sweet kiss when we were sure the coast was clear. I'm sure he was as happy about our relationship as I was, but with the spectacle of Ethan's mother in the offing, we both felt another revelation could be one too many in a household where alliances were already so delicately balanced, so resolved to keep ours for another time.

I should have been exhausted after so many hours in my least favourite pursuit, but even my antipathy to kitchens had been forgotten as my body ran on adrenaline, fuelled by the anticipation of pleasures to come. But all too soon it was time to go and see my mother. Ethan was meeting his that evening, and had gone to make sure Bianca was all right for tomorrow: a driver had been hired to bring her over to Lime Cottage.

I so hoped Ethan wouldn't be disappointed in his mother. I also hoped he'd invite her to Christmas dinner anyway: it would be interesting, to say the least.

I approached the hotel room warily, ever mindful that my mother's actions were inevitably loaded, and wondering what part I would be expected to play in her latest crisis; whatever, she was sure to make a drama out of it. So I was prepared for just about anything as I knocked on her door.

Anything except what transpired.

The first shock was that she wasn't alone – Sylvester was with her. Actually he was sitting holding her hand. She looked distinctly subdued and said she had something important to tell me.

I instantly jumped to the conclusion she was terminally ill – I mean what else was I supposed to think? And then she asked me what my relationship was with Ethan, and I was convinced she had lost her marbles. So I humoured her, gritting my teeth with frustration.

'He's my boss, Mother. I work for him. At present I'm looking after his children. But I've told you this already.'

She stared at me almost maniacally. 'You haven't...*slept* with him?'

'For god's sake Mother! What is this all about?'

Still the penny hadn't dropped.

'Ethan ...is...my son...your half-brother.'

After this point, I'm not sure what happened or in what order. I was totally speechless. One word kept going through my mind *Incest...Incest*...But my hearing seemed to be intact as the tale of my seventeen-year-old mother's affair with an American airman has imprinted itself on my mind in minute detail.

It was destined to be a sad story, and typically of my mother, she blamed everyone else for her plight – especially her parents who it seems would have adopted the baby boy if she'd let them. For some reason, after a second affair ended acrimoniously, she chose to have her son – whom she named Daniel – fostered. She said she just couldn't cope. But when she eventually, put him up for adoption, aged four (as Ethan had said) it was because her then fiancé (who was very wealthy), was not willing to accept a child by another man.

That relationship was doomed to failure, but soon after that she married my father – who I'm certain would have accepted any child, bewitched as he must have been. But that's water under the bridge, and as I've never been in that situation, who am I to judge?

I am utterly astounded. Especially by the implications of my near capitulation to my own *brother*...Well, she'd never hear it from me. And nor would anyone else. Ever.

I know my girlfriends will take it to the grave: we all know *far* too much about one another.

Of course, at this juncture, Ethan had yet to discover the truth.

Luckily, when I got back to Lime Cottage, still numb with shock, Mike had taken the youngsters for some last minute shopping, and Ethan was still out, so I was able to come round in my own time. Not that I've anywhere near come to terms with this mind-blowing development, and I'm writing this a week later.

There are just so many aspects to envision, so many ends to tie up. It also explains many things: for instance...as much as I wanted to...you know (I can't even *say* it now)... with Ethan, something always held me back. Was it more than self preservation?

It certainly explains why Ethan's expressions have often

put me in mind of Jamie: now I know the reality I can see they are *very* alike.

Talk about truth being stranger than fiction. You couldn't make it up.

On Boxing Day my sister rang to let me know my mother had been to Devon first to break the news to her, and had made Lizzie promise not to say anything to me until she'd had a chance to tell me in person. I give her due respect for that – but it would hardly have helped her case for me to have alerted Ethan that his birth mother was the woman who also abandoned me, albeit at a later stage in my development.

Of course, Lizzie was as stunned as me – not least because of the accident of fate that brought our half-brother into my life. The odds of that happening must be astronomic.

Apparently my mother told my brother before she left the States. No wonder she didn't suggest that the Weebles tagged along for Christmas. I bet his nose has really been put out of joint, knowing he's been usurped by a half-brother who is rich and famous. And slim. And good-looking.

Anyhow, on the Day of Revelation, I was expecting Ethan back before he went off to meet his birth mother, and my mind was in even more turmoil at the thought of having to face him, especially when it dawned on me he knew my opinion of the woman I call Mother.

My mother had suggested that I was there with her when she broke the news to him, but I turned her down flat. Now I'd had time to reconsider I thought it might have been easier than having to face him later, knowing that I knew. Does that make sense?

Happily for me, Mike returned before Ethan, and, having restrained the urge to fall weeping into his arms (seeing him brought all my emotions to the surface) I told him the improbable facts.

He is a diamond. He showed equal amounts of sympathy and common sense, suggesting the ideal solution would be for him to drive Ethan to his appointment with fate so he could be there to give him moral support, and also to pave the way for our meeting as siblings. In his arms I immediately felt calmer. And again weak at the knees, but this had absolutely nothing to do with the family theatricals.

There was only about an hour between Ethan coming back and leaving for his meeting, and I spent it soaking in the bath so I didn't have to see him.

I felt much better knowing I had Mike's support – not that I'd done anything wrong (well not quite), but it was just so weird, such a shock. I just kept saying to myself "Ethan Hammer is my brother, Ethan Hammer is my *brother*", and it still didn't really sink in.

Would he still want me to work for him? Oh god!! This means that Allie and Fen are my niece and nephew.

No wonder Fen reminds me of Jamie too.

It also means Leah and Jamie have two new cousins.

It is too much to take in.

The youngsters were riveted to Christmas Eve TV, and I waited in trepidation, listening for the car on the gravel.

When it eventually arrived, part of me wanted to run and hide.

Mike came through the door smiling reassuringly. Behind him Ethan stood, all manner of emotions crossing his familiar features. His eyes glistened as he held out his arms, and I fell into them.

It really was a brotherly bear hug, and when we drew apart we were both crying.

'I always new there was something special between us, Rosie,' he said.

Christmas Day was strange, to put it mildly. My mother (I suppose I should say *our* mother) and Sylvester came for dinner, most of which was cooked by Mike, Allie and Caroline as my emotional state ensured everything I touched turned to charcoal.

Of course, Allie and Fen not only had new aunts and cousins, they also, god help them, had a new grandmother.

My mother, once she'd recovered from the trauma of meeting her long lost son and his family, was soon back to normal, revelling in her role as Mother of Pop Star, and much more interested in his wealthy showbiz acquaintances than answering questions about her misspent youth, but Ethan didn't let it faze him.

Much later that night when the guests had left, and Bianca and the youngsters had gone to bed, I asked Ethan if he was sorry he'd opened this particular can of worms, and if he was disappointed.

'Nah,' he said, mellowed by an excess of the malt. 'I've got you and Lizzie as sisters, and Leah and Jamie. No, I'm not disappointed.'

'And…Mother?'

He shrugged. 'I don't know, Rosie. I can tell she's never been your dedicated homebody, but at least she didn't try to deny she had me – even if she did mess me up and have me adopted so she could marry some rich geezer.'

'Yes. I suppose she's not all bad,' I conceded. 'But you'll have to put your foot down or she'll be calling a press conference and moving in with you.'

'Jeez!' Ethan said.

'Well there's one really great thing to come out of this,' I said, and both men looked at me expectantly. 'It's going to make a brilliant ending for your book.'

What a year!

FIVE YEARS ON

Leah has just read this and thinks I should get it published. I might give it a go, so with that in mind, I suppose I ought to record how things are five years down the line because there's nothing more irritating than loose ends.

Well, after the dramatic finale to the year things never did quite return to normal – though I no longer believe there is such a thing. At least, *my* life has never been the same: it just gets better and better.

Leah is now working as a research scientist, still in Florida, and still with Dawn. They seem truly contented and have a wonderful lifestyle, and we see them one side of the Atlantic or the other a couple of times a year, which is great.

Jamie had a very successful couple of years on the pop circuit before deciding to produce music instead and is now a senior producer at Hammer Sounds, though I think he'll branch out on his own before long. He got married last year to a wonderful girl, Maria, who's in advertising – or she was until last month when she left to await the birth of their child.

I must be ready for grandparenthood because I wasn't the least traumatised when they told me about it. In fact I am quite chuffed and have even knitted bootees, though when we went shopping Maria was looking at designer trainers that would fit a doll, so perhaps my efforts will be wasted.

Bianca recovered completely – and she and Ethan remarried and are apparently very happy second time around. Ethan, is still rocking on, though mostly on the production side, and Allie (or Allegra as she became known professionally) became the face of Teen.Com (cosmetics) but soon tired of the modelling circus, and last year opted to go to university. She hopes to graduate with a BSc and specialise in sonic engineering. Her proud father is hoping she'll join Hammer as a sound engineer.

Ethan eventually won custody of Fen, and his rotten mother seems to have all but disappeared from his life. She's now on her third husband a "film director". Ethan says he's a porno producer and that Marnie's been spotted in more than one very blue movie. Anyway, Fen seems to be a well adjusted pre-teen. He's in the church choir and sings like an angel, and is also captain of the under 13's football team. He's the spitting image of Jamie, whom he idolises.

My mother went back to the States when she realised Ethan was not her gateway to the stars. She's still married to the long-suffering Sylvester, and we see her occasionally. Ethan's autobiography, by the way, was a bestseller, thanks in part to the publicity over his meeting with his mother, so she had her fifteen minutes of fame and has had to be content with that.

Of course, my part in the saga gave the tale an added twist - but was written under my precise direction so there was never going to be the slightest hint of anything untoward. And my friends remain as loyal and tight-lipped as ever.

Gina had a beautiful baby boy, Joseph, and loved motherhood so much, a year later she gave birth to another one, Samuel. I don't envy her having teenagers at 60, but she has plenty of help and is happier than she's ever been.

Heidi married Tiny who now has his own accountancy business - in fact he cooks the books for Hammer. And Martin has three children, which keeps him out of trouble and Heidi happily occupied.

And Maddy (surprise, surprise!) is queening it as Mrs Bernard Landseer and seems settled (if you call travelling from one exotic location to another settled). Mind you, she always used to say if marriage makes you miserable, you might as well be rich and miserable, so either way she's on a winner.

Simon? Well you wouldn't believe it but Angelica had *twins*! Kylie and Dannii (yes, it's even spelt the same!) I always said they came from his side of the family. He has aged considerably. And I can't help a smidgeon of smugness when I record that Angelica has put on about three stones. As she mostly wears a black tent she's now akin to an Avenging Angel.

And me? Well, I married Mike who, of course, is a partner in Hammer Sounds – which is doing very nicely, thank you. I work on the public relations/advertising side where I am able to utilise my creative skills, and since they are now greatly appreciated, I love it.

Caroline, who I love to bits, will be going to Uni this year - she wants to be a doctor. Maybe she'll specialise in geriatrics!

When Ethan moved back with Bianca, we bought Lime Cottage – so dreams do come true. So do astrological predictions, as per my Great Yarmouth tarot reading, even the part about the new baby – thank goodness it must have indicated the grandchild. Though we have just acquired Geoffrey Mark II, who is being whipped into shape (and taught to thieve) by his grumpy old mentor.

Anyhow, I must finish this now. I have to go and pack as we're all off to Maddy's villa in Cyprus.

And to think I was dreading being middle-aged.

Young free and single? You can keep it!